Shiva Naipaul was born in 1945 and educated in Trinidad and at University College, Oxford, where he read classical Chinese. He is based in London, but has travelled widely in India, Africa, the Caribbean and the United States, where he spent a year as a Guggenheim Fellow.

He is the author of *The Chip-Chip Gatherers* which won the Whitbread Award for Fiction, and *Fireflies,* winner of the Jock Campbell *New Statesman* Award, the John Llewelyn Rhys Memorial Prize and the Winifred Holtby Memorial Prize of the Royal Society of Literature in 1970. He has also written two books of non-fiction: *North of South* about a journey through Africa, and *Black and White*. His most recent novel is *A Hot Country*. These last two titles are also available in Abacus.

Also by Shiva Naipaul in Abacus:

BLACK AND WHITE
A HOT COUNTRY

Shiva Naipaul

BEYOND THE DRAGON'S MOUTH

STORIES AND PIECES

First published in Great Britain by
Hamish Hamilton Ltd 1984
Published in Abacus by
Sphere Books Ltd 1985
30–32 Gray's Inn Road, London WC1X 8JL

Printed and bound in Great Britain by
Cox & Wyman Ltd, Reading

For Alexander Chancellor

Contents

Beyond the Dragon's Mouth

I recall a fine summer afternoon, soft and blue and unportentous. It was my second year at Oxford. 1966 ... a year when skirts were extravagantly short; when it was fashionable for men to grow their hair long and affect a disdain for material comforts; when it was almost compulsory to smoke marijuana (or pretend that you did), to find common reality 'weird' and to show concern about the war in Vietnam; when adventurous youth was convinced it possessed a wisdom surpassing all previous wisdoms ... the best of times and the worst of times. I see myself, slim, stoop-shouldered, walking back to my rooms in College, having just been released from another unremarkable tutorial session. My feeble attempts to stitch together a point of view on the use of the inductive method in the construction of scientific hypotheses had made no perceptible impression on my tutor and had left me feeling a little jaded. Strolling along St. Giles, I was neither happy nor sad. I may have been thinking how pleasant it would be to get hold of a punt, to spend an hour or two on the river.

Approaching Broad Street, I suddenly became aware that something peculiar was happening to me. Inexplicably, my heart had started to race, my palms to moisten with sweat, my head to swim. I realised I was terribly afraid. But afraid of what? What was there to be so afraid of on this soft, blue afternoon? Dazed, barely able to maintain my balance, barely able to breathe, I huddled against the wall of Balliol. The summer sky, so benign, so unthreatening, was transformed into a wheeling amphitheatre of undefined menace; a maelstrom of annihilating vacuity. Staring at it, wave upon wave of raw fear swept through me. I imagined myself a body: a nameless corpse to be picked up from the street. It was as if all the secret terrors accumulated from birth had broken loose of their chains and come upon me in one overwhelming, retributive flood. How long I remained huddled against that wall, I cannot say. Maybe no more than a minute or two.

The worst of the panic receded. In its place came exhaustion, a sensation of such utter weariness and debilitation that, for an interval, I could do nothing at all, lacking even the small amount of strength required to lift my arms and dry my sweat-soaked forehead. Shoulders hunched, I remained half-collapsed against the wall, staring at the passers-by who, although they moved within touching distance of me, although I could hear the soft snatches of their laughter and talk, seemed remote and enigmatic creatures, holographic projections from an external world that had lost its solidity. When some semblance of strength was restored to my muscles, I made my way to a nearby pub and, swiftly, unthinkingly, drank three pints of beer. Returned to my room, I stretched myself out in front of the electric fire and, stupefied by the beer, went to sleep.

All the same, that night I found myself wide awake in the small hours, staring blankly into the darkness. For the first time I properly understood the meaning of the word 'desolation'; for the first time I felt myself to be entirely alone and helpless. Lying there, I noted with a start of dread the creeping onset of a fresh rush of the terror that had already become my familiar. It was too much for me. Throwing on my dressing-gown, I fled from the room out into the empty quad and hammered on a friend's door. I cannot imagine what he must have made of the trembling apparition standing on his threshold. 'I think I'm dying,' I said to him – or words to that effect. 'You must help me. I'm dying.' He reacted with commendable calm to the news. He made tea and we talked (what could we have talked about?) until the sky began to lighten. With the coming of the day, my agitation waned and I became gradually less afraid.

The calamity that had befallen me – at first sight so gratuitous an assault – was, I quickly realised, linked to an event I had tried to banish from my consciousness. Earlier that summer I had had a bad shock. Just before the start of the term, a friend of mine, a fellow student from Trinidad, had been found dead in his rooms at Balliol College. We had known each other from early adolescence, gone to the same secondary school, studied the same subjects. But, to understand the impact his death had on me, it is necessary to talk a little about Steve, to compare him with myself. Although we were roughly the same age, Steve had always seemed significantly older and wiser. He exuded a 'maturity', a dependability and sureness of purpose, that I could not command. In part, this must have been the result of his Presbyterian upbringing. (His family's Indian ancestry had, somehow, been almost completely effaced by their conversion to Christianity: I never thought of Steve as an 'Indian'.) Presbyterianism seemed to inculcate a special piety and discipline in its adherents; an uprightness of mind and body alien to the quasi-Hindu formlessness in which I was reared. Presbyterian households were stamped with a distinct family resemblance. There comes back to me the sheen of varnish, the smell of polished floors, the upright pianos arrayed with framed family photographs; the bringing forth on trays of glasses of iced soft drinks and the passing round on dainty plates of slices of sponge cake to be nervously dissected and speared with tiny forks. Pale-faced Presbyterian girls, accomplished in the gentle arts of music, embroidery and cooking, became wonderful wives. Droves of Hindus went to the bad. Muslims went to the bad. Catholics and Anglicans went to the bad. Presbyterians – so it appeared to me – never did, moving through life with an uncanny assurance and precision.

Steve was a true child of this milieu, an exemplar of all its virtues. As befitted his air of maturity, he was the first of my contemporaries to graduate to long trousers. Not content with joining the Sea Scouts (briefly, unhappily, I too joined that organisation), Steve also became a member of our school's Cadet Corps. Idling about the playing field, I would sometimes watch him marching in his starched khaki uniform up and down the asphalted tennis courts, a rifle aslant his shoulder. I was not alone in thinking these late afternoon manoeuvrings an amusing and faintly ridiculous spectacle. But Steve, in his military aspect, was not to be trifled with. Once, my mockery slipping out of bounds, he marched stiffly towards me with his rifle, bawled me out and half-threatened to report me to the headmaster if I persisted. After that, I behaved myself. Making fun of the Cadet Corps – and, by implication, the British Empire – was a serious charge. It was not too difficult to imagine the wrath it would call down upon me. Our English headmaster was a fierce and resolute chastiser of the wicked. It was taken for granted by the rest of us that Steve would one day be made Head Prefect; and, in due course, he was. Disappointingly, I was not even considered for the lower ranks of that august hierarchy. Someone (not Steve) muttered something about my lack of a sense of responsibility. My one consolation was that Steve was not as 'bright' as I was. Cold comfort! Because, despite this nebulous attribute, his future seemed assured in a way that mine clearly wasn't. Steve, there could be no doubt, would get the kind of results required for university admission and would make untroubled progress towards a good degree in a sensible, marketable qualification. It was assumed that, eventually, he would rise to the top of some suitably exalted bureaucracy, become a man of power and influence, and, in the ripeness of time, be rewarded with a knighthood or some barely less worthy honour. He was mantled in an air of inevitability.

His attitude towards me was nearly always tolerant, touched with a barely perceptible trace of paternal indulgence. If he occasionally seemed ridiculous to me, I too, on occasion, must have seemed more than a little ridiculous to him. When, for example, I proclaimed myself an atheist (this was in response to the crusading zeal of the Jehovah's Witness in our class), Steve merely smiled and refused to be drawn. Generally, he distanced himself from the ferment of Sixth Form disputation: there cannot have been a better Head Prefect. Not even the Jehovah's Witness – obsessed by his creed's hostility towards Darwinism – could provoke him into argument. I, on the other hand, allowed myself to be considerably provoked by him and, as a consequence, blundered into absurdity.

We both did well in the A-Level examinations; we both got into Oxford – I on an Open Scholarship which left me free to do as I pleased, Steve (I believe) on a more restrictive 'Development' scholarship which would have obliged him to return to Trinidad and work for the government. He elected to read Philosophy (for which he had no head), Politics and Economics (for which he had considerable head). I, with my usual perversity, opted for the more dubious realms of Philosophy, Psychology and Physiology, knowing a little about the first and nothing at all about the second and third elements of that strange trinity. At Oxford we went, to some extent, our separate ways. Steve was a devotee of Union debates, a joiner of societies. I was anxious to put Trinidad behind me, to steep myself in unfamiliar excitements. As a result, though we were on the most amiable terms, our friendship during that period was not all it might have been. Once a fortnight or so I might go to his rooms. He was unfailingly welcoming and would offer tea and toast and other nutritious things. More rarely he would come to my room – it was never as pleasant and well-ordered a place as his was and the food cupboard was nearly always bare. My hair was gradually lengthening, my credit account at Blackwell's Book Shop was gradually getting out of hand (increasingly impolite reminders were landing in my pigeon-hole), I was gradually discovering I had neither aptitude nor taste for what passed for 'psychology' at Oxford. Steve, so far as I knew, was untroubled by the kind of anxieties gathering about me. He remained fastidiously barbered and well dressed; he looked forward contentedly to harvesting a decent Second at the end of his three years and to returning home. I was losing any vision I might once have had of the future, drifting through an often alluring but chaotic present that promised to lead nowhere in particular. It is possible that a creeping uneasiness about myself made me avoid him. And yet, while we never talked of such matters, he was a consoling presence, a dependable point of reference and a link with the past – a past fast rushing away from me.

Then, with brutal suddenness, there he was: a corpse huddled on a bed; a body that had to wait a day or two to be discovered. (He had had a bad cold, perhaps swallowed too many aspirins, vomited in his sleep, choked and died.) I remember I was walking along the High Street when I heard my name shouted from the opposite pavement. Turning, I recognised one of Steve's friends. Waving, I walked on.

'Haven't you heard?' he shouted across the roar of the traffic.

'Haven't I heard what?'

'Haven't you heard that Steve's dead?'

I can still hear the roar of the traffic through which the news first broke upon me. I walked on.

'It's no joke,' came that voice again, speaking now close to my ear. 'Steve's dead. They found him yesterday, in his room. I thought you would have heard about it by now.'

Even now, nearly twenty years later, I still do not altogether accept it. The fact of his death remains unassimilable ... inadmissible. I know no other fact quite like it; no other fact so indigestible, so beyond the reach of acceptance. It is a void, a darkness, I instinctively circumvent. Conventional grief was strangled by sheer shock and disbelief. After that macabre exchange on the High Street, there were no tears. The only emotion I felt was terror. Terror for myself. If someone like Steve could be snatched away like that, could be so swiftly and so incomprehensibly annihilated, what about me? Wasn't I too at risk? Wasn't I too in imminent danger of being swallowed up and annihilated? My last vestiges of certainty and optimism melted away. The ground on which one walked was treacherous and unpredictable. Without warning it could open up beneath you and plunge you God knows where. His death was like a sermon. It quickened and stirred all my subterranean fears; it revealed to me regions of nullity I didn't care to know about.

His family arrived for the funeral. I recall a tormenting scene in a hotel room on a suitably bleak afternoon. Steve's father was calm and studiously matter-of-fact. His dead son featured little in the unreal conversation. We talked, if my memory serves me right, about the Boat Race. At some point – almost casually – it was suggested I might be one of the pall bearers. I baulked. Somehow, I managed to sit through most of the funeral service, staring at the coffin. But, towards the end, I could bear it no more. I fled from the church out into a rainy noon, bought a bottle of rough Spanish wine, drank it all in my darkened room and fell asleep in front of the electric fire.

When, some weeks later, I walked out of that tutorial, Steve had been relegated to the lower reaches of conscious memory. But it was a very different young man who arrived back in his room. His life had effectively been broken; his optimism, his illusions of wholeness, had been shattered under the most benign of summer skies. He would, somehow, have to start afresh. Another kind of life would have to be fabricated out of the ruins, a new self-understanding of what he was and what he wasn't and what he might be would have to be struggled for.

And what had he been, this young man? Out of what had he come?

Barely two years before, on an afternoon of intermittent rain, I had sailed out of Port of Spain harbour – a young man wearing a specially tailored grey suit, a tie of subdued stripe and carrying a brand new brief-case with bold, brassy fittings. I had stood on deck a long time, staring at the green flanks of the receding hills, turning from time to time to look at the Dragon's Mouth, the strait beyond which lay the open sea. For me, the moment represented the culmination of eighteen years of dreaming, of intense longing. In a sense, my life as I had so far lived it had been aimed towards this climactic afternoon. The vision of it had underlain almost every endeavour, its possible frustration almost every fear. At last I was escaping from the island whose narrow confines and tropical sameness had always seemed like a prison. What I had seen happening to so many before was now happening to me. It did not matter that I had no solid conception of the future lying in wait for me beyond the Dragon's Mouth, whose misty headlands framed the limits of the known world. The magical present was being savoured not as a promise of future bliss but as a triumph over a past enacted in the shadow of those hills I gazed upon : a triumph over the darknesses and confusions and despairs of child-hood and adolescence.

It was the narrow pursuit of examination success which, to a large degree, had dominated and darkened those years. This was less an educational process – in the broader meaning of that term – than a prolonged struggle, ruthlessly prosecuted, for survival. In a society so small and simple, so circumscribed in its perceptions and its aspirations, there was little other hope for release and emergence – unless, of course, you happened to come from a well-to-do family (mine was anything but that: my father, when I knew him, was an anguished invalid living on a niggardly pension from the newspaper on which he had worked as a journalist) or unless you happened to be what we, in our innocence, called 'white'. Those who were 'white' seemed to need only the most slender of intellectual resources to get on in life. Our 'white' girls (their miscegenated creaminess of complexion cannot be denied) entered beauty contests, were lauded as Carnival Queens and, if they were especially talented, progressed to the status of 'model'; their brothers strummed guitars on moonlit beach picnics and had offers of jobs from the banks and the more respectable business houses engaged in the Import-Export trade. It was rare to meet a bright white boy. Bright boys were either Indian, Negro – or Chinese. Those who weren't rich or weren't white had to be bright.

Rigour was applied from the tenderest age. The conception that learning could – or should – be 'fun', that it could – or should – be 'relevant' (but to what?) did not exist. There was no indulgence of what today would be referred to as the child's 'potential' and 'creativity' – no sand-boxes, no showy diagrams, no daubing of primary colours on virginal sheets of art-paper. 'A' was for apple. 'B' was for bat. 'C' was for cat. The cat inflexibly sat on the mat; and Dan was invariably the man in the van. The fact that you hardly ever saw an apple and that mangoes and paw-paws were not mentioned in the alphabetical catechism was neither here nor there. (I think we would all have been a little shocked and scandalised if mangoes and paw-paws had been mentioned: they belonged to a different, more intimate realm of being.) Learning was an abstract form of mental torture reinforced by spasms of physical pain. The leather strap and the chalk-stick were indissolubly linked. The system was not without its compensations. Most of us did actually learn to read and write and spell tolerably well, to add and subtract (so what if the teacher did sometimes say 'substract'?), to divide and multiply.

My first experience of school was a little shack in one of the yards adjacent to our house. It was an endearing example of Trinidadian private enterprise. I would wriggle through a gap in the rotting wooden fence. I would sit on a bench and practise my letters on a broken slate – the top right corner was missing. Daily my ears burned from being pulled and twisted. Teacher was not a cruel woman: she was merely doing what was expected of her. She was, I now suspect, hardly more literate than her charges. But she knew her alphabet, the demand for education was overwhelming and she had to earn a living somehow. I must have been barely five when I used to wriggle through that gap in our back fence with my broken slate. My memories are touched with the evanescent shadowiness of early infancy. But I can still recreate the pungent odours emanating from the nearby latrine and the sour-sweet aroma of the yellowing hog plums that littered the black mud surrounding the shack which passed as a school-house. Soon enough I progressed to another young woman who ran a larger establishment at the rear of a Chinese grocery. (The Chinese grocer's urchin of a son used to make faces at us through the cobwebbed grille that ran along the top of the wall.) She was called Teacher Van and was much admired for her strong and unsentimental arm. It was under Teacher Van's muscular guidance that I learned to read.

The distant goal of all this torment – oh, how distant! how fabulous a prospect! – was to become the winner of one of the four 'Island Scholarships', based on the results of the Cambridge Advanced Level examinations, awarded each year by the Trinidad government. The island offered no higher reward, no greater accolade than these. Island Scholarship winners were like gods among us. They were the elect, the anointed. Their photographs appeared on the front page of the local newspaper; they were fêted; girls of dubious but ambitious intent offered assignations amid the sombre glades of the Botanical Gardens. At Queen's Royal College – the secondary school I attended – the names of the winners were inscribed in black letters along the walls of the Assembly Hall where, once a week, wearing our thick navy-blue blazers in defiance of the tropics, the entire school would gather to be addressed by the Headmaster. Standing in packed, sweltering rows in that high-ceilinged hall, looked down on with amiable condescension by the sixth formers (we all knew who among them were the most likely candidates for glory) lining the balconies above us, we smaller boys would stare at the columns of names that had showered honour and fame upon our school. Some went back to the last quarter of the preceding century, a remoteness enhancing the lustre of their enshrined success. Nearly all were well known in our island life. The name of an uncle of mine was there; so, even more intimately, was the name of my elder brother. An intimidating burden of expectation weighed upon me. Monday after Monday, paying only desultory attention to the exhortations and rebukes issuing from the rostrum, I would let my gaze roam over the walls and wonder if one day my own name would be added to the pantheon, if I too would be immortalised and become an object of veneration to succeeding, thickly-blazered generations. (That was not to be – for, though I did win an Island Scholarship, I did so at another school which, regrettably, did not celebrate its heroes in the same way.)

But, long before one approached within striking distance of these glories, there were other obstacles to be overcome, each invested with its own special terrors, each threatening failure, the price of which always seemed to be extinction. Foremost among these was the College Exhibition, an examination you took about the age of ten or eleven. This provided the perilously narrow bridge that took you across the abyss from primary to secondary school – that is, to one of the two or three secondary schools worth going to. The others, mere 'high schools' of inferior status, had only the most exiguous academic pretensions: the best one could hope for after attendance at one of these was to be apprenticed in some inferior trade. That such a fate could possibly be lying in wait for me was unthinkable. The College Exhibition threw a long shadow, darkening the years of schooling preceding it. I would say that from about the age of eight it loomed before me, poisoning all joy. The protracted run-up to it was, perhaps, the unhappiest period of my childhood.

Normal school hours weren't considered long enough. At the end of the day there were the compulsory 'extra' lessons that could keep one confined for another couple of hours; and, during the holidays, there were the no less compulsory daily sessions of 'private lessons'. These, apart from anything else, provided our teachers with additional income. Economic benefit fused with sincere dedication. It was the agonising era of long division, of fractions, of decimals, of simple and compound interest; of dictation, spelling, 'comprehension' and what was eccentrically referred to as 'general knowledge'.

– What island is known as Little England?
'Barbados.'
– The Isle of Spices?
'Grenada.'
– A stitch in time saves what?
'Nine.'

– What do too many cooks spoil?

'The broth.'

– Spell Czechoslovakia ...

One's knuckles would be rapped with the edge of a ruler until they were bruised and swollen, angry fists would pound the back of one's head. I recall a memorable beating in front of a blackboard chalked up with rows of fractions upon which I gazed blankly, petrified into idiocy by a leather strap – dark and supple as a snake – thudding against the seat of my khaki trousers, burning through the material like tongues of flame, scalding my skin. (That particular leather strap had acquired an awesome notoriety among us boys. Rumour had it that the teacher soaked it nightly in a mixture of oils which endowed it with its peculiar pulpiness of texture and fieriness.)

At one point, the misery became too great. For nearly a month I absented myself from school, playing truant. So began one of the more eerie phases of my life. It was like ceasing to exist; like becoming a ghost even to oneself. My elementary school was located in an eastern district of Port of Spain (I lived in a western district of the town: I was sent to that school because my mother knew the head-master and admired his skills), near the Central Market. The market, a collection of cavernous halls – the fortress-like wall of one of these buildings bounded one side of the school's stony playground – had stamped its vagabond character on the locality. The immediate neighbourhood was anything but salubrious. Dingy tenements fenced in congested, filthy streets; piles of decomposing matter, animal and vegetable, clogged the gutters, wafting up miasmic vapours into the stagnant heat of noon; stalls offering for sale decaying mounds of dates covered with flies – abandoned cargo picked up for a song – obtruded on to the slippery pavements; red-eyed drunks lounged in the dark doorways of bars and cheap eating-houses, eyeing the drifting flotillas of women with shrill voices, skins shining and odorous with sweat ... I was too young to guess at the pleasures they offered in the alleyways.

For the first few days, a tattered canvas schoolbag looped over my shoulders, I roamed the crowded streets and the echoing halls of the market, slinking up and down the passageways between the long rows of stone counters – a vast mortuary spread out under the milky haze seeping through faraway skylights. I stared at gutted carcasses impaled on hooks: in the vicinity the water in the drainage channels ran rusty red and the air reeked of stale slaughter and discarded offal. Glittering fish filled blackened wicker baskets pearled with scales.

Escaping to the vegetable section, I lingered in the sodden aisles where women sold bunches of watercress, breathing in the astringency, half-listening to their staccato exchanges of gossip and obscenity. Nobody ever challenged me and my schoolbag. In that part of town you took life as it came.

But, after a couple of days, I grew tired of these explorations in and around the market. Becoming restless, afraid of being spotted, I began to wander farther afield, away from the market, venturing down the quieter, balcony-shaded streets leading towards the docks, moving past dim Chinese restaurants, curtained 'guest houses' and the usual bars where red-eyed men lounged in doorways, dissipating undefined longings and miseries into the hot afternoon. On Broadway I peered into godowns piled with sacks of rich-smelling cocoa beans – in those days, the island still had some interest in agriculture. Others sheltered bags of flour that coated the pavement with a powdery film which, when it rained, was churned into a glutinous slick. Elsewhere were heaped up piles of timber, stacked sheets of corrugated iron and big crates stamped with the hieroglyphics of the Import-Export trade. I liked the aura of mystery which enveloped those warehouses near the docks. Gradually, my ramblings became even bolder.

A succession of shadeless afternoons found me walking along the road that ran parallel to the harbour, staring at the ships' masts and flags and funnels showing above the rooftops of the dock installations; and – beyond – to the flats of reclaimed land won back from the pewter-coloured waters of the Gulf of Paria. Once or twice, tired out, my head aching from over-exposure to the sun, spots dancing before my eyes, I took refuge among the wild grasses that grew there, staring out over the grey water, following the movements of the ships that crept like fragments of dreams along the whitened arc of the horizon. Did I ever wonder at myself during those escapades? I do not know. There comes back to me, as I write about them, only the sensations of ghostliness, of invisibility; the compulsions of somnambulism.

But this vagrancy was too exhausting and whatever charms it had soon began to fade. Then I remembered something. On one of the streets near the market lived an ageing Indian couple, tenuous acquaintances of my mother. I had once accompanied her on a visit to them . . . they may even have been obscure relations. A receding aura of impropriety surrounded these semi-derelicts: they were runaways thrown together by an ancient and illicit passion that had led to marital treachery. Now it occurred to me that I might seek refuge with them. One morning, unable to face the prospect of roaming the streets, I presented myself at their door. The room they occupied was located on the ground floor of a tenement, approached via a tunnel – where a charcoal merchant conducted business – giving access to a confused and crowded courtyard where (so it seemed to me) children were always being beaten. I cannot imagine what I said to them, how I explained myself. However it was, they took me in without murmur.

I had stumbled on as perfect a refuge as I could ever hope to find. Both the man and the woman were absent nearly all the day. They must, I assume, have done some sort of work in or around the market, though I was never able to discover its exact nature. Even more conveniently, neither could be accused of being over-inquisitive. A hard life breeds an instinctive discretion. The room, lit by a single barred window placed high up on a wall, was murky even in broad daylight. Indeed, it was not so much a room as a cave. The amenities were rudimentary. At one end, protected by a folding screen, was a tarnished brass bed, its rickety legs standing in tins half-filled with water – a precaution against marauding ants and other ground-borne vermin. A table with an oil-lamp and two or three wooden chairs were the only other items of conventional furniture. For the rest, the gloom was randomly populated with boxes and sacks and bundles. I spent most of my time curled up under the table. Food was prepared on a coal-pot placed near the door. Around noon the woman would reappear and, crouching before the coal-pot, would fan the embers into life. I would watch her boil water in an old tin that had once contained cooking-oil, knead and roll out the dough for *rotis* (our Trinidadian equivalent of Indian bread), make *dal* and cut up and fry a mess of vegetables. Out of this I would be fed. The remainder she ladled into various improvised containers and took away with her. I saw the old man rarely. Stooped, toothless, purblind, he was generally mute on those occasions. Squatting on the dusty brick floor, he scooped up the food with his fingers from the enamel plate placed before him. It takes an effort to reconstruct the passion that must once have overwhelmed their lives, that had led to their ostracism and, ultimately, to this curious troglodytic existence in a tenement near the Port of Spain market. But some of the original ardour must have survived. For, when I saw them together, the woman displayed a tenderness that animated their silences and rose above the childish fumbling of the fingers in the enamel plate and the juices seeping down from the corners of the old man's mouth.

One lunch time there arrived a young woman – daughter-in-law as I later found out – wearing a dress of orange satin frilled with lace. A baby was propped on her hip. Sitting on the brass bed, she nursed the child. I was entranced by the sight of the milk flowing from her breast. Later, her husband – dark-skinned, oiled hair and gold watch gleaming richly in the room's poor light – arrived. To my dismay, he seemed surprised when he saw me curled under the table and stared at me with protracted curiosity. He muttered something to the old woman – who, turning briefly away from the coal-pot, glanced in my direction and shrugged. I was relieved when son and daughter-in-law went away.

The rhythm disturbed by this intrusion was restored. Another week or so went by. I lay under the table, reading and re-reading the few books I carried with me in my schoolbag. My favourite was *Homes Far Away*, one of the prescribed texts for General Knowledge. It described the lives (today we would say 'lifestyles') of exotic peoples – the Norwegians who farmed on the edges of vertiginous fjords; the Japanese who lived in fear of earthquakes and built houses from the flimsiest materials; the Swiss who rolled cheeses down steep mountain-sides; the Eskimos who lived in houses made from blocks of snow and fished through holes in the ice; and, most alluring of all, the Kirghiz who roamed the wide grasslands of Central Asia with their flocks and pitched tents of hide on plains rimmed by saw-toothed mountain ranges. Few other books have so enthralled me, penetrated so deeply into my fantasies. In that cave of a room I lay under my table, reading, dozing, staring at the window, following the subtle changes in the twilight flowing through the uncleaned glass, drifting off into reveries about the Kirghiz.

It could not last forever. One morning the young man returned. Once again he subjected me to a prolonged scrutiny. Once again he murmured agitatedly at the old woman as she crouched in front of the coal-pot, fanning the glowing charcoal with a square of cardboard. Once again she turned and glanced at me, nodding at her son. When I returned home later that afternoon my mother was waiting for me. My truancy had ended.

I returned to school a penitent, garbed – so to speak – in sackcloth and ashes. Somehow or other, though not with any great distinction (I was placed 166th in the island), I did manage to win a College Exhibition, thereby earning myself the cherished privileges of going to a decent secondary school, paying no fees and having at my disposal a small annual allowance for the purchase of text-books. Still . . . 166th. My family's relief was tempered by displeasure at that mediocre placing. The disgrace I had inflicted on our good name rankled enormously. In a fit of rage, a new pair of shoes I had been given was seized and tossed with vigour into a rain-dripping patch of anthurium lilies. '166th!' cried the furious aggressor. 'Our Mr 166th has the nerve to sit there with new shoes and look pleased with himself!' Considered levelly, I had been extremely fortunate. In another less benevolent, less democratic era, when only a handful of Exhibitions was awarded, I would not have made it. Contritely, I waded through the lilies and retrieved my shoes. They were a little soiled but otherwise unharmed.

On my first morning at Queen's Royal College, resplendent in my new blazer, the columns of names enshrined on the walls of the Assembly Hall represented not an inspiration but a burden of expectation almost too oppressive to contemplate. Many of the other boys lined up in sweltering rows must have been gripped by a similar anxiety. Stories about 'bright' boys who had gone mad or bad because they had failed by a mere mark or two to win an Island Scholarship featured prominently in the island's mythology. I remembered there being pointed out to me a wild-haired tramp of middle age who dressed himself in jute sacking and lived rough. His mania took the form of pretending that he was driving himself about in a motor-car. He would mime to perfection all the motions and gestures and petty harassments associated with that activity – the changing of gear, elaborately executed hand signals, the sudden stamping on brakes . . . everything. In this way, he travelled great distances, traversing the length and breadth of the island. Not surprisingly, it was asserted – but with what truth I have no idea – that this demented individual had narrowly missed winning a scholarship. 'That man,' I was told, 'had set his heart on studying doctor and driving about the place in a big-time car. If you could get him to slow down [he tended to 'drive' rather fast and recklessly] and talk to you, you will see how much Greek and Latin and that kind of thing he know.' I never did put him to the test; but to see that lunatic racing along the roadsides always aroused sensations of disquiet.

A doctor with a big car . . . Our ambitions in Trinidad were – and continue to be – simple and starkly defined. For us, a man could aspire to no grander title than that of 'Doctor'. To be so designated was a kind of beatitude. No loftier pinnacle of individual success could be envisaged. Doctors were rich and lived in large houses in the best suburbs; they had mown lawns of crabgrass patrolled by fierce dogs (once experienced, the ferocity of these suburban dogs will never be forgotten); their comforts were seen to by retinues of servants, frequently no less pugnacious than the Alsatians and Dobermann pinschers and Great Danes; many married foreign women, pale Irish girls who soon grew querulous in the tropical heat, treated their servants badly, imported overseas editions of the yellow press and developed all the airs and graces crudely associated with the memsahib. The submissive clientèle that flocked to their wrought-iron gates symbolised a power, a regality of status, that transcended the vulgar writing-out of prescriptions and the transfer of money extracted from knotted handkerchiefs. The lure of medical practice was not commonly associated with altruism. There were no Lydgates among us. Trinidadians are not by nature a philanthropic or scientifically curious people.

But, alas, not everyone who wanted to could become a doctor. The thoughts of such unfortunate ones would turn to the lesser kingdom of dentistry – almost as good as being a doctor, almost as glamorous. And, if you could be neither doctor nor dentist, there remained the law, distinctly third-best but, all the same, capable of bringing considerable respect. Much gold was also to be had from that quarter. Yet, there was nothing inevitable about that – and lawyers laboured under the further disadvantage of having no obvious titular splendour. Beyond these three professions our imaginations rarely ventured. When you had penetrated the realms of the law you emerged on to a foggy no-man's-land. Engineering, I would guess, was about as popular a choice – and only slightly less mysterious to most of us – as, say, electing to join the priesthood. This last vocation was not quite as uncommon as one might think. It has to be remembered that several of the best schools on the island were run by Roman Catholic teaching orders. This had its effect. The Island Scholars who chose to become priests formed a small but significant minority.

Trinidad did, oddly enough, have one distinguished institution of higher learning at that time – the Imperial College of Tropical Agriculture, to which came a few students from the hotter regions of the Empire. But, in fact, most of the students and teachers seemed to be British. They strolled about the grounds in short khaki trousers, smoked pipes, and stooped thoughtfully amid their neat little plots of experimental growth. No Trinidadian even feigned interest in that eccentric place. If it had been suggested – and no such outrageous sentiment was ever uttered in my hearing – that agriculture was an honourable course of higher study, we would have laughed; we would have judged it a symptom of insanity. For us, agriculture was linked with backwardness and degradation. It was an occupation best suited to the 'coolies' (i.e. Indians) of the countryside. Agriculture meant the hard labour in sugar-cane fields, villages of mud huts, illiteracy, the fetching of water from road-side standpipes, excessive rum-drinking, wife-beating and murder by cutlass. Agriculture (and I am talking mainly about the 'upwardly mobile' Indians: the blacks had long ago turned their backs on the land) was what you wanted to escape from; a bad ancestral dream. These attitudes were reinforced after the coming of Independence when the government, put in power by urban-minded, 'coolie'-despising blacks, ignored the Indian-dominated countryside, a process brought to completion by the onset of oil-fed prosperity in the late Sixties. Today, after a generation of 'development', Trinidad is neither the industrialised country it wanted to be nor the agricultural country it once was. It drifts towards disaster on a tinselly tide of imports. These include not only transistorised goods (the late Prime Minister, Eric Williams, declared that every home would one day be equipped with stereo-phonic sound) but sugar. All over the island you will see fields given over to neglect, ruined cocoa and orange groves. Our 'liberation' is turning into a nightmare. We cannot go back and, blinded by the greeds of insecurity and fear, we cannot discern any way forward.

My family, agonised by financial worry, looked at me and decided, without reference to my own inclinations or aptitudes (easily deduced from a long succession of school reports), that I should be a doctor. Not even in my wildest fantasies – in one of these I saw myself a 'pundit' conducting complex religious ceremonies of inordinate length; in another I pictured myself a sailor-boy who had run away from home – had I toyed with that possibility. Against all the evidence and overriding my protests, I was shunted into the science stream at Queen's Royal College. Suddenly, hopelessly, I found myself having to cope with physics and chemistry (I was never able to distinguish between the two), botany and biology (no confusion arose here – but it didn't help me much) and, most terrible of all, Additional Mathe-matics. The result was another near disaster, this time in the Cambridge Ordinary Level examinations. Once more, my family's reputation was tarnished by my academic disgrace. At this point I was surrendered to my fate. Liberated at long last from other people's plans for me, I fled – I must have been about fifteen at the time – from the science stream in which I had been so nearly drowned to the more 'humane' branches of study. I had entered the happiest and most rewarding period of my Trinidad education. Overnight, I metamorphosed into a 'bright' boy – though one, it need hardly be added, without any sharply etched prospects; overnight I was seen as a potential candidate for an Island Scholarship.

Intellectual excitement – or what passed for it – arrived. It came to begin with in the shape of Bertrand Russell – in particular his essays and *The History of Western Philosophy*, which last I discovered in my father's book-case. It was under Russell's influence that I declared myself an 'atheist' – not that I had ever been troubled by theological questions: mine was a singularly pagan up-bringing – and so given my friend Steve some amusement while scandalising the Jehovah's Witness in our class. Russell's *History* prompted a closer combing of my father's shelves. From these I disinterred, among the old-fashioned Penguins and Everymans, many hitherto unsuspected treasures, including works by several of the great men mentioned by Russell. I read (attempted to read) Locke, Hobbes, John Stuart Mill and other even more recondite authors (Boethius springs to mind). I became precociously familiar with names such as Kant, Spinoza and Leibnitz. My father's shelves led me in other directions as well. I foraged among the classic works of nineteenth- and early twentieth-century fiction, making the acquaintance of Flaubert and Balzac, Conrad and Anatole France, the monumental Russians; and, of course, Dickens. Precocity nurtured in me a febrile, inchoate iconoclasm – very silly because we were not advanced enough to have accumulated idolatries – fostered by my fondness for Dostoievski's novels. I read and re-read the 'Grand Inquisitor' sequence in *The Brothers Karamazov*; no less alluring was the murderous conceit of Raskolnikov. The old thrill returns whenever I pick up *Crime and Punishment* and glance at its opening lines. 'On a very hot evening at the beginning of July a young man left his little room at the top of a house in Carpenter Lane, went out into the street, and ...' That sentence always makes me want to write. (A few select authors have that effect. Most don't.) Hour after hour was beguiled away in our sunny, over-warm sitting-room. Sprawled in an armchair, I lost myself among words and notions whose import must frequently have escaped me. But I was happy. Happier than I had ever been. Those

stupefying yellow afternoons when the world around me receded
evoke some of the lines of a poem that entranced me when I was twelve
or thirteen.

> '...I dimly heard the Master's voice
> And the boys' far-off play.
> Chimbarazo, Cotopaxi
> Had stolen me away.
>
> I walked in a great golden dream
> To and fro from school
> Shining Popocatapetl
> The dusty streets did rule
>
> ...The houses, people, traffic, seemed
> Thin fading dreams by day
> Chimborazo, Cotopaxi
> They had stolen my soul away!'

It was an exalted form of truancy. I was up to my old tricks, seeking
escape from immediacy; shutting out an environment that seemed so
poor in possibility, the everyday reality of which was so tawdry and
confining. Russell and Dostoievski and Boethius had no meaning in
the sun-drenched sitting-room of No. 26 Nepaul Street, St. James,
Port of Spain, Trinidad. They were spectres unattached to anything I
saw around me, exisiting only within the covers of the books protected
by my father's glass-doored book-case. From a strictly practical point
of view, my time would probably have been as well spent reading
fairy-tales. Looking at the matter more broadly, the meaninglessness
extended to the commonplace gyrations of school life. How could any
of us, however 'bright', really hope to understand the grandiose
movements and conflicts of the European history we studied on
which the Cambridge Examination Board would one day be testing
us? How could we, whose lives were so primal, whose experience was
so straitened by simplicity, grasp more than the bare shadows of the
facts peddled to us by our schematic text-books? But life is sometimes
kind and it hid the void. Later, some of us would be sucked into that
void and become as panic-stricken as any drowning man; we would
realise the full implications of 'under-development'. Some of us
would never recover.

Eventually, my hunger for the arcane took me to a little bookshop on a quiet street near the Queen's Park Savannah. (In the part of London where I now live, such an establishment would not attract notice. They are ten a penny.) Devoted to the highbrow, it was unique in Trinidad. Its proprietor nursed literary ambitions and we soon became friends. Two or three afternoons a week I would cycle to his little shop and explore its small but ardent stock. Now and again, if I had the money, I would buy a paperback. (Some of those paperbacks have survived my migrations ... Henri Bergson's treatises on moral philosophy ... Nietszche on the nature of Tragedy and the 'genealogy of morals' ...) The bookshop, cooled by the breezes blowing from the hills across the Savannah, its monastic peace rarely disturbed by the intrusion of customers, was a most congenial haven.

My new friend seemed to know something about everything. It was he who introduced the word 'polymath' into my vocabulary. Our conversation – or, rather, *his* conversation – was wide-ranging and studded with erudite reference. As he talked, he paced round the room, picking books off the shelves, reading aloud some appropriate passage or the other to illustrate the point he was making. No matter what the subject – literary, scientific, philosophical, political – he was never at a loss for something to say. If Karl Marx (for example) crept into the conversation, he might produce the 'Critique of the Gotha Programme' and gravely support his argument with quotations from it. From Marx he might progress to a discussion of the 'Jewish problem' in nineteenth-century Europe, in the course of which he would probably reach for one of Hannah Arendt's books. Or, he might launch into speculation about the Theory of Relativity and from this move on to a disquisition – I don't remember how the connection was effected – on the nature of mystical experience. Mysticism, as I noted even at the time, exerted a strong subterranean pull on him. From him I first heard of Gurdjeff, Ouspensky and Krishnamurti. 'The world built up by the senses,' he said, 'is only a convenient fabrication, a crutch on which we lean. We must pay attention to it because it conditions our existence. But beneath it ... beneath it ... who knows what there is?' He talked about the 'middle eye' which was rumoured to be located in the middle of the forehead; I listened enthralled to his tales of yogis who had voluntarily entombed themselves for lengthy periods and emerged unscathed from the ordeal. Infected by his enthusiasm, I bought several books written by a man called Paul Brunton: this strange person appeared to have spent a lifetime roaming India in search of holy men with miraculous powers. From Krishnamurti he might digress to Annie Besant and the Theosophical movement, and from these to Gandhi and the struggle for Indian independence – at which point he was liable to extract Nehru's autobiography from the shelves. We indulged in a wild whirl, both exotic and rational. Often, as we talked, a deepening twilight would invade the little room.

Our friendship flourished to the extent that at one juncture he asked if I would like to look after the shop during his absence. The money offered was modest (about twenty dollars for the two weeks he would be away) but I was flattered by his trust and accepted. (This was the first of the two salaried 'jobs' I have had – the other happened some time afterwards in London when, for a few spectacularly unsuccessful weeks, I was taken on by a publishing firm engaged in the compilation of an encyclopaedia, the brain-child of an entrepreneur who liked comparing himself to Diderot: most of that wretched interlude was spent re-writing the commissioned entries on lichens and Leonardo da Vinci – I was working on the 'Ls'.) I enjoyed the monastic seclusion of the shop during those two weeks. Hardly anyone ever disturbed its sepulchral solitude and all day long I sat at the desk, fanned by the Savannah breezes, reading whatever took my fancy. I behaved like a child who had been let loose in a sweet-shop. All the same, it was impossible not to wonder how he managed to make a living out of it. The twenty dollars I was paid I spent on books. The economics of the transaction continues to puzzle me. Did he make a profit out of me? Or did I make a profit out of him? Or did we merely maintain the status quo? Many years later, on a brief visit to Trinidad, I made the pilgrimage to the quiet street near the Queen's Park Savannah. The bookshop had disappeared. Eventually, however, I tracked down my old friend. He was, I was pleased to find out, still involved in the book trade. But he was no longer the man I had known. He had had severe nervous troubles. The result was that his mystical tendencies had – so, at any rate, it seemed to me – taken over completely. We had no common language; in our different ways, we had become ghosts to each other. The world built by the senses, that 'convenient fabrication' we had talked about long ago in the twilit shop, had virtually ceased to matter to him; had virtually, so far as he was concerned, ceased to exist.

It was some fifteen years before that last saddening encounter my photograph had appeared in the newspaper. There, staring out of the front page, was no mere future doctor or dentist or lawyer. There was a future 'philosopher'! There, declaring himself before all, was a would-be unraveller of the mysteries of life and of the universe! The gawky adolescent in his grey suit and striped tie who, some months later, leaned against the deck rails, contemplating with an air of triumph the receding hills and roof-tops of Port of Spain, turning from time to time to gaze at the headlands framing the Dragon's Mouth, did not know his deep absurdity; did not know that his ship was not bearing him from darkness to enlightenment but from ignorance to confusion. He did not suspect that one day his own life, his own nebulous and unstable 'identity', would become – for him – the greatest mystery and challenge of all.

In one of my books I wrote the following about myself. 'At the age of eighteen (which was when I left Trinidad), I was haphazardly cobbled together from bits and pieces taken from everywhere and anywhere. The ugly parallel that suggests itself is one of those shanty town hovels built up from whatever dross comes to hand ... I had inherited no culture; no particular outlook; no particular form.' And, in a recent novel, one of the characters says, 'I grew up, you know, without allegiance to anything ... Every day I have to re-invent myself.' Both these statements, I am aware, have about them a glimmer of extremism. They may even, I dare say, convey to hostile eyes an inverted conceit. The latter I would deny. As to the former, what else is there to be said other than that I simply state a truth? that if I seem, on a shallow reading, to be extreme that is only because the condition I try to describe *is* extreme?

Culture – in its aggressively political aspect – is a term much used and abused. It is an ineffable something we are all expected to have, to express at every opportunity and to fiercely protect from outside interference: an inalienable birthright, you might say. Some 'cultures' are startlingly recent revelations – the Rastafarians who, a generation ago, did not exist now constitute a fully-fledged dimension of 'black-ness' and, to a credulous white audience, proclaim ganja-smoking an essential part of their 'heritage'. Even women (women, that is, as distinct from *men*) claim to have unearthed a culture of their own; a culture disguised by thousands of years of male domination. No notion is foggier or harder to pin down. In so far as I understand it, it seems, at bottom, to imply a specific state of collective 'being', intimately harboured by the individual representative of the specific tribe, expressing itself in certain specific tendencies, modes of behaviour and ways of 'knowing'.

In other words, it defies analysis. It can mean everything and therefore constantly runs the danger of meaning nothing. As such, it is perfectly adapted to the requirements of soap-box oratory and politics; as viscerally appealing as the 'women and children' rhetoric beloved by the demagogues of an earlier age. Militant blacks are hopelessly addicted to the notion. In fact, mere pigmentation -- one could call it melanism -- has come to be regarded as a major cultural attribute. In the old days this used to be associated with the now notorious and slightly discredited 'sense of rhythm'. Now, underwritten by tender liberal sensibilities, the sense of rhythm has been transmogrified into other superficially sophisticated concepts. The notion of 'Black Art' is conspicuous among these. (The London Borough of Camden will soon have a 'Black Arts Centre'. Mixing his metaphors, one of the critics of the scheme was reported as saying that there was every likelihood of the Black Arts centre turning into a white elephant.)

The Oxford English Dictionary offers some relief from all this. 'Culture,' it says, is 'the training and refinement of mind, tastes and manners: the condition of being thus trained and refined, the intellectual side of civilisation.' One sees straightaway the dangers embedded in this definition. 'Refinement' . . . 'manners' . . . 'intellectual' . . . these are like red rags to a bull. Already I can hear the accusations of 'élitism', 'cultural imperialism', 'class arrogance' ringing in my ears. Being of pacific disposition, I shall omit these contentious extensions of the definition and simply confine myself to culture as the training of tastes, '. . . the condition of being thus trained'. It is in that elementary sense I assert my own lack of a culture, that unnerving perception of having been disinherited a long time ago, of having been cut off without a penny and cast adrift. I was not trained to anything; I was heir to no coherent and clearly identifiable body of tastes, prejudices, loyalties and behaviour. The 'culture' that would have provided such a training did not exist. It was already largely disintegrated – reduced, at best, to a nostalgic ruin – by the time I was born, a state of affairs that deteriorated steadily as I grew up. I was a waif, inhabiting a make-shift world in which all the landmarks had been effaced, in which there were no maps and no guides.

The clannish, hierarchical Hindu past known to the older members of my family (a gap of nearly twenty-five years separates my eldest and youngest sisters) had all but dissolved by my day, been split up into its various, often warring, fragments, each of which rigorously pursued its own interests. By the time I was born, the living link with the countryside, with the sugar-cane estates of the Caroni plains, had been effectively broken. About that other life I knew virtually nothing. I was a town boy through and through. The country belonged to a vague pre-history. Admittedly, many of my father's relations continued to eke out a rural existence, maintaining the traditional connection with the world of the sugar estates. But they too, though more slowly and precariously, were transforming themselves. Older sons were taking to school-teaching and taxi-driving (some of my paternal first cousins combined both these trades), the girls talked of going to England and training as nurses and hairdressers, younger sons murmured about medicine and the law.

I was never especially close to my father's family. Somehow, they had remained in the background of the everyday scheme of things, marginal presences in my Port of Spain life. So peripheral were they, I often had no idea who was who – and, for the most part, that ignorance persists. From time to time one or another of my father's relations would turn up at our house; or, succumbing to impulse, we would take a Sunday morning drive down to Caroni and spend the day sitting and reclining in hammocks made of jute-sacking, staring out from the shade of thatched roofs at the dreary, rustling acres of sugar-cane. Again and again, kindly men and women, reddened by the sun, smelling richly of dust and wood-smoke and grass, would urge me to come and spend time with them. But nothing ever came of these invitations. A foolish citified pride and apprehension made me hold myself aloof from them. For a long time I did not understand that the wrinkled old woman whom we called 'Poowah' and who could speak barely a word of English and was most comfortable when squatting on the floor, chain-smoking cigarettes between cupped palms, succumbing to strangulated spasms of coughing that made her eyes water . . . for a long time I did not understand that she was actually my father's sister. Even when I grasped that fact, its significance never really sank in; it never really acquired any intimacy for me.

When we referred to 'family', we almost invariably meant my mother's family – my two uncles (remote patriarchs accorded a near idolatrous respect), my array of aunts (whom we respected but did not worship), and an army of first and second cousins. The ancestral past was represented by my grandmother, a figure of legendary ferocity and resolution. However, I knew her only as a blind, bed-ridden woman ending her days in the Port of Spain house of her elder son. Whenever I went there with my mother, she would take me up on to the bed with her, call me '*beta*' (son) and, drooling endearments from her toothless mouth, lavish upon me clumsy caresses. Her flannel vests were impregnated with camphor and she smelled strongly of the bay-rum with which she liberally bathed her skin. My mother, as a gesture of daughterly submission, would apply more bay-rum as they talked together in Hindi or, if it was demanded, massage her limbs with coconut oil. I couldn't have been more than five or six years old when she died – to me she had been hardly any more than an emanation of mysterious, medicinal essences. I recall a gaudily orna- mented open coffin placed on trestles in my uncle's sitting-room and, afterwards, the leaping flames and smoke rising from her funeral pyre on the banks of the Caroni River. A couple of years later I would once more be standing on the muddy banks of the Caroni. On that occasion I stared at the leaping flames and smoke consuming my father's body.

The break-up of the family seemed to accelerate with my grand- mother's death, aggravated in authentic peasant style by the quarrels and jealousies that took shape round the division of the inheritance – the bulk of which, of course, passed to the two sons. But there still remained land enough and gold and silver enough to stimulate vile rancour and innuendo, quarrels that would be exacerbated in due course by the (ostensibly) political differences that developed between my two uncles, one of whom (the younger) became Leader of the Opposition: the other didn't. But all of this lay a little in the future. For a while yet, our 'Hinduness', our awareness of ourselves as members of an exclusive and important clan, Brahminical princes among the Hindu community, came to life once a year or so when we all gathered for some days in my uncle's house (I refer to the uncle who didn't attain the Leadership of the Opposition – the other, during those years, was absent in England and famed on the island for his mathematical genius) where were enacted various religious rites. At any rate, these rites provided a kind of climax to the other, more earthly proceedings. I had no knowledge of the meaning or signifi- cance of these rituals. Religion, so far as it impinged on me, consisted of the protracted drone of a pundit chanting a language I did not understand from the sacred texts, the clouds of incense ascending from the flower-strewn *puja* mound, the ringing of bells and the tuneless trumpeting of conch-shells. Beyond this, my comprehension did not penetrate.

What I did like was the communal coming-together, that chaotic assemblage of aunts and first and second cousins under one roof; the sleeping together on the floor in the pillared space downstairs; the games of table-tennis and cards and pavement cricket; the food, doled out on freshly-washed banana leaves sparkling with droplets of water, served at long tables, and the pots of sweet, milky tea poured into blue-rimmed enamel cups; the women cooking over wood fires in the improvised kitchen set up in the back yard, hoarsely singing *bhajans* as they rolled out dough and stirred cauldrons of boiling rice and vegetables and lentils; and at night, if the mood was conducive, the singing would be done to the accompaniment of drums. I have never seen my mother happier than she was on these occasions, her mood an unstable compound of excitability, serenity and gaiety shared by all the aunts. They surrendered themselves body and soul to the collective entity that overwhelmed us all during those few days. The colonial-cosmopolitan world beyond my uncle's gates receded and became dim.

These interludes were my nearest approach to the past (or what I imagined the past to have been like), to its amniotic assurance, protection and solidarity. It was the closest I have ever come to feeling I 'belonged' to an organism larger than myself, to having an 'identity' accepted by myself and recognised and reinforced by others: the closest I have ever come to a *social* existence. But soon enough even these celebrations came to an end – I must have been about ten or eleven when that occurred – as loyalties frayed under stress and collapsed into open enmity between the rival factions centred on the persons of my two uncles. When these old wars did finally come to an end, there was nothing left. Gradually, imperceptibly, I lost touch with most of my aunts and cousins. Some of the former have died, gone away or simply sunk into the futilities of old age. Nearly all my first cousins are strangers to me, the bond between us broken beyond repair. If we passed on the street, it is probable that we would fail to recognise each other. India, as represented by its ties of caste and clan and shared memory, lasted less than sixty years in Trinidad.

My mother, naturally enough, continues to worship the divinities my grandfather brought with him when he adventured across the 'black water'. At Diwali, the Hindu festival of lights, she illuminates the house, as she has always done, with little oil-fed lamps of clay and cooks special food which she distributes to the neighbours. Some of this food she puts out for the shade of my father. Nor does she neglect to light a lamp on behalf of each of her seven children and she places the lamps in a semi-circle under the sacred *tulsi* (basil). Her Hinduism is there for everyone to see, but it is there in a very different way. On the whole, I think it can be fairly said, her worship is more detached and formal. She goes to a nearby temple with tiled floors and colourful effigies of the gods and goddesses imported from the factories of Bombay and Benares; a temple with secretaries, treasurers and committees. India, as such, has emerged into the light of day. She has visited it twice by jet plane, stayed in its five-star hotels, been cheated by its merchants and, in keeping with her piety, made pilgrimages to the holy places. Now, she talks of travelling to Alaska. For better or worse, she accepts her 'Trinidadianness'; she knows the prehistory played out on the Caroni plains is dead and can never be revived. The turbulent cosmopolitan-colonial world has triumphed.

St. James, the western district of Port of Spain in which I grew up, mirrored that turbulent cosmopolitanism. The area had once been a sugar-cane estate and the names of the streets – Ganges, Hyderabad, Bengal, Madras, Cawnpore, Lucknow, Bombay, Calcutta – were (I assume) the last surviving echoes of the indentured labourers who had toiled on its soil. But long before I was born its agricultural past had been forgotten; become, in fact, almost impossible to imagine. St. James, cut in two by the busy thoroughfare called the Western Main Road, was uncompromisingly urban, harbouring a variegated population none of whom could be classed as rich or, come to that, desperately poor: the beggars who used to come regularly to our gate on Friday mornings were not of the 'locality. It was neither an especially desirable nor an especially undesirable area in which to live. If you had the money, you moved out; if you didn't, you stayed and didn't feel too hard done by. This raffish ambiguity was not without its charms.

On the Western Main Road there were modest businesses – offering for sale bolts of cloth, random items of haberdashery and hardware, knick-knacks made in Hong Kong – owned by indolent Syrians, Lebanese and Indians. Chinese ran laundries and groceries and rum-shops. The grocery favoured by my mother had a Portuguese proprietor – he, however, taking fright at the prospect of Independence (we weren't able to appreciate such sentiments in those days), sold up eventually and took himself off to Madeira. The defection of the generous and kindly Mr Cardoso filled my mother with sorrow. Elderly Negro women operated road-side stalls heaped, according to the season, with oranges and mangoes and tamarinds as well as sickly items of home-made confectionery. Our cinema, the Rialto, fed us a steady diet of Western double features and did a decent trade. On Saturday nights there would be good-natured brawls outside the deliberately narrow tunnel that gave access to its pit section. True to its urban character, St. James was well-stocked with steelbands. However, our steelbandsmen, perhaps softened by the ambiguous nature of the environment, were not as tough or as fearsome as those who came from the more easterly parts of town; nor, as a consequence, was their music quite as good.

St. James differed in many ways from the neighbouring district of Woodbrook – where my uncle lived. Woodbrook with its quiet streets, its sprinkling of tiny squares, its neat wooden houses fronted by verandas with fretted eaves from which were suspended orchids and ferns in wire baskets, was definitely more respectable, more desirably 'residential' in every respect than was St. James. Lighter-skinned folk, families of clerkly status, school-teachers, they all showed a marked preference for Woodbrook. Not surprisingly, it was also a favourite haunt of Presbyterians. There must have been more pianos per square acre in Woodbrook than in any other district of Port of Spain. (I do not believe my street in St. James could have laid claim to a single piano.) It had, predictably enough, many fewer steelbands; while the Hispanic bias of its street names – Luis, Carlos, Alberto, Cornelio, Rosalino – further emphasised its pretensions. If St. James was very different from Woodbrook, it was no less different from a district like Belmont. This last was an altogether unpleasant place. Its faults can be traced back to distant events. Many of its original inhabitants were slaves rescued from foreign ships by the crusading zeal of the British Navy after the abolition of the 'Trade' in 1807 (for a while the area was known as Freetown). Belmont, as a result, was given to a querulous independence of spirit. In its tortuous alleys and lanes was nurtured a peculiar Africanised hubris – a sort of proto-Negritude – that was off-putting to the outsider. I hardly ever went there. My Trinidadian – the type with which I am most familiar – is the St. James-style Trinidadian: an individual eluding precise defini-tion. And the street on which I lived – defying facile sociological analysis – was a typical St. James street.

Shortly after I was born (that stirring event took place – at an hour now forgotten by my mother – in my uncle's Woodbrook house, in a room unflatteringly referred to as the 'pantry'), my father moved us to a small, box-shaped, two-storeyed house on Nepaul Street. Here I would spend the first eighteen years of my life. The house, situated not far from the corner where Nepaul Street met the Western Main Road – the Rialto cinema was a stone's throw away, on the opposite side of that artery – had the distinction of being the only two-storeyed structure on the street. But, then, there were no two houses alike. Some were bungalows of plastered, painted brick; others, bungalows of raw brick. Some were old-style wooden houses with jalousied windows and fretted woodwork; others were newer-style wooden cabins without jalousied windows and fretted woodwork. Some were little better than tumble-down shacks. The one feature possessed in common was the use of corrugated iron for roofing. It would be tempting to hazard the generalisation that the quality of the architecture improved towards the Western Main Road end of the street and degenerated as you went away from it. But even that optimistic statement cannot be considered as accurate. In the zone of brick several more or less discreet pockets of dereliction were to be discovered scattered about the untidy backyards.

Nor did Nepaul Street lend itself to a quick and easy racial stereotyping. Negroes were certainly the most numerous but they were not culturally dominant. There were (apart from us) some families of Indian ancestry to be found on the street; there were those who, depending on mood, might have described themselves as 'Portuguese' or 'Creole' or 'Coloured' (Trinidadians deploy that term in its South African sense); and there were those of an ancestry so wonderfully confused that they were impossible to classify: our language, so subtle in these matters, could not, nevertheless, be expected to cover every eventuality. There was, let me add for the sake of completeness, a Chinese family. They remained among us for about two years – but, having the money, they moved out. At any rate, there we all were: a completely arbitrary collection of human beings. At one extreme, picture my father with his glass-doored book-case lined with classical works of literature and philosophy. At the other, picture the Negro children, running wild and shirtless in dusty backyards, with navels protuberant. Picture their pig-tailed older sisters, maturing with startling rapidity, whose bellies would begin to swell at the age of fourteen or fifteen, as if in obedience to some inflexible law of nature. Children were easy to bear but childhood was short in St. James. We co-existed without animosity, but also without mutual comprehension; we were strangers to one another, linked by nothing except our physical proximity – by the stark, unaccountable fact of our having been washed up on the same street, one of many, many streets like it, in the capital city of a distant outpost of the British Empire.

Beyond our back fence was the spacious yard – a compound almost – in which I had had my first taste of Trinidad's pedagogic techniques. The compound was shared by an odd mixture of people. At the front, facing the Western Main Road, was a large and airy wooden bungalow with a wide veranda. It was a curiously bleak place, minimally furnished, its floorboards bare and unpolished. When I think of it I see cheap lace curtains fluttering in the breezes that rushed through its wide-open doors and windows. Here lived a tense and pale Indian jeweller, his plump, fecund wife and their numerous progeny. My family's attitude towards them was reasonably amiable but distant, my mother's attitude being tinged with faint traces of an hauteur verging on suspicion. It is interesting that my mother, fascinated like all Indians by jewellery, never called on the jeweller's skills. It was as if she did not entirely trust the family's credentials. Never, or hardly ever, did they come to our house. However, no objection was raised to my going over to them and amusing myself with the younger sons of the family. They were, as it had happened, the only playmates I ever had in the immediate vicinity, even though Nepaul Street, it goes virtually without saying, teemed with children. But it was assumed both by these urchins (denizens of the yards at the less salubrious end of the street) and by myself that no friendship could arise between us. Subsequent events would seem to justify my mother's unspoken misgivings.

In the nether regions of the compound beyond the jeweller's house was a barrack-like building whose dark, stifling rooms were rented out to a vagrant tenantry – women without men, children without fathers, men without women who slept drunkenly through the day, emerging from their dens at twilight to roam the Western Main Road. The portion of the barracks nearest us – the building extended to within a few feet of our back fence – was occupied by a wild-looking woman of indeterminate age and racial composition who had with her a copper-skinned girl of Negroid feature. Mahalia (as the child was named) was (I imagine) about five years older than myself. They may or may not have been mother and daughter. The precise relationship between them never became clear to me. However it was, the woman exercised all the sinewy rights of guardianship over the child who, most days, would be mercilessly beaten. I grew up with the sounds of

Mahalia's frenzied wailing and sobbing, accompanied by the orgiastic howl of her 'mother's' stampeding rage as she chased her up and down the black-earthed compound. It is doubtful whether Mahalia ever went to school. Daily I would see her walking to and from the standpipe, swaying under the weight of the buckets of water she carried on her head; I would see her diligently sprinkling then sweeping their portion of yard; I would watch her fanning the coal-pot put out on the steps leading to their room: between beatings Mahalia was a lively and energetic child. There were even moments of simian tenderness between 'mother' and 'daughter' – when the former would cradle Mahalia's head on her lap and deftly comb through it and pick out the lice.

If their relationship was obscure, no less so were their means of support. My mother had convinced herself – and me – that the woman was an adept in the black arts of obeah, her diabolical aptitudes freeing her from conventional necessities. The Devil, like God, looked after his own. She may have been right. Certainly the woman, inky locks of hair curling into ringlets, kohl-blackened eyes sunk deep in her feral face, looked the part. And there were inexplicable goings-on. Now and again I would hear incantatory invocations issuing through the open windows of the room; now and again we would come upon garlands of faded flowers lying on our side of the fence. These objects roused all my mother's superstitious terrors, though it was never explained why the evil creature should want to harm us. Taking care not to let these unsolicited offerings come into contact with her flesh, my mother would lever them back over the fence. The usual response to these acts of defiance was explosions of raucous merriment in which – sometimes – the brutalised Mahalia shared. This war between the powers of light and darkness was waged over several years. My mother, I am sure, would claim that the ultimate victory was hers. I keep an open mind.

Alas, St. James was St. James – a brute reality which not even the dark angels of obeah could dispel. When she was about fifteen, Mahalia's belly began to betray tell-tale signs of distension. The beatings that followed were among the most terrible that I can remember. Day after day Mahalia raced about the compound, pursued by her hysterical mother. 'I going to murder you! I going to chop off your hands and foot! Chop up that thing you have growing inside of you! I don't care if they hang me!' Then, quite suddenly, from one day to the next, the beatings stopped. A weird and unprecedented quiet descended upon the barracks – the dazed tranquillity, one may surmise, of exhaustion and despairing fatalism. The transformation was uncanny. Mahalia, now exuding a slatternly serenity, resumed the round of her domestic duties. She sprinkled and swept the yard, swayed under the buckets of water she carried from the standpipe, fanned the flames of the coal-pot. Once a week or so she would have her hair combed and the lice plucked out. Her mother, sunk in lethargy, would sit out on the steps looking at her or would wander about the compound singing to herself. I heard no sombre incantations floating out from the windows of the room; no faded garlands appeared on our side of the fence. She even tried to address a few civil words to my mother, to enlist her sympathy about the waywardness of girl-children. My mother, who had five of her own, was not responsive. The baby was born. Mahalia, a woman now, neglected her domestic tasks and did as she pleased, consigning the child to its grandmother. 'Mahalia running wild,' I heard her complain to one of the neighbours. 'She must have a man on every street in St. James.' All the same, she seemed devoted to the baby's welfare, bathing it, feeding it from a discarded beer bottle, rocking it to sleep on her shoulders, weeping over it as, instinctively, she searched its head for lice: it must have been the only gesture of tenderness she knew. One day Mahalia appeared with a man – who may or may not have been the child's father. They took the baby and went away. It was the last time I saw Mahalia. Solitude brought with it a half-hearted revival of the old ways. The incantations started up again and more garlands were tossed over the fence. But the dread they used to inspire had evaporated; their power had been broken. During those months of solitude and half-hearted witchery, she looked wilder and more dishevelled than ever, shrinking into a meagre parody of her old self; and, within a few months, she too vanished. 'I going to look for Mahalia,' she said. We never saw her again.

The malign star haunting the compound reached out to embrace the jeweller and his family. On visits to the house I would hear his normally placid wife sobbing in a bedroom. A horrible change had come over the jeweller. His air of pale tension, of recession from his surroundings, had gradually intensified. He would sit out on the veranda, staring at the traffic on the Western Main Road, his light-brown eyes filmed with lustrous vacancy. Sometimes he would look at me and not seem to recognise who I was. His children appeared to be frightened by him and avoided his presence. They were withdrawn and did not want to play. I began to keep away. There were rumours of wife-beating – and worse: it was bruited about that the jeweller was insane. Among us the mad aroused not compassion but rather evoked the most primitive fears. At some subconscious level we must all have sensed how perilously close we were to dissolution. I stopped going altogether. The situation deteriorated. Occasionally, agonised wails floated across the compound and I would hear the sounds of breaking glass; the crash of furniture being hurled about. A climax of sorts was attained when one of the older boys set upon his father, beat him up and fled from the house with his mother and the younger children. The family disintegrated. Soon, the house was completely abandoned. They also had disappeared forever from our lives. I would experience a shiver of disturbance whenever I passed by the house and saw its empty veranda, its shattered windows and useless lace curtains fluttering in the breeze. After a time the house was pulled down and, St. James being St. James, a rum-shop was built on the site. The barracks too was demolished. In its place came a two-storeyed house. Here the owner of the rum-shop installed a number of women – a lewd, languorous, bosomy harem – who may or may not have been his mistresses. Their protector, a choleric man devoted to his trade, fell periodically into a drunken ferment of jealousy and suspicion. He would appear among them, a red-eyed, half-naked apparition waving a cutlass. 'I going to chop all of you! You hear me? I come to chop up all of you today.' The women flapped and squawked like panic-stricken fowls. This happened about twice a month. The compound remained an enclave of disrepute.

If we regarded the jeweller and his family warily – withholding, as it were, full communion – this was even more the case with the family next door. Outwardly, they looked Indian. With that, all resemblance between them and us ended. They represented an extreme of deracination, of vacuity, which still fascinates me. They were, I would guess, vaguely 'Christian' – but of precisely which variety it is not easy to say. The act of conversion had left them culturally shipwrecked. It is highly improbable that they were Presbyterian. If that had been so, there would have been a piano in the house and they would have assiduously educated themselves. Their aspirations – they had few I could discern – were, at best, muddy, fluctuating and modestly pitched. They seemed to me to subsist within a bubble of inanity: to have come from nowhere in particular, to belong to nothing in particular (they lacked even the crudest racial self-definition) and to be going nowhere in particular. Their emptiness expressed itself in peculiar ways. Old Mr. S... was said not to have exchanged a word with his wife for uncounted years. The original cause of their silence – if there had been any such specific event – had long been forgotten, had long ceased to matter. From one day to the next they had simply stopped 'talking' to each other. Petulance had hardened into loveless habit and become a way of life. Maybe, they had come to the bleak realisation that they had nothing to talk about. Indeed, the state of conversation in that house was altogether perilous. You could never be sure who was 'talking' or 'not talking' to whom. For no apparent reason, the daughter would stop talking to her mother for months on end; and – again for no apparent reason – she would suddenly resume normal communication. Shifting allegiance, she would then stop talking to her father. There were interludes when she talked to neither. The sons were prey to the same malady. They exhausted every conceivable permutation of talking and not talking with each other, with their sister and with their mother and father. To know the exact state of affairs in the household at any given moment was almost impossible. Sometimes, communication seizing up completely, a shrouding silence would envelop the household. To compensate for this, someone would play the radio at its loudest volume, so banishing the funereal silence. These alternating tides of sociability and reticence could be extended to their neighbours. Inexplicably, the daughter or one of the sons would refuse to acknowledge my mother's greetings. One of these numerous cold wars – with the daughter – lasted for several years.

Old Mr S..., when I came to know him, was already an invalid – a mild-mannered, slow-moving, yellow-skinned man. Mornings and afternoons, dressed in striped pyjamas, he would sit out on the little veranda at the front of the house, staring out at the street with rheumy eyes. When he saw me playing in our yard, he might wave and smile. After a fashion he tried to be nice to me. Now and again he would call me over to him and, amazingly enough, endeavour to talk. Once – rather to my surprise – he concocted a 'telephone' out of two tin cans joined by a piece of string; another time he showed me how to make a kite. 'When I was a boy,' he confided joylessly, 'I used to fly a lot of kite.' It was the only item of autobiographical information he ever allowed himself. Most days, however, he didn't call me over to him and didn't bother to smile or wave. Shoulders hunched, he would just sit there on the sun-struck square of veranda, looking out blankly at the street, waiting for death. He may have had a story to tell – we are all supposed to have a story to tell. It is terrible to suspect that his life was so void of passion and interest and meaning that he may not have had one.

As for Mrs S..., she who had not been 'talked' to by her husband for uncounted years – she was indistinguishable from a domestic servant. I have a fixed image of her wandering about the yard barefooted (the soles of her weathered feet were incised by intricate networks of cracks and fissures), a kerchief wrapped round her head, clucking at the fowls and turkeys she kept, scattering feed and scraps of stale bread. I see her too picking up the rotting breadfruit fallen from the impressive tree that grew in the yard. That breadfruit tree was one of the landmarks of our street. It was, in addition, a source of friction. My mother felt – and she may have been justified – that its roots were undermining the fence and threatening to irrupt through the floor of the sitting-room. Be that as it may, the breadfruit tree was for us an undeniable and unprofitable nuisance. Its upper branches overhung our roof. At night we would be startled awake by the thunder of overripe breadfruit crashing down on the corrugated iron. My mother also objected to the debris that littered our yard and, not infrequently, blocked our drains. All of these irritations were aggravated by accusations of miserliness: seldom were we given a breadfruit. On occasion my mother would murmur darkly about pouring poison on its roots but, not being a malicious woman, never had the courage to perform the deed. It is possible that the tensions and bad blood provoked by the breadfruit tree may have accounted – in part – for some of the cold wars waged against us.

Mrs S... never went anywhere and seemed to have no friends or diversions. She bore her enslavement without complaint, never betraying any visible signs of rancour. Whatever emotions she might once have possessed had been strangled. Her physical appearance altered little over the years – one had the impression that she had been born old, over-worked and neglected; that she had emerged from some anonymous womb with a kerchief tied round her head. If I could not convincingly portray to myself old Mr S... flying kites in his boyhood, neither could I portray to myself the youthful desires and agitations of this unloved, blighted and abandoned creature. Her husband's death – that long-expected and passionless event took place not many weeks after he had made me the kite – wrought no changes in her life. The nothingness within which she was imprisoned was beyond the reach of alteration or mitigation. She continued to do as she had always done; to be what she had long become. When last I saw her some five years ago, she was still wandering about the yard in bare feet, her head wrapped in a kerchief, clucking at the fowls and ducks (the turkeys had disappeared). In the interval the old bread-fruit tree had died a natural death and been replaced by another equally vigorous specimen – the upstart, I was glad to see, had established itself in a less contentious area of the yard. Breadfruit no longer thundered on to our corrugated-iron roof; and its roots posed no threat to the floor of our sitting-room. 'You gone and grow into a man,' she said to me. (I had had to re–introduce myself because she did not recognise me.) My adulthood appeared to surprise her. As she looked at me, her faded eyes dimmed with reflective wonder at the fact. 'I remember you so high.' She smiled emptily, gesturing towards her knees. We had nothing else to say to each other. In a moment she had turned away from me and started clucking at the fowls and ducks.

On the same visit I saw Claudette again. She was a near relation of the S . . . household – as usual, the exact nature of the connection eluded me – and, for a time, had lived with them. Claudette was roughly the same age as Mahalia. Her hair was long and black and curling, her hips robust – and on her downy upper lip there would sparkle, whenever she was excited and intent, tiny beads of sweat. Claudette had been one of the acknowledged belles of the neighbour-hood, the pride of our street. She was sociable, laughed a lot and, as she entered her teens, took to dressing herself with a stylish insouciance. She would wear shorts and tight jerseys of alluring stripe and was one of the first to appear in 'pedal-pushers'. She was a flagship of high fashion. In the afternoons she would display herself on the veranda where, years before, old Mr S. . . had drifted to extinction. As she rocked there, she read much-handled copies of cheap English and American magazines, nourishing herself on the romances they purveyed. She was judged a bit too 'fast' for her own good and suspected of having notions unsuited to her station. Her reputation never diminished my liking for her. 'It have too much envious people in this world,' Claudette remarked to me, pursing up her lips – for a spell she treated me as something of a confidant.

Doubtless, it had to happen. Obeah had not been able to protect Mahalia and neither did her modishness and romantic fictions protect

Claudette. Not many months after Mahalia had disappeared from our midst, I noticed that Claudette's belly had begun to swell. She said, laughing at me from the other side of the fence, 'What you looking at so, boy?' and, persisting in her laughter, caressed the rotundity. She told me she was 'madly' in love and described her boyfriend as tall, dark and handsome. 'A real saga boy,' she giggled. (We used to call fancy men 'saga boys'.) She hadn't read all those magazines in vain: they came to her rescue, giving her a vocabulary and a way of interpreting herself. Not for Claudette the fleeting consummations of the back alleys! She took to reading magazines with photographs of rosy-cheeked brides. 'I planning to get married in white,' she said. The expression 'in white' was new to me, but I nodded know-ledgeably. 'Claudette is going to get married in white,' I informed my mother. She shrugged away the revelation with a puzzled frown and advised me not to stick my nose in other people's business. Whether or not Claudette had her wish I can no longer recall. If she did, it didn't do her much good. Black would have been a more prophetic colour. Long before I left Trinidad, I had begun to hear tales of her husband's drunkenness, his beatings and his infidelities. She had moved to another street and I saw her rarely. She had become one more harassed woman and I was, after all, still only a boy. Now after an absence of ten years, I was seeing her again. She lived with her children in one small room. When I met her a white kerchief was wrapped round her head – she had, I already knew, discovered the consolations of religion, become a member of a sect that encouraged frenzied devotional exercises. Her looks had gone to seed, though it was still possible to detect vestiges of her girlish beauty. 'We all have to accept the will of God,' Claudette said to me, pointing to the sky. 'I am the Bride of Christ now.' Pious bric-à-brac cluttered the tiny room. She reminded me that during all those years of suffering and betrayal she had remained loyal to her seducer. 'It is God's will,' she repeated. As she talked, beads of sweat began to sparkle on the downy upper lip of the Bride of Christ. I left her scattering feed and scraps of bread to her fowls, clucking her tongue at them. She had found another vocabulary, another way of interpreting herself and her fate.

There were three business enterprises on our street – or four, if you counted the donkey-drawn coconut-cart that arrived each afternoon and parked on the corner. In those days, our 'pavements', unlike Woodbrook's, weren't paved and the donkey, braying and snorting, grazed at will on the rough pasturage. The sour-sweet reek of its urine and droppings permanently tainted the air. The wire fence to which the donkey was usually tethered – the pasturage in the vicinity, fertilised as it was by the animal, tended to be rich and varied – enclosed the premises of a 'book centre'. This curious enterprise, so out of keeping with the character of the locality, did next to no business. On its shelves were soiled, superseded text-books and a rag-bag collection of books on improbable subjects – soil erosion, librarianship, numismatics; it stocked piles of tattered comic books (some of those did get sold), editions of *Time*, *Newsweek*, the *Reader's Digest* and the *National Geographic* that were years out of date; and there was also a leavening of softly pornographic material. In a glass case were displayed bottles of dehydrated ink, hardened erasers and cheap dip-pens with rusting nibs. It was run by a languid, semi-literate Negro with bulbous eyes who, as the day progressed, collapsed into sedate inebriation. I do not believe that any fresh items were added to the stock. Claudette, I assume, must have acquired many of her magazines from this source.

A Muslim family lived on the corner opposite from the book-centre. Our relations with them tended to be less than cordial: my mother has always found it hard to forgive the Muslims for their numerous invasions of India and for forcing the partition of the sub-continent. I am not sure that our Muslim neighbours, much preoccupied with the little flock of goats they kept in their backyard, were fully aware of the complex amalgam of historical, cultural and theological resentments directed at them from our house. We were all taken aback when, without any kind of warning, they opened a *roti*-shop on their veranda. Later, the enterprise being successful (it was admirably suited to the character of St. James), a red and yellow neon sign appeared on their roof. One day, being in a venturesome mood, I bought one of their *rotis*. My mother, discovering this, stared at me with a shudder of distaste bordering on revulsion. I took care not to repeat the mistake.

The third business enterprise was, perhaps, the most singular. It was sited in the 'creolised' middle reaches of the street, a comparatively unknown territory harbouring pockets of uneasy and careful respectability in its brick bungalows. Here, in a tiny wooden hut shaded by a tamarind tree, was a shoe-repair service. The 'shoe-maker' (so he called himself and so we called him) aroused our curiosity and our respect. I liked the exotic atmosphere of the hut with its oddly-shaped anvils, its antique tobacco tins filled with tacks and tiny nails, its pots of paste and sheets of virgin leather. The shoe-maker, sitting on his work-bench, tacks clamped between his teeth, head cocked appraisingly as he examined some worn-out sole, was himself an exotic sight in his sturdy black boots, khaki trousers, khaki shirt and pith helmet.

Taken by himself, he would have been a comprehensible – if slightly enigmatic – figure. Taken together with his family, he became a man of mystery. The shoe-maker was undeniably black. His wife and children, on the other hand, were fair-complexioned. You could tell at a glance that mother and daughter and sons had a distinct kind of 'class' – a class which, by definition, excluded the shoe-maker. The daughter had the carriage and intimidating mannerisms we associated with 'secretaries'. You could easily imagine her sitting behind a desk in a fashionable doctor's or dentist's office, polishing her nails all day. The more impudent street-boys ('rabs we called them) did not hesitate to wolf-whistle Claudette. It would not have occurred to them to do the same to the shoe-maker's daughter. Her class automatically exempted her from their lust. It was obvious that the shoe-maker had no place in that milieu. Sitting all day in his hut among the rotting heaps of old shoes, he gradually began to exude the musty air of a man unloved, unregarded and neglected. His fall provided one of the more disturbing and frightening spectacles of my childhood. It goes on haunting me. From our yard or an upstairs window, I would watch his unsteady progress along the street; I would watch him, deranged with rum, clutch at the lamp-posts and fences for support; I would watch the stains of urine soak through and spread down his khaki trousers as he lost control of himself; I would watch as he stumbled and fell and lay supine on the roadway, alternately laughing and weeping as he gazed up at the sky. His family's neglect degenerated into abandonment. His ruin was the most terrible of the dramas to unfold in our street.

The shoe-maker's hut (it was pulled down years ago – but life does have its genuine ironies: today, not many yards away, is a modern workshop turning out what it describes as 'footwear') was in border-country. Beyond it began that region of the street occupied by the dusty yards overrun with pot-bellied Negro children, unmarried mothers and would-be steelbandsmen. It was out of one of these yards that Cora (so I shall call her), a girl not yet adolescent, came to us – gifted away, it could be said, by her varicose-veined mother who earned a desultory living as a washerwoman. Purple-black and fine-featured, Cora was a strong, handsome and clear-eyed girl. We grew attached to her and she became – in so far as that was possible – an honorary member of our household. But Cora, however much we might cherish her, was of the street and we were powerless to prevent her going the way of the street. She must have barely turned sixteen when I first noticed the man on the bicycle. He came every afternoon to our gate and there, camouflaged by the poinsettia, they did their courting, talking in whispers and laughing softly. It was not long before Cora's belly started to swell. The familiar ritual was duly acted out. Her mother arrived, chased her around the house and beat her over the shoulders with a broom. Then, in the time-honoured fashion, there came calm and reconciliation. Cora's mother offered us another of her daughters as a replacement. In the ensuing years Cora had more babies by (I believe) the same man. But he stubbornly refused to marry her. In the end, like Claudette, she was to embrace the consolations of religion. Dressed in a white gown and white turban, she is to be seen standing on street-corners, banging a tambourine, summoning the sinners of St. James to repentance.

... A street, one of many streets like it, in the capital city of a distant outpost of the British Empire. On this street my father had died (he was only forty-nine) when I was seven years old. That day I had gone with my mother to my uncle's house in Woodbrook. We were there when the news was brought to us that my father was desperately ill. Stupefied, stricken with remorse, I remembered how he had smiled and shaken his head at me as we were leaving the house – he was gardening at the time, examining the stalks of some anthurium lilies. 'Why don't you stay with your father for a change?' he had asked, looking up at me. 'Your *mamoo* [uncle] can look after himself!' he winked conspiratorially at me. But I had not stayed to keep him company. Rushing back, we saw him stretched out in one of the upstairs bedrooms, lying on the pink counterpane he and my mother had bought one rainy Christmas Eve. A trickle of spittle dripped from the corner of his mouth. I didn't know it then, but he was already dead. Another Nepaul Street tragedy had been enacted. There were steady breezes that afternoon from the hills of the Northern Range and the curtains billowed and flapped in the small bedroom. I knew so little about this man who, in the unpropitious soil of St. James, had tried to make a garden; had grown carnations and orchids, had grafted roses, had planted trees. In our yard, there was a cassia whose sprays of golden blossom were beaten down in the rainy season, carpeting the ground with yellow; and, growing beside it, the ylang-ylang whose jade-green flowers would scent the air at night.

Having to return to Trinidad – to St. James – nearly always fills me with alarm. It brings on this nightmare – that, having once arrived there, I may never be able to get out again. I imagine myself trapped there forever. I become agitated in the overheated torpor of a St. James Sunday afternoon; when I hear, as I used to during my childhood and adolescence, the ravings of evangelical broadcasters, local and American, who, hour after hour, monopolise the radio, I see myself, sprawled on a bed, staring out through glass louvres at the cloud shadows moving across the slopes of the Northern Range, feeling drugged, somnambulistically aware of the howling voices threatening eternal damnation in a hell supposed to be even hotter than our little island.

I grew up in a no-man's-land. Suburban life with its ease and its unrelenting worship of American standards, American ideals, had not existed when I was a boy. Its assumptions and prejudices were unfamiliar to me. If I was like a fish out of water at a Hindu rite, I was no less a fish out of water at a drive-in cinema scented with the vapours of hot-dogs and hamburgers. Such definition as I do now possess has its roots in nothing other than personal exigency. Every day, I have to redefine myself.

Trinidad challenges my uneasy perception of what I am. It seems to mock me. When I stare at its hills, when I hear the Sunday threats of its evangelists, when I see Cora standing on a street-corner banging a tambourine, I become a boy again.

On a sunny summer afternoon I turned my back on Oxford. The future was not merely indistinct but murky. My dreams of philosophical wisdom had ended a couple of years before. For me, there were no tribal hopes or structures upon which to lean. I had no vision of myself: I would have to start afresh; to discover, unaided, my human possibility. In my meagre baggage was the beginning of a novel, the outlines of which had occurred to me one bilious and despairing afternoon as, sick in mind and body, I gazed at the mossy apple tree that grew in the unkempt garden of the flat I had been renting. It wasn't much to be taking away after four years, but it was better than nothing: it gave me, however unreliably, a reason to go on living. After some searching, my wife and I found an affordable bed-sitter off Ladbroke Grove – a London equivalent of St. James – not far from the Portobello Road. I bought a ravaged leather-topped desk with brass-handled drawers. This I installed in a corner of the room where the West London light filtered milkily through filthy lace curtains . . .

That is the beginning of another kind of story.

Stories 1969–1974

The Beauty Contest

There were two hardware shops in Doon Town, and the Oriental Emporium, proprietor R. Prasad, was one of them. There was nothing remotely oriental about the place, but the name had been given by Mr Prasad's father (a man noted for his flights of fancy) and no one cared enough to change it. The other, just a few doors away, was the more aptly named General Store, proprietor A. Aleong. Though selling the same goods, they had succeeded in competing amicably for many years, and Mr Prasad appeared to derive a certain pleasure in telling his customers, 'Me and Mr Aleong is the best of friends. Not a harsh word in ten years.' But of late relations had cooled. The trouble began with Stephen Aleong, who had been sent by his father to study business management in the United States, and had returned not only with pastel-coloured shirts, but new ideas as well. The first blow fell when the General Store put up a neon sign with flickering lights and the picture of a man dressed cowboy style who said: 'Darn me if this ain't the finest store in town.' Mrs Prasad agitated for a sign along similar lines. Her husband was open to new ideas, but having searched the depths of his imagination he surfaced with nothing. This tended to happen to Mr Prasad. He felt that in some inexplicable way, Mr Aleong's sign had gathered up all the possibilities into itself. The nearest he had come to success was to have a picture of the Three Wise Men riding across the desert towards the Oriental Emporium, which was to be lit by an ethereal glow. However, he suspected that this, apart from being derivative, was probably also blasphemous, and therefore he adopted an altogether different line of approach.

'The value of my service lies in the quality of the goods I sell,' he told his wife.

'Don't talk stupid, man, the both of you does sell the same things.'

'I'm a simple man, Tara, selling to simple people. You think they going to care about neon lights?'

But Mr Prasad had misjudged the simple people. They liked Mr Aleong's neon sign, and there was a perceptible drift of custom away from the Oriental Emporium. Then Mr Aleong did another revolutionary thing. It was the custom in Doon Town for shops to bring their goods on to the pavements, where the bulkier items were displayed. Mr Aleong stopped doing this. 'It lowers the tone of the place,' he explained to Mr Prasad. He renovated the front of the General Store and installed plate-glass windows, behind which the goods were now tastefully arranged by his daughter-in-law. From this alteration a new slogan was born: 'Pavements were made to be walked on.' This caught the public imagination and Mr Prasad's simple people deserted him in ever increasing numbers.

'That man making you look like a fool,' Mrs Prasad told her husband.

'You've got to admit it's original, Tara.' And Mr Prasad, who had recently been more than usually prone to denigrate himself, added, 'I don't know how it is, Tara, but no matter how hard I try I just can't think up original things like that.'

'Pavements made to walk on! You call that original?' Nevertheless, she wondered why it was Mr Aleong and not her husband who had thought of that.

'What are you going to do?' The reproach in her voice was unmistakable. Mr Prasad scratched in vain at the thin top-soil of his imagination.

'Why don't you expand?'

Mr Prasad seemed to be thinking of something else.

'You could buy up Mr Ramnath.' Her expression softened. 'Your trouble is you always under-rating yourself. Think big.'

The idea of expansion appealed to Mr Prasad. He thought big for a few moments, then his face clouded.

'It's a pity how Aleong change really. We used to get on so well together until that sonofabitch son of his begin putting ideas in his head. No fuss, no bother. What do you think get into him?'

'That's business. Aleong is a businessman, he not running a charity on your behalf, and it's high time you realise you was one too. Now what about Mr Ramnath?'

'I don't see how I could do anything there, Tara. Ramnath love he money, hard as nails that man.'

'Think big, man. Stop under-rating yourself.' Mrs Prasad was insistent, suddenly alarmed by the empty spaces she discerned in her own imagination.

'You may be right. Maybe I do under-rate myself.' The cloud lifted. 'I don't know what I would do without you, Tara.'

'Chut, man! You mustn't say things like that.'

They gazed happily at each other.

Mr Ramnath, the owner of the shop next door to the Oriental Emporium, sold chiefly bicycles. He conducted his business with a misanthropic glee which he lavished on colleague and customer alike. Mr Prasad, knowing this, was reluctant to approach him, and his wife had to fan the sinking flames of his ambition for several days beforehand.

Mr Ramnath was standing on the pavement outside his shop when Mr Prasad sidled up to him.

'Good afternoon, Mr Ramnath. I see you taking a little fresh air.'

Mr Ramnath spat amicably on the pavement, and taking out a square of flannel from his pocket, began to polish the handlebars of one of his bicycles.

Mr Prasad coughed sympathetically. 'Look, do you think we can go somewhere where we can talk?'

'What, you in trouble or something?' Mr Ramnath seemed happier suddenly.

'No, no. Nothing like that.' Mr Prasad laughed.

Even Mr Ramnath had his disappointments. He stared gloomily at Mr Prasad. 'Come on inside and tell me about it.'

Mr Ramnath sat on a stool near the cash register on which had been painted in neat black letters: 'We have arranged with the Bank not to give credit. They have agreed not to sell bicycles.'

'It's like this, you see, Mr Ramnath, I want to expand the Emporium . . .'

'Aleong giving you trouble, eh? I was thinking that something like that was bound to happen one of these days.' He brightened, and slapping his thighs let his eye roam fondly over the sign on the register. 'You want my advice?'

Mr Prasad shifted uncomfortably. 'Not your advice so much as . . .'

Mr Ramnath grinned. 'It's the shop you after, not so?'

'You could put it like that.'

'Ten thousand dollars, Mr Prasad, not a penny more, not a penny less.'

'Eh?' Mr Ramnath's alacrity to sell worried him.

'I say ten thousand.'

'You wouldn't consider . . .'

'Ten thousand, Mr Prasad. Not a penny more, not a penny less. This place worth its weight in gold.'

'I'll have to think it over and let you know.'

'That's the way, Mr Prasad; and be quick or I might change my mind.'

'He asking twelve thousand,' Mr Prasad said to his wife.

'It only worth eight.'

'I know. Don't worry, I go beat him down.'

'I can't offer you more than eight, Mr Ramnath.'

'Ten, Mr Prasad. Not a penny more, not a penny less.'

'He's a difficult man to budge, Tara, but I manage to get him down to eleven.'

'That place not worth more than nine.'

'You think I don't know that? Don't worry, I go beat him down.'

'I could offer you nine thousand, Mr Ramnath.'

'You know my answer, Mr Prasad. Not a . . .'

'All right, all right.'

'I think I could get him down to ten if I try hard enough, Tara.'

'It's not a bad price when you think about it.'

'I know that. Don't worry, I go beat him down to ten, you wait and see.'

'All right, Mr Ramnath, have it your way. Ten thousand.'

'In cash?'

'Yes, yes, in cash.'

'Consider this place yours, Mr Prasad.'

'Well, he come down to ten.'

'Good man. You see what a little firmness will do? Twelve thousand! Who did he take you for, eh?'

'I told you I could beat him down. All it needed was time.'

But the General Store was not resting on its laurels. The shop assistants appeared in uniform and Mr Aleong retired from the public gaze to the fastnesses of an office at the back of the shop. It was the next move, however, which really shattered the long-standing friend-

ship. Mr Aleong began to cut his prices. Mr Prasad watched helplessly
as the General Store, succumbing to a kind of controlled frenzy,
announced new give-away offers and bargains each week. His own
plans were proceeding feebly. When he had bought out Mr Ramnath
his wife's joy had at first known no bounds. The prospect which
opened before her promised a shop of palatial grandeur and spiralling
profits. She was disappointed. Mr Prasad did not know what to do
with the additional space. He demolished the dividing wall and spread
his stock more thinly over the enlarged area. The emptiness was
embarrassing, and later on he added a few secondhand items. After he
had done that his imagination spluttered and died, and his wife's
dreams of glory faded. Mr Prasad, sinking deeper into despondency,
found fulfilment in prophecies of doom for Mr Aleong, the General
Store, and more recently himself.

'Man, I know what you could do,' his wife said one day, visibly
excited. 'It's a great idea.'

'What?' The joy of life, never strong in Mr Prasad, seemed to have
deserted him entirely.

'You could enter someone for the Miss Doon Town contest.
Imagine you get a really nice girl, Miss Oriental Emporium – you
know they have to say who sponsoring them in a sash across they chest
– and if she win Aleong go come crawling back to you. He'll keep his
tail quiet after that.'

'But that need money, Tara, and anyway who go want to be Miss
Oriental Emporium?'

'Man, remember what I was telling you. Think big.'

And Mr Prasad did think big, and as he did so a vision of success
and revenge rose before him and the fires of hope kindled once again.

If one were to judge by the rancour it aroused, the Carnival Queen
contest was without doubt the most important event in Doon Town.
The winner was in due course offered up to the National Queen
contest, where she had been consigned by tradition to that group of
contestants universally acknowledged to have no chance of winning;
though their presence there did have one advantage: it gave the other
more plausible contestants an occasion to be magnanimous. One year,
the national winner, Miss Allied Electrical Traders Ltd, had said
afterwards, 'I thought Miss Doon Town looked stunning as Aphro-
dite,' and Mr Prasad had commented, 'It's she conscience bothering
she.' Such lack of grace was understandable. The competition had
degenerated into a self-lacerating exercise to which the people of

Doon Town felt obliged to submit themselves annually. Mr Prasad, as a member of the town's Chamber of Commerce, took a keen interest in the affair. 'You just wait,' he would say, after Miss Doon Town had made yet another poor showing, 'one day we are going to shock them out of their boots. Let us see who will be laughing then.'

And now, the more he thought about it, the more the conviction took hold of him that it had fallen to him to deliver the people of Doon Town from their bondage. His flights of enthusiasm scaled such heights that even his wife was worried.

'You forget Aleong. He entering this too, you know,' she reminded him.

'Aleong? Who is Aleong?'

The confidence that comes from a sense of divine protection and mission had descended upon Mr Prasad, and despite herself, his wife was impressed and eventually infected by his fervour.

Mr Prasad discovered in Rita, one of his former shop assistants, the candidate he was looking for. She worked in one of the big department stores in Port of Spain. Rita was good-looking in the generally accepted way, and her stay in the city had given her 'poise' and 'confidence'. Mr Prasad had no doubts about her suitability while she on her part was eager 'to show Doon Town a thing or two.'

'But what do you know about this beauty queen business, Mr Prasad?'

He had to confess he knew nothing.

'Well, it got to be done professionally for a start. Professionally.'

'Sure.'

'It's not simply walking across a stage, you know. It takes money and ... and know-how.'

The transformation in Rita's grammar and vocabulary since she left the Oriental Emporium surprised and unnerved Mr Prasad.

'Don't worry. I ain't going to spare no expense.'

'I know a hairdresser who is experienced in these matters. We better go and see her.'

'Sure, sure. Anything you say.'

Whenever Mr Prasad tried to speak 'properly' he ended up with a mock American accent. He was aware of this and it made him uncomfortable. He left Rita, his sense of mission and divine protection shaken.

The hairdresser was attractive and supercilious. She had been trained in New York.

'So much depends on what you parade as,' she told them. 'From my experience I would say it's either got to be Greek or Roman.' She stared at her long, impeccably polished fingernails. 'Or Egyptian, perhaps. That's quaint.'

Mr Prasad nodded, striving hard to control the threatening American intonations. 'What do you like, Rita? Greek or Roman or Egyptian?'

Rita pondered. 'How about Egyptian? Everybody will be doing something Greek or Roman.'

'You could be Isis for instance,' the hairdresser said.

'What's that? Some kind of god or something?' Mr Prasad asked.

Rita looked embarrassedly out of the window.

'A goddess, Mr Prasad. An ancient Egyptian fertility goddess.'

'You like Isis, Rita?'

'Isis sounds fine to me. It's original.'

'Now there's only one more thing,' the hairdresser held her fingernails up to the light and squinted at them. 'Do you have any hobbies?'

'I does ... I read a little.'

'We'll use that. What else?'

'To be frank ...'

'Modelling?'

'Well ...'

'We'll use that all the same. Now we must have something quaint or as you would say, original.'

'What's wrong with two hobbies?'

Rita looked out of the window.

'It's *de rigueur* to have three hobbies, Mr Prasad.'

'Try gardening,' the hairdresser suggested.

'But ...'

'No. We'll use gardening. It sounds bohemian. That always helps.'

'What's bohemian?'

'Mr Prasad ...' Rita looked out of the window.

'Well, she going to be Isis,' Mr Prasad informed his wife.

'Who's Isis?'

Mr Prasad was incredulous.

'It's an Egyptian fert ... fertiliser goddess. And she also have three hobbies, reading, modelling and gardening.'

'Gardening?'

'You've got to have something bohemian, you know.'
'Oh.'

Mr Aleong's plans remained wrapped in secrecy. Whereas Mr Prasad splashed the walls of the Oriental Emporium with pictures of Rita and the pyramids and talked incessantly of the competition, the General Store continued to prosper amid a reticence so blatantly discreet that Mr Prasad's conversations gradually assumed a tone at once hysterically boastful and anxious.

'Maybe you shouldn't have advertise it so much,' his wife said to him. 'That kinda thing does bring bad luck.'

'Bad luck! We go see about that when the time come. But all the same I know that man and he bound to be making mischief somewhere.' He peered at her. 'Do you think he bribing the judges?'

'No, man. We would be sure to hear about it if that was the case.'

'All the same.' And the shadows of suspicion chased each other across his face.

However, Mr Aleong appeared to have only the civic virtues on his mind. He issued a pamphlet appealing for 'common-sense and good order' on carnival days, reiterating what he called his 'unshakeable belief in the native tolerance and forbearance' of his fellow citizens. But about his entrant for the contest, not a word. 'He want to be Mayor,' Mr Prasad said.

The contest was held in a cinema. When the Prasads arrived they were conducted to their seats by a girl in mock tropical costume. The Aleongs were late. Mr Aleong smiled pleasantly at Mr Prasad and elbowed his way across to him. 'Well, Mr Prasad, the night we've all been waiting for.'

'Yes. I expect you have a little surprise for us, eh?'

Mr Aleong laughed. 'Oh no, Mr Prasad, nothing like that. For me it's just a bit of fun. I don't suppose you look at it any different yourself?' Mr Aleong patted him on the shoulder. Mrs Prasad frowned.

'The best of luck, old man. Oh, by the way, Mrs Prasad, you look ...' Mr Aleong, waving his arms delightedly, backed away in a cloud of good will.

'The son of a bitch,' Mr Prasad whispered.

There were ten contestants and they were to parade three times: in bathing costume, in evening dress and in a 'costume of the contestant's choice'. The last was crucial. The urbanity of the master of ceremonies, whose presence there was a concession to Doon Town, was paper-thin. His jokes, so successful in Port of Spain night clubs, tended to fall flat, and he had even been booed by the audience. The people of Doon Town were not kind.

'And now we come to the first important business of the evening – the parade in bathing costume attire.' The master of ceremonies rocked delicately on his heels as he made the announcement.

The first six girls sauntered across the stage. They looked identical and were evenly applauded.

'Contestant number seven, Miss Ma Fong Restaurant.'

Nothing happened.

He glanced hastily at his programme. His professionalism was at stake. 'Miss Ma Fong Restaurant.' Good humour and contempt struggled for dominion over him. He addressed the audience. 'I suppose she take Chinese leave.' They stared at him stony-faced. He grimaced and prodded the back-drop curtain. 'Where is Miss Ma Fong Restaurant?'

At last she appeared, wearing a bikini emblazoned with dragons. The audience gasped, and even the master of ceremonies was unable to control his astonishment. Rita, who came next, seemed pallid by contrast, and Miss General Store, though attractive, was conventional.

The parade in evening dress followed the same pattern, with Miss Ma Fong Restaurant again providing the focus of interest. While the other girls were content to wear eighteenth-century ballgowns, she slithered across the stage in a close-fitting red sheath with a daring slit up the sides. 'The world of Suzie Wong,' the master of ceremonies explained, 'and man, what a world.'

Mr Prasad's impatience melted into irritation. Rita so far had made no impact at all.

'It's that damn Chinaman. They too cunning, I tell you.'

The 'pageantry' (so the programme described it) of the final round unfolded slowly, the goddesses of the Graeco-Roman world following each other in ponderous progression.

Mr Prasad relaxed.

'These people have no imagination at all. With them it either have to be Greek or Roman. Like they never hear of Egypt at all, but . . .' he turned to his wife, 'they go hear tonight, eh?'

'You getting too excited. Control yourself, man.'

Miss Ma Fong Restaurant was disappointing. Being a Chinese pagoda did not suit her. Anyway, the pagoda was tilting dangerously.

'A Chinese pagoda,' the master of ceremonies intoned. 'From Pisa.'

Again the audience failed to respond. Miss Ma Fong glared at him, and the master of ceremonies, sheltering behind his professionalism, rocked delicately on his heels.

'Miss Oriental Emporium as Isis, the Egyptian fertility goddess.'

There was a rustle of interest. Rita walked circumspectly across the stage, her movements restricted by the shaped tightness of her costume, and the precarious balance of a squat head-dress surmounted by what looked like a pair of bull's horns. In one hand she carried a staff and in the other a scroll of what was presumably 'papyrus'.

'Isis?'

'But I never hear of that one before.' Whispers like these reached Mr Prasad, and he prodded his wife in the ribs and smiled.

'Miss General Store as Fruits and Flowers.'

Mr Prasad stiffened. The audience digested the significance of this before bursting into rapturous applause. Miss General Stores wore what was basically a grass skirt, hidden behind bunches of hibiscus, oleander and carnations. Her bosom and back were encased in banana leaves overspread with wreaths of fern and more flowers, and on her head she balanced a fruit-filled basket from which hung chains of roses reaching to the floor. People rose from their seats and applauded. Someone threw a straw hat on the stage.

'Original!'

'Fruits and flowers, a local thing.'

'Look, she have a real mango and orange.'

The voice of the master of ceremonies rose above the uproar. 'Ladies and gentlemen, you should be here to see this.' He had forgotten he was not on the radio. This time the audience did laugh. Miss General Store tossed a rose into the audience. A man shouted, 'Strip!' She blushed. Everyone knew then that Miss Doon Town would have to be reckoned with in Port of Spain that year.

The Prasads left the cinema before the results were announced. They drove home in silence and went to bed. The next morning they read in the paper that Rita had come third. She had hinted in an interview that she would have done better but for her sponsor. She was quoted as saying, 'You must have a professional, not an amateur to look after you in this business.'

When Miss Doon Town came second in the national contest Mr Aleong's fellow citizens expressed their gratitude by electing him their Mayor. His rise in fame was paralleled by a rise in his fortunes. The General Store became one of a chain, Proprietor A. Aleong, and above each of his establishments there blazed forth the slogan, 'The finest store in town'. Mr Prasad, who now owned Doon Town's only secondhand shop, would say, pointing to the General Store, 'Our one claim to fame. You wouldn't believe this, but there was a time when me and Aleong – sorry, I mean the Mayor – used to be good friends. I know it hard to believe what with all them stores and things he own now, but we used to be rivals in the same business. I and that man used to compete. Imagine that!'

He would laugh for a long time after he said this, but there was no unhappiness or regret in that laugh. Mr Prasad was content. After all, the Oriental Emporium *was* the only secondhand shop in Doon Town.

A Man of Mystery

Grant Street could boast several business establishments: a grocery, a bookshop that sold chiefly Classic comics, a café and, if you were sufficiently enthusiastic, the rum-shop around the corner (known as the Pax Bar) could also be included. On week-ends a coconut seller arrived with his donkey cart which he parked on the corner. The street's commercial character had developed swiftly but with the full approval of its residents. Commerce attracted strangers and the unbroken stream of traffic lent an air of excitement and was a source of pride. In time a group of steelbandsmen had established themselves in one of the yards, adding thereby a certain finality and roundness to the physiognomy of the street. However, long before any of these things had happened, Grant Street could point to Mr Edwin Green, 'shoemaker and shoe-repairer', whose workshop had been, until the recent immigrations, the chief landmark and point of reference.

From the first Mr Green had been considered by his neighbours to be different from themselves. There were good reasons for this. Grant Street lived an outdoor, communal life. Privacy was unknown and if anyone had demanded it he would have been laughed at. There were good reasons for this as well. The constant lack of privacy had led ultimately to a kind of fuzziness with regard to private property. No one was sure, or could be sure, what belonged to whom or who belonged to whom. When this involved material objects, like bicycles, there would be a fight. When it involved children, more numerous on Grant Street than bicycles, there was a feckless tolerance of the inevitable doubts about paternity. Young men in pursuit of virility made false claims, while at other times the true father absconded. No one worried, since in any case the child would eventually be absorbed into the life of the street. Romantic relationships, frankly promiscuous, were fleeting rather than fragile, and the influx of strangers accelerated this tendency. Unfortunately, the results then were less happy. Grant Street was communal, but only up to a point, and any attachment one of its women might develop for a man from another street was looked upon with distaste. The inevitable child became the centre of a feud. Paternity in the stricter sense was of course not the issue. To which street did the child belong? It was over this problem that argument and acrimony raged.

Mr Green had been deposited in their midst like an alien body. Not only was he married, but his wife, a woman of half-Portuguese, half-Negro extraction, was pale-complexioned, good-looking and 'cultured'. In the late afternoon when Mr Green had closed his shop for the day, she would bring an easel out into the yard and paint for an hour. She had a fondness for sailing ships sinking in stormy seas and vases of flowers. The street, to begin with, had gathered solemnly around her and watched. She enjoyed their bewilderment.

'Lady, why you does paint when it so dark for?'

Mrs Green would stare seriously at her questioner.

'It's the light. There's a certain quality to this tropical twilight which I find so . . . exhilarating.'

Her accent was 'foreign' and when she spoke her bosom heaved cinematically, suggesting a suppressed passion. This impressed her audience. Mrs Green also frequented the public library. On Saturday mornings the street saw her struggling under the weight of half a dozen books, the titles of which were conspicuously displayed. The women sitting on their front steps would laugh in awed disbelief and shout after her, 'Soon you go read up all the books they have in the library. You go have to begin writing them yourself then.' Mrs Green, looking martyred, would disappear into her yard.

All of this was curious enough, but what really intrigued the street was her attitude to Mr Green. They could not understand it. They were never seen together. During the day while he hammered in his shop, she was nowhere in evidence, while during her afternoon painting sessions, he in his turn seemed to have been swallowed up by the silence in their house. That silence was another cause for speculation. It was an unnatural, abnormal silence which many believed to be in some strange way a counterpart to the suppressed passion they thought they detected in Mrs Green's voice.

Nevertheless it was on her husband that the street's perplexity and wonder finally came to rest. The incongruities were not hard to find. Mr Green was spectacularly black, he was ugly, and he betrayed none of the outward signs of culture which his wife exhibited. Stated so baldly the problem was insoluble. That could not be tolerated. Therefore, the belief took shape that Mr Green was something other than he appeared to be. He was not a shoemaker at all; on the contrary, he was a man of the highest education who had chosen that lowly profession out of a profound and philosophic love for the 'simple life'. Mr Green, it was claimed, was in revolt against the hypocrisy and useless trappings of modern civilisation. Also for a time it was fashionable to uphold the theory that Mr Green spent much of his time in a trance, but that was soon abandoned as being too improbable. Nevertheless it did not hinder his transformation into a man of mystery.

His shop became the centre of romance for children on the street. It was a small wooden hut situated at the front of the house (itself an enlarged hut on stilts) under the shade of a tall tamarind tree. Above the door there was a sign which claimed he had the ability 'to fit all sizes and conform to all tastes'. This was a piece of rhetoric. As far as anyone could tell, Mr Green had not once been commissioned to make a pair of shoes; he simply repaired them. Inside there was a clutter of old, unreclaimed shoes overspread with dust. On a sagging work-table he arranged those recently brought in for repair and, always in the same place, an American trade magazine for the year 1950. Mr Green worked facing away from the light. He sat on a bench, holding several tiny nails between his teeth, occasionally extracting one which he would tack with exaggerated care into the shoe he was holding. After each such operation he examined the shoe from all angles and shook his head mournfully. The children crowding near him savoured the smells of leather in various stages of decomposition and the bottles of glue which lay open beside him.

Gradually from his conversations with the children a picture of his past was pieced together. He had lived in Brazil for many years where he had worked as a tapper on a rubber plantation. There he had met his wife, the daughter of the overseer, a hard and unfeeling man who kept his daughter a virtual prisoner and beat her regularly and viciously. She had begged him to take her away – he was the only foreigner working on the plantation – and together they had fled to British Guiana where she had borne him a child, a daughter. They had named her Rosa. The overseer having by that time repented, and they being extremely poor, the child was sent back to Brazil to live with her grandfather. In the meantime, they had saved sufficient money to buy a house and it was thus they had come to Trinidad and to Grant Street. His one sadness in life was never to have seen his daughter – 'a full and grown woman now' – and it was only the hope of seeing her again that kept him 'alive'.

This was a far cry from the picture that had been built up, and while no one really believed the story, it did have its attractions. Therefore the street pretended to believe that it believed Mr Green. He made their task easy. He was everything they expected him to be: kind, gentle, and a little sad. His eccentricities pleased them, especially his dress for occasions, which was invariable and immaculate. He wore a starched and ironed white tropical suit and a cork hat, and when he began taking the children for walks the men lounging on the corner murmured as he passed them, 'Make way for the Governor, everybody make way for the Governor.'

On his Sunday walks Mr Green took the children to the zoo and botanical gardens. They went early in the afternoon, marching in military formation behind Mr Green, who walked stiffly ahead of them. When they had come to the highest point in the Queen's Park Savannah, he would gather the children more informally about him and show them the sea and the ships in the harbour. 'The Brazils,' he would say, 'lie in that direction, and Venezuela, which from certain points you can see on a clear day, in that.' His arms extended in a sweep that embraced the harbour and the glittering sea beyond. When this ritual had been performed, they crossed the road to the zoo. He appeared to have a taste only for those animals he had seen in the wild. 'They call those jaguars? Who they trying to fool? I'll tell you about a jaguar I saw in Brazil one time.' And he would relate a long and tortuous tale. The birds, though, were his favourites and he was at his most lyrical when talking about them. 'They call those parrots? I've seen them in the wild. The colours of the rainbow and more besides. Wonderful creatures. They belong in the jungle,' and adjusting his hat he led them to the alligator pond, as if what he had just seen had been calculated to offend him personally.

Afterwards, they went to the botanical gardens, which, at six o'clock, would be nearly empty. There he allowed them to rest, and while they sprawled on the grass he wandered along the gravelled paths, staring up at the trees, occasionally bending close to read the labels attached to the trunks. Sometimes, perhaps struck by the sudden recall of an incident or a landscape long forgotten, he left off his examination of the trees and gazed abstractedly at the flag flapping limply above the roof of the Governor's house, itself hidden by a bandstand and the clumps of trees growing thickly nearby. At such times it was not difficult for the children to make believe that he was indeed the Governor, and that these were his private grounds. There was something truly proprietorial about Mr Green as he stood there, oblivious of their presence, hostage to some troubling recollection. However, a gust of wind through the trees or a fight among the children and the melancholy would be set aside, to be resurrected and resumed the following Sunday.

His shadow stretched out before him on the path, the harshness of his dress muted in the softer light, he led them through an avenue of trees to the greenhouses where the more exotic exhibits were on display and there showed them insect-devouring plants, fruit one bite of which sufficed to kill a man, and a tree that 'bled'. Mr Green lingered over these things longer than the children cared for. The botanical gardens, so alien, so distinct, seemed hardly to connect with the street they had left three hours before. It was a swept, ordered profusion, a region of shadow on cut grass and strange fruit made stranger still by Mr Green's heady fascination for malignancies they did not understand and which appalled and frightened them. Some of the children cried, but Mr Green, ignoring, or perhaps ignorant of their distress, touched and smelled everything, delighting in the heat and spray of water from the pipes, his suit and helmet tinted green by the light filtering through the vines that crept up the sides of the glass and spread out over the roof. He would leave only when one of the caretakers looked in and told them it was time to go.

If these visits were not the undiluted pleasures they ought to have been, there were some advantages to be had in associating with Mr Green. He was a skilled carpenter and built stools and chairs and desks which he gave to the children. However, the most prized of all his accomplishments were the telephones he was able to make out of bits of wire and old tins. This sustained his popularity and at the same time it allowed him to continue his excursions to the zoo and botanical gardens.

Time having smoothed the rougher edges, the street learned to accept the Greens, bestowing on them the respect that springs from incomprehension. Crowds no longer gathered to watch Mrs Green paint, and although the men lounging on the corner still shouted 'Here comes the Governor', when Mr Green appeared dressed in his white suit, it was done less from malice than a desire to acknowledge his presence. Yet the Greens did come to have one thing in common with their neighbours: they shared their unchanging way of life. In that life, no one ever got richer or poorer; there were no dramatic successes or, for that matter, dramatic failures; no one was ever in serious trouble. Basically, they were cowards. Now and again Grant Street spawned a prodigy, a policeman for instance, but that was considered an aberration and did not happen often. Nevertheless, unheroic as it undoubtedly was, the street did have its heroes: the man in the Western who, flying in the face of the odds, conquers all, and his corollary, the loser, riding off, but with dignity, into the sunset.

The Greens succumbed to this pattern. The shoe-shop maintained a steady trickle of customers; Mrs Green continued to paint ships in distress and vases of flowers; the same silence swallowed now the husband, now the wife; and the tamarind tree, a prisoner of its own maturity, grew no taller. The changes Grant Street knew centred on the succession of carnivals, of births, and of deaths. Marriage, like the policeman, was an aberration that occurred infrequently. Ephemeral groups of children called Charlie and Yvonne and Sheila gathered round Mr Green and were introduced to the wonders of the zoo and botanical gardens and they cried as their predecessors had done. Mr Green, in his turn, saw them grow up, become mothers and putative fathers, fading away from him to the street corners and front steps of hovels.

Therefore when Mrs Green started work as a receptionist to a doctor it was considered almost an infringement of the established order, and when he was seen to come for her in the mornings and bring her back in the afternoons, it amounted to a disturbance of the peace. It soon became apparent that her suppressed passion had found an outlet. All the symptoms were there. When the doctor brought her back in the afternoon they talked long and earnestly in the car before he left, and Mrs Green, who, though distant had always been friendly, now abandoned her friendliness altogether. One change led to another. The painting sessions stopped and so did the visits to the library on Saturday mornings. From these occurrences was dated the commercialisation that was to sweep Grant Street, as if there were some species of sympathetic magic at work connecting the two sets of events. And it certainly was the case that hard on the heels of Mrs Green's liaison the Pax Bar and grocery first made their appearance. Mr Green alone seemed unaware of what was happening. He worked in his shop as usual, smiled benignly at the children and took them out for walks. Unfortunately it was noted that he had recently begun to make more telephones than he had ever done. Mr Green's sadness ceased to be speculative. The street had its standards. There were limits to what anyone could do, and one of the unspoken rules in their relationship with Mr Green was that their standards did not apply to him: he had a role to fulfil. They felt not merely that his wife was 'wronging' him, but more peculiarly, that her manner of doing it was sordid. For them, morality was a matter of form, of 'style', and they did not approve of Mrs Green's style.

Grant Street's commercialisation proceeded apace, and in the rush of cars and business and the sounds of the steelband, the Greens receded. The steelband was the street's pride and had rapidly become the focus of its loyalties. They practised every night and were good enough to merit being recorded. The radio spread their fame and eventually even the American tourists came to marvel at the men who could produce such sweet and coherent sounds from oil drums. Mr Green, his accomplishments thrown into shadow by the influx of visitors, was deserted by his youthful congregation The telephones which he made in increasing quantities lost their market and lay in untidy heaps on top the trade magazine for 1950. He had to entice the children into the shop and as before tried to talk to those who did come about his life in Brazil and the daughter he longed to see, but they were impatient and not interested in these stories. Formerly, they had begged him for his telephones and compliance had had to be dragged out of him. Now to hold them in his shop he had to promise instruments of greater sophistication. The next day he would be sure to see his efforts abandoned in the gutter outside his house or being kicked along the street. He stopped making telephones and on Sundays he took his walks alone. One or two people remembered to say, 'Here comes the Governor', but it was done without any enthusiasm, and Mr Green to avoid them went another way.

One morning some workmen arrived and they produced the first noises to come from the Greens. A crowd gathered on the pavement to watch. The house was being pulled down. Mr Green was detached. He worked in his shop all day amid the crashing of timber and galvanised iron sheets. The doctor arrived to supervise the demolition, leaving later with Mrs Green and two trunks, an action sufficiently daring to mollify the neighbours. There was no silence for Mr Green to return to that night. The house was already roofless and instead he went to the Pax Bar.

Everyone there recognised him and looked up with unconcealed surprise when he went in. He bought half a bottle of rum and sat alone in a corner. He wore his white suit and did not remove his cork hat.

Towards morning Mr Green shook himself and got up a little unsteadily from his chair. He fixed his hat more firmly on his head and felt his way across the room, holding on to the sides of tables and backs of chairs in his path. The few remaining drunks eyed him disconsolately. 'Good night, Governor.' Mr Green went out into the dark, empty street. A chain of red beacon lights punctured the blackness of the hills. Grant Street was unreal in the stillness. Gazing up at the street lamps and the shuttered houses he walked slowly back to the workshop. He fumbled for a long time before he found his keys. There was no light in the shop and he lit a candle. Half-made telephones littered the bench and table. He picked up one, held the receiver to his ear and laughed. The trade magazine caught his eye. He leafed through it, glancing at the advertisements. The Baltimore Shoe Corporation claimed to be able to 'fit all sizes and conform to all tastes'. Mr Green laughed again and put the magazine back on the table. He closed the door, snuffed the candle and went to sleep on the floor.

When he awoke the demolition men were already at work. The doctor was giving them instructions. Mr Green examined his suit in the semi-darkness. It had changed colour, and circular brown patches showed where rum had fallen on it the night before. He started brushing it, then, frowning, he gave up the attempt. He opened late and worked until lunch-time, when he closed the shop and went to the Pax Bar. It was the last time Edwin Green, 'shoemaker and shoe-repairer', ever opened for business.

It was a small house and in three days the demolition was complete. The street salvaged what it could from the piles of timber laid out on the pavement. There was no one to stop them except the doctor, and even he, after an argument in which he called them 'carrion crows', allowed them to take what they wished. The new house took shape slowly. Grant Street had never seen anything like it. It was large and rambling in the Californian fashion, surrounded by a lawn and fenced in from the street. The outside walls were painted a bright pink, and wooden louvres were used instead of windows. There were wrought iron gates surmounted by wrought iron lanterns. But by far the most impressive innovation was the chimney on the roof.

Mrs Green returned when it was finished. She behaved as if she had come to the street for the first time. In the afternoons she watered the lawn while the doctor fussed with the potted plants and orchids which hung from the eaves. Mr Green was banished to his reservation. His shop had not been touched and stood in ramshackle and bizarre opposition to the modernity that seemed poised to devour it.

The street had long ago surrendered its illusions about him. The evidence to the contrary was too overwhelming, and anyway they did not need these illusions. Mr Green's fall had been public and obvious, and any private sorrow which he might still have had could not compensate for or hide his humiliation. Now all they could see was the physical shell whose disintegration they studied with a passive morbidity. Grant Street had a clear conscience. It had expressed its sympathy for Mr Green and its horror of what his wife was doing. There were many other things demanding their attention.

Mr Green lived in the shop. His revelries in the Pax Bar ended late in the evening, and as he crept down the street on his way home he sang noisily, pausing to swear when his steps stuttered uncontrollably. Occasionally he stumbled and fell on the roadway and then he would lie there for some minutes without moving. Sometimes he urinated as he lay there, taking fresh swigs from the bottle he always carried with him. He delivered his final orations outside the shop, laughing and cursing in turn as he kicked at the door until it gave way. Then, suddenly, he would fall silent and leaning against the fence, stare at the freshly watered lawn and the curtains in the new house drawn tight and secure. At noon the next day he emerged, his suit tattered and frayed beyond recognition, the cork hat dented and twisted at an odd angle on his head, to make the journey once again to the Pax Bar. Mr Green's metamorphosis had been quickly absorbed into the landscape. The world had come to Grant Street and it would take more than the ragings of a drunken man to disturb them.

Sunday afternoon was hot. The men on the corner had sought the shade of the bookshop and in the yards the children played and the women sat on their front steps fanning themselves and gossiping. The steelband maundered sleepily to itself; the Pax Bar would not open until evening. Grant Street was in limbo.

Tamarinds were in season and several children were collecting the fruit that had fallen off the tree and littered the yard in front of the shoe shop. Mr Green watched them from the doorway. His eyes were red and he blinked painfully in the harsh light. He reached for the bottle of rum on his work table, uncorked it and drank some. With a faint smile and still holding the bottle he approached the children gathering the tamarinds. He picked up a handful and offered it to one of the smaller girls. She shook her head and backing away began to cry. The other children retreated, dropping the fruit they had collected. Mr Green laughed, and stepped out on to the street. He looked at the house. The louvres were opened and even in the gloom he could see that the walls were covered with pictures. One stood out. It was a painting of a ship with only its rigging visible, on the verge of being totally annihilated by a mountainous sea. He threw the tamarinds in the gutter and started up the street. His walk was studied and tenative. The urine stains on his trousers showed clearly. He took another sip from the bottle and shielding his eyes from the sun he gazed up at the sky. There were only a few clouds about, and they were small and white. He quickened his pace when he saw the coconut seller turn the corner with his donkey cart.

The donkey, a shaggy, morose, under-fed creature, had been tethered in a patch of weeds. Mr Green stopped to examine it. He passed his hands over its shanks and patted it. The men in the shelter of the bookshop laughed. Mr Green turned to address them. 'Do you call this a donkey? Poor creature. I've seen them in the wild . . .' The rest of what he said was lost in their laughter. The coconut seller advanced on him. 'Mister, you better leave my donkey alone, or you go know what.' He traced patterns in the air with his cutlass. 'Friend, I was only pointing out . . .' The coconut seller spluttered into obscenity and Mr Green, shaking his head sadly, drank some more rum and walked away.

On the Queen's Park Savannah people were playing cricket and football and horses were cantering on the exercise track near the racecourse. Families out for their Sunday walk paraded amiably on the perimeter. Mr Green sat on a bench under a tree and stared at them, eyes half-closed. A clock struck four. He was tired and sleepy and beads of sweat watered his face and arms. An attack of nausea frittered itself away, but the tiredness, reinforcing itself, would not go. He opened his eyes. There was a breeze and the dust was rising in clouds, hiding the horses and people. The colours of the sky and grass melted and footballers and cricketers wandered through a golden, jellied haze. A voice unattached to a body spoke near him, then receded. Someone tapped him on the shoulder. A dog played round his heels and barked from many miles away. Beyond the Savannah the sea was a sheet of light. The sun fled behind a cloud and the sea was grey and rose up to devour him. He shuddered. For a moment the disoriented world re-grouped, but it needed all his energy and all his will to keep it that way. He let it dissolve and shatter. The rum was everywhere, flowing from chimneys and lanterns and tumescent seas, soaking his clothes. He kicked feebly and the bottle rolled into the dust. He got up. The ground shivered. He swam to the iron railings protecting the Savannah from the road. Another dog barked, a herald of the loneliness descending on all sides. Someone said, '... back in time for dinner,' and someone laughed. Weariness called on him to surrender, but he was already on the road, creeping between the cars, and not far away was a refuge of shaded green. A flag danced in the sky. The brown, lifeless hills wavered. A gust of wind blew through the trees; blossoms floated in the air; trees and trunks and labels whirled towards him. The tree-lined avenue was cooler and he was startled by his reflection looming up to meet him out of the foliage. In a moment he was inside. There was a sound of spray, and water dripped on to his hat and trickled down his face. The desolation deepened. Stalks and flowers stumbled in the effort to make themselves seen. He noticed the green light flowing through the glass, becoming one with his nausea, and he tried to remember why the children had cried. The tree that bled. He moved towards it, but darkness closed in, confounding his desire, bringing with it the smell of fruit even stranger than those he had described, of flower-laden jungles and muddy rivers, landscapes of the mind more real than any he had roamed. Then, mercifully, there was only the darkness.

When the caretaker found him he had been dead for an hour.

Two days later Mr Green was buried in the Mucurapo cemetery. His body, contrary to custom, had been kept in the funeral home, returning to Grant Street for the brief religious service which was held in the drawing room of the new house. Some hitherto unsuspected relations of Mr Green turned up and wept, but no one from the street was allowed in. They gathered on the pavement and stared through the louvres at the coffin.

The procession did not have far to travel and a sombre crowd of neighbours walked behind the hearse to the cemetery. Mrs Green drove in a car. The sky clouded and it began to rain, delaying the burial. It was already dark by the time it was completed and the few limp wreaths had been scattered on the grave.

Within a month the workshop was pulled down – it took one morning to do the job – and for days afterwards the children played with the unreclaimed shoes that had been thrown in the gutter. The tide of grass invaded the spot where the shop had been, and the fence was extended.

Grant Street prospered. The borough council gave it concrete pavements and running water, and the Central Government, a sewage system. Commercialisation had stimulated its ambitions and several of the residents built new houses, none of course as grand as the Enriques' (Mrs Green had remarried), but all with pretensions to modernity. The grocery had become a supermarket, the café a restaurant; and the steelband went on tours to the Bahamas and United States. Romantic relations were regularised, and there were even a few marriages. Children were still numerous, but the index had changed: they were more numerous than motor cars.

The street had undergone a series of changes that went beyond carnival and birth and death, and this had brought nostalgia. Grant Street had acquired a past whose sharpness had been softened by the passage of time and now glowed with a gentle light. Those who were no longer there or had died shared that softness and were transfigured by it. Mr Green had left no physical reminder of his presence to trouble them and as a result his legend revived. His style of death, a memorial to his dreams, was beyond reproach, and in the end it redeemed him. Put in another way, in terms of the Westerns Grant Street loved, he had ridden into the sunset.

The Political Education of Clarissa Forbes

Clarissa Forbes had a mind of her own, a peculiarity sufficiently strange for her family to have recognised and sanctified it. The source of this independence of spirit was a mystery to her family, her friends, and, in due course, her employers. But first to bear the burden was her family.

The Forbes were poor and relatively humble. There had been a time when they were poorer and straightforwardly humble, but a new government had been voted into favour with help from people like the Forbes and in an initial flush of gratitude decided, among other things, to build new roads. The Forbes benefited from this.

Mr Forbes was a semi-skilled manual labourer, chronically out of work and compelled as a result to do jobs like sweeping the streets and cleaning windows, which he considered to be beneath his dignity. However, with the advent of the new government, the situation improved.

The extensive road-building programme left Mr Forbes with little spare time, but that spare time he spent not in a hovel wracked by the coming and going of cars and lorries, but in a new house, another of the government's gifts to its supporters, laid out side by side with other houses minutely similar to itself and inhabited by people indistinguishable from the Forbes.

Mr Forbes was understanding. 'If we was not all the same, there is bound to be some unreasonable people who go be sure to get up and ask why Tom different from Dick and Dick different from Harry. This way, nobody have reason to complain and we all happy.'

Mr Forbes was only partly right. True, his wife was happy. She applauded these sentiments. 'If everybody was like you, Ethélbert, there wouldn't be no trouble in this world today.' Clarissa, however, was less easily swept off her feet.

'Huh. I just don't understand people like you two. Is as if you have no sense of pride, no dignity, wanting to live and be just like all these foolish people you see around you.' She was sprawled on the sofa reading a copy of a cheap English magazine given her by a school friend whose aunt had emigrated to England.

'But what you mean, Clary?' her father objected gently. 'Don't tell me you prefer that other place we used to live in.'

'I do in a way, if you must know. At least there we was different, not living exactly like everybody else.'

'I just don't understand you, Clary.' Mr Forbes scratched his thinning hair, always a sign of perplexity. His tone, nevertheless, was mild and questioning. The disharmony his daughter had injected into the idyll he had been painting was not an entirely unfamiliar experience.

'Well take this, for instance.' Clarissa flourished the cheap English magazine. There was a picture on the cover of a woman in a bikini, sitting on a rock and gazing into the far distance. 'You should read this and get an idea of how other people does live abroad, the different kinds of thing they does do.' Clarissa sat up. 'You know, over there they does go to places like Spain and Portugal for they holidays. Have a look at that.' She thrust the magazine near her father's face and showed him another photograph, this one in colour. It was a picture of dozens of pale-skinned people gathered round the edges of a swimming pool. The sea, in the distance, was hidden by a jungle of umbrellas. 'Tell me, where we does go for we holidays? I never even set foot in Tobago once in my life. We never hear of that kind of thing. But over there they does take it for granted.'

Mr Forbes studied the photograph carefully. 'It look very nice,' he said. 'Let me see it, Ethélbert.' Mr Forbes gave his wife the magazine. 'Yes. Ethélbert right. It look very nice.'

Clarissa snatched the magazine from her mother. 'You don't have to tell me that. I know it nice.' She flicked through the pages of the magazine in search of further evidence. 'Ah yes. All you ever hear of Torremolinos?' Her parents shook their heads. 'I thought so. That's exactly the kind of ignorance I mean. And another thing. Here we only have horse racing, not so?' Her parents nodded. 'Well over there in England they have something else. Greyhounds. You ever hear of that?'

Mr Forbes scratched his head. 'Greyhound is a kind of dog, not so?'

'That's right, Pa. You smarter than I thought. Everybody does go to the dog races over there.'

'Dog races?' Mrs Forbes was incredulous. 'You mean they does race dogs against each other?'

'I remember now,' Mr Forbes said. 'They does call it greyhound racing.' Mr Forbes was pleased with himself, hoping this display of knowledge would further impress his daughter.

'That's right, Pa. I glad to see you know a few things.'

'And they have jockey riding these dog?' Mrs Forbes inquired.

Mr Forbes laughed loudly, slapping his thigh.

'No, Ma. They does have an electric hare out in front which the dogs does chase around a track.'

Mrs Forbes did not fully understand, but she was happy to let the matter drop. Mr Forbes, however, was determined to press home his advantage. 'Hear she. Jockey riding dog. Have to be a very small jockey or a very big dog.' He spluttered into fresh laughter.

Clarissa warmed to her theme. 'Someone like you, Ma, if you was living in England, could go in the evening to one of them bingo halls.'

'You mean they have places where they does only play bingo?'

'Every night without fail,' Clarissa assured her.

Mr Forbes whistled. 'I could go to the dog races and Maisie could go to them bingo halls.'

'Exactly,' Clarissa replied.

'I think I would really like them bingo halls.' Mrs Forbes, closing her eyes, surrendered to the seductive pictures of her imagination.

After this the Forbes were more circumspect in singing the praises of their new home in front of their daughter. Each new issue of the cheap English magazine brought its fresh dose of invective and a further unsettling of the Forbes household. To avoid this, Mr and Mrs Forbes did as much as was within their power to placate Clarissa. They responded with the same look of simple-minded amazement to everything she said, the same expressions of astonished incredulity and the same anxiety lest their ignorance should annoy her. Unhappily, try as they might, they could never quite escape the taint imposed on them by the limitations, the 'inferiority' as Clarissa never tired of describing it, of their situation.

Nevertheless, Mr Forbes's political consciousness continued to grow, doubtless stimulated in part by his daughter's incessant attacks. Despite Clarissa's scorn or, most probably, because of it, he developed in response to the pleadings of the politicians a sense of the injustices done to him in years, centuries, gone by. And this by the very people Clarissa would have him imitate. For the moment, however, he was reticent. Mr Forbes was still unsure of his ground.

This process the Prime Minister called 'political education', and to put his loyalty beyond all reasonable doubt and also as an expression of his gratitude for all the government had done for him, Mr Forbes joined the Party. He adopted its tie, whose motif was a yellow sun (presumably rising) over a blue sea. For some time Mr Forbes kept this a secret from Clarissa and listened in silent submission to her ravings about Torremolinos, the greyhound races and the bingo halls. But as the months passed his confidence grew and he began wearing his tie on Sundays when he went to the local Anglican church with his wife. Clarissa did not accompany them. 'It too low class,' she told her parents. 'If I go to any church at all it got to be Catholic.'

Mr Forbes was an admirable pupil. 'Nowadays,' he said to his wife, 'it ain't have a soul who going to push we around like they used to before. Let them just try it and the P.M. go take care of them.' Then he explained the facts about slavery and colonialism as described by the Prime Minister. Mrs Forbes applauded and was unable to decide whom she loved more, her husband or the Prime Minister. In time, Mr Forbes joined the ranks of the active Party workers and scoured the countryside showering leaflets on the peasants. His enthusiasm stimulated gossip about the Party nominating him to run for the local council. Unfortunately, though, to Clarissa's unbounded relief, he was not chosen. She was aware that people in the best circles rather despised the proletarian character of the present government and her father's activities had consequently become a great drain on her pride. Clarissa reproached him.

'You mean after all I teach you, you still think that running for the local council is the greatest thing in the world?'

Mr Forbes was apologetic. 'I didn't have anything to do with it, Clary. It was other people who was talking, not me.'

'People like you will never learn,' Clarissa said despairingly.

Mr Forbes hid his disappointment well and vowed to his wife that he would continue to serve the Party faithfully. Mrs Forbes, however, was greatly distressed by the turn of events and her fervour for the Prime Minister abated perceptibly.

'You been working for these people so long, Ethélbert, breaking your back to please them. You would think they could at least give you a seat on the council as a kind of reward.'

'These decisions have to go through a lot of channels we don't know about, Maisie, and I feel sure that if they didn't give me a seat it was for a very good reason.'

'But you would think the Prime Minister . . .'

Mr Forbes waved his hands angrily. 'He don't have nothing to do with this. You think he ever even hear my name? He is a busy man. And another thing, if I was a councillor I couldn't take you with me to functions and things like that. Is not that I insulting you, but you don't have . . .' Mr Forbes, scratching his head, searched for the right words.

'I know what you mean, Ethélbert. But you could have take Clary with you.' Mrs Forbes was not used to compliments and by the same token she was only able to recognise the crudest insults. Political education had hardly made any impact on her.

'Me!' Clarissa cried, looking up with a start from her magazine, 'Me! What you take me for, Ma?'

'Your mother was only using you as an example, Clary.' Mr Forbes was embarrassed.

'I hope so! I really hope so! Anyway, what's the point in working yourself up over a stupid thing like that for? Who would want to be a councillor in a stupid place like this? If you was in Port of Spain I could understand. But in a place like Paradise. It beats me!' She gave the rocker on which she was sitting a gentle push with her feet and creaking demurely back and forth continued reading her magazine.

Mr Forbes, catching his wife's eye, shook his head sadly. In a world where the cheap English magazine was not to be denied, the Forbes, husband and wife, had come to feel themselves and their activities insignificant and Lilliputian. They began to wish Clarissa would leave home.

The object of their concern was not particularly prepossessing. Clarissa's face was moon-shaped and faintly scarred by chicken-pox. Her round, black eyes were heavy-lidded and hemmed in by the bulging flesh that pressed in upon them from her cheeks. She had a boxer's build, squat and thick-set, her diaphragm giving the impression of having been added to the rest of her as an afterthought. As a result, one thought of it as being misplaced, another person's property which Clarissa had appropriated and turned to her own uses. Yet it was the attentions allegedly paid to this unlovely exterior which ultimately were to lead to the gratification of her parents' unspoken wish.

Clarissa, despite her irredeemable unattractiveness, took great care with her appearance. She was extremely vain. This, however, had not always been the case. As a child, she had shown little inclination to improve upon her looks and indeed, up to about the age of sixteen she had tended to emphasise her ugliness by the clothes she wore and the way in which she carried herself. Clarissa had, in other words, made a fetish of her ugliness. Then she met the girl whose aunt had emigrated to England and who, unaware of the revolution it would stimulate, introduced her to the cheap English magazine. Overnight Clarissa's world was transformed.

The first symptom of this transformation was her obsession with personal hygiene. Her cleanliness became mythical. She bathed twice each day, once in the morning before she went to school, and again in the evening before she went to bed, when, to the never-ending wonderment of her parents, she followed the exhortations of the toothpaste manufacturers and brushed her teeth as well.

Her clothes, which she now chose with the greatest care, were always neat and well-ironed and her hair, which formerly she kept plaited close to her scalp, she let down and attempted to comb straight with the assistance of the village hairdresser. Clarissa took copies of the English magazine to her and explained she would like it done just as in the particular photograph that had caught her fancy.

'That style not make for hair like ours, Clarissa.' The hairdresser herself had adopted an 'African' hairstyle. Her political education was well advanced.

'I don't see why. Why only they must have it for?'

'Because they have softer hair than we, Clarissa. That's why. Look, I'll draw a picture so that you could see the difference.' The hairdresser illustrated the difference with two rough diagrams. 'You see how theirs does fall without any trouble? Now you try doing that to ours and see what go happen.'

Clarissa twisted her face sourly and glanced quickly away from the sheet of paper. 'You only making that up,' she said. 'You just like my father. I don't see why you can't use a really hot comb. That bound to get it straight.'

'But it might burn you.'

'I don't care. Is my head that go be burning. Not yours.' Clarissa stared wistfully at the photograph in the magazine.

The hairdresser was resigned. She did as she was told and applied a very hot comb. Clarissa grimaced but did not complain. 'You see what I tell you,' she said, gritting her teeth, 'our hair not really all that different.' The hairdresser was silent. When it was all over, she brought a mirror and Clarissa examined the result. Her cheerfulness disintegrated instantly. 'You call yourself a hairdresser? Like you out to spite me or something?' She began to cry.

'You looking just like one of them Amerindians you does see in British Guiana,' the hairdresser giggled. And then, being a woman of some sensitivity, she realized her mistake and added, 'I was only joking, Clarissa. Don't mind me. It not looking all that bad.' She compared it with the picture in the magazine. The resemblance was tenuous. 'I could fix it up for you in no time at all.'

'You do it on purpose,' Clarissa sobbed. 'You was jealous of me. Everybody in this place jealous of me. You 'fraid that I was going to look too pretty, so you take the chance of spiting me.'

The hairdresser endeavoured to soothe her. 'Come, Clarissa. Don't cry. I'll fix it up for you so it wouldn't look too bad. I'll give it a few curls and it will look real nice. You wait and see.'

Thus Clarissa had no alternative but to submit to a more discreet hairstyle, more in keeping, as the hairdresser put it, 'with our stiff kind of hair'. In the end, all was forgiven. Paradise had no other hairdresser.

However, Clarissa's programme was not confined to improving her appearance. She stopped going to any and every film that happened to be on at the village cinema. Now she went only to light American melodramas and musicals; every other kind of film she considered beneath her. Westerns, especially, she condemned as 'unrefined'.

In addition, many of her friends fell under the withering contempt of Clarissa's new austerity. One of the few survivors was the girl whose aunt had emigrated to England. Without her, Clarissa's supply of the cheap English magazine would have been strangled at its source. Her reputation in the village grew. Young men took to roaming near the house in the hope of catching a glimpse of the renovated Clarissa and their girlfriends, when they saw her on the street, usually on her way to school or, if to the hairdresser's, with a copy of the magazine rolled under her arm, shrieked insults at her: the kind of insults which Mrs Forbes would have had no trouble in understanding.

Clarissa thrived. Her favourite place of repose was the little veranda at the front of the house where, in the afternoons after she had returned from school, she rocked gently in the sunlight, filing her nails and reading. The boys would arrive on bicycles and leaning against the gate try to hold her in conversation.

'Hey, Miss Forbes, give we a smile, eh!'

'You looking real sweet today. How about a little kiss?'

Clarissa would frown into her magazine, brushing imaginary flies away from her face. Then, with a shiver of annoyance, when the chorus seemed on the verge of melting away, she would rise and say, 'I don't see why you hooligans can't leave decent people alone. I can't even read in peace in my own house now.' And she would flounce inside, slamming the front door.

Clarissa's academic pretensions were never very great, but she took a stubborn pride in her poor performances, refusing to believe that they indicated any more than her own preoccupation with matters of greater importance and the spiritless mediocrity of those around her.

One day she returned home from school earlier than usual, and throwing her books on the floor, collapsed on the sofa with apparent disgust. Mrs Forbes was concerned. 'Clary! You sick or something?'

'Sick! I wish I was.' She stared at the books scattered on the floor. 'It's not me who sick, Ma. Is the people who live in this town sick, if you ask me.' She searched in her pocket for her nail file.

'Somebody trying to take advantage of you?'

'He would have if I had given him half a chance. Vulgar beast!' She filed minutely at her nails.

'Who you talking 'bout?' Mrs Forbes knelt down and began collecting the books.

'One of them masters at school. He was trying to be fast with me this afternoon.'

'You mean ...' Mrs Forbes gazed in scandalised disbelief at her daughter.

'That's right, Ma. If I had give him half a chance he would have rape me right there and then.' Clarissa studied the neat edges of her nails. She did not appear to be particularly shocked or distressed. She relished using the word 'rape' and Mrs Forbes, consequently, was inclined to treat what had happened as merely an echo from that larger, melodramatic world which Clarissa inhabited. It paralysed her normal response.

'I going to leave that school,' Clarissa added. 'I can't stay there after today. Anyway, that place don't have anything for me.' She replaced the file in her pocket and hugged herself. 'God! I can't tell you how much I wish I was abroad some place. Torremolinos. That's where I should have been born.'

'But that kind of thing might still happen there, Clary,' Mrs Forbes ventured timidly.

Clarissa was appalled. 'People like you does never learn,' she said. 'How many times I have to tell you things different over there?'

Mrs Forbes acknowledged her mistake and said no more.

Mr Forbes's reaction when he heard the news (he had been to a

Party meeting) was similar to his wife's, but nevertheless he felt it his duty to go and see the schoolmaster. Clarissa was not pleased.

'What's the point of doing that, Pa? I leaving the place after all and I didn't even give the man a chance to touch me. I suppose he was just overcome by desire. That does happen to men sometimes, you know. I sure even you does feel like that sometimes.'

Mr Forbes was enveloped in a thickening mental fog. 'Overcome by desire.' Attempting to gain a securer foothold, he pushed it away from his mind. 'All the same,' he continued tentatively, 'it not right to have a man teaching there who is liable at any time to grab you in the corridor and . . .'

'I didn't say anything about a corridor, Pa. Maybe he's frustrated.'

'Look here,' Mr Forbes replied with abrupt resolution, 'I going to have it out with that man whether he frus . . . whether he is like what you say he is or not.'

The schoolmaster was jovial about the affair. 'I don't know how Clarissa get an idea like that into she head, Mr Forbes. I treat she the same as I does treat all my pupils. And anyway, she tell me the other day that she was leaving school, so I thought I could ask she to go and see a film with me. Mind you, if she was still going to be my pupil I would never have dream of doing a thing like that. It wouldn't have been ethical, if you see what I mean.' He gestured attractively with his cream-coloured palms. 'Not ethical at all, Mr Forbes. But I don't see where she get this idea about my wanting to rape she from. Is not a nice thing to say about a man, you know, Mr Forbes. Is not a nice thing to say at all. That kind of gossip could ruin people, especially a man in my position.' He rubbed his palms together, wagging his head mournfully from side to side.

Mr Forbes was convinced by the sincerity of this defence and he returned home to Clarissa worried and confused.

'He say he only ask you to go to a film, Clary. And besides, you had make up your mind to leave school. You didn't tell we anything about that.'

Clarissa shrugged her shoulders. 'That's not the point,' she replied, but did not bother to elaborate.

'Anyway,' Mr Forbes persisted, 'it would have been unethical for him to try to do a thing like that.'

'I don't like all them big words,' Clarissa said, 'and anyway, I don't like talking about such things. It's better to leave that sort of thing to the other girls. Let them keep their "men".' She twisted her mouth in distaste. 'If I ever go with anybody it will have to be for love and love alone. I'll only become pregnant in wedlock.'

Clarissa's alternating use of the vernacular and that other vocabulary which stifled the judgement baffled Mr Forbes. Torn between the crudity of the former and the elegance of the latter, he listened uneasily to his daughter. Again he strove for the concrete.

'But did he really try to . . . to . . .' Mr Forbes scratched his head and avoided looking at his daughter.

'Really, Pa! Next you go be accusing me of lying.'

'Well I just wanted to . . .'

'If you must doubt me. Yes. He did want to have sexual intercourse with me. But I'm a virgin and will remain one until the day I get married.'

Mr Forbes's perplexity deepened. Sexual intercourse. Virgin. The gap between him and his daughter widened. It was not Clarissa's knowledge of the world that worried him: it was the way she communicated this knowledge. Somehow she managed to make the world seem a much more threatening and mysterious place than he had ever imagined it to be. He dropped the matter and awaited with mounting impatience Clarissa's decision to leave home and begin that inevitable pilgrimage to the land of her dreams.

For some weeks, however, Clarissa did nothing. She remained at home, clean and fragrant, rocking with determined obstinacy on the veranda, occasionally taking time off to rail at the smallness and pettiness of Paradise.

'Look at this place,' she exclaimed, 'a main road with a lot of houses on either side. What do they expect people to live here and do, eh?'

'Me and your father live here all we life. We never complain about it,' her mother answered.

'That's because you and he have no ambition.'

For the first time, Mr Forbes lost his temper.

'It's because we know we place. For people like we it all right, but for people like you . . . well, you could only make trouble for yourself and everybody else. You is the sort of person who have to wait for people to spit in your face before you come to your senses.' Mr Forbes watched his daughter narrowly. 'Why don't you go to Port of Spain, then and live with your aunt?'

'With Auntie Selma! You must be crazy or something, Pa. She does live in John-John with all kinds of louts and riff-raff. What you take me for, Pa?'

'You might find a nice job there and get married,' Mr Forbes went on. His tone was simultaneously conciliatory and goading.

'I could see you out to insult me, Pa. If all you want to do is get rid of me why don't you say so right out instead of beating round the bush?'

'Who say we want to get rid of you?' Mr Forbes replied soothingly.

'Get married!' Clarissa snorted. 'What do you take me for, eh? You think I like all these girls you see running round Paradise?'

'Nobody say that. We know you different.'

'I'll make up my mind in my own good time, you hear. Nobody going to push me around.'

Nevertheless, Clarissa announced her decision the following week.

'I think I'll go and find work in Port of Spain after all. I sure to meet a different class of people there.'

'That's a good idea, Clary,' Mr Forbes said.

'You don't have to tell me that, Pa. I know.' Clarissa was filing her nails. 'I'll go and be a nurse to some rich people children. They does do that kind of thing down there, treating you like one of the family.'

'You need qualifications to be a nurse.' Mr Forbes fingered his Party tie. Political education had gradually enlarged his idea of the complexity of things (due in large part to his failure to gain a seat on the local council) and he derived some comfort from being able to hint at the snags in any undertaking.

'I will learn, Pa. I not stupid you know.'

In Port of Spain, Clarissa discovered that while the wealthy did indeed want 'nurses', they were, none of them, prepared to treat her as one of the family. She would be subject to all sorts of regulations and restrictions which, needless to say, she found offensive. The charms of the Opposition faded and she detected in her heart small, but undeniably sympathetic sentiments towards the government. Clarissa, however, was not yet prepared to surrender to these baser instincts. She would compromise.

Day after day she ran her finger down the classified column of the newspaper. Too many of them asked for 'servant'. That was taking compromise too far, since for Clarissa it was metaphor alone that made the present world habitable. She persevered until at last she noticed that the Gokhools wanted a 'maid'. Clarissa arranged to be interviewed.

The Gokhools lived in a large, rambling house in Woodlands. It was surrounded by a well-watered lawn and two cars were parked in the garage. She hesitated on the pavement, studying the other houses on the street, nearly all as prosperous as the Gokhools'. Unconsciously she had allowed an expression of mild astonishment to form on her face, then, suspecting this, her eyes narrowed into a harder stare.

She rattled the gate. A small white dog came bounding out of the house, barking furiously, a frail woman in pursuit. 'Stop that, Nelson. Get back to your kennel.'

Nelson, ignoring her, barked frenziedly at Clarissa.

The woman looked at Clarissa. 'You are the girl who come for the servant job we advertise?'

Clarissa, shrinking into her obstinacy, nodded briefly.

'Come inside, then. Nelson bark is a lot worse than his bite. Pedigree dogs tend to be rather highly strung, you know.' The woman tittered, and Clarissa opened the gate, her hostility focused on the yapping dog. Nelson subsided instantly, cowering behind the woman who had bent down to stroke him.

'So you are the girl, eh?' She examined Clarissa's clothes with the barest slinking displeasure. 'You ever do servant work before?'

Clarissa shook her head, gazing, her eyes dull and lifeless, at the woman crouched at her feet.

'I'm Mrs Gokhool.' The woman stood up, smoothing her skirt. 'Come this way into the kitchen where we can talk.' Mrs Gokhool, adopting a more business-like manner, led the way briskly, leaving a faint trail of perfume in her wake. Clarissa shambled negligently behind her. They entered the kitchen, a spacious tiled room, obviously newly built. All the equipment was electric and extremely modern. Clarissa had to struggle to control the look of astonishment that was about to descend on her again. The expression she assumed implied that nothing could surprise her. Mrs Gokhool threw herself into a chair.

'We had to send the last girl away because she got pregnant.' Mrs Gokhool twirled a strand of her hair around her fingers. 'She was having a baby, that is,' she explained, smiling more genially at Clarissa. 'My husband didn't want to have yet another mouth to feed and anyway she started having all kinds of riff-raff hanging round the house. It's amazing how quickly that kind of thing can happen. Overnight.' Mrs Gokhool wrinkled her brows and smiled up at Clarissa. 'But I don't expect you are the sort of girl to go and do a thing like that.' As she had done earlier, she glanced at Clarissa's clothes with the same hint of muted displeasure. 'Still,' she waved her hands, running her eyes over the shining kitchen equipment, 'all that's over and done with now, thank God.' She sighed. 'Well, I suppose what you really want to know is what your duties would be if we decide to give you the job.'

Clarissa stood withdrawn and unmoved before Mrs Gokhool.

'You wouldn't have to do any cooking. I have someone else for that.' Mrs Gokhool paused, waiting for a reaction, but none forthcoming, she went on. 'But you would have to help with the washing up. Adeleine suffers from rheumatism and it's not good for her to be in water too much.'

Clarissa's gaze travelled over the varnished wooden ceiling, returning to rest for an instant on the tip of Mrs Gokhool's nose, before settling on the floor. She gave the impression of not having heard a word.

'Your main job, though, would be the cleaning of the house, the making of the beds in the morning and looking after the children generally. Saturday afternoons will be yours and you can do anything you want then, within reason of course. There's a cinema just across the road.'

Clarissa had drawn herself tightly together as if striving to efface the image of the woman speaking to her. Nelson came running into the kitchen and crawled under the table. Mrs Gokhool picked him up and put him on her lap. She stroked his long, furry ears. 'Naughty boy. I thought I told you to go to your kennel.' She turned to Clarissa. 'You just leave school?'

'Uh huh.'

'Your parents still alive? This last girl we send away was from the Belmont Orphanage.'

'Uh huh.'

'What does your father do?'

'He's a councillor.' Clarissa hardly parted her lips as she spoke and the sounds emerged as if wrapped in cotton-wool.

Mrs Gokhool, herself a supporter of the Opposition, was condescending.

'A councillor! That's nice. So you come from an important family?' She grinned at Clarissa.

Clarissa twisted her face sourly. She did not answer the question. Instead she asked whether she would have a room of her own if she, and Clarissa laid special emphasis on this, if she 'decided to take the job'.

Mrs Gokhool looked at her queerly. 'Yes, yes. I was forgetting. Come and I'll show you.' She got up hurriedly, Nelson sliding from her lap, and went out through another door into the backyard and pointed at a small, low shed with a corrugated iron roof kept in position by strategically placed stones. Next to it was Nelson's kennel with 'Home Sweet Home' painted in neat red letters on the front. Clarissa stared at it, trying to disguise her interest. She had never seen a kennel before, not even in the cheap English magazine.

'It's not as bad as it looks,' Mrs Gokhool grinned cheerfully at Clarissa. She was referring to the shed, not the kennel. 'It's much better inside than out and it has everything you will need. The other girl was very happy until she began getting ideas above her station.'

They went inside, having to stoop slightly so as not to brush against the roof. The shed was furnished with a bed and a battered wardrobe. Along one wall there was a sagging bookshelf, filled with old text-books. The floor was of bare concrete and there was no electric light. 'You will have to use candles, but I don't suppose you do much reading anyway, so that doesn't matter.'

'I read a lot,' Clarissa said.

'Do you? Oh, I forgot to ask. What's your name?'

'Clarissa.'

'What do you read, Clarissa?'

'All kinds of things.'

Mrs Gokhool giggled. 'Well, you won't have much time for that here, Clarissa. But what little reading you like doing you can do in the daytime. It's a nice little room, don't you think? The electric light is the only drawback.'

What Clarissa thought was written plainly on her face. She did not attempt to hide her disappointment. She puffed out her cheeks and with that look of sourness that had become habitual to her, stared morosely round her future surroundings, refusing to be drawn by Mrs Gokhool's forced enthusiasm.

Mrs Gokhool giggled uncomfortably. 'It used to be a chicken-run at one time.' They went out into the yard.

'When do you think you can start work? If you want the job, that is. I have lots of other girls like you breathing down my neck.'

'Tomorrow. I can start tomorrow.' Nelson sniffed at her heels.

Mrs Gokhool promised to have the room cleaned. 'I'm sure you will like the rest of the family. My husband is the easiest man in the

world to get on with, once you do your work properly.' Mrs Gokhool
escorted her to the gate. 'Till tomorrow then, Clarissa.'

'So you going to be a nurse after all,' Mr Forbes mused. 'Well, I must
say that really surprise me.'

'I keep telling you I not stupid like you think.' Clarissa was
arranging her clothes with great care in a suitcase. 'People know they
can't push me around.'

'They giving you a uniform to wear?' her mother asked.

'Nothing like that, Ma. The woman say they going to regard me as
one of the family. Mind you, I don't think I going to stay with them all
that long. What I really want to do is a commercial course.'

'But you haven't even start the job as yet and you already talking
about leaving. You is a funny girl, Clary.' Mr Forbes scratched his
head.

'A long time ago I set my heart on a commercial course. I don't want
to be a . . . a nurse for the rest of my life.'

'What you want to do a commercial course for?'

'What do you mean, Pa? I going to be a top class secretary one of
these days. I don't mean any ordinary secretary like you does see
running about all over the place. I mean really top class. I intend to
work in a bank or something like that.'

'You ever see a black person working in a bank?'

'You wait and see,' Clarissa said. 'Mrs Gokhool say she going to use
she influence to find me a really first-class job some place. They is
important people, you know.'

'They sound really nice. You is a lucky girl, Clary.' Mrs Forbes
looked at her daughter admiringly.

'People know they can't push me around,' Clarissa insisted.

Clarissa and the Gokhools were destined not to like each other. At
almost every point her duty came into conflict with her dignity. They
quarrelled on the first day when Mrs Gokhool insisted that she wear a
special blue and white uniform when taking the children for walks.
Clarissa refused.

'I don't want everybody taking me for a common servant, Mrs
Gokhool.'

'But what do you think you are, Clarissa? You mustn't forget that I
am employing you. Just because your father is on some borough
council or other and you want to take a commercial course – I don't

know who put that idea into your little head – that doesn't make any difference you know.'

'I not a common servant, Mrs Gokhool, and you wait and see, I going to take a commercial course, no matter what you say.'

'Why you working for me then? I didn't ask you to take the job. If you feel like that you shouldn't have come here in the first place.'

'I doing a job for money, Mrs Gokhool. But I not nobody's servant. I won't let anybody kick me around.'

'You must be mad.'

In the end it was Mrs Gokhool who capitulated and Clarissa took the children for walks dressed as she pleased. She avoided those places where the other 'maids' on the street congregated with their charges; but, in the succeeding weeks inevitably having to meet and talk with them, let fall that she was a friend of the family and doing them a favour. Thus having established her position relative to them, they no longer sought to chat and gossip with her about their employers. However, the full flight of Clarissa's fancy was reserved for the rheumatic Adeleine with whom she was in daily contact.

'I'm really a kind of au pair girl,' Clarissa told her.

'A what?' Adeleine had not heard of such things before.

'An au pair girl. They have them in places like England and that.'

'Oh. But I never hear of them in Trinidad before, Clarissa.' Adeleine was as guileless as Mrs Forbes, slow to suspect or take offence and willing to believe anything she was told.

'Is not a common thing as yet. But it just starting to happen here. I'm not really a servant at all, you see.'

'I understand now. But . . .' a doubt formulated itself hesitantly in Adeleine's mind, an unusual thing with her, 'but I don't see you eating with them and things like that. You does eat in the kitchen just like me and the other girl who used to be here. How is that?'

'That's because,' Clarissa replied readily, 'I like keeping myself to myself. I don't like mixing with all different kinds of people. I is a fussy person. I like to pick and choose.'

Adeleine nodded slowly. At last she understood. From then on she kept a suitable distance between Clarissa and herself.

These rumours drifted back to Mrs Gokhool. She liked them even less than Clarissa's refusal to wear a uniform. Nevertheless, she bided her time and said nothing. These stories were an unfailing source of amusement to her friends and they urged her to keep her on for a while longer. 'You can't get rid of such a gem,' they said.

But the causes for mutual complaint grew apace. Mrs Gokhool also read magazines, though of a different kind, and, like Clarissa, they were the source of many of her ideas on elegant living.

'I want you to call Jerry Master Jerry from now on,' she informed Clarissa one day. 'I don't think you should be so familiar with him.'

Clarissa laughed, unfeignedly astonished and amused by this latest directive. 'But I so much older than him,' she protested.

'That's not the point. At this rate you will be calling me Mavis soon.'

'You older than me. But Jerry?' She burst out laughing again.

'Master Jerry.'

'But Jerry . . .'

'Master Jerry.'

'. . . he is not even ten years old and I is seventeen.' Clarissa puffed out her cheeks, shaking her head, and Mrs Gokhool knew she had lost again. She did not retail this 'story' to her friends. It was embarrassing and she was not even sure whether they would approve. They might laugh at her, not at Clarissa. Therefore this refusal rankled more than the rest.

Reluctant as she was to fall back on her father's political teachings, nevertheless Clarissa's injured pride fled there to nurture its grievances. She had divided her world into two quite separate spheres: a present full of injustice, a future laden with promise. The one fed the other. The nature of this future was unclear, except for her conviction that, in it, all wounds would be healed. In the meantime, hoping to further extend her horizons and prepare herself for that great day, she read, furtively, all Mrs Gokhool's American magazines and experimented with her expensive perfumes. Mrs Gokhool caught her. 'So, like you want to take my place as mistress of this house, Clarissa?'

'I was only trying the perfume out, Mrs Gokhool.'

'What make you think this kind of perfume is for you, child? That is proper French perfume you know. I just don't know who is putting all these grand ideas in your head.' She took the bottle away from Clarissa. 'This sort of thing wasn't meant for people like you.'

'I don't see why.' Clarissa puffed out her cheeks.

Mrs Gokhool stared at Clarissa for some moments without speaking. Her status had never been seriously called into question before. 'Get this into your head, girl. You are not like me. We are not the same kind of people.' She paused, scrutinising Clarissa's face, before turning away discomfited by what she saw there. She lowered her voice. 'Look, here, Clarissa. I don't want you to feel I'm doing you down, but what I'm telling you is going to be for your own good. My husband is, as you must know, an important man. We belong to . . .' Mrs Gokhool groped for words, her eyes wandering painfully over the room.

'I know,' Clarissa replied. 'You believe that you is really high-class people and I is some kind of dirt which you can sweep anywhere you want. That was what you wanted to say, not so?'

'That is not what I want to say, Clarissa.' Mrs Gokhool's composure was cracking fast. 'I've been very reasonable with you before now. Believe me when I say that none of the people I know would stand from a servant . . .'

'I is not a servant, Mrs Gokhool. I doing a job for money.'

'. . . none of them would stand from a servant what I have stood from you. You would've been out on your ears after two minutes.'

'I is not a servant,' Clarissa intoned, but she seemed to be trying to convince herself rather than Mrs Gokhool.

'. . . there was that business about Jerry, for instance, then your telling everybody that you were a friend of the family. A friend of the family! And not wanting to wear a uniform . . .'

'I is not a servant . . .'

'. . . and what was that phrase you used? An au pair girl? For a servant you have a lot of false pride. Not wanting to call my son Master, well I never . . .'

Clarissa roused herself. 'I wouldn't call that boy Master if you was to pay me a million dollars. Not even for a million dollars, you hear.'

'Look here, girl!' Mrs Gokhool shouted suddenly. 'Watch how you talking to me. I'm not your equal, get that straight. My husband is a rich, important man. He has more money in his pocket alone than you will ever see in your entire life and I'm employing you and that means you are my servant. My servant. Get that straight in your head.'

'Having money don't make you God, you know. And he only get that money by robbing poor people. But the government going to fix all of you soon.'

'Who going to do that? Your councillor father? Is he going to come and dispossess us?'

'I warning you not to insult my father, Mrs Gokhool . . .'

Mrs Gokhool took a step nearer Clarissa. She spoke slowly, measuring each word. 'You are a servant, Clarissa, not a friend of the family as you keep lying to everybody on the street. A servant! A servant! A servant!'

'I'm not yours or anybody's servant, Mrs Gokhool. My father is a respectable man. He didn't want me to take this job in the first place and if he ever get to hear of the way you treating me . . .' Clarissa glowered at her. Mrs Gokhool laughed shrilly.

'He's going to come and beat me up. Don't tell me.'

'That's the sort of thing only you would do.'

'Oh! So you are more respectable than us now. Good. I'm grateful to you for telling me. You have any work for me to do? Maybe I could wash your feet for you and spread a red carpet everywhere you walk.'

'I didn't come here for you to insult me, Mrs Gokhool.'

'Sorry, Miss Clarissa. Sorry.' Mrs Gokhool bowed her head low, bringing her palms together in mock obeisance. 'Well, I don't suppose we can continue to be honoured with your presence.'

'Don't think you can tell me to go, Mrs Gokhool. I make up my mind to leave here a long time ago.'

'Don't let us keep you, Miss Clarissa.'

'Stupid, stupid people,' Clarissa muttered and stumped heavily out of the room.

'Clarissa!' Mrs Forbes, astonished, watched her daughter come stumbling up the path. 'What happen?'

'I give up the job.' Her tone was matter-of-fact. She threw her suitcase on to the steps.

'But why? I thought they was such nice people wanting you to be like one of the family and that.'

'Nice people!' Clarissa spat, and pressing her lips tightly together, kicked the suitcase. 'They wanted me to be too much like one of the family, if you ask me. The woman husband try to rape me.'

'You mean to say . . .'

'Exactly, Ma. You hit the nail on the head. He wanted to sleep with me.'

Mrs Forbes gazed more with puzzlement than with alarm at her daughter. 'Sleep with me.' The phrase echoed in her ears. She had never heard it put like that before. Her judgement clouded.

'Imagine that,' she murmured, unable to suppress the note of admiration creeping into her voice. 'Imagine that. A big, respectable man like that wanting to . . . to sleep with you.'

Mr Forbes when told was tempted to intervene. Clarissa dissuaded him. 'It's not that important, Pa. After all, for a man, especially a frustrated man, to want to sleep with a woman is only natural.' And he too, falling victim to the magic phrase, decided the matter was outside his competence.

During the time she had been at the Gokhools', Clarissa had saved sufficient money to enable her to enrol for the commercial course she had long set her heart on. She relented on the matter of accommodation and in the end agreed to live rent-free with her Auntie Selma in Port of Spain.

'When I finish this course,' Clarissa declared, 'I could get a job anywhere in the world. And not any old job either. You mark my words.'

Clarissa bought all the necessary books and a fountain pen. The books she covered carefully with waterproof paper and her name she wrote on specially chosen pink and white labels. It looked extremely pretty. Each day Clarissa wore a different coloured cotton blouse and a neatly pressed skirt. She was the best dressed girl at the college, and for a month all went well. The reports she sent home were enthusiastic. She even dropped hints about being 'dated' by the man who ran the college. Her parents, poring over the cryptic language, marvelled at their daughter's success.

Unhappily Clarissa was dogged by the same kind of mediocrity that had crippled her performance at school, and, to make matters worse, thrifty though she had been at the Gokhools', she had been buying too many clothes and cosmetics and thus was unable to finance more than her first month's attendance. She was summoned by the head of the college.

'Now, Miss Forbes,' he said, 'you owe us fees for four weeks. We are not running a charity here, you know.'

'I expecting some money soon, Mr Roberts, in another month or so. I'll pay you then.'

Mr Roberts shook his head mournfully. 'A bird in the hand is worth two in the bush, Miss Forbes, and your birds are too much in the bush for my liking.' The phrase pleased him. He smiled dreamily, playing with his thin beard. 'I will tell you something, Miss Forbes. I was a very trusting man when I first began running this business and everybody was taking advantage of me right, left and centre. Hundreds of dollars are still owing to me all over the place. I'm sorry, but I must have it now.'

Clarissa fixed her eyes on the floor. 'I not the sort of person to run away without paying, Mr Roberts. Give me a chance. I'll be getting money soon.'

'I have heard that story too many times, Miss Forbes. Anyway, your work here doesn't justify my giving you a chance.'

Clarissa closed her eyes, her lips pinched together. She seemed to be trying to ward off some unpleasant image or memory.

'You mustn't think me hard-hearted, Miss Forbes, but I must draw the line somewhere.' He spoke as if from a prepared speech.

'I'll do anything you want me to do, Mr Roberts. Just give me one more chance.' Clarissa's eyes strayed over his face.

'What are you suggesting, Miss Forbes?'

Clarissa did not answer. Her eyes, leaving him, swept across the walls and ceiling.

'You're a nice girl, Miss Forbes, and you take a lot of care of yourself. I can see that. But don't go and spoil it . . .'

'I'll do anything you ask, Mr Roberts. Anything.' Clarissa no longer struggled to hold back her tears.

'No, Miss Forbes. That won't do. It's a bad policy to get . . . how shall I put it? . . . to get involved with one's students in this kind of business. I speak from bitter experience.' Mr Roberts, unruffled by her tears, stared steadily at Clarissa, displaying the professional concern of the undertaker.

'You is a stupid, stupid man. I could tell you how much people try to make it with me, getting down on they knees and begging me. Is not everybody I does offer myself to and don't think I haven't seen how you been watching me out of the corner of your eye these past few weeks.'

'I'm surprised to hear you talk like that, Miss Forbes. Truly surprised.' And he could not resist adding, 'If I was watching you it was only because you hadn't paid your fees.'

'You're a stupid, stupid man. Don't believe you will ever have another chance with me. I warning you. Your face not all that pretty.'

'I never said it was, Miss Forbes.' He got up. 'I think you better take your things and go. You can pay me when you get the money you were talking about.'

'You is a real nigger!' Clarissa screamed. 'Is people like you who is the cause of our people downfall, making everybody treat we like servant. They should throw you in jail. In jail, you hear!'

'Yes, Miss Forbes, I hear. But you better go now before you say anything you will really regret.' Mr Roberts pushed her gently towards the door.

'In jail, in jail,' Clarissa whimpered.

'Here, Miss Forbes. You are forgetting all your nice books.'

'You could eat the damn books, for all I care.' Clarissa brushed her tears away in quick violent movements. Then, pushing him aside, she ran abruptly out of the room, slamming the door hard behind her.

Once more Mrs Forbes was confronted by the sight of her daughter struggling up the path with her suitcase.

'You finish the course already?' she asked.

'I give it up.'

'You give it up? But think of all that money you waste, Clary.'

'Is not my fault. Is the blasted man who own the school to blame.'

'You mean . . .'

'Yes. That's right. He try to rape me like the rest of them.'

Mrs Forbes nodded. This time Mr Forbes did not even suggest intervention.

Clarissa sought and found comfort in the pages of the cheap English magazine. However, she was altogether quieter and more withdrawn. Her parents, especially Mr Forbes, were distressed by the change in their daughter.

Mr Forbes was not an entirely stupid man. It struck him as distinctly odd that three quite different men at one time or another should have tried to rape his daughter. He studied her. She was not beautiful. He mentioned this to his wife and she agreed. 'I never think of it like that before,' she said. Mr Forbes brooded over Clarissa's history and, as he brooded, his distress gave way to ill-temper. His political education was by now very far advanced.

'Clary,' he said one day when she had been more than usually reticent, 'what would you say about my paying your passage to England?'

Clarissa brightened. 'You really mean that, Pa?'

'Yes.'

'That's the place I feel where I really belong. Living in a flat and that sort of thing.' Mr Forbes scowled. 'Mind you,' she went on, 'what with all that rain and fog and thing is not an easy life. But I really feel that's the kind of life I was made for. Still, it's expensive getting there.' She glanced doubtfully at her father.

'Not if you take one of them immigrant ships and travel third class.'

'Immigrant ships! Third class!' Clarissa flung the copy of the magazine she was reading on to the floor. 'What do you take me for, Pa?'

'Shut up, child. You'll do as I say or not at all. I'm damn tired of all your stupid prancing around the place. Is high time you learn some respect for me.'

'Ethélbert!' Mrs Forbes groaned, alarmed at the prospect of their daughter's scorn falling on their heads. She worried needlessly. Clarissa did not rise to the bait. Her reply was defensive, self-pitying.

'You just like everybody else, Pa. Trying to take advantage of me.'

'Nobody taking advantage of you. Is your . . . is your . . .' He flung his arms about excitedly.

'Ethélbert,' Mrs Forbes groaned, 'don't excite yourself so.'

'Keep quiet, Maisie, and mind your own business.' He turned again to face Clarissa. 'Is your damn colonialist mentality that taking advantage of you. Yes, that's what it is. Your colonialist mentality.' It was a phrase the Prime Minister had employed recently against a renegade Minister who had embezzled large sums of money and fled to Switzerland. Mr Forbes waved a threatening finger in front of Clarissa's face.

'You always blaming your failure on people wanting to rape you. Well, let me tell you something. You got to have sex appeal for people to want to rape you and you have about as much of that as I have. But you go to England and we go hear how much of that kind of nonsense you go still be talking when you come back.' The magazine caught his eye. He picked it up from the floor and flipped rapidly through the pages. 'Is this what you consider so great? Is this where you does get all your stupid ideas from? You should be shamed of yourself. Let me see.' He read aloud from the magazine. 'They met on holiday in the Riviera, he, unmarried and bronzed as a Greek god, a happy-go-lucky man of the world, she, good-looking and with a husband suffering from leukaemia . . .'

'Give me back my magazine, Pa. What I read is my own business.' Clarissa lunged at him.

'Tell me first what all this Riviera business got to do with a little nigger girl like you, eh?'

'Give me back my magazine please. Please.' Clarissa wrung her hands. Mr Forbes let the magazine slip through his fingers and fall on to the floor. Clarissa picked it up and hugged it close to her bosom.

A few weeks later Clarissa took passage to England on an immigrant ship, third class.

London was not all Clarissa expected it to be. True, there were fogs and days when it drizzled without cessation. But the fogs were not as thick or as yellow as she had been led to imagine and there were many days when it did not rain. Neither did Clarissa share a flat with a friend. She lived in a bed-sitter in a dilapidated immigrant section of the city. Her landlord, a West Indian, charged her six pounds a week for it. It had peeling wallpaper, a leaking ceiling and a stove that filled the room with smoke. She had no friends. The cheap English magazine, and others like it, existed in abundance, but she had lost her taste for it. Where were the Greek gods? The leukaemia-stricken husbands? The world pictured there hardly corresponded with what she saw around her every day, and on the rare occasion when the veil did lift, Clarissa took fright and ran away.

She was two months finding a job, as a ticket collector on the Underground. Week after week she stood outside her cubicle, her hands stretched forth to trap the stream of tickets thrust at her. At nights she crept slowly back home, cooked supper and went to bed to the accompaniment of the trains that rattled past beneath her windows. Her landlord was sympathetic.

'I know how lonely it does get when you away from home so long and all by yourself. But you does get accustom in the end, like me.'

'I leave a good home to come to this,' Clarissa replied. 'My father is a councillor. He would dead if he was to see me living like this.'

'I been here ten years. Take me a long time to save up to buy this place.' He surveyed the decaying room with pride. 'Ten years,' he repeated. 'Is warming to meet a really nice local girl like you after such a long time. From the moment I set eyes on you I know you had class. Real class. What you say your father is?'

'A councillor.'

'A councillor. Yes. You is a girl with real class.' He put his hand on her shoulder. Clarissa did not protest. 'I tired of these English girl.' He felt her hair. Still Clarissa did not protest. The landlord grew bolder. He swayed slightly as he bent low over her.

'You want to sleep with me?' Clarissa asked suddenly.

The landlord, taken aback, laughed. 'Real class,' he said.

'You want to sleep with me?'

'What a funny girl you is.'

'You want . . .'

'Yes, yes.'

And so Clarissa Forbes lost her virginity. But it was not for love and certainly it was out of wedlock.

Clarissa worked hard and this time she did not spend her money on clothes and expensive perfumes.

'But what you killing yourself so for?' the landlord asked.

'I going back home. I saving up for a tourist-class passage.'

'But, Clarissa . . .'

'No, Frankie. You was enough.'

A few weeks later she was back home.

'You see them dogs race?' her mother asked.

'No, Ma.'

'No bingo halls either?'

'No, Ma.'

'And I don't suppose you ever get to that place you was telling we about. Torr . . . something or the other.'

'No, Ma, I didn't manage to get to Torremolinos.'

'And nobody try to . . .'

'No, Ma. Nobody try to rape me.'

'But like you didn't do anything at all while you was there?'

'It was too cold out there, Ma,' Clarissa replied. 'It was much too cold.'

Mr Forbes's political fortunes had improved during Clarissa's absence. Recognition of his unswerving devotion to the Party came eventually and he was, after all, elected to the county council. Clarissa was proud of her father, and Mrs Forbes, whose ignorance was still an embarrassment to her husband, gratefully gave way to Clarissa who accompanied him on all important official occasions. And thus she too was brought to the attention of the branch Party. Her international experience stood her in good stead.

'We need more people like you,' the local party manager confided to her. 'People with experience of conditions abroad will be an asset to the Party.'

Clarissa was flattered. She joined the Party and was unanimously elected secretary of the Paradise Women's Federation. The head of the local branch visited the Forbes often. The rumours circulated. He proposed. Clarissa accepted.

'Your daughter is a terror,' he said to Mr Forbes some time after they had been married. 'A real fanatic about everything local. She does say that she wouldn't even let our children read any of them foreign magazines. Yes, man. Clary is a real terror.'

'It take she a long time to learn,' Mr Forbes confessed. 'There was a time . . .'

'I owe it all to my father,' Clarissa interrupted hastily. 'He it is who teach me all I know. He was my first political mentor, right through from my childhood . . .' Clarissa elaborated. Her voice drifted sonorously through the sitting room.

Mr Forbes laughed and patted his daughter. He settled back more comfortably into his armchair and as he listened to her conversation, his judgement clouded, but in a manner he was quite content to leave well alone.

The Dolly House

The neighbours had seen Roderick first: a dark, slender young man with the beginnings of a manly air and a moustache. A gold watch was slung loosely on his wrist and he was neatly and nattily dressed. He had come to look at the single room with jalousied windows and doors, which, because it was divided by partitions into a warren of tiny cells, its owner called a house. It had been unoccupied for some months.

They examined Roderick with interest; while he, pretending to be oblivious of their scrutiny, inspected the property with an air of knowing, businesslike efficiency. Using a measure – the kind that shoots out several feet of limber steel at the press of a finger – he strolled purposefully about the muddy, poultry-soiled yard, recording lengths and breadths and heights in a red notebook. He pounded the woodwork with his fists, crawled among the supporting pillars and examined the floorboards for signs of decay. He frowned, drummed thoughtfully on his head with the pencil and scrawled more jottings in the notebook.

'What are you taking all them measurements for, Mister?'

Roderick surveyed the faces staring at him from the surrounding windows. 'I like doing things properly,' he answered. 'Sci-en-tif-ically. I don't believe in hocus-pocus.'

The neighbours were impressed.

'Like you thinking of renting the place, Mister?'

'Not renting.' Roderick pounded the woodwork and listened. 'Buying.'

The neighbours were even more impressed.

'Buying!' They assessed him. 'What somebody like you thinking of buying house for?'

Roderick did not answer immediately. He scrawled another observation into his notebook, muttering to himself and frowning. 'I getting married,' he announced casually when he had done. And then added offhandedly: 'A married man must have somewhere for his wife and family.'

The neighbours stared at him. '*You* getting married? But you hardly out of short pants!' They laughed. 'You bound to be making joke with us, man.'

Roderick was peeved. 'I don't see what's so funny about it.'

The neighbours were conciliatory. 'Don't take offence. Is just that you look too young to be thinking already of wife and family and what not.'

'I'm twenty years old,' Roderick said sourly, putting the notebook into his shirt-pocket.

'And your wife-to-be? How old *she* is?'

Roderick grimaced and departed without another word.

They had their first glimpse of Clara the following week when Roderick brought her to see the house. An arm circling her waist, he led her somewhat defiantly – he was aware of the neighbourly scrutiny – into the yard and up to the front steps of the house.

'This is it,' he said. 'What you think?'

'It's nice,' Clara replied. 'It's very nice.'

'A bit on the small side,' he conceded. 'But that's not the main thing. The construction' (he kicked one of the supporting pillars) 'is basically sound. What I like best about it is the possibilities. This place has a lot of poss-i-bil-ities.'

Roderick waved his free arm optimistically.

'I like it,' Clara murmured. 'It's very nice.' She pressed closer against him.

The neighbours gaped.

'So this is the wife to be, eh!'

Clara blushed, raising and lowering her head quickly. She clung to Roderick, endeavouring to conceal herself as much as possible from their naked curiosity. There was much laughter.

'Don't be bashful, doux-doux. What you hiding yourself behind him for? Come where we could see you.'

Roderick had done his best to outface them. However, they could not be outfaced indefinitely. 'You don't have to be frightened,' he whispered. 'Let them look at you.' He removed his arm from her waist and stepped back, giving them an unobstructed view. Having done so, he looked round challengingly. 'Yes,' he said aloud. 'This is my wife to be.'

Clara bowed her head. Roderick, who was of average height, seemed to tower over her. A rich, unschooled mass of curling black hair spilled in natural ringlets across a smooth forehead. It emphasised her childish aspect; as did the prim, oval face and upturned nose. Her eyelashes were thick and curving, veiling her brown eyes. Prominent veins buttressed her narrow neck: it seemed that the weight of her abundant hair might almost prove too much for that neck to support. Her legs tapered down to tiny feet. The wind stirred the folds of her light cotton frock and she smoothed it absently with the hand which bore the engagement ring. The ring flashed when it caught the sun.

This slip of a girl was soon to be a wife! This slip of a girl was soon to possess a husband!

'She must still have a few milk-teeth!'

Kindly laughter floated from the windows.

'What's your name, doux-doux?'

'Clara.' Her voice was an undertone.

'And how many years you have, Mistress Clara?'

'Sixteen.' The ring flashed.

'Your mother and father – what they have to say?'

'That's enough questions,' Roderick said.

But Clara answered. 'They don't approve.' She exchanged an uneasy glance with Roderick. 'We having a love marriage.'

The neighbours clucked their tongues. 'Ah, doux-doux. A love marriage. I hope the both of you know what you doing.'

A month later a truck backed into the yard. A sheet of tarpaulin protected the furniture stacked on its open tray. Clara was huddled affectionately against her husband in the high driver's-seat. Roderick jumped out and eased his wife gingerly to the ground. Then he hauled off the tarpaulin. There was revealed a wardrobe, a rolled mattress, a double bed, a chest of drawers, a two-burner kerosene stove, assorted pots and pans; and, crowning it all, a cane-bottomed rocking-chair. The latter was resplendently new but the rest had obviously been acquired on the cheap: they were ancient, battered things.

'How you going to carry all that inside your dolly house?' the neighbours enquired.

'We'll manage,' Roderick said. He stripped off his shirt.

'You'll manage, eh! Don't be stupid, man. Just take one good look at the doux-doux.'

Roderick, despite himself, obeyed. He looked at Clara. His assurance wavered.

'And you is no superman either, come to that.' They eyed his naked torso.

'We'll manage all the same.' Nevertheless, he stared disconsolately at the massed furniture.

'Tcha!' They sucked their teeth. 'Stubbornness will be the death of you. Wait there.'

Their faces disappeared from the windows. The women trooped into the yard. 'We'll help you carry it to your dolly house.'

'This is a nice-looking rocking-chair you have here,' one of the women said to Clara.

Clara beamed. 'You like it? It's he who buy it for me as a wedding present.' She pointed proudly at her husband who was struggling up the front steps under the weight of the mattress.

The woman grinned.

Every morning at eight o'clock, Roderick, dressed in the khaki uniform of a sanitary inspector, wheeled his bicycle out of the yard. Clara, her arm linked in his, walked with him out to the road. There, unashamed and undaunted by the passers-by, they kissed each other goodbye. Clara spent the time until his return in the evening – the day for her was, essentially, nothing but a waiting and longing for his return – performing the necessary wifely duties and chatting to the neighbours over the rotting wooden fence, giggling girlishly at all their jibes. They had had to teach her those necessary wifely duties. For Clara, they had not been overly amazed to discover, did not know much about anything.

'Like your mother didn't learn you nothing at all?' they asked.

To which Clara replied that her mother had tried; but that she could not be bothered to pay a great deal of attention.

'Telling us!' the neighbours retorted. 'But now you give yourself a husband you have to pay attention – even though you had a love marriage with him.' Their lectures were grave. 'He is the only thing you have to have on your mind from now on. Because no matter how much a man in love with you, he will still expect you to be able to cook his food and wash his clothes.'

These were unpalatable truths but Clara accepted them without complaint. The neighbours set in train her domestic education; and Clara, urged on by the threat of forfeiting her husband's love, learned with remarkable rapidity.

The daily routine accomplished, Clara readied herself for Roderick's homecoming. Sheathed in a petticoat, she splashed herself with buckets of water in the corrugated-iron cubicle near the back fence which served as a bathroom. After her bath, she dressed and sat on the front steps combing out her hair, letting it dry in the sun. Finally, she powdered and 'made up' herself. The morning kiss of farewell was matched by the evening kiss of welcome; and, as Roderick wheeled his bicycle into the yard, Clara provided him with a running account of the day's adventures.

From the neighbours' point of view, the house next door remained a dolly house. Clara and Roderick were playing at life: playing 'wife'; playing 'husband'. Life, as the neighbours knew it, was something hard and intractable; a maze of thwarted desire. Thus they could not treat the young couple seriously. It was impossible to put the two on an equal footing with themselves. Equality would have required of Roderick and Clara a knowledge – or if not a knowledge, at least an awareness – of the quicksands that might be lying in wait for them. But neither knowledge nor awareness seemed to be present in the smallest degree: they had no notion of tragedy. This ignorance did not diminish the neighbours' fondness. They did not wish the slightest harm to befall the young couple. Indeed, had it been within their power, they would gladly have conferred upon them an eternity of blissful play in their dolly house.

Not even Clara's pregnancy could make them alter their attitude. Improbability was merely being piled on improbability: from playing wife Clara was only about to make the natural progression to playing mother. She thrived on her pregnancy and discussed with them suitable names for the child.

'I hope it's a boy because then I could call him after Roddy. What's another nice name for a boy? I can't think of any.'

The neighbours tried to discourage these speculations: they were superstitious; they felt fate was being needlessly tempted.

'Leave all that until the child born, Mistress Clara. Is never good to count your chickens before they hatch.'

'It's not a chicken I going to have,' Clara said, contemplating her swelling stomach delightedly.

The neighbours clucked their tongues.

Their fears were unfounded. When the time came, Roderick called a taxi and took Clara to the General Hospital. A week later she was back home – with a baby girl. Her initial disappointment at the child not being a boy was soon quelled by the praise which the neighbours lavished on mother and infant. There was no formal christening – Roderick dismissed the suggestion as a piece of hocus-pocus; but, at the insistence of Clara, he did agree to have a small party to mark the event.

All the neighbours were invited. In addition, Clara asked some of her old schoolmates; while Roderick, less prodigal, contented himself with the friend whom he had chosen to be best man at his wedding. Archie appeared to be – so far as it was possible to tell – the only person in the world outside (that mysterious world to which Clara consigned her husband every morning and from which he was returned to her every evening) with whom Roderick was on anything like intimate terms. In fact, apart from a shared interest in things mechanical, they were a strangely contrasting pair: Roderick, slender to the point of being gaunt and reticient to the point of being surly; Archie, plump to the point of being fat and flamboyant to the point of being vulgar in dress and manner.

Clara presided from the rocking-chair, cooing to the baby and smiling amiably at everyone. Archie, behaving like a host, distributed the cigars he had brought and poured the drinks.

'Come on, ladies,' he would shout from time to time. 'Drink up! Drink up!'

The room filled with smoke and laughter and the smell of rum. Roderick, a little drunk, flourished his cigar and began to enlarge on his plans for the future now that he was a father. The neighbours listened attentively: they had never seen him in so expansive a mood. He said he intended to build an extension; to install a 'real' bathroom and a 'real' kitchen. Clara beamed at her husband in the thickening haze. Her face was barred by the sunlight falling through the jalousied window under which she was sitting.

'That is what I liked about this place from the first – the poss-i-bil-ities. All it need is some imagination to make this into what people would call a desirable residence.' The cigar stabbed the soupy haze. He repeated the phrase, rolling his *r*s. 'A desir-r-rable r-r-residence.'

'Imagination – and money,' a neighbour ventured. 'You might have the imagination. But where you going to get the money from?'

'I will. Don't you worry.'

They studied him sceptically.

'America is the place for money,' Archie said. He rubbed his reddened eyes and swayed a little as he spoke. 'If is money you after, America is the place.'

'But I hear it not so nice for black people,' another neighbour observed mournfully.

'Am-er-ica.' The glow of Roderick's cigar had been extinguished. He tapped it and watched it shed its load of dead ash on the floor. The guests were oddly subdued.

'You shouldn't throw ash on the floor, Roddy,' Clara scolded mildly.

Roderick grimaced. 'I'm still a young man,' he went on, as if speaking only to himself and with a sudden access of belligerence. 'I don't intend to remain a sanitary inspector all my life. I don't want to spend the rest of my life spraying drains, throwing lime down cess-pools and poisoning rats. That is no kind of life for a man.'

'That remind me of something I wanted to tell you,' Clara said. 'Now we have a baby I don't think you should keep all that rat poison hanging about the place.'

He paid her no attention. 'I have a brain. A good brain. Why should I let it rot? The world . . . the world is such a big place. It have so many things a man could do. So many things for a man to be.'

Clara looked up at him, surprised. 'I never hear you talk like that before, Roddy. What get into you so sudden?'

His mouth contracted. 'Do you want me to remain a sanitary inspector forever? Is that what you would like the father of your child to be?'

'You know I want whatever you want, Roddy. Whatever will make you happy.' Clara smiled timidly at him. 'But up until now I thought . . . well, it's just that I never hear you talk like that before. That's all.'

'You like living in this shack? You like bathing yourself with a bucket instead of a real shower?'

'We been happy,' Clara said. 'And that is what count most. So long as we happy I don't mind living in a shack or bathing with a bucket.' She appealed to the room for confirmation and support.

The neighbours nodded approvingly. But they were solemn. The party spirit had fled from the room.

'That is the kind of talk I would expect to hear from stupid country people,' Roderick said.

An uneasy silence ensued during which the neighbours pondered the speeches they had heard and Roderick twirled his dead cigar. It was the baby who came to the rescue: she began to cry vociferously – as if the silence disturbed her.

They were recalled to the purpose of the gathering.

'Ssh . . . ssh . . . I not going to starve you.' Clara unbuttoned her blouse and proffered a full breast.

'What name you choose for the baby?' one of the old schoolfriends asked.

'Paulette,' Clara replied.

Everyone agreed it was a pretty name.

'Come on, ladies. Drink up! Drink up!'

The neighbours channelled their attentions to the feeding operation. They cautioned and recommended and praised. Clara giggled. Archie filled the empty glasses. Roderick relit his cigar. Soon the talk became cheerfully general.

The next year Clara was pregnant again. It astonished the neighbours that so fragile a frame could produce babies with such apparent ease.

'I praying for it to be a boy,' she confided to them. 'Roddy would like a son. Somebody to follow in his footsteps.'

'Tcha!' they rebuked her. 'Leave that to God. He know best whether to give you a boy child or a girl child.'

'Roddy say it's nothing to do with God,' Clara replied. 'He say it's to do with something he call the genes.'

The neighbours crossed themselves and rolled their eyes heavenward.

Clara wept copiously when she was delivered of a second girl. The neighbours sought to console. 'Is not your fault, doux-doux. Nobody could blame you because is a girl child. Roderick is a intelligent man. He will understand.'

This time, however, Clara was not to be so easily comforted. 'It's all my fault,' she wailed. 'I let him down.'

The neighbours were right. Despite his unscientific desire for a son, Roderick was sensible about it. With all the patience and resourcefulness at his command, he explained to Clara that it was not within her power to determine the sex of her child; her 'foetus' as he called it. Consequently ('though I admit a boy would have been nice') she could not be held responsible. But, he added as a footnote, the wonders of modern science were such that in the not too distant future . . . etc. . . . etc.

Clara was inconsolable. 'I know it's all my fault,' she wailed. 'I let you down.'

Roderick gave up; and Clara's distress remained acute until he was driven to relent and permit a final assault on the recalcitrant genes. 'But remember I mean final,' he warned. A third child was going against his principles: Roderick was fond of denouncing the practice of indiscriminate child-bearing. 'It's because they have no self-control that all these stupid country people will go on starving and being stupid.'

And Clara's luck held! The third child was a boy. Even Roderick – stern in the preceding interval – could scarcely disguise his pleasure. The child was named after his father. Clara's happiness was now complete. In the eyes of the neighbours, they were still the enchanted couple playing at life in their dolly house.

Yet it was the very completeness of Clara's happiness which worried the neighbours. Her happiness was too perfect; too simple. In that perfect simplicity lay its great strength – and, alas, its fatal weakness: for it depended on everything remaining more or less the same. Her happiness was not adaptable. It could never accommodate itself to a change of circumstances. The neighbours knew that things never remained the same. All was flux. Once let that happiness fracture and it would vanish all of a piece. It would be as if it had never existed. Clara, they saw quite clearly, could be easily – and dreadfully – hurt; though they could not predict from what quarter that hurt might descend; what awful shape it might assume.

Roderick's outburst at the 'christening' had not been forgotten by the neighbours. It could not be lightly dismissed. From time to time it surfaced to haunt them. Unconsciously – against their wills – they searched for fresh signs of restlessness in him. The evidence did not reassure them. Roderick, they observed, had slipped gradually into the habit of treating his wife much as he treated his children. This was not a deliberate policy of his. On the contrary: in conformity with his progressive views Roderick had accepted the theory that a wife was not a mere 'chattel' – as he expressed it – but a 'companion'. Confronted with Clara, the theory collapsed. She agreed with auto- matic (and unfeigned) enthusiasm to everything he said or did. Clara had willingly sunk herself in his authority and, with the passage of time, she was increasingly hypnotised by it. His theories having been sabotaged, the decline from the heights was inevitable. He could be magisterially stern with her in moments of displeasure; and, occa- sionally, he exceeded magisterial sternness.

One morning – it was a Saturday and Roderick was not at work – a wandering preacher came into the yard. There was nothing extra- ordinary about this visitation. Such characters were a familiar and accepted part of the social scene; a kind of travelling circus providing an innocuous diversion. Robed and bearded, they were an exotic sight. Clara was a trifle disappointed by this one: he was neither robed nor bearded but conventionally dressed and carrying a briefcase. He looked more like a door-to-door salesman than a preacher. It was only the big silver cross hung round his neck which belied the resemblance. He was tall and thin and stoop-shouldered.

Clara greeted him banteringly. 'I never see a preacher dress like you before. You look more like a salesman.'

He bowed gravely. 'I'm a salesman for the Lord. How a man dresses is not important. Our souls go unclothed before God.' He opened the briefcase he was carrying and drew out a magazine from it. 'I would like you to read this.' He held it out to her. Clara hesitated. 'Take it – it is given free of charge.' He smiled.

Clara accepted the magazine from his outstretched hand. She saw Roderick approaching and fumbled guiltily with it.

'What is all this?'

'I take it you are this lady's husband?' the preacher enquired politely.

Roderick was not welcoming. 'That's right. But I want to know who *you* are and what *you* are doing in my yard.'

'My name is Horatio Reuben and I am a servant of the Lord.'

Roderick turned to Clara. 'What's that he give you?' He took the magazine from her and leafed through it, his expression darkening as he did so. 'So this is the kind of nonsense you like to fill your head with. You not interested in what I try to teach you. You prefer to addle your brain with this rubbish. Eh? Answer me.' He shook her.

'It's only a magazine, Roddy. What's the harm?'

His indignation waxed. 'Only a magazine, you say. What's the harm, you say. How do you know there's no harm in it? Who tell you that? Tell me!'

'How can God's Word possibly do any harm?' Reuben asked with undiminished politeness.

'If you know what's good for you, you had better keep out of this, Mr Preacher.' Roderick ripped the magazine in two and flung it at Reuben's feet.

'Blasphemer!'

Roderick advanced on him. 'Haul your tail from my yard, Mr Preacher.'

Reuben retreated with as much dignity as the circumstances permitted.

'You shall regret having done this,' Reuben shouted when he had gained the safety of the road. He waved a clenched fist. 'God will not suffer his servant to be humiliated by the likes of you.'

'Make sure,' Roderick said to Clara, 'that that is the last time you ever let him – or anybody like him – enter my yard. I won't have it.' He shook his head at her. 'I can't help feeling that all my efforts are completely wasted on you.'

Clara clutched at his arm. 'Please, Roddy. Don't say things like that. I don't mean to be always letting you down. But . . .' She started to cry.

He gazed at her with a sorrowful, surrendering anger, still shaking his head.

Acting on the assumption that there was nothing a man could do or understand which was beyond the capacities of an 'intelligent' woman, Roderick had tried to instruct Clara in the elementary principles of mechanics. She was not an amenable pupil, accusing him of 'confusing' her. Her concentration would quickly wilt and, rather than listen, she preferred to run her hands through his hair. 'Please pay attention,' Roderick would plead, fending off her flirtations. 'Pulleys are no joke business, you know.' Ultimately, he was forced to give up his attempts to educate her. Hence Clara was deprived of place and function in this important area of his life. She was simply an obstacle to his efforts to 'improve his mind'.

Even though she boasted about her husband reading books laden with numbers and mysterious diagrams, it was apparent to the neighbours that Clara was not overly keen on Roderick's determined struggle to educate himself. His reading seemed to stir a latent unease in her and, either through wilful neglect or an apprehension dimly formulated, she refused to credit it with any real significance; refused to admit the danger. For instance, she had never referred to the incident with the preacher: it appeared to have slid completely from her memory by the next day. She confined herself to saying things like: 'I wish Roddy wouldn't read so much. I'm sure it's not good for his eyes.'

For a while it was Archie who filled the gap of 'companion' left vacant by Clara's desertion. He would come on Sunday mornings and crouch on the front steps with Roderick. Together they would work through various complicated calculations and have long and earnest discussions. Clara was not jealous. Glad at her release, she was content to circle hennishly around them, bring cups of tea and shoo the children away. Then, without warning, Roderick suffered his second desertion: Archie suddenly announced he was going to America.

'Sorry, old man.' Archie looked guiltily at him.

'You have nothing to be sorry for,' Roderick said quietly.

'I know I should have tell you before but ...' Archie laughed nervously. 'Well, to be frank, I wasn't sure how you would take the news.'

Roderick laughed heavily.

'I thought you mightn't take it too well,' Archie said.

'I don't know why you should think that,' Roderick replied.

Archie rested a hand on his friend's shoulder. 'Thanks, old man. I was so worried that you would ...'

Roderick gathered up the books on the step. 'No use for these today.' He removed Archie's hand from his shoulder and carried them back inside.

Roderick did indeed appear to take Archie's desertion in his stride. But it unnerved the neighbours when, throwing his books aside disgustedly, he paced aimlessly about the yard in his short, fraying khaki trousers and vest, his sabots clicking; plucking at the leaves on the bushes with unnecessary violence, his mouth contracted. The click of those sabots sounded like a warning in their ears. They could interpret its message; Clara, it seemed could not.

And what could they tell her? After all, they could be wrong. In any case, Clara would not have believed them. Even worse, she would not have understood. She would have scorned their fears. Therefore, they said nothing. Impotent observers, they could only hope for the best. Above all, they did not wish to hasten by foolhardy meddling that which they feared. They suspected that, if and when the eruption did come, it would do so suddenly; as suddenly as it had come at the christening: like the crash of thunder in a clear sky.

But nothing untoward occurred and the fear, though it did not vanish, lessened. On the surface at any rate, life in the dolly house proceeded smoothly. Motherhood had filled out Clara's figure. Her breasts had expanded to ample and womanly dimensions and her arms and legs were well fleshed. She had become altogether sturdier. The changes wrought were not negligible – but they could not be described as dramatic. Now she could, without arousing incredulity, pass muster as a young wife. However, as mother of three, Clara was still not convincing.

She looked after her children reasonably well – as reasonably, that is, as the salary of a sanitary inspector would allow. She was not afraid to beat them when the occasion demanded. The spectacle of an angry Clara pursuing her children around the yard with a broom caused the neighbours much amusement. Clara herself, realising how comic and absurd she must appear to them, would sometimes pause in the midst of one of these sessions and share in the merriment before resuming the chase. These beatings were done largely at the instigation of Roderick: he was a kind but not a lax father. 'If you spare the rod you spoil the child,' he said to her. 'That is a sci-en-tif-ic fact.'

Despite the additional cares imposed by the children, Clara managed to maintain most of the rituals of the early days of their marriage intact. She walked out to the road with Roderick in the mornings and delivered on his lips the kiss of farewell; and the evening found her waiting to give him the kiss of welcome. Once or twice a month, having left the children with the neighbours, they went to the pictures. At four o'clock on Sunday afternoons, after dressing carefully, the entire family would set out on a leisurely parade around the Queen's Park Savannah. As a special treat, Roderick would buy them all coconuts from one of the many carts which lined the perimeter of the park.

The extension had not been built; the kitchen stayed a lean-to shed tacked on to the house; Clara had not ceased to splash herself with buckets of water in the corrugated-iron cubicle near the back fence; and Roderick never stopped talking about the possibilities of the property. Still, they were not years totally devoid of achievement: there had been a few tangible improvements. Celebrating a marginal increase in his salary, Roderick painted the partitions of the house white and repaired the broken slats in the jalousies; and, after an orgy of measuring and jotting in his notebook, he had slowly and painstakingly raised the wooden fence to the front. The wood was not new – he could not afford that – but it looked as good as new. Clara and the neighbours brimmed with admiration.

'It's because I do it sci-en-tif-ically it turn out so well,' Roderick commented, surveying his handiwork with ill-concealed pride.

The neighbours had almost persuaded themselves to forget their fears; had almost come to believe that Clara and Roderick led truly charmed lives in their dolly house, when the crash of thunder came out of a clear sky.

*

After three years in America, Archie returned to the island. During the first year he had written regularly to Roderick; the second year saw a gradual tailing-off in their correspondence; and, latterly, there had been nothing at all. 'He become a real sweet man' was the verdict of the neighbours when they heralded his unexpected entry into the yard with cries of warm greeting.

Archie was dressed in a suit of black-and-white houndstooth check. A thin, cultured line of moustache adorned his upper lip. His loss of weight gave him an air of springy, dandified alertness. He radiated confidence, knowledge and success. Next to him Roderick felt as though he were made of a heavier, earth-bound material. He greeted his friend awkwardly.

'And how's the Dawson family?' Archie grinned affably at Clara and the children. He was sitting in the rocking-chair, the seat of honour.

'All of us fine and well,' Clara said. She too smiled affably and turned to Roderick for confirmation as she spoke.

'You back for good or . . .' Roderick's tone was heavy and a little sullen. He stared at the shimmering houndstooth.

Archie laughed loudly and slapped his thighs. 'Not on your life, old man. Not for all the tea in Boston harbour. This is just a little holiday to see how the old folks are getting on.' He winked at Roderick. 'Gotta fine woman in Noo York City keeping my bed warm.' He tucked a finger into the fob of his trousers, leaning farther back into the chair. 'I'm through with this dump.' He shivered with prefabricated distaste.

'You think it's a dump?'

Again Archie laughed loudly. 'I don't *think*, old man. I *know* it's a goddam dump.' He half-closed his eyes and smiled as if at some lascivious memory. 'Whaddadump! Whaddadump!' He drummed on the arms of the rocking-chair.

'A dump. . . .' Roderick echoed, savouring the word.

'Tell me something.' Archie opened his eyes and stilled the motion of the rocking-chair. 'How much are you earning these days in that so-called job of yours?'

Roderick told him.

'Peanuts!' Archie snapped his fingers in his confident, knowledge-able and successful way and set the rocking-chair in motion again. 'In Noo York City you would be earning nearly four or five times as much for the same work.'

'It's enough for our needs,' Clara intervened. 'We don't need more.' She glanced appealingly at Roderick. He was silent, staring intently at Archie.

'Any man could do wonders over there if he had a bit of initiative,' Archie flowed on. 'Of course, it's a little hard at first. I'm not denying that. But if you could stick that out . . . why, old man, it's a land of limitless opportunities. The sky's the limit over there.'

'They don't like black people,' Clara put in, dredging up the flotsam of another conversation.

Archie laughed. He was a little contemptuous; a little pitying. 'I can tell you a story or two about some of those white chicks. Some of them are really hot for it. . . .' His eyes closed lasciviously.

'Lim-it-less opp-or-tun-ities,' Roderick echoed.

'We have enough for our needs,' Clara said. 'We don't need more.'

Archie shrugged.

'Let me get you something to eat,' Clara said.

Archie dismissed the offer with a small flutter of the hand. 'In Noo York City. . . .'

'Something to drink then,' Clara urged with a hint of desperation. 'Something to drink if not something to eat.'

They ignored her.

'It's easy for you to come here and say these things, Archie.' Roderick's voice was leaden with reproach; and something more than reproach. 'You don't have a family.'

'Quite right, old man. I was forgetting. Let's drop the touchy subject.' He smiled amiably. 'How are the mechanics coming along?'

Roderick did not answer the question. He stared at the shimmering houndstooth.

It was a difficult evening. Neither for husband nor for wife was the reunion a great success.

The following evening Roderick was late home from work. This was virtually unheard of and Clara was frantic.

'Maybe he had an accident. Maybe he dead!'

'Tcha! The man must have a good reason.'

'But he was never so late before.'

'There have to be a first time for everything, doux-doux. Keep calm.'

It was past ten when Roderick wheeled his bicycle into the yard. Clara, notified by the neighbours, rushed out of the house and overwhelmed him with her tears. Roderick brushed aside her lamentations and cries for explanation. He did not let her kiss him. 'Let's go inside,' he said brusquely. 'I want to talk to you.'

The neighbours strained their ears but they could hear nothing.

In the morning Clara was unusually subdued. She and Roderick did not kiss goodbye.

'Did he say why he was late?' a neighbour called anxiously over the fence.

Clara was silent. There were tear stains on her cheeks and her eyes were puffed and red.

'What's wrong, doux-doux? What you been crying for?' They could not control the catch of fear in their voices. 'He didn't tell you why he was late? It can't be some woman friend. . . .'

Clara shook her head. 'It wasn't a woman friend.' She spoke so softly they could barely hear what she was saying. 'He was drinking with Archie.'

'Archie!'

Relieved laughter rolled across the yard.

But Clara was weeping.

'Doux-doux . . . doux-doux. It was only Archie. A man friend. What could be so bad about that?'

'I wish he had never come back. I wish Roddy had never know him.' Clara thumped her breast. 'Archie only bring trouble for me. So help me God, I could take all that rat poison Roddy does keep in the kitchen and poison him. Kill him dead with it!'

'What a thing to say, doux-doux! You not yourself this morning. What happened between them that upset you so?'

'They was talking about America. Archie was telling him he could get a good job over there and about all the things he could do if . . . if. . . .' Clara broke down afresh.

'If what?' The neighbours' alarm had free rein now.

'I don't know. . . . I don't know. Why you asking me? You must ask Roddy.' Clara ran inside.

The fear defined itself and it deadened their hearts.

Overnight the spell of enchantment had been lifted from the dolly house. Clara's happiness burned up and vanished. Life changed. Her girlish giggle – like the morning and evening kiss – fell into neglect. They stopped going to the pictures. There were no more walks with the children around the Queen's Park Savannah on Sunday afternoons; no more coconuts. Old joys had soured. The break in the pattern of their lives had been abrupt and radical. Roderick was sullen and hostile. Often he was late home from work, provided no explanations and refused to eat the dinner Clara had cooked. Nightly the neighbours listened to Clara crying. At weekends Roderick paced the yard and his sabots clicked.

Then the shouting began.

'How you expect me to stay like this? A man must have some ambition in this life. Otherwise he might as well be dead. I never wanted to stay a sanitary inspector all my life. It have so many things a man can be in this world if only he put his mind to it. I have to take my chances where I find them.'

'And what about me?' Clara replied, shouting too. 'What about my chances? Where will I find my chances? You just can't leave me like that. A man with a wife and three children just can't up and go whenever he feel like it.'

'You said once upon a time that you would want whatever would make me happy.'

'But not this, Roddy. I can't let you do this thing to me. I can't.'

Roderick shifted from anger to entreaty. 'It will be for only two – or three years at the most. Why you can't give me that? Why you have to be so selfish?'

'You calling *me* selfish.' Clara laughed bitterly. 'That's a good one.'

'I'm a young man, Clara. I have a good brain. I can feel it beating inside my head. I don't want to let it dry up and rot from idleness. That would be a crime.'

'What about me?' Clara persisted. 'What you want to do to me is also a crime. I'm young too. I only have twenty-three years. What you expect me to do while you in America improving yourself?'

He embraced her. 'You have to be patient. It's not for ever. When I come back we'll still be young. There'll be time for everything then.'

'There won't be time for nothing,' she said. 'You don't love me any more.' She extracted herself from his embrace – so warm yet already so distant! 'You tired of me. I let you down. That's why you want to go and leave me.' She raised her voice. 'You want . . . you want all those white chicks!' She began to whimper but would not let him touch her.

Roderick groaned and cursed.

She loved him. Why could he not understand that simple thing? Beyond that there was nothing more to say; beyond him there was nothing left to desire. If she was fond of her children it was because she saw scattered bits and pieces of him in them. Her maternal pride had no greater satisfaction than to hear somebody say that one of the children looked 'just like Roderick'. It was through him that she loved them; through them that she celebrated her love for him. Her fondness did not root itself directly. Perhaps that was wrong. But she could not help it. Her passion was like a consuming, fiery wind. She questioned neither its origin nor its purpose: it was sufficient unto itself.

Clara remembered the night he had asked her to marry him. They had gone to the Trade Fair because Roderick wished to see the engineering exhibits. Every day on her way to and from school she had been passing the site near the harbour which had been selected for the fair-ground. They had set off at dusk to join the jostling queues. The fair-ground glowed and shimmered in the dark like an outpouring of incandescent gas. It seemed to hover weightlessly in the air; transparent and crystalline. Clara gazed in ecstasy at the floating towers, domes and cupolas whose curves were sinuously defined against the black sky by the electric glare. The multicoloured, foaming plumes of the fountain arched in rods of pencil-thin spray. Flags flapped and fluttered from tall white poles. Clara was afraid to take her eyes off it, fearful that the wraith might disintegrate and vanish. Somewhere a band gusted into life amid a steady thumping of drums and the crash of cymbals. A twinkling glass globe revolved above the entrance.

Inside they could not hear themselves talk. All around them voices hummed with wonder and admiration like telegraph wires. Each booth, tent and gaudy pavilion sent forth its own tributaries of sound to swell the main stream. They strolled slowly down the central promenade lined with cardboard palaces decked with tinsel and strings of coloured bulbs. They crossed an artificial lake by a tiny footbridge. Clara leaned against the railing and stared at the dark leaves of the water-lilies. Real fire shot from the chimneys of a miniature oil-refinery. The colours were intoxicating, transfiguring ordinary objects into subtle but harmless mysteries. Fire would not be hot enough to burn. Water would not be deep enough to drown. A fall from the tallest tower would not hurt. It was a dream of unblemished joy and happiness. Clara's head swam pleasantly. As they approached the fountain, the stinging spray blew into their faces. She sat on the rim of the basin and dangled her feet in the cool water; while Roderick wandered off to study the exposed engine of a tractor revolving on a pedestal.

The fair-ground resolved itself into a rapturous blur. She had a vague recollection of standing in a steaming tent and peering between sweating shoulders at the antics of a performing monkey; of biting into an ice-cream the coldness of which hurt her teeth; of the crunch and slip of gravel underfoot; of wet, shining grass; of trampled mud. High above the floating towers, domes and cupolas she could always see the foaming plumes of the fountain. No object or moment of time was distinct from another. The former were all one and the latter all simultaneous.

They stood by the picket fence enclosing the ferris-wheel. The rims and spokes were strung with coloured bulbs. Clara watched it go round, listening to the clatter of its engine and the screams and laughter of those riding on it. Every few minutes it halted its revolutions and disgorged some of its giddy cargo while those with tickets rushed and scrambled for the empty seats.

'I would like a ride,' she said.

They bought their tickets and waited. When it stopped they dashed into the enclosure and climbed into a swaying cabin. They started to rise. A cool current of air fanned her face and the lights of the fair-ground spread out far below. At the top she had a glimpse of the ships in the harbour and those anchored farther out to sea. The harbour and the ships sank out of sight and the lights of the fair-ground rose up to meet them.

Suddenly she was terrified. She shut her eyes and grasped Roderick's hand. The sound of the engine grew louder; then faded. They were rising again. She opened her eyes and closed them immediately. The cool air played on her cheeks. Her stomach heaved. Roderick was speaking close to her ear but she could not hear what he was saying because of her giddiness and the screams and laughter ringing about her. She could no longer tell whether they were going up or down; standing still or going round. The cabin seemed to pitch and toss in every conceivable direction. It plunged into interminable headlong dives and then shot upwards as if it had been loosed of its moorings and catapulted into space. She was screaming. 'Don't let go of me! Don't let go of me!' It was a senseless, nightmarish chaos. She was aware of Roderick's warm breath on her ear. He was saying something to her. Having soared upwards to infinity, the cabin was hurtling downwards in one of its interminable dives when, quite unexpectedly, the vicious motion was arrested. Their journey had ended. But the sensation of falling into bottomless blackness persisted. She stumbled from the enclosure, her head spinning, hardly able to draw breath.

Roderick caught her. 'What's the matter, Clara?'

'Don't let go of me! Don't let go of me!' Gradually, she grew calmer. 'I was so frightened up there. So frightened.'

'It's all right now,' he said. He seemed mildly impatient. 'Didn't you hear what I was saying to you on the ferris-wheel?'

She shook her head.

'I was saying we should get married. What do you feel about that?'

There was trouble when she returned home late that night.

'You been with that man?' her mother asked.

'Yes.' Clara was defiant.

Her mother hit her.

'You won't be able to do that much longer,' Clara said. 'We going to get married.'

'Over my dead body, you little. . . .'

'You can't prevent us.' And then, seeing that her mother was about to strike her again, Clara told a lie. 'Because I having a baby for him.' As if to prove the truth of her assertion, Clara vomited: it was not difficult; her stomach still heaved.

Now Roderick was letting go of her; and the senseless nightmarish chaos of that evening was closing in again. 'Let him go,' the neighbours counselled. 'Let him get it out of his system.'

'He will never come back to me,' Clara said.

'The man love you. He bound to come back.'

'If I let him go,' Clara said, 'if I let him do this thing to me, I will never see him again.'

'Listen to us, doux-doux. You shouldn't take on so. We women somehow always seem to need less than men to be happy. You have to give a man his head from time to time. Otherwise. . . .' They gestured wearily.

'I will never see him again,' Clara said. 'And, even if I do, what difference will that make? It will still be like not seeing him.'

The neighbours did not understand. They were startled by the odd conviction with which she spoke. 'How you mean, Mistress Clara? When the man come back to you as he bound to do. . . .'

'I not sure myself what I mean,' Clara said. 'But it's something I feel deep down in my bones.'

'Shush. You talking nonsense, Mistress Clara. The man basodee about you. Crazy!' Nevertheless, she frightened them.

'It won't make no difference,' Clara repeated.

They stared hopelessly at her.

The neighbours did not care to apportion blame. Life alone could be blamed; the process of living. They grieved for them both.

In the seventh year of his marriage, Roderick Dawson, driven forward by the brain he could feel beating so warmly within his head, resigned his job as sanitary inspector with the borough council and, leaving behind him a wife and three children, departed for America. The possibilities of the house had been realised after a fashion: it served as security for the loan required to pay his passage.

Clara did not cry – as she had done more or less without interruption during the days preceding his departure. The time for tears was past: the hurt was too deep.

To survive, Clara took in washing. Her clients were some of the more well-to-do families in the district. She had gone from door to door peddling her services at a price undercutting the majority of her rivals in the trade. Commissions, as a result, had been plentiful. She washed on Mondays, Tuesdays and Wednesdays; and did the ironing on Thursdays, Fridays and Saturdays. On Sundays the various consignments were packed neatly into cardboard boxes and delivered. The work for the following week was collected at the same time. Paulette was her mother's chief assistant in these labours: she it was who did the fetching and the carrying, skilfully balancing the boxes on her head.

Clara did not trade gossip with the neighbours over the fence. She had discarded frivolity: her energies were consumed by her work. The neighbours saw her bent over the washtub, concentratedly scrubbing and wringing; and afterwards pegging the sodden clothes out on the washlines, the soap-stained wooden clips clenched between her teeth. She was remote. Roderick was never mentioned – except by the children. 'When is Pappa coming back?' they would ask. Clara would generally respond to their enquiries with a more dogged application to whatever she happened to be doing. Sometimes she slapped them hard on the mouth. Her silence was like a denial of his existence; a denial of the past; a denial, even, of grief.

Once a week the postman brought the envelope with the red, white and blue border. Ignoring the children's clamour, she would tear open the envelope, cursorily skim her eyes over the written sheets and then squash it into her bosom. Roderick wrote with undiminishing enthusiasm about America – his letters were like effusions from someone on holiday. He was having a busy time. By day he worked in a meat-packing plant; by night he took a course in mechanical engineering.

'How is he getting on?' the neighbours would ask.

Clara never replied. They would have preferred to hear her rail and curse: almost anything would have been preferable to her impenetrable silence about him.

And there was something else about which she would say nothing: the regular visits of Reuben the preacher.

Horatio Reuben was an assiduous saviour of lost souls: they were, in a manner of speaking, his stock-in-trade; his reason for living. With unflagging zeal, he scoured the city in search of his quarry. For months, one of the chief topics of conversation on the street had been Clara. The merits and demerits of her case were still being zestfully discussed and dissected when Reuben surfaced on one of his periodic tours of inspection.

'Is not we you should be trying to save,' he was told. 'You should go and preach instead to the young lady up the road who husband leave her just like that and went off gallivanting to America.'

Reuben's appetite was whetted. 'Which lady?'

They launched into the details of the story. Reuben did not wait for them to finish. He recalled Roderick's violent reception and the blasphemies he had uttered. Reuben was not unaccustomed to being met with a certain amount of rudeness and hostility. In his type of work he recognised it was unavoidable (there was much sin in the world) and he made allowances for it. Up to a point, they were part of the challenge of the job. Roderick had overstepped those limits. Reuben could not think of his threats and blasphemies without flinching. As he walked quickly up the street, the memory only rankled but also angered him afresh. However, Reuben indulged this luxury: had he not been harshly dealt with?

Clara was pegging clothes out on the washlines when he arrived. She did not recognise him immediately.

'What you want?' She did not stop what she was doing.

Reuben smiled. 'Have you forgotten me, Mrs Dawson?'

Clara frowned suspiciously at him. 'How you know my name?'

Reuben approached to within a few feet of her. 'The last time I called, your husband was somewhat . . . somewhat abusive.'

Clara squinted at him. Then recognition dawned. 'Why! It's the preacher.'

Reuben tilted his head graciously. 'The very same. The name is Horatio Reuben – in case you have forgotten.'

'I don't have time to waste, Mr Reuben. I'm a busy woman.' She indicated the dripping clothes strung out on the washlines. 'I have to work hard to keep my children bellies full.'

'I won't take up too much of your time.' He waved sympathetically at the washlines. 'I appreciate how hard you have to work. But no one should ever be too busy to hear the Word of God.'

'The Word of God isn't going to help me keep my children bellies full, Mr Reuben.' She moved away from him towards the washtub.

'I have heard about your tragedy.' Reuben's voice planed downwards. 'I am here to bring you comfort, peace of mind and repose.'

Reuben sang rather than spoke. Comfort. Peace of mind. Repose. They were like hymns. His words touched the core of her grief, reawakening it from its hibernation. Suddenly she wanted to cry out her despair to him. She restrained herself.

'Go from my yard, Mr Reuben. Neither you nor anybody else can help me.' Clara drew a wet hand across her forehead. She was giddy.

'But that is why I am here – to help you.'

'Please go from my yard. Please.'

Reuben grasped her arm firmly. 'Let me take you inside. You don't look too well. Perhaps you should lie down.'

She tried to push him away. 'It's nothing. Only a little giddiness. It will pass away.'

'All things will pass away,' Reuben said. 'Even this grief.' He took firmer hold of her arm. 'Let me take you inside.' He was adamant and Clara too weak to resist.

He led her to the house, guiding her up the front steps. Clara, refusing to lie down, slumped into the rocking-chair. Reuben sat beside her, resting his briefcase on the floor. He rubbed his bony hands and looked solemnly at her.

'Suffering is our common human lot.' He crossed his legs. 'We can only be saved by obedience to the Word of God.'

Clara's mouth drooped. 'Why did your God make me suffer so much?'

'He's not only my God, Mrs Dawson. He's your God too. Thy people shall be my people, and thy God my God.' Reuben stood up, shoulders stooped. He was gigantic in the small room. 'Our sufferings are sent to us as a trial; a test of our faith. Your . . . your husband, (Reuben's lips curled in involuntary distaste), was sent to try *you*. Why? That I cannot say. The Lord moves in mysterious ways. But know that the greater our suffering in this world, the greater shall be our reward in the next.'

'I don't care about the next world,' Clara said. She raised her head and scanned the towering figure looming above her.

Reuben sighed. He sat down beside her again. 'I see you are one of those who believe only in the things of Caesar. That is the source of all evil and misery. Free yourself of that attachment. Cleanse yourself of an unworthy desire for a. . . .'

'For a what?' Clara asked.

Reuben checked himself. He pulled a handkerchief from his pocket and dabbed his face with it.

Clara's eyes were fixed on him.

'The flesh must be mortified – it must be denied – if the soul is to be saved.' Reuben jumped up from the chair. He was very excited. 'Let me help you cure yourself of this disease. For make no mistake. That is exactly what it is. A disease!' Reuben was standing over her like the very incarnation of the God he claimed to represent. 'The source of your suffering is attachment. In this case, attachment to . . . to a most ungodly man. . . .'

'My husband,' Clara said. 'My husband. My husband. My husband.'

'Your – husband.' The use of the word seemed to require effort. 'But still, for all that, a mere mortal. Attachment is a weakness of the flesh. Mortify the flesh and kill attachment. When attachment dies, so does suffering. They are two sides of the same coin.' Reuben spoke with hypnotic, catechistical authority. Clara felt herself sinking into it.

She looked away from the stooping, gigantic figure. His words were not easy to follow. But that hardly mattered: their message, the promise they held out, was clear enough. To be rid of this pain! With this strange man's assistance it might be cured. She was prepared to try any remedy.

'Do you have a Bible?' Reuben glanced around the room. Before Clara could answer he smiled and said: 'A stupid question. Pardon me. A man like that would not have been likely to keep such a thing in his house.' He opened his briefcase. 'I shall give you mine.' He placed on her lap a leather-bound volume stamped in gold. 'Now I shall leave you. I have no wish to take up any more of your precious time.' He locked the briefcase. 'But I shall come again. Soon.' He bowed and went out.

Reuben began coming to the house every Sunday – Clara's day of relative rest. They would remain closeted together for as much as two hours during which time the children were banished to the yard. What went on inside the little room no one knew for certain: their voices never rose above a whisper and the curtains were kept tightly drawn.

These visits perturbed the neighbours. They were sufficiently familiar with Roderick's hatred for 'idle preachers' to be amazed at his wife's behaviour: his lessons must have had even less effect than they had imagined. But, more than that, they did not like Reuben himself. The sessions with him seemed to debilitate Clara. She would emerge from them pale and preoccupied; indifferent to the needs of the children and to what was going on around her. It was as though Reuben had been feeding on her in the interval; siphoning off her vital juices into himself.

'You should stop seeing that man, Mistress Clara. Drive him from your yard.'

'Mr Reuben is a great comfort to me,' Clara replied.

'He no good for you,' they insisted. 'He only going to make matters worse for you in the long run.'

Clara looked at them dismally. 'Let me be the judge of that.'

'What about Roderick? You know he don't like people like that.' They watched her closely: to mention Roderick's name was a calculated risk.

'Roderick! Roderick!' Clara jeered. 'Who is this Roderick you and everybody else always talking about? What he have to do with anything?' Her face was made ugly by the warring anguish and rage distorting its features.

Nevertheless, it pleased the neighbours that they had managed to stimulate a response of some kind.

'He is your husband,' they said. 'The man you love.'

Clara blocked her ears.

'What are you going to do when he come back?'

'Who tell you he coming back?'

'Who tell you he *not* coming back?' they countered.

Clara turned from them.

'Like you don't want him to come back?'

'Why can't you leave me alone?' Clara cried softly. 'Why?'

The postman steered his bicycle to the kerb, tinkling the bell on the handlebar. Excited shouts rose from behind the wooden fence and the raggedly dressed children charged through the gate and surrounded him, grabbing at the mailbag slung across his shoulders. The postman parried goodnaturedly.

'What is this at all! I don't have no letter address to any of you.' Laughing, he slid from the saddle. 'Where's your mother? Is she I have a letter for.'

The neighbours leaned out of their windows and watched.

'And I don't have no letter for any of you either,' the postman said, looking up at them and laughing in the same goodnatured manner.

'Letter for you, Mamma,' the children shouted. 'Letter from Pappa.'

Clara came from the side of the house, walking slowly towards the postman. Her arms, from the elbows down, were covered with soapsuds. Strands of tangled hair formed black, interlocking veins on a forehead moistened by sweat. The postman surrendered the airmail envelope whose distinctive red, white and blue border the children had come to know so well. He looked at her – as did the neighbours who now leaned farther out of their windows – with an air of vague expectancy; as if the letter were common property and its contents to be divulged there and then. Clara turned away and walked quickly to the house. The children ran after her.

'Get away from me!' Her arms flailed out.

She went inside and sat down on the rocking-chair. She tore open the envelope. Her eyes skimmed over the sheets of paper. Abruptly, she crumpled them into a ball. She rose from the rocking-chair and stared distractedly around the room. Going to the jalousied window she looked out at the road, her back to the clamouring children.

'What Pappa say?' They mobbed her.

Their mother did not answer. She gazed out at the broken, yellow day.

'Did Pappa say when he was coming home?'

'Keep away from me! Keep away from me!' Still holding the crumpled ball of the letter, she ran out of the room. Dodging the wash-lines, she stalked barefooted across the muddy yard to the washtub.

Clara thrust the letter into her bosom and plunged her arms up to the elbows in the grey, soapy water.

Clara was not prepared for the announcement in Roderick's letter. She had stubbornly closed her mind to the possibility of his return and its implications for her. To think about it would have served no purpose; made no difference. Her burned-up happiness was beyond recapture. Reuben had told her it was an ensnarement: he had given her a whole new vocabulary. The things of Caesar, her attachment to a piece of mere mortal flesh – these had been the cause of her suffering and misery. Her 'happiness' had always been an illusion. He had taught her a bitter knowledge; but, despite his constant assurances, it had given birth only to bitterer despair. Try as she might, Clara could not shake off that despair. At every step it lay in wait for her. Roderick's return would intensify her sickness. It was not possible to re-embark on that voyage. That was asking too much. The ship was broken in two. But memory would not be stilled; and the renunciation Reuben demanded (why did everyone have their own demands?) was not possible either. That also was asking too much of her. The heavenly spaces were inhuman; terrifying. She would never be at home in them.

Intermittently, for one or two hours at a stretch, Clara would feel she had come close to the state Reuben desired of her. Her other life dimmed to insignificance and eased its grip on her. She saw Roderick as a kind of mirage and Reuben's God – she could never separate Reuben from his God – was very near. She had only to reach out and she could embrace Him. But these interludes were short-lived. Reuben's God would recede from her and be swallowed up in the darkness. Then it was He who seemed a mirage and mere mortal flesh was all that there was or ever could be.

Her distraction was complete by the time Reuben arrived on his Sunday visit. Immediately he walked into the room, Clara thrust the letter at him. Her face was drawn and sallow and her hands trembled. Reuben looked curiously at her, read the letter calmly and returned it to her. He sat down and crossed his knees. Idly swinging his free leg, he smiled at her.

'What I going to do, Mr Reuben?' Clara stuffed the letter into her bosom from force of habit.

'You should know the answer to that by now,' Reuben replied equably. 'The Lord is testing you.'

'What is the answer, Mr Reuben? You must tell me.'

Reuben raised his eyebrows.

'I don't know what to do.' Clara wrung her hands. 'I been so confused. I don't feel I know anything any more.'

Reuben's earlier assurance faltered. His smile faded. He uncrossed his legs. 'Do you mean to say that even now – even now! – you will allow yourself to be tempted and led astray?' Reuben levelled a black finger at her.

Clara lowered her head. 'I wish you would understand, Mr Reuben. . . .'

'Understand what?' Reuben spoke with gathering fury. 'That you haven't learnt your lesson? That you wish to be ensnared yet again? That you wish. . . .'

'No!' Clara blocked her ears. 'But. . . .'

'But what?'

'I not sure that I have the strength, Mr Reuben.'

Reuben was silent.

Clara got up from the rocking-chair and went to the window.

'The Devil drives,' Reuben muttered.

She came away from the window and subsided on the floor close to his chair. 'So you won't help me, Mr Reuben?'

'I can't help you if you refuse to help yourself.' Reuben was cold.

She began to weep.

Reuben shut his eyes to her tears. 'Have you prayed?'

'Day and night.'

'And?'

'It didn't help.'

'Then you must pray some more.'

Clara stared desperately at him.

'At the first test you trip and stumble.' Reuben waved his arms angrily. 'And for what? For *who*? A blasphemer! All this for a man who insulted God's servant. My efforts have been wasted on you. Wasted!' He was shouting now and jerking his arms wildly.

Clara suddenly sprang up from the floor. 'You understand nothing! Nothing!' She was shouting too. 'You're just like the rest of them.'

'I understand all too well,' Reuben replied, becoming calm again and smiling sardonically at her.

'No. You don't understand a thing! You don't care what happens to me. All you can think of is how you wasted your efforts. That was what *he* thought as well when I let him down.' Clara circled round him, brushing her tangled hair away from her face. Her tears flowed freely. 'He use almost the exact words to me that first morning you come here and give me the magazine. Almost the exact words.'

'Do not compare me with that . . . that. . . .' For once Reuben was at a loss for the apt phrase.

'I'll compare you with who I like. At bottom you and he are just the same. You both have. . . .' She circled round him. 'Yes! That's it. You both have *ideas*.' She seized with despairing triumph on the word. 'Wherever I turn it's only ideas, ideas, ideas. But what about me?' She gazed at him frenziedly. 'Why is it I have no ideas like you and he, Mr Reuben?'

'I've warned you before not to compare me with that son of Satan.'

The leather-bound Bible he had given her lay on a tiny side-table next to the rocking-chair. Clara reached down, picked it up and hurled it at him with all her strength. Reuben dodged successfully. He uttered a nervous laugh as he bent down to retrieve it.

'I shall pray for you,' he said.

'I don't want your prayers. They're no good to me. No good at all. Now take your Bible and go. I never want to see your face here again. Get out of my sight!' She pointed at the door.

'Is that your final word?'

'That is my final word.'

Reuben departed.

After he had gone, Clara collapsed into the rocking-chair. She kicked it into motion. Her shining forehead puckered. She fished out the letter from her bosom and clasped it in her palms. Bars of sunlight and shadow, thrown from the jalousied windows, patterned the bare, dusty floorboards. The rocking-chair – which had long since lost its glitter and acquired the decrepit appearance of the other furniture – creaked back and forth in rhythmic sequence. The ring she was wearing flared when it caught the sun. Her face moved from shadow into light and then into shadow once more.

Clara disappeared from view. The neighbours were reluctant to intervene. They had already given all the solace they could. There was nothing more they could do. They took charge of the children who – abandoned by their mother – maundered about the yard unwashed and unfed. Clara seemed to notice neither their presence nor their absence. She noticed nothing. Hour after hour, with scarcely a twitch of a muscle, she sat on the rocking-chair, her hands resting flat on her lap. When she could no longer bear to be still, she got up and stared at the road. Roderick's letter, forgotten, lay undisturbed where it had fallen on the floor hours before.

Then came the evening of the second day when Paulette, sent by the neighbours to check on her mother, fled screaming from the little room and tumbled down the steps into the yard. The neighbours did not pause to question the hysterical child but shook her aside and dashed into the room. Clara was sprawled across the bed, her fingers clawing the bedclothes. She was drained of colour. A metal container had spilt its contents on the floor.

'The rat poison!'

The dose was not fatal. The doctors at the General Hospital pumped her stomach out. Every day the neighbours took it in turn to go with the children and visit her.

'You should have let me die,' she said to them.

'Foolish, foolish, doux-doux,' they chided. 'What a way to talk. You have so much to live for and you want to die.'

'I have nothing to live for.' She was unmoved; unrepentant. Her hollow eyes stared out at them from a pinched, ravaged face.

One afternoon they said: 'Look. We bring a present for you. All the way from America.'

Roderick, dressed in a smart brown suit and wearing a gaily coloured tie, bent down to kiss her. She shrank away from him.

'But doux-doux ... doux-doux. . . .'

Roderick placed the bunch of red carnations he had brought her on the bedside table.

Clara, her head sunk into the pillow, watched him impassively. Neither spoke.

The neighbours were afraid to look at them; afraid especially to look at *her*. Those brown eyes were shorn of their bridal innocence. It was not easy to decode the message they carried. Her ordeal did not betray itself on the surface: it had been pushed back out of sight and buried deep in their brown depths. Yet it was plain that that ordeal lived on within her. It was flesh of her flesh. She was suffused by it. Desolation was like a curtain drawn between her and the world. Those eyes proclaimed her isolation; proclaimed that what she had been through could never be adequately told. She was a traveller who, unaccompanied, had undertaken a bizarre and dreadful journey across a strange land.

'What happened?' Roderick said to the neighbours when they were on their way back home. He was bewildered. 'How. . . .'

'You men don't know anything about we women. It might take less to make us happy. But it have some things. . . .' They clucked their tongues. 'Better not to talk about it. It was a terrible thing to have to witness. Terrible! So the less said the better.'

To the neighbours, Clara seemed possessed of a knowledge surpassing theirs. She was no longer a child. But she had paid an inordinate price for the privilege. Their present and future silence would be part of their respect; part of their homage.

To Roderick, who had stared at her in speechless astonishment, there seemed to be no bridge existing between Clara and himself. That bridge had been washed away along with much else. When? How? But he would never know. She could never tell him because they spoke in different tongues and there was no one to translate.

Mr Sookhoo and the Carol Singers

Mr Sookhoo, a short, fat man with a pot belly and a bushy, black moustache, drove the only truck in the village. He carried anything people would pay him to carry: furniture, sand, gravel; and, when the village headmaster asked, he took the schoolchildren on excursions to the beach, sugar-cane factories and oil refineries. It was a way of life that Mr Sookhoo found entirely to his liking: he was his own boss.

He was rocking slowly on his veranda, scraping thoughtfully at his teeth with a toothpick, when his wife appeared through the doorway.

'Eh, man. For the past two days all you doing is sitting here and rocking. Mr Ali tired ask you to carry that gravel to Port of Spain for him. What's more, he pay you for it already.'

'Ali could wait.' Mr Sookhoo continued to pick his teeth. 'So you been wondering what I been doing these past two days, eh?' He tossed the toothpick over the veranda rail and Mrs Sookhoo followed its flight with interest. 'All you could see was me rocking. But there was something else I was doing. Somthing invisible.' He smiled slyly at her. 'I was *thinking*.'

'Thinking!' Mrs Sookhoo weighed the significance of this remark. It worried her. 'Be careful, man. I sure it not good for you.'

Mr Sookhoo laughed scornfully. 'Now and then a man have to do a bit of thinking. Otherwise . . .' Losing the thread of his argument, he shrugged.

'I still think you should deliver that gravel to Mr Ali.'

'Ali could go to hell.' Mr Sookhoo expanded his chest.

'But what get into you so all of a sudden, man? I know all this thinking wasn't good for you.'

Mr Sookhoo waved a finger at her. 'I just been working out a master plan. Tell me – how many days it have till Christmas?'

Mrs Sookhoo frowned. 'The radio say it have about twenty-seven or so shopping days to go.'

'Right!' Mr Sookhoo gazed fiercely at her. 'Christmas is coming and the geese is getting fat. Time to put a penny in the old man hat.' He took another toothpick from his pocket. 'Believe me when I tell you the geese is really going to be fat this year. And it going to have so many pennies in the old man hat by Boxing Day that you will bawl when you see them.'

Mrs Sookhoo could not disguise her alarm. 'What get into you so sudden, man?'

'Tell me,' he went on, scraping vigorously at his teeth, 'tell me how much children it have in the school?'

'Twenty, thirty . . .'

'To be on the safe side, let me say it have twenty-five. Twenty-five divide by five is five. Agree?' Mr Sookhoo tossed the toothpick over the veranda rail and, as before, his wife followed its flight with interest. He got up from the rocking-chair and leaned against the rail, staring up at the sky. 'So that if I divide them up into five groups and say each time they sing they get a little dollar or so . . .'

'What you intending to do, man? You sure is legal?'

He ignored her. '. . . and say each group sing about ten time a night for twenty or so nights . . .' Here the magnitude of his calculations so affected Mr Sookhoo that he let out a prolonged whistle, slapped his stomach and spat on a rose-bush. 'Of course I'll have to take the cost of the gasoline into account.' A shadow crossed his face. 'Still . . .'

'You going to land in jail, Sookhoo.'

'Chut, woman! People like hearing little children sing. Once you could organise it properly, it have a lot of money in it. All this carol singing need is organisation.'

'You forgetting one thing.'

'What?' Mr Sookhoo asked sharply.

'You is a Hindu.'

He laughed. 'Who is to know that in Port of Spain? It have hundreds of Christians out there who look just like me. Like you never hear of the Reverend Hari Lal Singh?'

'I still don't like it. And another thing. All them children you does see singing carol singing for charity.'

'That is what they would like people like you and me to believe. All that money they does collect going straight into their own pocket. Charity!' Mr Sookhoo spat disdainfully on the rose-bush and went inside.

Mr Sookhoo changed into his best suit and left the house pursued by his wife's anxious enquiries. He walked the half-mile to the village school with a quick, firm step.

Mr Archibald, the headmaster, stared at him suspiciously from behind the pile of copybooks he was correcting. He was well aware that Mr Sookhoo grossly overcharged him for the school's excursions.

'Good afternoon, Head. How is life with you these days?' Mr Sookhoo hummed under his breath.

'As usual.' Mr Archibald was guarded. 'I think I know that tune you're humming', he said. 'Christmas is coming and the geese are getting fat. Time to . . .'

'First time I hear of that one, Head. You wouldn't imagine how sometimes I does regret not having a education. It must be a great thing.'

Mr Archibald looked doubtfully at him. 'I suppose you have a reason for coming to see me, Mr Sookhoo?'

Mr Sookhoo leaned his elbows confidentially on the desk. 'I'll come straight to the point, Head. They asking me to organise a charity.'

Mr Archibald dried his forehead with a handkerchief, a symptom of his incredulity. 'They asking *you* to organise a charity, Mr Sookhoo? Who asking you to organise a charity?'

'The Deaf, Dumb and Blind Institute. They want me to help organise a little carol singing for them.'

'I never knew such an Institute existed.'

'Is a new thing.'

'Ah. But why *you*, Mr Sookhoo? Not that I want to be rude, but to be frank . . .'

Mr Sookhoo smiled gallantly. 'I not offended, Head. I know that my life – up until now that is – hasn't been exactly perfect. Like most men I have a few faults . . .'

'A few!'

Mr Sookhoo laughed. 'I don't know how to say this, Head – it going to sound funny coming from a man like me – but, all the same, I think I finally see the light.'

'What light?'

'Head! How you mean "what light"? That don't sound nice coming from a man like you, a man of education.'

Mr Archibald's vanity was touched. 'Sorry, Mr Sookhoo. But, as you yourself said, coming from a man like you . . .'

'Sooner or later a man have to set his mind on higher things,' Mr Sookhoo intervened solemnly.

'That is something nobody can teach us, Mr Sookhoo.' Mr Archibald's eyes swept vaguely across the ceiling. Then they hardened, assuming a more businesslike expression. 'But why *you*, Mr Sookhoo?

That is what I still don't understand. Even accepting that you have
seen the . . . the light, it's very odd that the Deaf, Dumb and Blind
Institute should ask you to . . .'

'Transport, Head. Transport.' And he added hastily: 'Don't think
I is the only one. I only in charge of one area, you understand. This is a
big operation they have plan.'

Mr Archibald nodded. 'Where do I come into it?'

Mr Sookhoo leaned closer to him. 'Not you so much as your pupils.
This is a chance for them to help out a worthy cause by singing a few
carols. My truck is at their disposal. Don't worry – is I who going to be
paying for the gasoline.'

Mr Archibald stared at him. 'I really don't know what to say, Mr
Sookhoo. Your generosity is overwhelming.' He fluttered the handkerchief before his face.

Mr Sookhoo grinned broadly. 'You teach them to sing a few carol
and I take them to Port of Spain in the truck free of charge. That's a
deal.' He held out his hand.

'Your generosity is overwhelming, Mr Sookhoo.'

'Is because I see the light,' Mr Sookhoo said.

It took Mr Archibald a week to teach his pupils a repertoire of six
carols. Mr Sookhoo went to the school every afternoon to listen to
them practise. Standing at the back of the classroom, he would shout
encouragingly at them. 'That's the way, kiddies. Remember it's a
worthy cause you singing for.'

Mr Archibald, beaming, would swing his baton (in fact a whip)
with renewed vigour.

The first expedition into Port of Spain was a gay affair. Mr
Sookhoo polished his truck and drove to the school. Freshly washed
and dressed in white, the children looked convincing. Mr Archibald
provided them with candles. 'I felt it was the least I could do
considering you giving the gasoline,' he explained to Mr Sookhoo.
They drove to one of the richer suburbs of the city and Mr Sookhoo
parked his truck discreetly in a narrow side-street. He gathered the
children about him, dividing them into groups of five.

'It have two things I must tell you about,' he said when he had
finished. 'First and most important – don't mention my name to
nobody . . .'

'Why?'

Mr Sookhoo glowered at the questioner, a small, earnest boy.

'Because I is a modest kind of person, that's why. If they ask you who send you say is the Deaf, Dumb and Blind Institute. And if they say they never hear of that before, tell them is a new thing just open up. You understand?' The children nodded confusedly. 'Second. Try to get a dollar each time you sing. When they pay you, stop. What would be the point in singing more after that, eh?' Mr Sookhoo giggled. The earnest boy gazed sternly at him. Mr Sookhoo, catching his eye, turned away in discomfort. The groups dispersed and, fetching a deep sigh, he took a toothpick from his pocket and scratched contentedly at his front teeth.

The choirs met with immoderate success. Their renditions were listened to attentively and no one gave them less than a dollar. In all, Mr Sookhoo collected just over forty dollars. He was jubilant.

'Good work.'

'Mr Sookhoo \. . .' the earnest boy began.

'Later, sonny, later.'

'Have a look at that, woman.' Mr Sookhoo displayed the night's takings to his wife. 'Forty dollars in hard cash. And how? By using the brains God give me. By thinking. That's how.'

'Some people does call it embezzling. They bound to find out sooner or later what you doing.'

'How they go find out?' Mr Sookhoo folded the notes and put them in his pocket.

Success stimulated ambition. 'We going to start earlier and finish later,' he informed the children the next day. The choirs were not quite as gay as they had been the night before, but they set about their task without complaint. That night Mr Sookhoo collected fifty-five dollars. He could hardly contain himself, counting the notes again and again. 'Orgainisation was all it needed,' he said to himself.

'Mr Sookhoo . . .'

'Later, sonny, later.'

Mr Sookhoo prospered for a whole week. He had collected over three hundred dollars. And there were still many shopping days to Christmas. And there were still several suburbs waiting to be plundered. His eyes glittered. 'You going to end up in jail, Sookhoo,' his wife warned. He laughed and continued his calculations.

Early one morning Mr Archibald came to see him.

'How things going, Mr Sookhoo?'

'As well as could be expected in the circumstances, Head.'

'You not collecting enough?'

'Is a hard business, Head. These rich people tight, tight with they money.'

Mr Archibald dried his forehead with a handkerchief. 'You know Horace?'

'Which one is Horace?' Mr Sookhoo's heart sank.

'A thin little boy. He say that you working them down to the ground and that you collecting one hell of a lot of money.'

'I always thought he was a trouble-maker.'

'That boy is my brightest pupil, Mr Sookhoo. He's going to go far.'

'They is the worst kind.' Mr Sookhoo spat on the rose-bush.

Mr Archibald cleared his throat. 'You sure you being honest and above board with me, Mr Sookhoo? I mean this Institute really exist, not so?'

Mr Sookhoo gave the headmaster a pained look. 'Head! Head! How you could say a thing like that to me? A man of your education to boot!'

'Just put my mind at rest, Mr Sookhoo. You really see the light?' Mr Archibald spoke in a whisper.

Mr Sookhoo rested a comforting hand on the headmaster's shoulder. 'Honest to God, Head. I really see the light.'

Mr Archibald relaxed. He was anxious to believe Mr Sookhoo. 'These children working real hard,' he said. 'You could buy them a little sweet drink and ice-cream every day. I'm sure the Institute wouldn't mind.'

'Anything you say, Head. But I'll have to tell the Institute about it.'

'I could do that for you. I don't want them to think you're cheating them.'

'Don't bother yourself, Head. They trust me.'

Mr Archibald smiled and left the house.

The following night – it was the second week of their carolling – Mr Sookhoo took the children to the Trinidad Dairies. He bought them a Coca-cola each. When they had finished Mr Sookhoo got up to go.

'You forgetting something,' Horace said.

Mr Sookhoo instinctively felt for his wallet. His hand caressed the square lump. 'What it is I forgetting, Mr Know-All?'

The children gathered in an expectant circle.

'Mr Archibald tell you to buy ice-cream for we.'

Mr Sookhoo scowled. 'They don't sell ice-cream here.'

Horace appealed to the other children for support.

'I just see somebody buy a ice-cream,' one of them said.

'Well, I say they don't sell ice-cream here. And therefore they don't. You understand?'

'I know for a fact they does sell ice-cream here,' Horace insisted. 'To tell you the truth, I believe you trying to cheat we, Mr Sookhoo. I believe you keeping all that money we been getting for yourself.' Horace pouted insolently.

For a moment Mr Sookhoo hesitated, resisting the temptation to slap Horace. Finally he said: 'You little sonofabitch!'

'All you hear what he call me? You hear?' Looking greatly aggrieved, Horace walked away from the bar.

'I feel like letting that sonofabitch find his own way home.' Unhappily, he could read no sympathy on the faces of the choir.

Mr Archibald had a visitor.

'I come to ask a favour of you, Headmaster.'

'I will do anything in my power to help you, sir,' Mr Archibald replied primly.

'I'm involved in charity work ...'

'I myself have been having a little experience of that.'

'Have you? Well, I was wondering if your pupils would care to sing carols for my charity. We choose certain schools each year ...'

Mr Archibald smiled sympathetically. 'I'm afraid we're already booked up this year. I'm sorry.'

'I understand. As I always say at times like these, one charity is as good as another. The unfortunate, no matter what their affliction, are always to be succoured.'

For some seconds both men savoured their goodness.

'Incidentally, Headmaster – and I hope you don't mind my asking you ...'

'Not at all, sir. I have no secrets.'

'What charity are your pupils singing for?'

'The Deaf, Dumb and Blind Institute. I believe it's a new thing just opened up a few months ago.'

His visitor started. There was a long silence while they looked at each other.

'That's very strange, Headmaster. You see, I work for something called the Blind Institute. But the Deaf, Dumb *and* Blind Institute ...

luckily I have a list of accredited charities here with me.' He took a pamphlet from his pocket and scanned it.

'I feel quite faint.' Mr Archibald fluttered his handkerchief.

'Pardon me for saying so, Headmaster, but I think you've been taken for a ride.'

'I really do feel quite faint.'

Trinidad is a small island in a small world.

When Mr Ali saw the group of children led by Horace coming confidently up the path towards him and singing 'Silent Night', he lost his temper.

'Stop that blasted racket this minute!'

The choir stuttered into silence, their candles guttering in the wind. Loose gravel shifted under their feet. It had been their rudest welcome to date.

'Tell me who it is send you to disturb my peace.'

'Is the Deaf, Dumb and Blind Institute what send we.'

'The Deaf, Dumb and Blind Institute, eh! Try me with another one.'

'Is a new thing. Just open up these last few months,' one of the children ventured timidly. He looked round for Horace, their acknowledged leader. But Horace had detached himself from the group and stood to one side, lost in contemplation.

'You have any identification?' Mr Ali was very threatening.

The child cringed. 'Ask Horace over there. He will know.'

Mr Ali strode over to Horace. 'Tell me who send you,' he shouted. 'And remember no lies, if you not careful I'll skin the whole lot of you alive.'

Horace smirked. 'Is Mr Sookhoo who send we.'

'Mr Sookhoo! He have a moustache and big belly?'

Horace nodded.

'And he does drive a truck?'

'He park just down the road waiting for we to come back.'

'And what about this so-called Institute? It have any truth in that?'

'Mr Sookhoo make that up.' Horace's smirk intensified.

'What a tricky bugger, eh! So that's why he wasn't delivering my gravel. Come and show me where Mr Sookhoo is, Horace. I have a little outstanding business to settle with him.'

Horace, abandoning his candle, skipped eagerly down the path, followed by Mr Ali and the nonplussed choir.

Mr Sookhoo was sitting in his truck, sucking a toothpick and occasionally looking at his watch. A notebook lay open on his lap covered with scrawled calculations. The confused sound of children's voices reached him. 'How come they so early tonight?' he wondered, peering into the rear-view mirror. He stiffened. The toothpick hung limp between his teeth.

'Mr Sookhoo! I so glad I manage to catch up with you at last. I been longing to have a chat with you.' Mr Ali's voice floated sweetly on the night air.

'Believe me when I say you still have a lot of catching up to do,' Mr Sookhoo muttered. He flung the toothpick out of the window. The engine stammered into life and the truck lurched away from the curb, gathering speed.

'Don't think you getting away this time, Mr Sookhoo.'

'Mr Sookhoo! Mr Sookhoo! Wait for we! Wait for we!'

The cries of the choir faded behind him, drowned by the noise of the engine.

'Woman, bring your clothes quick! I think we have to go away from here for a while. Things hotting up.' Mr Sookhoo raced up the steps to the veranda and stood there catching his breath.

'Good evening, Mr Sookhoo.' Two large policemen came strolling casually through the sitting-room door, flourishing torches.

Mr Sookhoo clutched at his heart. However, he recovered himself quickly. 'Why is you, sergeant.'

Mr Archibald trailed behind them, accompanied by his visitor. Mrs Sookhoo, her cheeks wet with tears, brought up the rear.

'Man . . . man,' she moaned.

Mr Sookhoo paid her no attention. 'Why, Head – you here too. And I see you bring a friend with you as well.'

'You deceived me, Mr Sookhoo. A most cruel deception.'

Mr Sookhoo gestured resignedly.

'I really thought you had seen the light, Mr Sookhoo.' Mr Archibald seemed on the verge of tears.

The sergeant produced a notebook and licked the tip of his pencil. 'Mr Sookhoo will see a lot of lights in jail,' he said quietly and started to write.

Mrs Sookhoo moaned louder.

'This gentleman,' the sergeant went on, indicating Mr Archibald's visitor, 'is from the Blind Insitute. Show him your card, Mr Harris.'

Mr Harris showed Mr Sookhoo his card.

He refused to look at it. 'I know all them tricks,' Mr Sookhoo said. 'Ask him how much money he does make out of it. Go on. Ask him.'

Mr Harris flushed. 'I get paid a salary for the work I do, Mr Sookhoo. Legally. Just because I work for charity doesn't mean I can live on air.'

'Living on air my arse! You see the expensive clothes he wearing? I could tell you where he get the money to buy all that.'

'This is to add insult to injury,' Mr Harris said.

'I should warn you, Mr Sookhoo, that everything you say will be taken down in evidence against you.' The sergeant scribbled energetically.

A sleek motor-car stopped outside the gate. Horace and Mr Ali entered out of breath.

'Ali! Like is a party we having here tonight.'

'I not in a party mood, Mr Sookhoo. I come for all that money I pay you to deliver my gravel.'

'What gravel is this?' the sergeant asked interestedly.

Mr Ali outlined his grievances.

'The plot thickens,' the sergeant said.

'Man, remember how I did tell you all this thinking would be bad for you. Remember . . .'

'Go and do something useful, woman. Bring me a toothpick.'

Horice sidled up to Mr Archibald. He tugged at his trousers. 'He didn't buy we any ice-cream either. And you should have hear how he insult me when I remind him.'

'Don't worry, Horace. Mr Sookhoo is going to get what he deserves.' Mr Archibald patted Horace.

'I think you should expel that boy from your school, Head. He's a born sonofabitch.' Mr Sookhoo spat on the rose-bush.

'You hear the kind of thing he does call me?' Horace exlaimed aggrievedly.

The sergeant closed his notebook. 'You better come to the station with us, Mr Sookhoo. You could make your statement there – for what it's worth.'

Sandwiched between the two policemen, Mr Sookhoo was escorted to the waiting car. He waved to the small crowd that had assembled on the pavement.

'Don't say I never warn you, Sookhoo.'

Mr Sookhoo smiled at his wife. 'You didn't bring me that tooth-pick.' He laughed.

The car drove off.

'The Good Lord is just. Isn't he, Horace?' Mr Archibald curled an affectionate arm around the boy.

'Yes.' Horace grinned and thought with delight of the ice-cream Mr Archibald had promised to buy him.

The Father, the Son and the Holy Ghost

Flea looked at the dark, pinched face and the tiny shrivelled legs, like twigs, kicking in the air. Carmen lay beside the child, her skin shining, and watched him with exhausted eyes which yet were vaguely questioning and pensive.

Flea, a short and wiry man, with closely cropped, curling black hair and arms tattooed with big-bosomed mermaids, shook his head sorrowfully and sighed. 'So, this is what God decide to do to me,' he said. He gazed at the child, his face wrinkling with dismay. It started to scream. 'I wonder what God expect a poor sailor like me to do with this one. Another hungry mouth to feed.' He lifted his woe-struck eyes up to the ceiling and let them rest there.

Carmen laughed. 'I don't see what God have to do with all this, Flea. I could see your true feelings as plain as daylight in your eyes. I don't know why you does always be pretending to have children all over the place. You should be thankful for even having one, instead of rolling your eyes up like that.'

Flea's features having composed themselves, his gaze returned to the screaming child. 'What you mean "pretending"? I is a sailor now, you know. Not some stupid carpenter. Don't forget that. Things very different out on the high seas. The sea does change a man. A sailor is a lot different from other people.' His gaze roamed up the wall and his eyes contracted thoughfully. 'In a way,' he said, 'we is really wicked men. Take my captain, for instance. He have a child in nearly every port in the West Indies. He was telling me just the other day that Spanish women is the worst of all, and I think I agree with him. You yourself have a little Spanish blood, not so?' Carmen nodded. 'You must know for yourself what I mean then. I wouldn't tell you a lie.'

'I must say, I never know you to tell the truth, Flea. Sailor indeed! You only been working on them boats for six months now, so I don't see how you could have any other children, unless they does fall down out of the sky.' Carmen giggled. 'I bet you never even went as far as Jamaica.'

'What you mean I never even went as far as Jamaica? I been further. To Cuba. Havana. That's how I come to know about Spanish women.' He sucked in his breath. 'They know how to do things over there,' he said. 'A man don't stand a chance with them.' Carmen laughed.

'You trying to make me jealous, Flea?'

Flea felt ashamed of himself and resentful. He knew Carmen to be an ultra-cool and experienced woman of the world, so absolutely sure of herself as to be incapable of any paltry feeling like jealousy. It had put her far beyond him and it made him powerless before her. He was aware that beyond this was a long dead love, a passion played out in the shadows of her youth, full of romance and heartache. Such at any rate was the story. But Carmen never talked about it. It may have been an invention, perpetuated by Carmen for her own secret purposes.

Flea was silent for a time. Then he said, 'And I been to Jamaica twice as a matter of fact. You could ask the captain, if you doubt me.'

'I wouldn't trust what your so-called captain say either. If anything, he sound like an even bigger liar than you.'

The child continued to scream.

'And anyway,' Flea added, 'is more than six months since I went to sea. Is nearly a whole year since I stop working in old Ramchand sawmill.' He scratched the tip of his nose. 'You think the child hungry?' he asked, peering at it with sudden concern.

Carmen lifted the child off the sheets without ceremony and unbuttoning her bodice, brought its lips to the almost black nipples of her breast. It fell to with a contented gurgle. Flea watched her. She was a good-looking woman. Her face was round and full and she had big, dark eyes and a fine, straight nose. She radiated health. Flea remembered what Felix, his predecessor in Carmen's affections, had said about her. 'That woman have the biggest thighs I ever see. Big like lampposts. But soft, man, much softer. That Carmen is a real thoroughbred. You can't beat the Spanish blood in a woman.' Felix had carved languid patterns in the air as he spoke. It was then that Flea, who had never seen her, fell hopelessly in love with Carmen.

At that time both he and Felix had been working in old Ramchand's sawmill. Carmen cooked for the Ramchands and Felix, who in his capacity as foreman had access to the old man's house, had made such good use of his time there that a child had resulted from these visits. When the sawmill had started to run into serious difficulties (from its inception it had been threatened with disaster), old Ramchand had taken to having his lunch brought to the office, in the belief that a more prolonged physical presence there would, in some mysterious way, halt the slide to chaos. Punctually at one o'clock Carmen would appear, a bright, flowered scarf fluttering on her head, bearing the little white enamel containers wrapped in napkins. To Flea, she was an apparition of pure delight risen freshly each day from the sawdust. Day after day Flea had watched her flitting, light as a butterfly, among the piles of timber and the ugly, growling heaps of machinery. From afar he had gazed at those thighs, big as lampposts, and in imagination explored their yielding softnesses. His chance for closer acquaintance came one day when Felix was absent on business. He got into conversation with her and offered to share his lunch. Flea exerted all his charm. Perhaps it was the hopelessness of his passion; perhaps it was the absurdity of his ambition; perhaps Carmen was touched by his simplicity; it is impossible to say, but whatever it was an intimacy of sorts was established. Unfortunately it was not long after this that the sawmill had gone out of business and Flea, having listened long to Carmen extolling the masculinity of sailors, had taken reluctant leave of his mistress and gone to sea in the guise of a ship's carpenter.

For a moment, thinking of these adventures, his eyes filled with pride and he traced with a finger the outline of the mermaid imprinted on his left arm. Then, a worried frown distorted his features.

'You see much of Felix while I was away?'

Carmen shifted the baby's head. 'On and off. But not since the baby born though.' The child sucked noisily.

He leaned over Carmen and peered closely at the child's face. 'You sure this child is mine, Carmen? I don't find it resemble me all that much. It look more like Felix if you ask me.'

Carmen raised her head interestedly. 'You really find it resemble Felix?' she asked, scrutinising the child's face with a curiosity greater than she normally allowed herself.

Flea shrugged. 'I think it have his nose.'

Carmen giggled. 'So, it have Felix nose. I wonder who else it resemble?' Her giggle changed into a high-pitched laugh. The child having had its fill, had fallen asleep, its lips stained with milk. Carmen rested it gently beside her and buttoned her bodice.

'What you laughing at? What it is you find so funny, eh? Sailors like me don't stand much for that kind of behaviour, you know. You think I was sending you all that money to support another man child?'

'Don't get on such a high horse, Flea. I just find it funny that you should say he have a nose like Felix. That's all. Come to think of it, I never really notice Felix nose at all when I was going with him. What it like?' Carmen choked on her laughter.

Flea cursed under his breath, striding up and down the narrow room, examining with displeasure its furnishings.

'Anyway,' Carmen went on, brushing a tear away from the corner of her eye, 'since when twenty dollars is a lot of money?'

'Is twenty dollars more than you deserve. I don't believe that child is mine. The nose give it away. You would think that the baby would at least have my nose . . .' Flea gestured futilely.

'You right. Is Felix child.'

Flea turned pale.

'I only joking,' Carmen said soothingly. 'The child is yours, Flea. Yours.'

'You sure you not fooling me?'

'I wouldn't do a thing like that, Flea. I already have one child by Felix, as you well know. So, what I want another one by him for?'

Flea relaxed. Carmen's logic, though dismal, was convincing and, above all, Flea wanted to believe her. Nevertheless, the thought that had been nagging him ever since he had entered the room returned.

'Where you get all this fancy furniture from?' Flea pointed at a dresser, obviously new, with swing mirrors.

'I buy it secondhand,' Carmen replied, glancing carelessly at it.

'It look brand new to me. And I recognise the workmanship as well. You can't fool me so easy.'

'After the business collapse, old Ramchand was selling off all kind of thing dirt cheap.'

Flea looked doubtfully at her. 'I don't see Mistress Ramchand allowing he to do that. She's a real tigress when it come to money. She refuse to pay me for the last two weeks I work in the sawmill. Say they didn't have any money. I had a lot of dealings with she in my time.'

'All the same,' Carmen insisted stubbornly, 'old Ramchand sell me that dirt cheap. It was a kind of favour.' She smiled, 'When you going away next?'

'It depend on what happening to the child. We got to think about that.'

'We?'

'What you mean "we"?'

'You think I is a millionaire or something, Flea? I didn't keep the child I make for Felix. So why should I keep the child I make for you, eh?' She might have been a potter talking about his pots.

'And so, you expect me to keep the child?'

'You could always send it to the Belmont Orphanage.'

Flea was glum. He scratched the tip of his nose. 'I think that would be a wrong kinda thing to do. After all, the child is mine, not so?' He looked searchingly at Carmen.

'You think is the Holy Ghost who came in here one night?'

Flea could not suppress a smile. 'Don't worry, Carmen. I know the child is mine,' he said. He walked across the room to the window and looked out. The yard was black and muddy. Some ducks were fishing in the turbid pools of water. He smiled. Paternity sat lightly on his shoulders. A lifelong ambition had been realised. Not only had he a child but, what was even better, it was illegitimate. There could be no doubt about it now: he was a true sailor, one of a gallant fraternity much admired by Carmen, and Felix and the rest could no longer laugh at him. However, Flea's love for the child was only notional. The idea of paternity was all that appealed to him. For the rest, his son was an encumbrance. He saw that clearly. Flea was aware of someone staring at him. A woman was walking past below the window and craning her neck at him. When he caught her eye she smiled familiarly. That smile disturbed Flea and he came away from the window.

'Why that bitch laughing at me?'

'Who?'

'That bitch who does live next door to you.'

'Go and ask she. Not me.' Carmen's eyes gazed with unabashed serenity at him.

He brightened. 'You could go back to work with old Ramchand. That will give you enough money to keep the child.'

'But didn't I tell you they fire me? The moment Mrs Ramchand see my belly swelling up with another baby, she order me out of the house. Without so much as a by-your-leave. She didn't pay me either.'

'Why don't you give it away to somebody then?'

Maternal pride stirred fitfully in Carmen's breast. 'But what you think it is, man? You think it was a sack of flour or potatoes I was carrying in my belly for nine months? Try and remember that is your child as much as mine. I wonder how you does treat all them other children you claim to have all over the place.' Her lips formed into a smile, half-mocking.

'Hear she talk now! Who was just saying to give it away to the Belmont Orphanage?'

'I was only making a joke.'

'I tell you what,' Flea said, 'why don't you give it to the Ramchands?'

A curious look seeped over Carmen's face when Flea said this, but she remained silent, as if following a quite separate train of thought. Much of this escaped Flea's notice. 'You remember how I used to break my back working in that rundown sawmill? They owe me something for all those years' faithful service. Old Ramchand used to underpay me like crazy, but I never complain once. Mind you, it wasn't him to blame. He have a kind heart. I mean, take that dresser he sell you so cheap, I bet Mistress Ramchand would have rather dead than do that. She have him under she thumb. You must know yourself how she does insult him in front of total strangers. I tell you, sometimes I used to blush for the poor man.' Flea lowered his voice confidentially. 'You know why she never had any children by him?' The dreamy look had not yet left Carmen's face. 'Because she find him too black and ugly. That's why. Poor fella. Nobody want a child more than he. You could take my word for that. A man need some comfort in his old age.' Flea stopped and studied the sleeping child. 'He need this boy more than we. After all, in nearly every port from Port of Spain to Kingston I have two or three children calling me daddy . . .' Flea raised his eyes to the ceiling, swept along to such an extent by this wave of sentiment that he had actually come to accept the altruism of his motives. A tear rose to his eyes.

Carmen, roused from her reverie, laughed, though the curious expression had not entirely left her face. 'You should have been an actor, man. You would have put the whole of Hollywood to shame. None of them could ever have hoped to compete with you.'

The following day Carmen went to see Flea. He had spent an uneasy night, greatly troubled by his conscience. His sentiment had shifted its ground. Flea had come to believe that he had a profound love for the child. Carmen, her flowered scarf fluttering, settled like a butterfly on his bed.

'I been thinking about what you was saying yesterday, Flea.'

Flea was glum. 'What about?'

'About giving the child to the Ramchands. I think is a good idea.' Carmen twiddled the buttons on her blouse.

'I change my mind about that,' Flea replied. 'I think is a wrong kinda thing to do.'

'But you is a sailor, Flea. You going to be away for months on end. You call that being a father?'

'I don't have to be a sailor. I could set up as a carpenter.'

'You is not a true sailor at all. I disappointed in you.' Carmen untied her scarf and shook out her hair. It settled, a dark, restless mass, on her shoulders. 'All the sailors I know . . .'

'But . . .' Flea's despondency deepened.

'And you have all your other children to think about,' Carmen said.

Flea cast a despairing glance at her. 'I like this child the best, Carmen.'

'I thought you was feeling so sorry for old Ramchand.'

'Ramchand could look after himself.'

'All the sailors I know is generous, carefree men. Devils!' Carmen's eyes flashed. 'Wicked men, as you yourself tell me. You is not a true sailor at all, Flea, a mouse not a man.'

'But . . .'

'No buts. Be brave. Be generous. Be a sailor! If you think I going to waste my life living with you and looking after this child, you have another think coming.'

'You mean to say you will walk out on me just like that?'

Carmen played with her scarf. 'It wouldn't be the first time I do something like that, Flea.'

Flea thought of those thighs, big as lampposts, walking inexorably away from him and his heart ached.

'You sure the Holy Ghost had nothing to do with this child, Carmen?'

Carmen gave one of her high-pitched laughs, but she did not answer his question.

'The child is mine, not so, Carmen?'

'Stop asking stupid questions and go and see old Ramchand.' She began winding the scarf about her head.

'Why me? Is you who want to give them the child. Not me.'

'The child is yours too, Flea. You must accept some of the responsibility. And anyway, I don't feel like meeting Mrs Ramchand. She tell me she would call the police if I ever set foot in that house again.'

Mrs Ramchand was a thin, fine-boned woman. The structure of her face was delicate: the high cheekbones, the bright almond-shaped eyes, the flawless olive complexion. Only one thing could be said to detract from her looks: her narrow pinched lips which she always kept tightly pressed together. Even when she smiled (a rare occurrence) this rigidity was apparent, lending her face an air of profound insincerity. Mrs Ramchand was not a likeable woman. Flea's information was correct. Mrs Ramchand despised her husband. As Felix had once said to Flea, 'She hate the very dirt old Ramchand does walk on.' She admired two things to the exclusion of all else: wealth and fairness of complexion. Unfortunately, one of the first lessons that life had taught her was that these two things did not invariably go together. Mr Ramchand was a compromise. He was rich but at the same time dark and inescapably ugly. This dissonance had provided Mr Ramchand with a fertile source of metaphysical meditation and formed the theme of all her lamentations. Compromises are never inspiring and from the first day of their marriage Mr Ramchand had found himself the object of his wife's never-ending scorn. He had gone the way of all compromises. She had, as Flea said, refused to bear him any children. In front of guests she would say, 'The reason why we don't have any children is simple. You ever see a man uglier than my husband? Look and see for yourself.' She would then give a guided tour of her husband's infirmities. Mr Ramchand would shrink into himself and submit to the silent scrutiny of the assembled company, usually his wife's relatives.

When Flea presented himself, Mrs Ramchand examined him scornfully from head to foot. Having satisfied herself, she pursed her lips and stared at him.

'Is your husband I come to see, Mistress Ramchand.'

'He not home, Flea. He gone to Port of Spain to waste some more of my money. You could talk to me. What concern him also concern me.'

Flea shifted uncomfortably from foot to foot and gazed distrustfully at her. 'Well . . .'

'Time is money, Flea. At least my time is.'

'But is your husband I come to speak to, Mistress Ramchand. I'll come another day.' Flea started to move towards the door.

'You won't come another day, Flea. You not going to leave this place till you tell me what it is you come for.' She darted ahead of him and blocked the door. Her agility unnerved Flea. 'Now,' she said, 'you going to tell me what kind of underhand business you and that scoundrel trying to cook up behind my back.' Flea was silent. 'Tell me!' she shouted suddenly. Flea cringed. 'You and Hari planning some mischief together? I thought these last few months he was looking all kind of secretive and worried. Jumping at the slightest sound, looking at me out of the corner of he eye. The both of you figuring out some new way to throw more of my money down the drain? Eh? Tell me.' Although Mrs Ramchand had come to her husband with no personal fortune, she had fallen, without effort, into the habit of thinking of her husband's wealth as entirely her own, free to dispose of as she saw fit – normally to her relatives.

'It have nothing to do with what you say. You remember Carmen?'

'You think I could ever forget that prostitute my husband bring here to cook? I surprise she didn't poison me. The way that bitch used to look at me, laughing at me behind my back . . .'

Flea chose to ignore these remarks. 'You know she was . . .'

'I know, I know. You would think being a prostitute she would know how to take care and avoid that kind of thing. But stupid people is stupid people, I suppose.'

Flea drew himself up to his full height, which made him look slightly ridiculous. Realising this, he lowered himself to his customary hunched stance. 'I would not have you speaking of my Carmen in that way, Mistress Ramchand. I would have you know . . .'

'Your Carmen, Mr Flea?' Mrs Ramchand's nostrils twitched scornfully. 'You mean she was going with you too? You mean you let she fool a sensible man like you?'

'I would have you know, Mistress Ramchand, that my Carmen is . . .'

'Your Carmen! Your Carmen was leading you round the place by the nose.' Mrs Ramchand was pitying.

'Nobody could ever lead me round by the nose, Mistress Ramchand . . .' Flea paused, his confidence checked. 'That nose . . .' he said, half to himself.

'What nose you talking about, Mr Flea?'

'Nose? Did I say something about a nose?'

'That's what I thought. That woman making you take leave of your senses.'

'I must have been thinking about something else, Mistress Ramchand. I have a lot on my mind these days. What I wanted to say was . . .' He stopped and looked about him. He heard Felix's languid voice. 'Thighs big as lampposts. But soft, man, much softer.' His heart ached.

'I don't have all day to stand up here talking to you, Mr Flea. I not an idler like my husband. Say what you have to say. And if Madame Carmen send you here to ask me to take she back, you shouldn't waste your breath. Once I make up my mind even God – note that – even God won't make me change it. He could fall down on his knees and beg, but even He won't make me change it. So now you know the kind of woman you dealing with.' Mrs Ramchand had put such energy into this declaration of faith that droplets of sweat appeared on her upper lip.

Flea drew a deep breath. 'Is nothing like that,' he assured her. Mrs Ramchand was unable to hide her disappointment. She wiped the droplets away with the sleeve of her dress.

'Well?'

'What I wanted to say was that I am the father of that child.'

'You, Flea? But how you could be sure about a thing like that? Especially with someone like Madame Carmen.'

'I sure. That child is mine. It certainly wasn't the Holy Ghost.' Flea could not suppress the worried smile that accompanied this declaration.

'What?' Mrs Ramchand, leaving the doorway, approached Flea and thrust her face close up to his. It was one of her favourite tricks with Mr Ramchand. 'What the Holy Ghost have to do with all this?'

Flea withdrew further into the depths of the room. 'That's the whole point, Mistress Ramchand. The Holy Ghost have nothing to do with it at all.'

'You don't sound too sure to me, Flea.' Mrs Ramchand clapped her palms against her hips and laughed loudly. Flea's poise crumbled altogether.

'What you laughing at so, Mistress Ramchand?'

'You must excuse me, Flea.' Mrs Ramchand quickly recovered herself. 'But with someone like Madame Carmen I wouldn't rule the Holy Ghost out of the picture.' She spluttered into fresh laughter. It was not often that the world afforded Mrs Ramchand such pleasure.

'I tell you the child is mine, Mistress Ramchand. Why would I lie about a thing like that? I don't stand to gain anything from doing that. The child have all my features.'

'All right. All right. So you think you is the father of the child. What that have to do with me?'

'We was wondering if you would like to keep the child.'

'What! You sure I hear you right the first time, Flea?'

'Is the least you could do for me. Since Carmen get fired, she hardly have a penny to spend on sheself, much less on the child. Is you who responsible for that. And don't forget how hard I used to work for you down at the sawmill.'

'You mean how hard you used to work at cheating me. Robbing me right, left and centre. If you had the chance you would have run away with the whole place, lock stock and barrel.'

'I never rob anybody,' Flea replied with glum defiance. 'I is an honest man and I used to do an honest day's work. In fact you didn't pay me for the last two weeks, but I not the sort of man to remind you of that. I not even asking for it.'

Mrs Ramchand snorted. 'And what you think you doing now? Praying in church? And what about you? You have a job, not so?'

'Sailors don't get pay much, Mistress Ramchand. Anyway, I have a lot of other children to look after already.'

'You?' Mrs Ramchand brought the full weight of her scorn to bear on Flea. 'You have other children? Don't give me that one, Flea. What woman go like you?' She laughed as before, her palms resting on her hips.

At that moment, Mr Ramchand came into the room. He was a short, very dark man and, although he had a disproportionately large, moon-shaped face, his eyes were little more than bloodshot slits. His nose was flat and spreading, as if it had been melted by the heat and later congealed into its present shape, and his nostrils were shaped like cavernous triangles, dark caves out of which peeped clotted strands of greying hair. Flea's face brightened. However, when he saw Flea, Mr Ramchand stumbled in astonishment, his face clouding over. With one eye on his wife, he retreated back to the doorway.

Mrs Ramchand glanced disdainfully at him. 'Don't run away, Hari. It was you who Flea come to see in the first place.'

'Me?'

'I think you should know what Flea come here to ask. You remember that child the cook was having?'

'Cook? What cook?' Mr Ramchand asked in a soft, debilitated whisper.

'Don't tell me you don't remember Madame Carmen, Hari. That prostitute you yourself bring here to work for we.'

'Oh, Carmen. Yes. I remember she.' Mr Ramchand's voice crackled from the doorway. He avoided looking at Flea who was staring intently at him and wrinkling his brows.

'Well, Flea say he is the father.'

Mr Ramchand jumped and stammered something.

'Speak up, Hari. I can't hear what you saying.'

'Nothing. Nothing.'

'Stop wheezing like that then. Mind you,' Mrs Ramchand went on, 'I don't believe for a moment that he is the real father.'

Mr Ramchand retreated out into the passage. He uttered a shrill laugh and fell silent.

'I is the father, Mr Ramchand,' Flea said.

'Come into the room, Hari. I not going to bite you this morning.' Mrs Ramchand tittered.

Mr Ramchand shambled hesitantly into the room.

'What we would like to find out,' Mrs Ramchand said, 'is the name of the Holy Ghost.'

Mr Ramchand seemed to shrink into himself.

'Anyway, that is neither here nor there.' She looked at her husband. 'The point is that Flea is asking me to keep a black and ugly child in my house. You ever hear more?'

'The child not so black and ugly as you think, Mistress Ramchand.' Flea felt the nagging pull of paternal pride.

"It not?' Mr Ramchand's agitation had lessened.

'What you think it is, Mr Ramchand? Carmen have a lot of Spanish blood in she.'

That seemed to please Mr Ramchand. He rubbed his palms together and smiled.

'I don't see what you have to be smiling at, Hari. Whether Carmen have Spanish blood or not is nothing to do with you. So I don't see what you grinning all over your face for. I sure the child is a lot prettier than you.'

The smile faded from Mr Ramchand's face, though he appeared less perturbed than usual by this rebuke.

'What sex is this child, Flea?'

'That's the best part of the whole business, Mistress Ramchand. It a boy. Boy-children is a lot less trouble than girl-children. You take my word. For instance, in Puerto Rico . . .'

Mrs Ramchand signalled him to be silent. 'I don't want to hear about your so-called children in Puerto Rico, Flea. So you say the child not bad-looking?'

'It resemble me, Mistress Ramchand. It have all my features.'

Mr Ramchand looked strangely at Flea.

'You is not the best looking of men, Flea. In fact, to be frank with you, I could think of only one man who is uglier than you and we all know who that is.'

Flea's pride was too heavily involved for him to bestow any sympathy on Mr Ramchand. 'I never said I was the handsomest of men, Mistress Ramchand.' He pouted sullenly, scratching the tip of his nose.

Mrs Ramchand turned to her husband. 'What you think of the idea, Hari?'

Mr Ramchand cleared his throat. 'I don't think is such a bad idea. Is up to you of course, but I feel we bound to need somebody to look after we in we old age.' Mr Ramchand's agitation had returned with all its previous force and his voice trembled and crackled as he spoke.

'You could bring him up here as a kind of houseboy,' Flea added encouragingly, if not eagerly.

'A houseboy,' Mrs Ramchand considered. Servility, in any of its forms, invariably appealed to her. It was what she understood best and now it exercised a kind of magical influence over her. 'All right, Flea,' she said with a show of reluctance, 'you bring the child and I'll have a look at it.'

Flea brought the child the next day and Mrs Ramchand looked at it.

'What you think of it?' Flea asked.

Mrs Ramchand, turning the child over as if it were roasting on a spit, clucked her tongue distastefully.

'This child is ugly like sin, Flea. In fact, it might be even uglier than that. And it so black too. I never see such a black child in all my born days. It almost as black as Hari. You ever see such a black child, Hari?'

Mr Ramchand glanced quickly at the child and said nothing. His eyes, after a sleepless night, were like red cracks.

Flea pouted. 'It have hundreds of children in Africa a lot blacker than he, Mistress Ramchand. You don't have to take it if you don't like it. Nobody forcing you.'

'Don't be hasty, Flea. It not all that black. Houseboys don't have to be pretty.' And, as Flea was leaving, she called after him. 'What you say about all them really black people in Africa, it have any truth in that?'

'I only see them in pictures,' Flea said. 'But from what I can see there some of them black like coal.'

'Like coal!' Mrs Ramchand was astounded.

She looked at her acquisition and shook her head sadly.

'Come on, Flea. I haven't seen you smile for a whole week. Woman troubles? Have some more rum. That will make you happy.' Felix, tilting the bottle with an unsteady hand, poured some rum into Flea's glass. 'Drink that up, man, and tell Felix what on your mind. Rum is the best medicine for woman troubles. When you have enough experience of that kind of thing, you will agree with old Felix.'

Flea frowned morosely at the rum and drank it down in one gulp, drying his lips with the back of his hand. 'I have enough experience already,' Flea said.

'Don't fool yourself, man. If you was really experienced, like me, you wouldn't let what a woman say trouble you. Ignore them and after a while they go come running to you.'

'When you love a woman,' Flea said, staring balefully at the bottle of rum, 'it hard to behave like that. And anyway, the woman I thinking of would never come running to anybody.'

'Is Carmen you talking about?'

'Who else?'

Felix grinned. 'You letting she bother you?'

Flea looked up in surprise. 'I never hear you speak like that about she before.'

'You will learn in time, Flea. It have a million women like Carmen in this world.' Felix snapped his fingers.

'When you fall in love, you will see things in a different light.'

Felix laughed. 'Till that time come,' he replied and snapped his fingers again. He leaned back in his chair and gazed up at the rows of glittering bottles behind the bar. A silver chain gleamed through his shirt and a gold identity bracelet glittered loosely on his wrist. He wore a wide-brimmed hat which was set firmly on his head. Felix was dressed in the height of fashion.

For a while, they were silent. Then, with an abrupt nervous movement of his whole body, Flea said, 'Turn your face up to the light, Felix.'

'Why? Like you take up painting these days, Flea?'

'Turn your face to the light. I just want to see something.'

Felix turned his face towards the light, striking a comical pose as he did so. Flea studied the upturned face. He shook his head sorrowfully. Felix laughed.

'Satisfied now?'

Flea nodded and poured himself some more rum.

'What's the matter with you, man? Tell Felix. We is old friends.'

'The Holy Ghost is the matter with me.'

'The Holy Ghost? Like you turning religious, Flea?'

'Is only a joke.' Flea, smiling mournfully, tore away the label from the rum-bottle and rolled it into a ball. 'Tell me something, Felix, Carmen have any other men?'

'Hundreds of them. Carmen know how to butter she bread.'

'I don't mean that. I know lots of them does hang around she like flies. I mean this other man who she does never talk about.'

Felix was thoughtful. 'To tell you the truth, Flea, I don't believe that man ever exist.'

'But she had a child by him, not so?'

'So they say. They say he used to be a sailor. One night in a storm he fall overboard and drown.'

'Who say that?'

'People.'

They looked solemnly at each other.

'And how is Carmen baby, Flea?'

'It fine. It fine,' Flea replied, shaking the rum in his glass.

'You wouldn't believe this, Flea. But, you know, I haven't been to see she since the child born. I too smart for that kind of thing.'

'I don't see why you should have to go and see she. Is not your problem.'

Felix' solemnity vanished. He laughed happily. 'I glad to see you learning fast. Hit and run. That's the way to do it. Still, I'll go and see she and the child one of these days.'

'It don't have much to see,' Flea said. He blinked nervously several times and rubbed his stomach.

'What you mean it don't have much to see?' Felix, fingering his silver chain, narrowed his eyes suspiciously. It was a trick he had picked up from a gambler in a popular Western.

'It belong to the Ramchands now. It going to be their house-boy when it grow up.'

Felix leapt from his chair. The customers looked up in alarm.

'Let me hear you repeat what you just say, Flea. My ears must be fooling me.'

Flea was calm, resigned almost to this latest development. 'I say I give it to the Ramchands. It going to be their houseboy when it grow up.'

Felix swooped down suddenly and lifted the table. The bottle of rum rolled off and clattered on the floor. However, it did not shatter. The rum flowed in a brown stream over the tiled floor.

'Come on, Flea. Stand up and fight like a man.' Flea remained sitting. He scratched the tip of his nose. Felix turned away from him in disgust and addressed the customers. 'You hear what this man gone and do? He gone and give my child – note what I say – he gone and give *my* child away to strangers. And for what, I ask you? So that he could get a good education? So that one day he could become a doctor or lawyer? Nothing like that. He going to become their houseboy when he grow up. Imagine that! If it was his child I wouldn't mind, though that would be bad enough. But imagine giving another man child away to become a houseboy. Just like that.' Felix snapped his fingers. 'Tell me if I don't have the right to smash his face in for him. Tell me!' Felix swung his clenched fists through the air. Although he showed all the outward signs of uncontrollable fury, he made no move to carry out his threat, remaining frozen in the dramatic pose he had assumed at the start. Flea watched him impassively.

'Is my child,' he said softly, speaking into his glass. 'I have a right to do with it as I like.'

'You hear him? You hear him? You ever hear such shamelessness in your born days? His child! As if he could ever have a child. Women does scream and run and hide when they see him.'

The customers laughed. One or two of them came closer, to get a better view.

'Fight! Fight!' The murmur spread round the bar. More of the customers left their tables and crowded round the combatants, urging them on. The barman watched worriedly from behind the counter. 'I won't have nobody fighting in here,' he shouted. 'As it is the police already threaten to close we down and I not going to lose my job for any sons of bitches like you two. I got my wife and family to think about. You hear that?' He lifted the lid of the counter and came quickly towards them. 'Go outside and fight on the pavement if you bitches have to fight. But if you make another false move in here, I'll get the police on to you. I'll call the police.'

'Don't worry, Mister,' Felix said, grateful for any excuse. 'I won't be the cause of you losing your job. I have nothing against you and your family. I go fix this sonofabitch somewhere else.'

The barman returned muttering to the bar.

Felix rested his hands on the table and glowered at Flea. 'That child is my child, Flea. You hear that? Is my child. I is the man who Carmen really love. She would lick my boots for me if I was to give she the chance. What you think was happening when you was spending all the time gallivanting around the place in some boat or the other? You think Carmen went and join a nunnery because of you? Is me she love. Is me. You can take my word for that. Come with me. Let we go and see she now and ask who is the child true father. Come.' Felix attempted to grab Flea by the elbow. Flea pushed him away.

'You lying, Felix. You fooling yourself if you think is you Carmen really love. Is my child. It have all my features except maybe for the nose.' Flea's voice rose hardly above a whisper.

'And I could tell you who that nose belong to, Flea. It belong to me. That is my nose you was seeing.' Felix thumped his chest.

'You never even seen the child. So how you know that?' Flea's confidence was returning. 'The child nose not shaped like yours at all. This child have a flat and spreading nose.'

'All baby have nose like that. Come. Let we go and ask Carmen who is the child true father. Like you frighten of the truth, Flea?'

Flea got up slowly and walked unsteadily out of the bar. Felix once again addressed the company. 'Come with us, gentlemen. You will be the judges of the case. Come and see for yourselves.' Felix, accompanied by some six or seven men who had taken up his invitation, followed Flea out of the bar. There was much good-natured laughter and speculation on the way to Carmen's room. Felix was in high spirits.

Carmen was brushing her freshly washed hair when they arrived outside her door.

'Watch me, fellas,' Felix said. He pushed his way past Flea and walked boldly into the room, surveying the furnishings with a proprietorial air. He went up to the startled Carmen and even as she had begun to protest at this invasion, folded his arms around her waist and kissed her on the nape of the neck. She pushed him away roughly. Felix stumbled into the middle of the room and stood there grinning with just a hint of sheepishness.

'You are drunk, Felix.' She looked at the men crowding the doorway. 'Who is all these people you bring here with you? Who tell you you could come barging into my room with all these riff-raff, eh? Eh?' Carmen lowered at the mob. Flea came into the room, his face set and tight.

'You too, Flea,' Carmen said, pouncing on him. She sniffed his breath. 'And smelling like a rum factory as well. I wouldn't have expected this kind of behaviour from you.'

'I have nothing to do with all this, Carmen. Believe me.' Flea crossed his heart. 'Is Felix you must hold responsible. Is he who invite all these people here.'

Carmen turned on Felix. 'Well, Mr Big Mouth, what you want?'

Felix was embarrassed by his reception. 'Is really Flea fault,' he said. 'None of this would have happened if it wasn't for Flea.'

'I don't know which of you to believe. You are two of the biggest liars in the whole of Port of Spain.'

One of the mob started to clap. 'Some woman.'

'That's right,' Carmen shouted. 'And if the pack of you don't leave my room right this minute, I go "some woman" you all right.'

'That is what we want you to do, darling.'

Maidenly modesty had not entirely deserted Carmen. She blushed and in order to hide her confusion, rounded again on Felix. He fingered his chain haplessly. 'Well, Mr Big Mouth, you haven't answered me as yet. I want to know why you bring all this riff-raff to my door.'

'I go be frank with you, Carmen. This miserable man Flea is going about all over the place claiming that he is the father of your child. I want you to tell these gentlemen the truth. I want them to hear that I is the father of that child from your own lips.'

Carmen reddened and her eyes, laden with accusation, gazed at Flea. 'So, Flea, after all the kindness I show you, this is how you paying me back. Spreading my name all over Port of Spain, trying to shame me. I should have known better than to trust a man like you.'

'You see what I mean, gentlemen . . .'

'Shut up, Felix. I going to deal with you in a minute. Now, Mr Flea, tell me what you been saying.'

Flea scratched the tip of his nose. 'I ain't been saying nothing bad about you, Carmen. In fact is Felix here who been saying really bad things about you. He say it have a million woman like you in this world and that you dying to lick his boots for him, only he wouldn't let you . . .'

'He lying! He lying!' Felix screamed. 'I didn't say nothing like that.'

'Shut up, Felix. Go on, Flea. Tell me what else Mr Felix was saying about me.'

'He was saying that the best policy with women was to hit them and run . . .'

'He lying! He lying. I didn't say nothing like that.'

'I tell you to shut up, Felix. Go on, Flea.'

'It don't have much more to say, Carmen. Except that I wouldn't say nasty things about the woman I love with all my heart and soul . . .'

Carmen blushed. There were cries of derision from the doorway. Flea paused in confusion and traced with a finger the outline of the mermaid on his left arm.

'So, Mr Felix. It have a million woman like me in this world. You does hit them and run, eh! Well, let me show you what hit and run really is.' She raised the hairbrush. Felix cowered, shielding his face with his hands. The hairbrush landed with a solid thump on his shoulders. Felix danced out of the way. Carmen ran after him, hitting out with the hairbrush, her hands flailing wildly in all directions. 'This is what I call hit and run,' she panted in his wake. 'This is what I call hit and run.' The crowd cheered and chorused encouragement. Felix flitted about the room. 'Flea was lying, Carmen. Flea was lying.' Finally, out of breath, Carmen gave up the chase.

There were whistles and more clapping from the doorway. A man in a red jersey ran into the room and before Carmen had a chance to realise what was happening, shook her hand and ran out again.

'That's the way. Give it to him good.'

'Some woman.'

Carmen sought in vain to disguise her pleasure at these compliments.

Felix, having to some extent regained his composure, though keeping well out of Carmen's reach, said with a show of his former bravado, 'Now you have had your fun, Carmen, tell these gentlemen who is the real father of the child.'

'But what the hell you think it is, Felix?' She lunged at him with the hairbrush. Felix dodged successfully. Tired out by her exertions, she decided to confine herself to abuse. 'What the hell you take me for, eh? You think I is some common kind of market woman? Well, you have another think coming if you think that. You think I have no morals? And why the hell you bring all these people here for, eh? Eh? You think is a circus I running? Well, let me tell you something, Mr Hit and Run. If you think is a circus I running here, you is the chief clown . . .'

The mob could hardly contain itself. There was further whistling and clapping. The man in the red jersey turned a somersault.

'What a woman!'

'Give it to him real good! That's the way.'

'Get out of here, you hooligans. Get out! Otherwise I'll get the police on to you. This is molestation.'

'She know a lot of big words too,' the man in the red jersey said.

Carmen flung the hairbrush at them. They scattered as it crashed against the wall, but soon regrouped, though at a more discreet distance. The mob was cowed, though the man in the red jersey did manage a forced laugh.

'You refusing to tell these gentlemen who the real father of that child is, Carmen?'

'Like you haven't learnt your lesson as yet, Felix. You more stubborn than a mule.' Carmen advanced threateningly on him. 'Get out of here, Felix. I warning you. Don't provoke me. Take these people with you and go from here.'

Felix dashed to the doorway and squeezed himself in amongst the mob. 'Come, gentlemen. Since she playing stubborn, we'll go and do the next best thing. We'll go and have a look at the child itself. To Mr Ramchand, gentlemen.'

There were cries of approval from the doorway.

'Felix! What the hell you think you doing?'

But Felix pretended not to hear her. The procession filed out of the house, Felix at its head. Flea and Carmen looked at each other.

'Carmen . . .'

Carmen waved him away irritably. She picked up her scarf from the dresser, holding it lightly between her fingers, as if undecided about what she must do next.

'But Carmen . . .'

'No time for talk now, Flea.' Carmen hurriedly changed her bodice. Flea angled his head discreetly.

'You playing the gentleman too late in the day,' Carmen said. The scarf had fallen on the floor. Flea picked it up and handed it to her. 'No time for that,' she said, flinging it on the bed, where it settled gently in a yellow heap; and without even looking at herself in the mirror, she ran out of the room.

Flea laboured after her, clutching, for some strange reason, the hairbrush. 'Carmen . . .'

Carmen tossed her head impatiently and ran on in front of him, her hair streaming behind her. 'I tell you already that this is not the time for questions, Flea.' She said something else, but her words were carried away by the wind. Gathering up her skirt, she quickened her pace.

They caught the procession about a hundred yards from the Ramchands' house. The mob had grown. Felix had taken off his shirt which he was now using as a flag. His back shone with sweat and the silver chain glinted in the bright sunlight. He was singing loudly, skipping out from time to time into the middle of the road and dancing. The Ramchands, attracted by the noise, came out on the veranda. When Felix rudely pushed open the front gate, Mrs Ramchand screamed at the top of her voice and boldly advanced down the path to intercept him.

'This is private property. I order you to leave this minute.' She came up to Felix and thrust her face under his chin. Mr Ramchand watched from the verandah. Felix stopped singing and draped his shirt over his arm. Carmen and Flea, breathing heavily, stood next to him. The mob, its enthusiasm checked for the moment, formed an untidy circle around them.

'We come to see the child, Mistress Ramchand,' Felix said.

'What business is that of yours, Mr Felix? I not going to answer one question till you ask these louts to leave my yard. Otherwise, I'll call the police. Hari, go and bring the police.'

'To get the police he'll have to get past all these people, Mistress Ramchand.'

'You threatening me, Mr Felix?' Mrs Ramchand pressed her lips together.

Mr Ramchand, who was leaning as if mesmerised over the veranda rail, remained where he was. His eyes were fixed on Carmen.

'These gentlemen,' Felix began.

'Louts, Felix,' Mrs Ramchand interrupted him. She counted. 'To be exact,' she said, with an air of triumph, 'you have twelve louts here with you and one prostitute.' She smiled pleasantly at Carmen.

'I will not have you insult my Carmen in front of all these strangers, Mistress Ramchand,' Flea said.

Carmen rested an arm lightly on his shoulders. 'Don't worry, Flea. Insults don't bother me.'

Mrs Ramchand's face contracted into a sour smile. 'Get these louts and prostitutes out of my yard this instant, Mr Felix. Or I'll make Hari go and call the police. Hari, go and bring the police.' She gave her husband one of her withering looks, but Mr Ramchand seemed not to notice. Carmen engrossed all his attention.

'These gentlemen,' Felix said, 'will leave your yard the minute you show us the child. Isn't that so, gentlemen?'

'That's right, Mistress Ramchand,' the gentlemen chorused. 'We will leave your yard the minute you show we the child.'

The man in the red jersey bowed low from the waist.

'Stop playing the fool, Sammy,' Felix said.

Mrs Ramchand hesitated. 'And what so important about the child all of a sudden, Felix? I never see people make so much fuss over such a black and ugly baby. Though Flea was telling me the other day that it have people in Africa blacker than coal.'

'Flea, as you must know by now, Mistress Ramchand, is a born liar. Still, forgetting that, whether the child ugly or pretty don't matter. The point is that I is the real father of that child. Not that sonofabitch liar Flea.' Felix spat.

'But I thought you and he was good friends, Felix.'

'Not after what happen today, Mistress Ramchand.'

'That sound to me like the pot calling the kettle black,' Mrs Ramchand replied. This witticism pleased her and her lips compressed themselves into a smile. 'Then, you is the father of this child? But Flea swear to me on his bended knees that he was the father of the child.'

Felix laughed. 'Flea, as I told you just now, Mistress Ramchand, is one of the biggest liars to ever walk the face of this earth. A man like he doesn't hold anything sacred ...'

Flea started to protest, but Carmen again rested a restraining hand on his shoulder.

'He would sell his old grandmother for five cents,' Felix went on smoothly as if reading a prepared speech, 'if he wanted a packet of chewing gum. A man like he does stop at nothing to get what he want. You yourself know how he used to behave down at the sawmill, always hanging round the cash-box and that kind of thing. But his greatest crime, for which one day he'll fry in hell, was to give away another man child to become a houseboy.' Felix lowered his head. 'I could forgive him all the rest,' he concluded, 'but I can't forgive him that.'

'Hear! Hear!' Sympathetic growls circulated among the mob.

'I, not Flea, is the true father of that child. These gentlemen here will be the judges. A child must resemble his father, not so, Mistress Ramchand?'

Mr Ramchand, looking dazed, sank down on a rocker. Carmen stared at Felix.

'So, Felix, you is the Holy Ghost?'

Felix laughed. 'Ah. Now I understand what Flea was talking about this morning. Yes, Mistress Ramchand. I suppose I is the Holy Ghost.'

'But the child is our property now, Mr Felix. You shouldn't be so careless about things like that. Say I refuse to give it back to you. What you go do then?'

'Then it will be a police matter, Mistress Ramchand. They call it kidnapping. Is one of the most serious crimes you could commit. You are keeping my son, my own flesh and blood, under false pretences. In some countries they does hang you for that, you know. And I not joking either.'

Mrs. Ramchand blanched.

'Don't get me wrong,' Felix continued. 'After we settle this matter we could come to some little arrangement about the child. But I'm not exaggerating about this kidnapping business, Mistress Ramchand. Just last week I think it was, they hang somebody in New York – or they put him in the gas chamber, I can't remember which – for kidnapping a little boy, the son of some millionaire or the other. You must have read the case in the newspapers. I think they was going to make him a houseboy as a matter of fact.' Felix fingered his chain.

'Bring the child, Hari. You hear what Felix say? I sure you wouldn't want them to hang you for such a black and ugly child.' While she regarded her husband's fortune as entirely her own, she took good care to see that his misfortune remained entirely his.

Mr Ramchand appeared not to hear. He dried his forehead with a handkerchief and looked around wildly. Carmen too was distracted. Flea twiddled the hairbrush and stared down at the ground.

'Like you deaf or something, Hari? I say to bring the child. Is enough as it is being the wife of a ugly man like you. You want to make me the wife of a criminal on top of all that?'

The mob laughed.

'They does hang you for taking people children away from them, you know, Hari. You yourself must have hear what Felix say.'

Mr Ramchand disappeared into the house. There was an excited buzz of conversation among the mob. Mr Ramchand took his time. When he returned to the veranda with the baby wrapped in a blanket, the slits of his eyes were almost invisible among the folds of his face. He cradled the child in his arms, hugging it close to his chest. It was screaming. Carmen ran up to him and took it. Mr Ramchand sank as he had done before into the rocking-chair and mopped his brow with a handkerchief.

'I must say I don't think this child resemble you all that much, Felix. Maybe you is not the Holy Ghost after all.' Mrs Ramchand giggled.

'We will soon see about that, Mistress Ramchand. Gentlemen! Compare the features of this child with mine. It's a little darker, I grant you that, and maybe the nose is a little flatter than mine. But then, every baby that was ever born in this world have a nose like that. Apart from that though, it's a mirror image of me, not so?'

Flea remembered something. His face puckered and raising his head slowly, he gazed first at Felix, then at Mr Ramchand. His eyes shone.

'I know who it is the child resemble the most,' he declared suddenly. Everybody looked at him in surprise. The mob's chatter died away. Carmen bit her lower lip. 'And is not Felix either. That nose, all those features belong to . . .'

'Flea,' Carmen said, 'stop shouting like that. You frightening your son. That is no way for a father to behave.' She cooed to the child and kissed it.

Flea stuttered into silence, twirling the brush. Mr Ramchand was drying his forehead furiously.

'You lying,' Felix shouted. 'That's the second time today somebody decide to tell a lie against me. I is the father. These gentlemen will support me.'

'You is not the father, Felix,' Carmen replied calmly, still cooing to the child. She felt it was her turn to harangue the mob. 'You want to tell me, gentlemen, that I don't know who the father of my own child is?'

The mob grunted approvingly. The man in the red jersey performed another of his somersaults and skipped excitedly around the yard.

'She right. She must be right. All woman must know who the true father of their child is.'

Mr Ramchand got up from the rocker and stood at the top of the veranda steps.

'Anyway,' Felix said, 'the child you give me is a hell of a lot prettier than the child you give he. I never thought a woman like you could make such an ugly baby.'

Carmen shrugged. 'In that case, you have nothing to quarrel about then.'

Felix fell silent.

Several of the mob came up and shook Flea by the hand and slapped him heartily on the back. Flea grinned weakly at them and twirled the hairbrush.

'You can't trust these sailors an inch,' one of them said. 'Real devils when it come to the women.'

Carmen walked up the path to Mr Ramchand. He came down the steps to meet her. Without a word, she handed him the child. Mr Ramchand took it without a word and, cradling it close to his chest, disappeared into the house.

'As it is,' Felix was saying, 'apart from this child I have by Carmen, I have more than enough of them to call me daddy nearly all over Trinidad. So ...' He looked towards the heavens and gestured hopelessly.

'We must celebrate this,' the man in the red jersey said. 'I always thought Felix had a big mouth. Still, I glad everything turn out right in the end.'

'Yes,' Flea said, 'everybody happy now. Even Mistress Ramchand.'

'Come on, Flea. I can't stand here waiting for you all day.' Carmen held out her hand to him. Flea clasped it gently. And they went, without further ado, out into the street.

The Tenant

Pankar the jeweller was a well-known and respected figure, admired as much for his technical and artistic skill as for his honesty. This was no mean achievement. Jewellers as a class were under constant suspicion of cheating their customers, or if not, of harbouring the intent to do so. This attitude was not confined to what was supposed to happen in their workshops. It extended to their everyday lives as well. The jeweller was a marked man, never more than one step away from abuse or arrest.

Pankar was determined to avoid this. Given to calculation, he had catalogued what he considered to be his colleagues' shortcomings. For a start, they were too friendly. This did not inspire trust. Therefore, Pankar was austere and distant, taking charge of his customers' gold with the greatest reluctance. Secondly, they were too democratic: they accepted everybody's custom. This also did not inspire trust. Therefore, Pankar only did work for people of a certain class. Finally, he disliked the gaiety and opulence of their shops. Pankar's shop was small and dark. All anyone could see were the instruments of his trade and Pankar, dressed in soiled overalls, seated at a cluttered table, peering through his magnifying glass. He was a great success.

He had been the aberration in his family. Among them there had never been a hint of artistic inclinations, and Pankar himself had shown no early signs of possessing any spectacular gifts. He had run away from school when he was fourteen and gone to live with an aunt who had quarrelled with the family. She was a mild woman, and being slightly afraid of Pankar, she let him have his way. He smoked and drank and seduced the girls in the neighbourhood. Between these bouts of dissipation he was moody and silent and confessed to having a religious vocation. He talked with priests and for a time flirted with the idea of becoming a Roman Catholic. They gave him numerous pamphlets which he read carefully. But eventually his more worldly energies reasserted themselves and Pankar put away the pamphlets and behaved as before. This time, however, he added a refinement: he joined a gang which specialised in breaking windows and petty theft. He was caught and sent to a detention centre for three months. There, the religious urge reasserted itself, accompanied by an intense, a morbid, interest in his abilities. He questioned one of the social workers closely.

'You feel I have a talent for anything?'

'Everybody have a talent for something.'

This answer did not satisfy Pankar.

'You don't understand me. I mean a special talent, a . . . a gift.'

'Who can say? You got to put your hand at something before you can know whether you have a gift.'

'And you think if I try my hand I'll find something?'

'Determination can move mountains.' She examined his hands. 'You have delicate fingers. You ever think of taking up jewellery?'

Pankar was inspired. It seemed to him that this was the revelation he had been waiting for. When he was released from the detention centre, she found him a job as apprentice to a famous jeweller in Port of Spain. He learned quickly. 'It's a gift from God,' he told the social worker. She was impressed and advised him to set up on his own. 'They will come running after you, once they know. You'll be a rich man in no time.' 'It's not money I after,' Pankar replied, 'but before I do anything like that I must find a wife. I want a nice simple girl. The uglier she is, the better.' In two months he found one. Dulcie was overwhelmed by Pankar; she was simple; and above all, she was ugly.

Pankar's asceticism infected his other activities. He lived, with monastic devotion to his trade, in a tiny room above the shop, which he shared with his wife. She was a thin, querulous woman, whose two pregnancies had ended in miscarriage. Pankar, cushioned by his asceticism, quickly recovered from these initial failures. He even derived some consolation from them.

'You know,' he said to his wife one day, 'sometimes I does think it's a blessing in disguise that we don't have any children to bother we. To do the kind of work I does do you need to be a sort of priest, lock away from the world and temptation. It's a kind of religion really.'

Dulcie was not moved by this declaration of faith. She hated the tiny room, with its narrow bed, unadorned wooden tables and enamel cups and plates.

'Look at it this way,' she replied, 'I don't know anything about being a priest, but I want to say this. You have all this money you save up which you don't do nothing with, with the result that the two of we living like a set of church mice. You not living like a priest, you living like a miser.'

'You in too much of a hurry, Dulcie. Buying a house is not like spitting, you know. It's an investment and you got to make sure it's a sound commercial proposition.'

'Well you better hurry up then. I sure if it wasn't for this damn place I wouldn't be so sick all the time and we could have ...'

'Calm yourself, Dulcie. The room have nothing to do with all that. I don't think God wanted you to have children. Just have some patience and remember I making this sacrifice for your sake, not mine.'

But Pankar was not to be hurried, even when making a sacrifice. As in everything else, he was strict and methodical. He went to see nearly all the houses that were advertised in the newspapers, but there was invariably something the matter with them.

Then he was told about a house for sale on the Western Main Road, a most unlikely place to seek the religious life, but Pankar seemed not to mind that fact. At that moment, commercial considerations were uppermost in his mind, and it sounded promising. The prices in the area were rising steadily and the house itself, though not grand, was decent and spacious. There was only one drawback. It shared a communal yard and water supply with two sets of tenants, occupying two barrack-like rooms to the rear. He took Dulcie to see it. She was appalled, not by the house, but by her future neighbours.

'What kind of people you bringing me to live with, Pankar?'

'You does worry too much, Dulcie. I'll have them out of here in no time. You wait and see.'

They moved in.

Their neighbours were the Smithers, a cowering family of Grenadians, who lived in one room with their three children, and Mrs Eugenie Radix, who lived alone. Pankar's optimism was not entirely unfounded. He had sufficient money to hope to buy them out. The Smithers were easy. They jumped at Pankar's offer and left within weeks. Mrs Radix, however, was intractable. Dulcie claimed to know this would be so from the moment she first set eyes on her.

Eugenie Radix was a tall, dark woman of half-Indian, half-Negro extraction. She was about forty, the possessor of a ponderous bosom, thick, full lips, and long black hair which fell in uncontrolled curls down her back. It was not obvious how she earned her living. During the day, she wandered through the yard, dressed in a loose smock, torn in places, a bucket propped against her hip, singing to herself.

She was proof against all Pankar's persuasions and blandishments.

'I don't hold it against you, mind, but it go take more than the offer of a few extra dollars to get me out of here. Anyway, what harm you think an old woman like me could do to you?'

'It's not me that worried,' Pankar confessed, 'it's the wife. She nervous, you know.'

'What, she think I want to eat she?'

'I wouldn't be surprised.' Pankar laughed. They were sitting in her room, surrounded by pots and pans and old Chinese calendars. The air was sweet and oppressive, burdened with the odour of stale incense. Mrs Radix had one book in the room, the Bible, which was well thumbed. The cover had been torn away. The kettle steamed in the coal-pot. She was making him tea.

'You believe in dreams?' she asked suddenly, as she was pouring the boiling water into the tea-pot.

He was taken aback by the question. 'Well, I never really think about it.'

'You know, is a strange thing, but I had a dream the other night which tell me that the two of you was moving in here. I could have describe you before I ever set eyes on you, tall, a little grey hair, fair.' Mrs Radix opened her eyes wide in amusement. Pankar sipped his tea slowly. The subject had aroused his interest.

'You does interpret dreams, then?'

Mrs Radix giggled. 'You trying to find out my secrets, eh? I go tell you one thing though, the people around here believe I is some kind of a devil woman. They believe I does work obeah and black magic.' She grinned happily at him.

'You does interpret dreams?' Pankar was insistent, ignoring these other disclosures.

'Like you really interested in that. Why, you been having funny dreams of late?'

He gazed at her over the rim of the tea-cup. 'Well, I don't know if you could call them funny . . .'

'Come, let me see your palms.' She held his extended palm and studied it, frowning and running her fingers along the lines.

'You see something bad?'

'No, no. Nothing like that,' Mrs Radix reassured him. 'You have a long life line and your heart line strong, very strong.' She shook her head. 'Still, all is not plain sailing. You have to have your troubles like the rest of us.'

'I going to have a bad sickness?'

Mrs Radix smiled. 'You turning as white as a sheet.' That seemed to please her. 'No. No sickness. But tell me your dream.'

Pankar described his dream. Mrs Radix, her eyes exploring the features of his face, nodded from time to time. When he had finished, she said, 'Well, the water is a good sign and the way you was crying mean you will be happy. Dreams is a funny thing. They does say exactly the opposite of what they want to say. If you dream you sad, it mean you going to be happy; if you dream you happy, it mean you going to be sad. Is a mystery really, but that's the way it is. It need someone who is a expert to tell you what they mean exactly.' Pankar listened eagerly, his face tight and serious. 'If you ever have any more dreams like that you must come and see me. I'll tell you exactly what they mean.'

Pankar's dreams obsessed him after this meeting. On waking up in the morning, he turned them over in his mind, trying to unlock the secrets which, he suspected, lurked in every minor detail. Invariably, he failed and was driven back to the superior knowledge and guidance of Mrs Radix. She never failed him. To have to live through a day, unsure of what it held in store for him, a prey to fallibility, gradually assumed the dimensions of a dreadful punishment. Dulcie looked on, disturbed, disapproving, envious.

Dulcie's relationship with Mrs Radix, taking a different path, developed more slowly.

'She's a prostitute, I tell you,' she said to Pankar, when they had been living there for a week. 'You see how she clothes tear to show she belly? I really don't know what kind of gutter people you bring me to live with.'

'Do you know what a prostitute is, Dulcie? You ever see any men visiting here?'

'Where does she get she money from then? Don't tell me she does shake if off the plum-tree. The only thing I ever see she shaking is she backside.'

'She might be married for all you know and separated from she husband. That kind of thing does happen, you know.'

Dulcie winced. 'Huh! Could you ever see any man marrying she? Still, you never know. All you men is the same.'

Pankar was silent. He appeared to be thinking about something else.

Mrs Radix, despite Dulcie's efforts to get rid of her, was friendly and open towards her; even, one might be tempted to say, anxious to please. When she came to fill her bucket at the tap, she beamed good-naturedly at Dulcie who would be watching her sourly from the kitchen window. One day she stepped up to the window, the empty bucket rattling on her hip.

'I been wanting to talk to you for a long time, but I was frighten to think you might feel I was interfering, but I want you to know that I truly glad and thankful that those other people sell the house to you and move out of here.' She paused, as if to see what effect this implicit declaration of good will would have on her listener. Duclie stared, still sour, her eyes full of mistrust. 'They was so unpleasant to me,' Mrs Radix went on, ignoring her hostility. 'Well, he wife was anyway.' There was another pause.

'Why?' Dulcie was unable to resist asking. She had vowed not to encourage Mrs Radix in conversation.

Mrs Radix laughed, happy to gain a response. 'You may well ask, my dear.' Dulcie winced. 'She get the idea into she head that I was trying to take she husband away from she.' Mrs Radix grinned pleasantly at Dulcie, inviting her to savour the improbability of the accusation. 'Imagine that, my dear! As if an ugly old woman like me could take away anybody husband from them.' Dulcie gazed indecisively at her. Perhaps Mrs Radix was mocking her. She smiled weakly.

'Yes ... well, I better go and cook the food now. Pankar go be coming back from work soon and he go lose he temper if the food not cook.'

'You don't have to tell me, my dear. All these men does behave just like spoil children. I know that even without having a husband. My brother used to be just like that. He was a real little baby, just like Pankar.'

Dulcie moved away from the window, and Mrs Radix, singing, went to fill her bucket.

'You know,' Dulcie reported to Pankar that evening, 'that woman had the bold face to come up and talk to me this afternoon.'

'What wrong with that?' Pankar, never a great eater, toyed with the food on his enamel plate. It was one of the things Dulcie held against him.

'She was telling me about some confusion she had with the people who used to live here before we.' Pankar made circles in the rice with his spoon. 'The wife thought she was trying to take away she husband.' Pankar looked up. 'And another thing. She was calling you Pankar, as if she is your equal.'

He shrugged. 'What wrong with that? You want she to come and kiss my feet?'

'I wish you would eat the food I does cook for you.' She stared irritably at the circles of rice, and getting up suddenly, went out of the kitchen.

Mrs Radix courted Dulcie with a rising fervour. There was a plum-tree growing near her room, whose fecundity was the marvel of the neighbourhood. She claimed sole rights over it and allowed no one to pick the plums, which when in season hung in thick yellow clusters from the branches. She had warned them about this on the very first day. 'Is I who plant that tree and I doesn't let anyone, man, woman or child, touch it without my permission.' Nevertheless, Mrs Radix did not hoard her fruit. One day she appeared with a basinful of over-ripe plums outside the kitchen window and offered them to Dulcie.

'For you,' she said. Dulcie accepted the gift, but again she complained to Pankar about Mrs Radix's effrontery.

'I don't know who it is give she the idea that she own that plum-tree. Is our property, not so?'

'Why don't you just eat the plums and keep quiet, eh?'

Another day Mrs Radix leaned confidentially against the window sill. 'Call me Eugenie,' she said, 'Friends shouldn't call each other by their second name.'

When she told Pankar about this latest overture, he replied, 'You say that the other woman thought she was taking away she husband from she? It look more like the other way round to me. Soon I go have to start worrying that she taking away my wife from me.'

She looked at the circles he had carved in his rice. 'I really wish you would eat the food I does cook for you.'

But, despite herself, she had begun to warm towards Mrs Radix. 'Those plums were real nice, Eugenie.'

'I glad you like them, Dulcie. I chose them especially for you.'

For several weeks the friendship blossomed. Dulcie discovered in Mrs Radix unsuspected virtues and talents and in return she received buckets of plums and had her dreams unravelled. Mrs Radix promised prosperity, happiness, good fortune, and here and there, for good measure, a minor tragedy was mixed in. Any thoughts Dulcie might have entertained about getting rid of her were submerged in the seductive atmosphere of their friendship and the mutual exchange of confidences through the kitchen window.

*

Unfortunately, Mrs Radix had not confessed all. The initial revelation occurred one evening, when Dulcie saw her friend clad in a long white preacher's gown, a candle in her hand, a garland of red hibiscus on her neck, walking, as in a dream, through the yard, intoning a chant whose words she could not understand. Dulcie choked on the greeting that had already formed on her lips and ran softly out of the kitchen. There was a full moon and the yard was bathed in a blue light that washed over the roofs of the neighbouring houses. She followed Mrs Radix to her room, which was lit by rows of candles. An improvised altar, draped with a piece of gold cloth, had been erected at the top of the steps. It was bedecked with brass images of animals and Christ on the Cross and hung with hibiscus and oleander. Mrs Radix bowed low before the altar and prostrated herself, uttering low, ecstatic moans and lifting her hands towards the bright sky. Dulcie, mesmerised, followed her every movement, then abruptly turning away, she ran, through the contorted shadows of the plum-tree, back to the house.

The doubts which she had only so recently stilled assailed her anew, their former animosity exaggerated, but now, in addition, edged with a superstitious fear. Dulcie lived through all the agitations of a lover betrayed. 'If she had only tell me before,' she kept repeating to herself, 'it wouldn't have been so bad. But she had to be underhand about it, and there I was telling she everything about myself and Pankar. All we troubles and everything.'

Some days went by before she had the courage to describe to Pankar the events she had been witness to.

'That woman,' she concluded, 'if you could call she a woman, that is, is a witch, not a prostitute.'

'I glad you make up your mind at last. But you never know. She might be both.'

'Eh?'

Pankar grinned at her.

'Well, I don't claim to know, but whatever she is I don't like it. I always thought there was something fishy about she and since you don't want to move she out of here . . .'

'What give you that idea, Dulcie?' he seemed genuinely interested in her answer.

'I haven't seen you doing anything about it. You always going there telling she what you dream, asking she for advice, sucking up . . .'

'You is a fine one to talk.'

'If you want she to stay why don't you out with it and say so?'

Pankar winked at her. 'Okay. You right. I do want she to stay.'

'I don't like those kind of jokes.' She knew he was not joking. The prospect of losing Mrs Radix alarmed her probably as much as it did him, and aware that nothing she said could alter the situation, she felt free to continue the attack. It was soothing exercise and helped her to believe that she could defy and in defying, exorcise the evil influence.

'I don't see what so difficult in getting she out of here. Somebody else would have had she out of here in two twos.'

'She have a lease on the place, Dulcie. You can't fight a lease. Anyway, what harm she do you? She's a very religious woman, that's all.'

'Bring out a writ, then. Forget the lease.'

'A writ?' Pankar was amused. 'Do you know what a writ is?'

'Writ! Lease! You only making excuses. Let we build a fence then, since we so powerless.'

'You want to deliberately insult she or something? But what she do to you that you want to behave so? The trouble with people like you is once you don't understand or appreciate something, you does begin to get on a high horse and condemn. It's sheer ignorance and jealousy.'

'Me jealous of she? Huh! You must be crazy. What it is she have that I got to be jealous? Tell me.' Dulcie was unable to hide her distress. She watched, frustrated, perplexed, as Pankar traced curious patterns in the rice. 'Jealous! Me! I remember when we had first come here you was running your mouth all over the place about how quick you would have she out of here. Now all of a sudden . . .' She stopped speaking and bent low over his plate. 'What you drawing there?' Pankar scrubbed out the patterns. 'She working she magic on you, you know. She go have you in she power soon. "Imagine an ugly old woman like me taking away somebody husband",' she mimicked Mrs Radix. 'She good-looking, too, eh? Big bust, not so?' Dulcie extended her arms.

'You have a dirty mind, Dulcie.'

Dulcie laughed bitterly, and thought of her own pitiful under-developed breasts.

Mrs Radix stayed locked in her room an entire week. On the third day Pankar went to visit her. His knock had not been answered, and he was about to go away when Mrs Radix opened the door. She invited him in. The windows had been shuttered and the room was lit by a single candle burning feebly on the dresser. Crushed flowers littered the floor. Mrs Radix sat on the bed. She seemed thinner and her hair was even more tousled than usual. There were black rings under her eyes. They looked as if they had been painted on.

'I suppose you been wondering what happening to me.'

Pankar did not answer. He studied the confusion in the room.

'You ever hear about the Rosicrucians?'

'A little bit.' One of the Catholic pamphlets had mentioned them in passing.

'Well, is partly that and partly Baptist. The powers I have is something I was born with.'

Vague religious sentiment stirred in Pankar.

'You mean the Spirit does take you sometimes?'

'It does take me every full moon, as you see for yourself.'

'And so you always in contact with It?'

Mrs Radix nodded. 'It does guide me all the time.' She waved her arms. 'Come and sit on the bed by me. You too far away.' Pankar sat next to her. 'The Spirit does exhaust me and sometimes I does have to stay in my room like this for days.'

'One time I wanted to become a Catholic. I used to go and talk to all them priest in the church.'

Mrs Radix pressed her lips tightly together and frowned. 'Catholic no good. I used to think like that myself one time, but in the end the Spirit tell me that wasn't for me. One day the Spirit going to call on me to serve Him all the time and when that day come I going to leave this place and go somewhere very far away, like a pilgrim. But that day ain't come as yet. That is why I was telling you it would take more than a few dollars to get me out of here.' Mrs Radix laughed. 'Don't look so embarrassed. I know it wasn't your fault. Catholic not for you, Pankar. You is different kind of man. The Spirit tell me that.'

'It really say so?'

Mrs Radix sprawled full length on the bed. 'You mustn't ask so much question. It does get angry when you do that.' She raised her hand and rested her palm on his neck. 'This is the only true way. You got to do what the Spirit mean for you to do.' She drew his face down to hers. Her skin smelled of flowers and stale incense. 'I glad Dulcie like the plums I give she.' The rings under her eyes disappeared into her wrinkles as she smiled up at him and drew his face yet closer.

Dulcie watched impatiently for signs of Mrs Radix's reappearance. She was envious of the privileges accorded Pankar and was several times tempted to go and knock on her door. But it was not pride alone that dissuaded her; she relished her resentment and the pain it caused her, and in proportion as she did this, so much sweeter by contrast were her visions of the ultimate reconciliation.

The morning she emerged, Mrs Radix walked slowly through the yard, gently swinging the bucket from her hips. She smiled pleasantly at Dulcie, who was staring at her from the kitchen window. However, Eugenie, instead of stopping to talk, went straight to the pipe and started to fill her bucket. Dulcie closed the window with a bang. Mrs Radix filled the bucket and returned to her room. Dulcie was devastated by the coolness of her reaction. Whatever she had been hoping for, Eugenie, clearly, was not prepared to give it. She set about planning her defences.

Since she was not allowed to build a wall, she decided to make a garden. She would retaliate by magnifying her presence. The soil was not particularly fertile; it was hard and yellow, but with application and the liberal use of fertilisers, she succeeded in coaxing from it roses, hibiscus, oleander, canna lilies and lime and orange trees. Soon, Mrs Radix was blotted from view by the flowers and trees. Even Pankar was pleased. He said it improved the value of the property. Duclie worked in the garden in the afternoons. She had bought a watering-can and a set of garden tools. She hoed and raked and weeded, and every evening at six she watered the flower beds. Mrs Radix renewed her overtures of friendship.

'I don't think you planting the hibiscus right, Dulcie. It look as if it need some more manure.'

Dulcie scraped away at the soil, not answering. Nevertheless, she was flattered by these attentions. Mrs Radix modified her approach.

'But the canna lilies looking really nice, though, together with all them other trees you plant. I think you have a hand for gardening. I been peeping at you these last few months and I feel sure about it. What do they call people who good at growing things?' Mrs Radix puckered her brows. Dulcie gazed up at her, flushed with excitement. Eugenie had been 'peeping' at her!

'Ah yes, Green fingers. I read that in the paper the other day. You have green fingers.'

Dulcie blushed. 'You only joking with me.'

Mrs Radix shook her head. 'You know me better than that, Dulcie.'

Dulcie flushed again. 'You really think so?'

'I won't answer until you call me Eugenie.' Mrs Radix frowned pettishly at her.

'You really think so, Eugenie?'

'Yes, man. Not everybody could do what you do.'

'All it need is a little effort, really. But you know people don't like to apply themselves to anything these days.'

'Is strange that you should say that. Me and Pankar was talking about that kinda thing the other day. He was saying a jeweller have to be a kind of priest, but that most people don't appreciate that. But I was saying that all three of us was at bottom like that. You is a gardener, he making jewel and I praying and making contact with my god. Same thing really, eh? We all have that one thing in common – doing the thing we have to do.'

It was still and extremely hot in the yard. Only an occasional car on the Western Main Road disturbed the mid-afternoon silence. Through a gap in the wooden fence Dulcie saw across the neighbouring yard into a side street, empty and silent. A small, dry wind shook the leaves of the lime and orange-trees and ruffled Mrs Radix's thin white smock and strands of tangled hair. Lulled by the heat, the old resentment stirred fitfully in Dulcie. Her desire to please and be accepted by this woman was wounding and offensive to her sensibilities. It was, she knew, a one-way traffic with very little return. Yet, instinctively, she had come to recognise the power, the attractions, wielded by Mrs Radix. Unfortunately recognition had come too long after surrender for it to matter. Perhaps it would have made no difference in the first place. Recognition merely served to emphasise the inequalities, the essential hopelessness and pointlessness of the battle. And a battle it was, for Mrs Radix commanded not the affections, but something more elemental: the pull, inexorable, irresistible, exerted by the strong on the weak. Dulcie had found herself competing, not with her, but with Pankar. Logic had been reversed, and husband and wife had been transformed into rivals struggling each with the other to become the first object of their tenant's concern. Painfully she imagined their conversations and pictured the intimacies she exchanged with him in the privacy of her room. Pankar had nearly been right after all. Given the opportunity, Eugenie would have taken her away from him.

She half-listened to what Mrs Radix was saying and to the sounds of her smock flapping in the wind.

'Do you want some flowers, Eugenie?'

'I wasn't suggesting . . . but that would be nice. I could use them in the room.'

Dulcie recalled the performance of that strange rite, the altar draped with gold cloth, the garlands of hibiscus and oleander draping the necks of those idols. She felt that her offer made her part of what she suspected was a blasphemy, the work of the devil. It was her initiation, her token of good faith. Heavy with guilt and discomfort, she gathered and presented a bunch of her favourite flowers to Mrs Radix. After that, whenever Mrs Radix asked she got the flowers she wanted.

The strange rites went on, more frequently than before. On moonlit nights the same solitary procession through the yard would be repeated, and Dulcie would watch the glimmer of the candles through the trees. She could never escape a feeling of acute discomfort when she remembered that it was her own flowers that dangled from the necks of the idols and decorated the altar at the top of the steps. But Mrs Radix was always so charming the next day, and Dulcie invariably overcame her scruples. They became friends again, and it was Mrs Radix who carried her into the house and put her to bed the day she fainted in the garden.

Dulcie's pregnancy shocked everyone. Pankar paled when she told him.

'But how come you having a baby all of a sudden?'

'You should know.'

He was silent.

'What's the matter with you, Pankar? You looking as if you see a ghost. Have I kill priest or something? I thought you would be . . .' But Dulcie failed to convince even herself.

'Calm yourself, Dulcie, it's only the shock. You know how.'

That night he went to see Mrs Radix.

Pankar worked hard, returning from the shop later than usual. He insisted on sleeping in a separate room.

'After what happen I got to purify myself,' he explained to Dulcie. 'To do the kind of work I want to do you need to be clean in mind and body.'

She detected the voice of Mrs Radix in all that he said, but she was afraid to question him.

'Don't talk like that, Pankar. It does make me frighten.'

'That's only because you ignorant of these matters.'

Dulcie bowed her head. Even at second hand, Mrs Radix could not be denied.

The only furniture Pankar would allow in his room was a bed and a chair. He removed all the pictures (photographs of friends and family) and in their place hung a crucifix he had made himself. The floor he scrubbed white.

'Purity,' he said. 'Purity.'

It had been a bad month for Dulcie. She had been vomiting every day and in spite of her pregnancy she looked strangely worn and emaciated. They were having dinner when Pankar took a small, very ornate box out of his pocket.

'I got something to show you, Dulcie.'

'What?' She was listless, playing with her food. Pankar, on the other hand, had of late developed an appetite. With an exaggerated delicacy and caution, he opened the lid of the box and taking out a gold amulet, laid it flat on the palm of his hand. The light from the naked electric bulb reflected sharply off it.

'Bring it closer, Pankar. I can't see.'

'No, no. You come here.' And she had to lean close over him to see what it was.

'Do you know what that is, Dulcie?'

It had been delicately carved. In the centre there was a picture of Christ on the Cross surrounded by the signs of the zodiac.

'No.' She looked ill and pregnant. She drew away quickly. 'What you doing, Pankar? What you showing me that for?'

'It's an amulet. You know what they use for?'

She shook her head.

'It's a charm. It does bring good luck.' He held it up to the light. 'It take me a long time to make this and it's all for you.'

She raised herself heavily from the chair, and never taking her eyes off him, backed slowly to the window.

'I don't want that thing, Pankar. You dealing with obeah and I is a clean-living woman. Give it to Eugenie. She would know what to do with it.'

'Eugenie? But it's not she who making a baby, Dulcie.'

They were both standing near the window now. A white figure swirled through the darkness outside, bucket rattling.

'What you trying to do to me, Pankar? What has that witch done to you?'

They heard the tap running, the water drumming into the bucket. She tried to drag the amulet from his hands. 'Come, come, man. Give that thing to me and let me throw it in the dustbin where it belong. Give that . . .' Her voice trailed away. The tap went silent and this time the white figure lurched ponderously through the darkness. Dulcie, clutching at her stomach, stumbled out of the kitchen. Pankar laughed softly.

Dulcie painted white crosses on all the doors of the house. Every morning she prayed in the nearby Roman Catholic church and before going to bed she recited novenas. When Mrs Radix came to ask for flowers she refused. Eugenie was not offended.

'I see you putting crosses on all your doors. But why for, Dulcie? I never know you was a Christian.'

'You should know the answer to that.'

'Me?'

'Yes. You and he. Your innocent face doesn't fool me.'

'But what's the matter with you, Dulcie? What get into you so suddenly?'

'Don't put my name in your mouth.'

Mrs Radix was distressed. She eyed Dulcie disconsolately. 'You know what I think? You too old to be having a baby. People always say that when you over forty and making a baby you in for trouble. The Lord knows why, but that's the way it is. You should have take the amulet that Pankar spend so much time making for you, but . . .' Mrs Radix waved her arms resignedly and gazed at Dulcie's swollen stomach, pitying, regretful. Dulcie felt the spell descending. She walked away and from her bedroom window saw Mrs Radix cutting flowers. She sank wearily on the bed and closed her eyes.

Dulcie was too ill to look after the house, and it was Mrs Radix who cleaned and did the cooking. She wandered freely about the rooms in her torn smock, dusting the furniture and singing softly to herself. At night she and Pankar rocked on the veranda, marvelling at the number of cars that went by on the Western Main Road. 'This area getting busier and busier,' Pankar murmured admiringly. 'Prices sure to be rising.' Later on in the evening when the traffic had lessened, he discussed his dreams with her. Sometimes they spent the night in her room. Dulcie had confined herself to her bedroom. She ate little of the food Mrs Radix brought and left outside the door, convinced they were planning to poison her. Too weak to move around, she spend much of the time lying flat on her back, staring up at the ceiling, listening to the flutter of the bats roosting in the eaves.

The baby was born deformed. Some of its toes were missing and it could not cry properly. The day after it had been born Pankar came into the bedroom. During the previous month he had visited her only once or twice a week. Mrs Radix she saw not at all. Dulcie, haggard and yellow, was feeding the baby. Pankar studied them.

'A fine son, he said. 'You should be proud and thankful to God.'

The baby sucked at its mother's breast with difficulty.

'Let me hold it.' He approached the bed and leaning over, attempted to shift the baby's head from her breast.

She stayed his hand roughly. 'You leave the child alone.'

'It's my child, too, Dulcie.'

'Your child! That's the best joke I hear for a long time.' She twisted the baby's face away from the nipple. It tried to cry but could not. 'Look at that, Pankar. That's your work and that woman's as well.'

'You shouldn't speak of Eugenie in that tone, Dulcie. She was only trying to help you, but you was too obstinate. If you had listen to what she was saying in the first place, all this wouldn't have happened.' He pointed at the baby's deformed feet. She raised herself from the bed, fixing the baby in her arms.

'Stop torturing me, Pankar. It's you and she who make this child come out like this and you know that.'

'You don't know what you saying, Dulcie.'

'It's you and that ... prostitute you bring inside the house to live with you. Obeah and amulets. "Look, Dulcie, I make this amulet specially for you!" ' She mimicked his voice.

'You don't know what it is you mocking, Dulcie. Control yourself.'

'Control myself! What do you take me for, Pankar? A whore like she, taking away other people husbands? A obeah woman?' Dulcie's voice rose to a scream. Mrs Radix came running and stood in the doorway. 'Well, I not nobody's whore, you hear, and I not nobody's witch either. I is a decent self-respecting woman, not a shameless whore!'

Pankar laughed. Her face contorted.

'I'll show the two of you how to laugh.' She raised the child.

'Dulcie!'

'Don't touch me. I not pure enough for you. Remember?'

Pankar grabbed at the baby. But he was too late and Dulcie too agile. The child fell with a thud and lay wriggling on the floor. Its mouth writhed soundlessly in its tiny pinched face.

'Well, you not laughing?' She was crying. 'I thought you and Angel Gabriel over there would be grinning on both sides of your face.'

Mrs Radix patted Pankar on the shoulder. 'Come, come, is best to leave she to sheself. A long time ago I was telling she that people as old as she shouldn't be making babies. It does do strange things to you.'

Dulcie stiffened. For an instant she seemed poised to fly at Mrs Radix, but only for an instant. Almost immediately, the tautness slackened, and remembering what she had done, she looked down at the baby, squirming at her feet. She bent down and, picking up the child, she collapsed limply on the bed with it, at the same time peering anxiously at its agitated features. The next day, taking the baby with her, she left the house.

After Dulcie had gone, Mrs Radix moved in. 'Somebody got to look after him,' she told the neighbours. They did not believe her, but were afraid to say so, afraid, in fact, of what she might take it into her head to do to them. Her powers had been sufficiently displayed to silence any criticism. Pankar worked harder than ever, and was unusually friendly to everyone. They did not trust him, although, in his case, they were less afraid to say so. Nevertheless, they were cautious, anxious not to offend Mrs Radix.

Pankar renovated the shop. It was no longer dark and crowded and there were many pieces of glittering jewellery under glass, showing the old artistic and technical skill. He even employed a pretty secretary. Yet, some of his former clients withdrew their custom. Despite this, Pankar smiled and appeared to prosper. He bought a car, repainted the house, and in place of the garlands of hibiscus and oleander Mrs Radix wore necklaces of an intricate and occult design. Then he was accused of adulterating a client's gold and taken to court.

Pankar was brave in his own defence, supported no doubt by the presence of Eugenie among the audience. He explained to the magistrate that he was a man of God, that his talents as a jeweller were dedicated to the service of the spirits (at this point Mrs Radix gazed benignly at him and fingered the necklace she was wearing), that the gold he had 'appropriated' would do more for the soul of the 'donor' than any rings or bracelets he might have made for him. The magistrate was not convinced. Pankar had to pay a heavy fine and in the ensuing scandal he was forced to close his shop. The neighbours were appalled by what they considered the magistrate's foolhardiness. He had flouted Mrs Radix. Doom must surely follow. They sat back and awaited the catastrophe. Nothing happened. On the contrary, the magistrate was mentioned in the New Year Honours List and commended for 'services rendered to the noble cause of justice'.

'Somebody really got to look after him now,' Mrs Radix said.

Pankar continued to do occasional work for the faithful, those people whose admiration for his genius had only been augmented by the recent events. But most of his time he spent in the garden. He added to the fruit and flowers Dulcie had planted, introducing carnations and bougainvillaea, anthurium lilies and frangipani, and was no less assiduous than his wife had been in the application of fertilisers. As a result, the garden flourished.

Pankar was disturbed. He had had an extraordinary dream which woke him up in the middle of the night. Together with some friends of his childhood he had been driving along a narrow road carved out of the sides of a precipitous cliff. Below them stretched a bare, treeless plain, lit by a sun made peculiar by the extreme yellowness of its light. Bordering this plain was another mountain, squat and table-topped, with a covering of green on the surface of its plateau. Its slopes were scarred by a constellation of black holes, entrances to caves running under the plateau, and numerous sand-filled craters. Magically, they were transported across the arid plain and found themselves standing outside the entrance to one of the caverns. He entered the cave. Inside was a thick, grey darkness, and in the centre of the floor he saw that a turgid, oily pool of water had been gouged out among the rocks. Near the edge of the pool was a platform of smoother rock. He dived, fully clothed, off the platform. At the bottom of the pool he found discs of a greyish, glutinous substance. They were threatening, malevolent. He swam quickly back to the surface. For a time he lay on the platform, powerless to move. The whole atmosphere of the cave, dank, dark, exhaled disease. His friends laughed at him. Their laughter grew louder, more hysterical. He struggled, trying to raise himself off the rock, but his body refused to obey. The laughter around him swelled. He cried out.

It was then he had woken up, shivering and frightened.

'What happen? What frighten you so?' Eugenie gripped his arm.

'Nothing, nothing. Don't worry.'

'You had a bad dream?'

'I tell you is nothing.'

Pankar, afraid to sleep, remained awake until day-break, listening to the bats scurrying in the eaves.

The next morning he worked in the garden. Eugenie, leaning against the fence, watched him.

'I think you have a hand for gardening, you know.' Pankar was weeding the anthurium patch.

'Don't come telling me I have green fingers, Eugenie.'

He studied the sun-darkened face with the thick, full lips, hovering above him. They both laughed, but without any enthusiasm.

'We must not joke about that. It might bring bad luck.'

He stared at her, the laughter drained from his face. She frowned and he resumed his weeding.

'You behaving very odd, you know. Since last night.'

'I need rest. I tired.'

Mrs Radix raised her eyebrows sceptically.

'Tell me what it is you dream last night.'

'I tell you I didn't dream anything.'

'Well, you don't have to bite me. I only trying to help.'

Pankar laughed. 'I feel I hear that somewhere before.'

'Watch what you saying.' Mrs Radix raised her voice.

Pankar straightened himself abruptly.

'I not taking any orders from you, Eugenie. Mind how you speak to me.'

He spoke softly, as if he were gently reasoning with her.

'And who is you to give me orders, eh?' She stood before him, belligerent, uncompromising. 'Ask yourself who it is teach you all you know. That scrawny woman with no breast at all who you used to call your wife?'

'Mind how you speak of Dulcie.' He too raised his voice.

She laughed, loud and scornful. 'Hear him talk now.' She seemed to be addressing not him, but the neighbourhood. 'Why don't you go back to she, since you like she so much? Why don't you go back, eh? I won't try and stop you. Go on. Give it a try. Go back to she!'

He walked away from her.

'You going?'

'Yes.'

'For good?'

Pankar did not answer. He quickened his pace. Eugenie's laughter was soon lost among the roar of the traffic on the Western Main Road.

Pankar walked a long time. He followed the side streets down to the Quevedo Avenue and continued down some more until he came to the waste land near the docks. There was no shelter from the sun here. Only a thin scrub vegetation grew on the poor soil, recently reclaimed from the sea. He walked slowly through the knee-high grass to the sea wall. The smaller ships, those that trafficked among the islands, docked here. He sat down on the sea wall. Apart from himself, it was deserted. Two schooners, small, dirty ships, were anchored near the pier, about a mile away. The warehouses were empty. Pankar closed his eyes and listened to the water lapping against the stones and, as it penetrated the crevices, the small sucking sounds it made. Cold shivers ran down his back, despite the heat. He dozed from time to time, waking with a start. A large ship gradually disappeared over the horizon. The tide rose, and the water, licking at the stones, crept up the wall. The sun spread out across the water. It grew cooler and darker. He fell asleep.

Someone was shining a light on him. It was a policeman. He regarded Pankar with mild curiosity.

'What going on with you, mister? You drunk?'

Pankar shook his head.

'You sick? If you stay here like this you bound to catch cold.' The policeman bent down to take a closer look at him.

'You don't look too good to me, mister. Why don't you go home?'

Pankar stood up.

'All kinds of funny people does come here in the night. Couples, you know. I does use my torch light to flush them out. For a moment I thought . . .' The policeman licked his lips. 'You don't look well to me at all. Come on, go home.' He patted him encouragingly on the shoulder. Pankar stepped off the wall.

'You going home?'

'Yes.'

'If you do these kind of things too often, you go worry your wife to death, not so? Think about that, man.'

Pankar, stumbling through the grass, laughed, and waved the policeman good night.

Eugenie was preparing dinner when Pankar arrived.

'You just in time,' she shouted as he was coming up the steps. 'I had made up my mind to eat it all if you wasn't back by seven o'clock.' Pankar sprawled on the bed and stared at the floor.

'You looking as if you dog tired. A little food go do you good. Like you take a really long walk?' She studied his face. His eyes were bloodshot. She smiled. 'Anyway you come back in time for your food and that's the main thing.' She served him the food. Pankar rested the plate on his knee.

'Eugenie . . .' Pankar made circles in his rice.

'What?'

Pankar scratched his head. 'You know, I had such a funny dream last night . . .'

'Tell me,' Mrs Radix said.

Lack of Sleep

Last night I dreamt of my own death. From my window, I saw a hearse parked outside the front door and, though I was far from being dead, it was evident it had come for me. Mrs Maundy, dressed in black, was calling out impatiently from the front steps and anxiously scanning the empty street. She urged me to hurry while there was no one about and reminded me that to keep the hearse waiting was an expensive business. Typical. 'I'm not ready,' I cried out to her. 'Send it away. I'm not ready to die as yet.' Most dreams fade the moment you wake up but this one remains fresh in my mind.

It is several days now since I have been able to get a good night's rest and I am at my wits' end. How cruel it is to have to get out of bed so early in the morning and be forced to crouch in front of the electric fire waiting for Mrs Maundy to come and clean the room. If only she would let me sleep a bit longer the nightmares, I am sure, would disappear of their own accord. What a delightful thing sleep is! That hour or two of rest I am able to snatch towards morning is much too vital to be interrupted and squandered so recklessly. But that, needless to say, is precisely what happens to me.

The effects of all this have not been altogether lost on Mrs Maundy. She is an observant woman. However, she won't let herself be affected by me. Not her. She doesn't like the smallest inconvenience. Mrs Maundy never swerves from the letter of the law as laid down by herself. That, by her book, is a crime. About three days ago she said to me, 'You'd better watch yourself. You're much too jumpy for my liking. It makes me nervous when old people get like that. You should go for a long walk. Use up all that excess energy you have.' I replied that my jumpiness, as she chose to call it, had nothing to do with excess energy but was due, purely and simply, to lack of sleep. 'Huh!' she retorted.

The trouble is that my room, being at the top of the house, is the first to be cleaned in the morning. Mrs Maundy firmly believes it is easier for her to work downwards rather than upwards. Certainly it may be easier for her. I don't deny that. Nevertheless, at my age you would have expected her to show a little more consideration. But no.

She wakes me – me! – while she allows Herbert, that dreadful son of hers, to go on sleeping peacefully on the first floor. 'Is this fair?' I asked. She stared at me scornfully. 'Herbert is a working man,' she replied. 'What work do *you* have to do?' I had no wish to drag Herbert further into the argument. That, I suspected, was dangerous ground. And not only because I feared to antagonise his mother. Above all, I felt it would not be wise to get on the wrong side of Herbert Maundy. Yet Mrs Maundy regards herself as the soul of kindness. I have listened to her working herself into a fine froth over the treatment of those she is fond of describing as 'our senior citizens.' I can't square it with the way she treats me. But that is Mrs Maundy all over.

Risking her wrath, I reminded her of the avowed concern and suggested – as politely as I could – that right under her very nose was a golden opportunity to display it by working upwards for a bit ('to tide me over this difficult patch' was how I put it) instead of downwards and so giving me a few extra minutes of precious rest. She did not take at all kindly to the suggestion and, for a moment, I thought she was going to lose her temper and shout at me – as she does to the other tenants now and again. That would have been hard to take. If there is one thing I am unable to tolerate, it's people shouting at me. When that happens a kind of raging black cloud seems to envelop me. Thankfully, she didn't shout. 'Are you trying to teach me my own job?' she asked frigidly. I let the matter drop. The Day of Judgment would find her working downwards and not upwards.

Yesterday morning she again said, 'You're altogether too jittery for my liking. It makes me nervous. If you don't want to go for a walk then go to the cinema. See a nice film. Or read a book. I don't care what you do – within limits, of course. Only, for God's sake, stop being so jittery. I don't want you dying off on my hands in the middle of the night.'

Dying off on her hands in the middle of the night! How could she bring herself to speak to me like that? You don't say that sort of thing to a man in my position. It's insensitive. Downright insensitive. As if I could help it if I died. Recently I have noticed that Mrs Maundy has fallen into the habit of taunting me about death. It has become one of those perverse games she likes to play with me. She always manages to introduce the subject into our conversations nowadays. She enjoys observing the effect it has on me. 'I can see you don't care to talk about it,' she would remark sententiously, 'but all the same you should prepare yourself for it. Get yourself into the right frame of mind. It's no good pretending you're going to live forever.'

She treats death as if it was something unnatural and obscene. I remember what happened when Mr Maundy died. For some days none of the other tenants was aware that he had died and if I had been out at work like the rest of them, I don't suppose I would have known either. We hadn't even been told he was ill. Everything was hushed up. It was in the middle of the afternoon when there was hardly anyone about on the street I saw the hearse drive up to the front door and wondered who it could be for. There was a solitary wreath on the coffin. Two hours later, having, as you might say, disposed of the body, she was back, stern and white-faced. By evening she appeared to be perfectly recovered. I expect it will be like that when I die. No crowd of mourners. No tears. Perhaps not even a solitary wreath.

Keeping as calm as I could, I assured her I was merely suffering from lack of sleep. My jitteriness, my jumpiness, whatever it pleased her to call it, had nothing to do with dying and would she be so kind as to refrain in the future from making such callous remarks. 'Believe me,' I said, 'the last thing I would want to do is die on *your* hands in the middle of the night.' However, Mrs Maundy doesn't recognise sarcasm. It's a blind spot with her.

But enough of this. I have no desire to dwell on this subject. It depresses me.

I offered to do without the privilege of having my room cleaned every morning. Not that it is a privilege. Strictly speaking, it is my right and her duty. I pay an extra ten shillings a week to have it done. This fact doesn't prevent Mrs Maundy from behaving as if it were an imposition I personally inflict on her and from which she gains no advantage. That too is Mrs Maundy all over. She rejected my proposal out of hand, saying she had yet to meet an old person who knew what cleanliness meant. 'Not that I am blaming the little dears,' she meandered on in that sickening, sugary way of hers. 'All the same, you must admit old folk do tend to let themselves go to pieces. I hear too many stories about your sort passing over and the body not being discovered for days.' She shook her head and smiled. 'I can't afford to take any chances.' She giggled. 'In any case you pay for having your room cleaned and I don't want it to be said of me I cheat anybody out of their fair due.' 'Ah, Mrs Maundy,' I was on the point of replying, 'you cheat me out of my fair due of sleep and, what's more, you enjoy doing it.' Naturally I held my peace. 'Now, now. None of your cheek.' She squinted slyly at me and wagged a finger in my face. 'Cheek?' I was puzzled. She laughed. 'If by any chance you're planning to worm your way out of paying the little extra. . . . I've been in this business long enough to know all the little tricks and schemes you tenants can get up to.'

I protested. Ignoring her unsavoury reference to bodies not discovered for days, I insisted that I was not planning to worm my way out of anything. The extra ten shillings a week I paid for having my room cleaned was a trifling consideration compared to the precious sleep I was losing. I was perfectly willing to sacrifice it. To waive my right and relieve her of an onerous duty. 'An old man like you,' she said, 'with nothing to do all day but sit up there and stare out of your window – and, let me add, with the sunniest room in the whole house – and you object to getting up a little early. That is the only sacrifice I want you to make.' I was sorely tempted to answer her thus: 'Thank you for mentioning that. Don't forget on top of everything else you charge me an extra five shillings because it is the sunniest room in the house. It's a bit much to make a profit out of that sort of thing. But since you make a profit out of it you should learn a lesson from the sun. It works its way *upward* in the morning. Take note of that. Upward. Not downward.' I restrained myself. A long speech would have exhausted me. And, as I have already remarked, Mrs Maundy is impervious to sarcasm. Anyway, she had such a queer expression. I was puzzled. It was almost as if I had spoken my thoughts out aloud. 'I'm only jittery because I don't get enough sleep,' I said. 'Nonsense,' she replied, moving to the door and continuing to look at me with that queer expression. 'Old people don't need much sleep. Everybody knows that.' There the matter rested. How can you fight such blind obstinacy? It was the closest she and I had ever come to having an open disagreement. Which just goes to show how bad things are with me. How can she say that old people do not need much sleep? That is a lie. A fabrication.

But no! I must control myself. I must be calm. My nerves really are in shreds. I jump at the slightest sounds. Sometimes I forget what I am doing. My thoughts wander disconnectedly and inconclusively. Most worrying of all, I find I cannot say for certain whether I have actually done or said something or simply imagined myself doing or saying it. Are these the infirmities of old age? Or do they herald the onset of a horror I dare not think about too much? Not merely death – though that is horror enough. But I refuse to think about it. Not now. It has all become so confusing for me of late. My dreams can seem so real, so compellingly vivid. On the other hand, what I do when I am awake can assume all the fantastic, disjointed qualities of dreams. What a torture it is. Frequently I have seen Mrs Maundy stop and stare at me with that queer expression. 'What is it?' I ask anxiously. 'What are you looking at me like that for?'

One incident in particular obsesses me. To tell the truth, it is that which has reduced me to my present state. I had gone to the pub on the corner. Often I go there at lunch-time for an hour or two. I find it a nice change from my room and it relaxes me to see different faces and listen to the chatter of different voices. Opening the front door and walking down the steps helps to remind me that my room is the habitation of a free man and not the cell of a man imprisoned. Mrs Maundy doesn't approve of these excursions, though she herself isn't above the occasional pint. 'Wasting all your money on beer,' she would say, wagging her finger in my face. 'But just you wait. One day I shall be told you have no money left to pay the rent and then, I suppose, you will expect to live off my charity. You old people!' As if I would ever allow myself to live off her charity. That would be a fate worse than death. Still, I don't let her prevent me. A man must stick up for himself. And the fact that Mrs Maundy disapproves adds a keen edge to my pleasure. It may even be the whole pleasure.

I was sitting at my usual table in the saloon bar staring at the whirling patterns traced on the coloured glass of the windows when I suddenly became aware of someone standing in front of me. I had noticed this lady many times before without paying more than a cursory attention to her. She was one of the fixtures of the pub. An explosive cascade of bright red hair foamed down to her shoulders. It had doubtless been dyed or bleached to that striking colour. Her lips were usually daubed with some gaudy preparation not always in harmony with the painted eyebrows. To me she was virtually an extension of the coloured glass. I looked at one as I looked at the other. She was not very pretty. Flesh running to seed prematurely, bruised by indulgence. She glowed with a dull, cosmetic sheen. Perched on a bar-stool, she would survey the regulars with a kind of defiant but inviting lewdness. When she was bored, she preened and ogled herself in the mirror behind the bar. She drank a great deal. All of this I noticed because it was impossible not to. But, beyond that, I never paid her too much attention. Not until now.

'How about buying me a drink, grandfather?' She pushed up her hair and stared into the mirror. 'I'm skint this morning.' Without invitation, she sat down next to me.

The regulars were amused. 'Watch out! She's expensive, that one.'

I was so astonished – and embarrassed – by this focusing of the pub's attention on myself, I didn't know where to look.

'Don't pay any attention to them, grandfather.' She put a blue-veined hand on my coat-sleeve and stroked it gently. 'They're just jealous of you.'

I couldn't remember when last somebody had stroked me like that. My skin tingled. How soothing it was. How soothing to be stroked so gently. 'Buy me a drink, grandfather.' I must have implied assent by some subtle, surrendering motion because she immediately turned towards the bar. 'A whisky and soda, Fred. Double.' The barman gazed enquiringly at me. I must confess I blanched when I heard the order. But while she stroked me like that and while wave upon wave of stale, body-scented sweetness washed over me, I could do nothing else. Her presence encompassed me. The barman, receiving no sign to the contrary from me, shrugged and went away to pour the drink. The regulars shook their heads sadly but it was as if they did so from a receding distance.

'What's your name?' I asked.

'You can call me Sally if you like. Call me anything. Whatever takes your fancy.' She turned again to the bar. 'Hurry up with that drink, Fred. I'm parched.' Fred brought the drink himself. 'Now that is what I call real service.' Sally grinned up at him but he did not smile back. His face was blank. In one gulp she finished the drink, screwing up her face. She ordered another. This time Fred did not even look at me.

'I will call you Sally,' I said. 'I like the name.'

Sally laughed. Fred brought the second drink. She drank it as she had drunk the previous one.

'I like how you stroke my arm, Sally,' I said.

'Do you now, grandfather?' She stroked me now with the merest hint of roughness. 'Then you can buy me another drink.'

'I'm not sure I can afford it, Sally. There's the rent, you see. . . .'

She took her hand away abruptly. The painted mask was hard and closed against me.

'Don't be like that, Sally.' I did not want my skin to stop tingling. It was like ceasing to exist.

'Then buy me another, grandfather.'

There was no alternative. I was powerless, a victim of my craving for existence. For life. I ordered a drink for her and one for myself. Money flowed out of my wallet. After the fourth drink she said, 'That's better. Now I feel human again.'

'So do I, Sally,' I said. 'You make me feel human again.'

Sally tittered. Her moist fingers lifted my coat-sleeve. She stroked my bare skin. Then it was I had my inspiration. It came to me in a flash. Just like that. Perhaps the drink had something to do with it. I began to chuckle to myself. I was thinking of Mrs Maundy. What an apt revenge it would be to take a woman like this back to her respectable lodging-house, to inject into its astringent smells these waves of stale, body-scented sweetness. I was trying to picture Mrs Maundy's face as her nose picked up the corrupting trail of vapour. Imagine. This woman! In Mrs Maundy's house. I nearly strangled on my laughter.

'What's up, grandfather? Are you drunk?'

'I have an idea, Sally.' I brought my laughter under control. 'Why don't you come back to my room with me? It's not far.'

'Hey!' Sally exclaimed. 'Hey!'

'Not for long,' I coaxed.

'If you buy me a bottle of wine, grandfather,' Sally said. 'Anything for a bottle of wine.'

On the way out I bought a bottle of wine. Blank-faced Fred wrapped it in a sheet of brown paper. I tucked the bottle under my arm. As we walked back to the house Sally whistled and sang, which caused people to look at us curiously and disapprovingly. I believe she too was a little drunk after all those whiskies. But I was past caring. And whenever I thought of this woman desecrating Mrs Maundy's house, I laughed out loud.

I quietened Sally when we reached the area railings. The house watched us in stony silence. I unlocked the front door as quietly as I could and peeped in. The hall was gloomy and empty. I started at the sight of some white envelopes strewn on the red carpet. Steadying my jangled nerves, I signalled for Sally to follow me. She crept in, a hand clapped over her mouth to stifle her giggles. I stooped to pick up the envelopes, then changed my mind. What was the point? No letters ever came for me. I led Sally up the lightless stairs to my room at the top of the house. She settled herself on the bed. Now she had come I wasn't sure what to do with her. She seemed more than ever a garish apparition. Reclining on my bed, she was as startling as the envelopes strewn on the hallway carpet. Somehow my idea didn't seem so funny any more. I was frightened.

'Hey, grandfather. What's up with you? You look as if you've seen a ghost. Uncork the wine. Let's drink each other's good health.'

'Yes,' I said, striving to shut out the fear. 'The wine ... the wine. . . .'

We drank the wine, clinking glasses. It was cheap, rough stuff and it made me sleepy.

'Come, grandfather. Come and sit beside me.' She patted the bed and heaved herself over to the wall. Where she had lain the sheets were warm and scented. I nestled my head in the folds of her fleshy shoulders. She smelled of decaying roses. Her lips brushed the nape of my neck. Her presence encompassed me.

'There is something I must know, Sally.'

'What is that, grandfather?'

'Are you real, Sally? Or do I dream you?'

Sally laughed. 'Poor grandfather.' She eased herself from me and sat up. 'Does it matter?'

'No,' I said after a while. 'Perhaps it doesn't.' And, truly, it didn't seem to matter. Not just then anyway.

'Nothing matters,' Sally said.

I watched her like a child and it was like a child that I took into my mouth the speckled, ivory breast she proffered.

'Oh, Sally! I'm so old, so desolate and so frightened I won't be able to pay my rent.'

'You and your rent.' She wrenched her breast from my mouth.

I groped blindly for it.

'You've had enough, grandfather.' She clambered out of the bed and crossed to the wash-basin. She peered into the shaving mirror, pushing up her red hair and adjusting her clothes. Her hair flamed in the ugly glare flooding in from the window.

'Don't go so soon, Sally. Stay a while longer.'

Sally laughed. She came back to the bed. 'I won't be going until you pay the five pounds you owe me, grandfather.' She held out her hand.

I was dumbfounded. 'For what, Sally?' Why do I owe you five pounds?'

'For the use of my beautiful body,' Sally said.

'But I don't have five pounds to give you, Sally,' I said. 'If I do I won't have anything left to pay the rent with. You have no idea what Mrs Maundy can be like when it comes to that.'

'Pay up, grandfather.' The mask was hard again. Closed against me.

I gave her my last five pounds. 'You are heartless, Sally,' I said. 'You have no pity for an old man.'

'No,' she said. 'I have no pity.'

I listened to her footsteps fading down the stairs. From my window I watched the pitiless lady walk quickly up the street.

This is how things stand with me at present. Therein lies the source of my sleeplessness and my nightmares. Today Mrs Maundy will expect me to hand over the rent. She will not ask for it directly. She never does. 'It makes it all so crude and mercenary,' she says. Nevertheless, she will be expecting it. A week in advance to be paid on Friday. That, despite her mock delicacy, is one of the laws from which she never swerves. And I have nothing to give her. My consolation is that I may have imagined the whole thing. Dreamt it. But, if that is the case, then where has the money disappeared to? I can't even lay hands on my wallet. It has vanished. I have looked on top of the wardrobe. Under the bed. I have crawled, scraping my knees, combing every inch of the floor. I have searched high and low for it. It is slowly driving me mad. Possibly I am already mad. Yes, that is the word. That is the thought I dare not think.

Because even if Sally belonged to one of my dreams it is only the mad who dream so vividly. Oh pitiless lady, did I invent you? Did I spin you out of my longings? Maybe, as you suggested, it doesn't really matter. For, imaginary or real, and pitiless as you were, I still yearn to lay my head on your sweet-smelling breast and sleep, like a child forever. My life ebbs for lack of you, Sally. When I think of how you stroked me and how my skin tingled, I want to scream and scream and scream. . . .

No! No! I must stop travelling round in this despairing circle. That is the recipe for madness. I refuse to work myself up into a frenzy as I crouch here like a supplicant, vainly holding out my clammy, freezing hands in front of the electric fire.

This desire to scream scares me. The man who lives in the house opposite, he screams. Like me, he has a room on the top floor. But facing north as it does, the sun rarely shines into it. Mrs Maundy constantly threatens to have them – whoever 'they' might be – 'cart him away.' I often wonder where they take such people and what they do with them. She would not hesitate to let 'them' cart me away if I began to scream like him. Therefore I mustn't. I must be sensible and control myself. 'He shouldn't be allowed to upset decent people,' she says, 'screaming and carrying on the way he does. It's a disgrace. Mind, I'm not saying I'm not sorry for him and all that. He served his King and country in two world wars. But that is no excuse for upsetting decent people. He should be locked away for his own good.' Locked away for his own good! Such is the extent of Mrs Maundy's gratitude to a man 'who served his King and country in two world wars.' She told me he had been a prisoner of the Japanese during the last war. The experience had driven him insane. He stands for hours at that window of his jumping up and down like a jack-in-the-box and screaming until he is hoarse. 'You yellow bastards! You yellow bastards!' Terrible phantoms must patrol the darkened spaces of that deranged mind. What a lot of madness there is in this city. It's quite appalling.

My head is aching. It's horribly cold and damp in this room despite the fire. Mrs Maundy will be here any minute, rattling her keys like a jailer. Yes. Here she comes, predictable as some infernal clockwork. How I loathe the slow, heavy, martyred tread with which she climbs the stairs. Like doom itself. She could move with greater speed if she cared to. There is nothing to prevent her. She is always boasting about the fine state of her health.

She enters, as is her wont, without knocking. I have successfully conquered the irritation which this used to cause me. She leans in the doorway, leering at me. 'What a smell! You would think I hadn't cleaned this room for days. You could at least draw the curtains and get some light in here.' She crinkles her nose. 'Poof! What a smell.'

'Does it smell like roses?' I ask, half-eagerly, half-fearfully.

'Roses indeed!' She giggles. 'Rotting roses maybe.' She shakes her head at me. 'And there you are grumbling about me cleaning it for you.'

'It's not that I grumble about,' I say. 'It's. . . .'

'I know. I know. You're a lazy old man.' She pulls the curtains. The light dazzles me. I close my smarting eyes. 'It snowed during the night, did you know?' I open my eyes. The roofs are white with it. The gardens are white with it. The pavements are white with it. I am oddly thrilled at the thought of all that whiteness blanketing the city. 'I hate snow in the town.' Mrs Maundy's voice breaks rudely into my reverie and scatters it. 'Out in the country, though, it's very beautiful. Nothing to beat our English countryside is what I always say.'

That's Mrs Maundy all over. Giving her opinions about everything. She bristles with opinions. Who gives a damn about what she thinks of the snow in town or country? She probably never set foot in the country in her entire, godforsaken life. Now she is staring at me with that queer expression again. 'What is it?' I ask. 'What are you looking at me like that for?'

'You're a funny one,' she says. 'And getting funnier every day by the looks of it.'

'How do you mean, "funny"?'

'Oh nothing, nothing,' she replies hastily. 'It all comes out in the wash, I expect.' She considers me wisely.

'Listen, Mrs Maundy,' I say with sudden decision, 'there is something I have to tell you.'

She props herself against the broom and stares at me interestedly.

But my courage declines as rapidly as it had arisen. 'Another time,' I say, glancing evasively about the room. 'When you are less busy.' Thankfully, she does not press me. My cowardice disgusts me. I begin afresh. 'It's to do with ... with....'

'With what?' She eyes me with visibly intensifying interest.

'Nothing,' I say. 'It's not all that important anyway.'

She wags a finger at me. 'You have something weighing on your conscience. I can tell that a mile off. Out with it!'

'Later,' I say, 'at breakfast.'

'You old people are so secretive.' She busies herself with the cleaning. I go to the window and look out at the snow-covered street. In my mind's eye I see the pitiless Sally walking quickly up it.

I have my breakfast in the poky little dining-room, covered with flowery paper, on the ground floor. As I descend the stairs the smell of brewing coffee drifts up to meet me. I collect my newspaper from the table in the hall and shuffle into the dining-room, pretending to be absorbed in the headlines. I don't look at the other tenants who all have their heads bent low over their plates. We never greet each other. That is the established practice in this house. I slide as noiselessly as possible into my chair. Herbert Maundy sits next to me. He is a dour, unfriendly man. I don't recall ever having seen him smile. Once or twice I have met him on the street and he betrayed not the smallest sign of recognition. Mrs Maundy describes her son as a 'working man.' But what Herbert Maundy works at is a mystery to me. Even his mother is reticent about it. All I know is that he leaves the house on a bicycle which, when it is not in use, he keeps carefully covered with a sheet of canvas. However, it is not the unresolved mystery of Herbert's employment which disturbs me. It is his eyes. They are of a mesmeric blue-grey colour – the colour you sometimes see in a thundery sky. Lifeless and yet threatening. Cold eyes unwarmed by any human sympathy. He never seems to be seeing what is directly in front of him. Those eyes, unbending, inflexible, see only what they choose to see. They have the glazed expression of the blind. But Herbert Maundy is not blind. That is why he frightens me. He invades my nightmares, presiding over them like the Angel of Death. And he frightens not only me, I suspect. I have observed that his mother watches him warily and never speaks a rough or even mildly scolding word to him.

Mrs Maundy is talking about the snow – though to no one in particular. She brings me a tiny glass of orange juice and a rack with three thin slices of cold toast.

'How would you like your eggs this morning, dear?' She invariably calls me 'dear' when the other tenants are within earshot.

'Scrambled,' I say, without holding out any great hopes.

'If *you* had to scrub the pots and pans you wouldn't want scrambled eggs, you old dear.' She twists my ear playfully. 'Why don't you have some nice fried eggs instead? I have two keeping warm in the oven and it would be such a waste. . . .'

I nod resignedly, giving in to her blackmail. She brings me the two rubbery fried eggs. This is another of the perverse games she likes to play with me. Dangling non-existent choices. She leaves me and starts to fuss around Herbert.

'Is your egg right for you, Herbert dear?'

Herbert is having boiled eggs. For some reason he always has his eggs done differently from the rest of us.

'Yes, mother. They're just right.'

'Some more toast?'

'No, thank you, mother. I have quite enough.' Herbert slurps his coffee noisily. He is a messy eater. Mrs Maundy doesn't dare complain when he spills things. But if I do I never hear the end of it.

I cannot concentrate on my newspaper this morning. For distraction I turn to the pair of ragged budgerigars perched in their cage on top of a dark-stained chest of drawers. Like those of us sitting at the table, they pay no attention to each other. Passion has long been killed in them. They resemble waxen images. Unfortunate things. You should be wheeling freely through the African jungles – or wherever it is you come from. What a fate for you to have fallen into the clutches of Mrs Maundy. You should not have let her imprison you like this. I lift my gaze to the photograph of the fluffy white Persian cat hanging on the wall above the cage. The dead blue eyes stare back at me. I am reminded of Herbert and look away. The budgerigars are motionless in their cage. They will probably die soon. Just as well. But how cruel that they should die in captivity. Perhaps you are dreaming of the warmth and freedom of your tropical home. What an indignity for you to die in a cage. Ironically, Mrs Maundy proclaims herself an animal lover. Every year, with loud trumpeting, she sends off a five-pound postal order to the RSPCA and another for three pounds to the Donkey Sanctuary. 'The poor dumb creatures,' she would say. 'I feel so sorry for the poor dumb creatures.'

'You haven't touched your food, dear.' Mrs Maundy bustles about me. 'Waste not, want not. That's my motto.'

I have no appetite but, to avoid a lecture, I apply myself with as much enthusiasm as I can summon.

There is a clatter of cups and saucers as Herbert bangs his fists on the table and levers himself upright. Though this is an habitual flourish of his, the signature with which he ends every meal, it has never ceased to jar. I sit, tensely expectant, waiting for it to happen. This morning it is particularly bad. My nerves ripple in a radiation of fine, needling pain. The goose pimples rise. My ear drums reverberate with the lingering echo. I shut my eyes, biting on my lower lip.

'So jumpy, dear. So jumpy.' Mrs Maundy pats me on the back. She seems to be amused. Bending down confidentially, she whispers, 'We will wait till they all clear out, dear. Then you can tell me what's on your mind.' However, it is a whisper calculated to carry. The tenants glance up furtively.

Herbert jumps up noisily from his chair, dabbing his lips with a spotted handkerchief. 'I'll be off now, mother. See you later.' He goes out from the dining-room. Mrs Maundy follows him with her eyes. Herbert's footsteps thud ponderously along the hallway carpet. The front door opens and slams. The walls shake and ornaments rattle. In a sense, I am glad there is at least one person in the world who frightens Mrs Maundy. I regard it as salutary. Still, that is cold comfort to me. Between the two of them, taunting mother and dead-eyed son, I feel trapped.

One by one the others finish their breakfast and Mrs Maundy removes the dirty plates and glasses, piling them on the draining-board. These successive departures and Mrs Maundy's journeys between dining-room and kitchen are like the swings of a pendulum ticking away the seconds to the doom which is about to devour me. I am seized by panic and try to eat more quickly. The intention is frustrated. Husks of dry toast lodge in my throat and almost succeed in choking me. I cough and splutter.

'I hope you're not dying, dear,' Mrs Maundy calls out from the kitchen amid a clinking of cutlery. 'Remember our little secret. You're only allowed to die *after* you've told me.' She stands in the kitchen doorway and laughs.

The last of the tenants has finished. He rises, bids Mrs Maundy goodbye and departs. I am alone. Alone with Mrs Maundy! She comes in from the kitchen to take away the remaining plates. I struggle to my feet as she does so, pushing my plate aside. The taste of oily egg circulates nauseatingly at the base of my throat.

'Are you *through*?' she asks, staring in disbelief at my plate.

'I'm not very hungry this morning,' I manage to say. 'My stomach is upset.' I hold on to the chair for support. My legs feel unsteady.

'Ungrateful old man,' she says. 'You don't appreciate what I do for you. You wouldn't get as much as what's left on your plate in most establishments. They will give you a continental breakfast. Have you any idea what a *continental breakfast* is?' She breathes indignantly at me. 'What I provide costs me a pretty penny, let me tell you.'

Murmuring apologies, I run out of the room. My legs make the decision rather than me. Mrs Maundy pursues me to the foot of the stairs. 'Wait!' she cries. 'You still haven't told me that little secret of yours.'

'I have no secrets,' I reply, pausing on the first landing. 'I have no secrets at all. . . .'

'It will all come out in the wash, I expect,' she says. 'Never mind.'

What relief courses through me when I finally reach the haven of my own room. I lock the door and collapse against it, fighting to steady my nerves and ward off the nausea. There is a burning tightness in my chest. I listen to see if Mrs Maundy has followed me. But I do not hear that slow, heavy tread. I relax somewhat. I cross to

the washbasin and examine my face in the shaving-mirror. How pale
and wild and hunted it looks. Not the face of a man in serene old age. I
open the window wide and thrust my head outside. The fresh air is
reviving and I inhale deeply. The morning is clear and crisp and the
blue sky is without a cloud.

It occurs to me I should go for a walk in this lovely weather. It
would probably do me good to get out of the house for a bit. To taste
once more my dwindling freedom. I dress hurriedly and sneak down
the stairs, hoping to avoid Mrs Maundy and her inevitable questions.
But, as luck would have it, I stumble on her in the hall.

'I thought you were ill,' she says, blocking my passage.

'I'm just going out for a short while,' I reply, hating myself for
behaving like a prisoner. 'To the park. It might clear my head a little.'
She looks at me in sceptical silence. Then, like a jailer, she makes way
reluctantly. She watches me as I open the door and go down the front
steps to the street.

'Take care you don't catch a chill,' she shouts after me. 'At your age
that could prove fatal.'

The sunshine has lured many people to the park. After the walk, I
am tired. I sit on a bench and try to read the newspaper I have brought
with me. A chill wind is blowing. Bloated pigeons peck at the crumbs
a woman is scattering on the snowy grass. She laughs ringingly as the
pigeons swarm greedily about her feet. Several people are exercising
their dogs. In the blue distance beyond the farthest line of trees a mist
is forming, shot though by the copper sun. Suddenly I have the
absurd notion I am invisible and seeing everything in slow motion.
The dogs, the people, the pigeons, the woman's ringing laughter seem
unrelented elements of a fantasy in which I have no part. At one
moment I am a giant watching the antics of a pygmy race. At another,
I am the pygmy and they are giants and I am terrified of being
crushed. I have to remind myself where I am and what I have come
there to do. 'Only the park,' I assure myself repeatedly. 'Only the
park.' I do my utmost to concentrate on the newspaper. The words
refuse to yield their sense. They perform a blurring dance on the
paper. I try to recall the sound of Mrs Maundy's voice. But that too
possesses an alien quality and is soaked up in the hallucinatory
sensation. It is as though life itself – not simply *my* life – is ebbing,
rushing away from me into a black limbo. But the strangest thing of all
is how calm I am. I seem to be standing at a certain remove from
myself and noting, with a kind of dispassion, even my own terror.

Yes, it is that dispassion which is the strangest thing. I pinch my arm but the skin is numb and I feel no pain. My heart is racing and my head is spinning. What shame, I think, to die in front of these people. Without a name. Without a past. Another body. 'Help me!' I want to shout. 'I am dying without dignity. You must help me!' The woman with the ringing laughter scuttles towards me. 'Can't you see you're scaring away the birds?' Her words are like an antidote. The chaos recedes. The world gradually comes into focus again. I rise from the bench, leave the park and walk slowly back to my room, buffeted by a raw wind.

Mrs Maundy is cleaning the hall. 'The return of the prodigal son,' she says.

I do not answer her but go straight up to my room. Opening the window, I look out. The snow is melting. On the street the brown slush is furrowed by the tracks of cars. Water drips from the black branches of the chestnut trees. The weather has changed. This swift transformation of the white morning alarms me. Storm clouds flurry across the sky as if propelled by a malevolent god. The grey light is probing and harsh. Then I hear my neighbour opposite.

'You yellow bastards! You yellow bastards!'

I shut my window quickly and turn my back on him. Lying down on the bed, I close my eyes, praying for sleep.

I wake with a start. Someone is in the room. A prowling, hostile presence. 'Who is it? Who is there?' I raise my head cautiously from the pillow. Herbert Maundy is standing over me. He fixes me with his dead, blue-grey eyes. 'What do you want with me? I have done nothing to you.' He does not reply. His head inclines towards me until I can see only his eyes. They are as menacing and ominous as the sky itself. 'I've done nothing to you. If it's the rent your mother sent you for tell her I can pay. I'll find it and pay her in full.' He does not answer. I cannot escape the dead eyes of my Angel of Death. 'Why can't you speak? Why don't you *ever* speak to me? Say something. Say anything. You shouldn't frighten an old man ... a dying old man.' The awful eyes dim. They grow distant. Herbert vanishes as soundlessly as he came. For a time I lie there, unable to move. The room is cold and dark. It is late. Soon I will be called to account. The wallet ... the wallet....

I dash to the wardrobe and frenziedly ransack the pockets of my coat, my three pairs of trousers, my two jackets. Nothing. I drag a chair over and, hauling myself on to it, sweep my hands across the top of the wardrobe. Nothing. I fall on my knees and thrust my hands into the gap between it and the wall. I insert my arm as far as it will go. Nothing. Nothing but cobwebs and dust. Still on my knees, I crawl over every inch of the floor. Nothing. I lie flat on my stomach and grope under the bed. Nothing. Nothing. Nothing. If only I had some evidence one way or the other. The wine bottle for instance. I start to cry.

'What *are* you doing down there?' Mrs Maundy has made one of her silent invasions.

Why can't you leave me in peace, I want to say. Why can't you and your son leave an old man in peace. This is my room. I have always managed to pay the rent for it. Surely I can do what I like in here. On my patch of earth.

'I was hunting for my shoes,' I say. 'I can't seem to find them anywhere.' I haul myself effortfully to my feet.

She has that queer look again.

'What is it?' I ask. 'What are you looking at me like that for?'

'If you want to find your shoes it might help if you switch on the light,' she replies. She flicks the switch.

The light. I had not realised. And it is cold too. I had forgotten how cold it was. Clasping my arms about me, I shiver.

'I came up to see you earlier,' she says. 'But you were asleep.'

'Asleep . . . yes, yes, I was asleep.' I do not look at her.

'Since you haven't had any lunch,' she says, 'I thought I would ask you to have some tea with me. Yyou must be hungry.'

'Tea,' I repeat stupidly. 'You want me to have tea with you.'

'I've baked a lovely cake.' She smiles cheerfully. 'With nuts and raisins.'

I fight my surging anguish. 'I'll be down in a minute,' I mutter. 'Just let me find my shoes and I'll be down.'

She points to the floor near the foot of the bed. 'There they are,' she says, not troubling to conceal her amusement. 'Now don't be long.' She wags her finger at me and goes, not closing the door.

Tea indeed! A lovely cake with nuts and raisins! I am too well acquainted with Mrs Maundy's little tricks to be taken in by these blandishments. She is planning one of her perverse games with me. I don't believe for a minute she is concerned about my hunger. Anyway, I am not hungry. Her acts of 'kindness' do not fool me. Their purpose is clear enough. To fox me. To throw me off my guard. I remember the day, some months ago, when, out of the blue, she came up here and presented me with a book of crossword puzzles. 'To keep your mind occupied,' she said. 'It's bad for old people to get bored. The Devil always finds mischief for idle hands.' But then, like now, it wasn't genuine concern for my well-being that prompted her. Not at all. Her joy consisted in watching the confusion into which this act of apparent generosity threw me. Her invitation to tea isn't very different. She knows something is wrong and, most probably, she knows it is to do with the rent. Mrs Maundy can sniff these things out. She is an extremely clever and observant woman. However, she won't come right out and say so. That isn't her style. She must have her fun first. Play cat and mouse with me. And only when she has wearied of the amusement will the trap be sprung without further ceremony.

'Yoo hoo up there! What are you doing?' Mrs Maundy's strident tones drift up from the hallway. 'The tea will be undrinkable if you don't come down straight away.'

'Coming! Coming!' I shout back. I try to make myself as decent as I can as quickly as I can. My fingers are fumbling and awkward and my palms are moist. I feel feverish. The journey down the stairs is like the journey of a condemned man to the scaffold. Mrs Maundy is waiting for me in the hall.

'Ah! There you are at last, you old dawdler.' She hustles me into the sitting-room. Two arm-chairs are drawn up in front of the small, brown-tiled fireplace. The banked-up coals glow orange in the grate. A round table on spindly legs is placed between the chairs. I see the virgin cake, the teapot sheathed with its woollen cap, two cups and two saucers, a shining knife. They are arrayed like the instruments of my impending execution. The room is crowded with furniture. I sink down in one of the arm-chairs and gaze at the fire. My doom sounds faintly in my ears like the crash of distant but approaching thunder. Mrs Maundy, chattering gaily, pours the tea and cuts meagre slices of the cake.

'Isn't this nice and cosy? After a hard day's work to relax in front of a cheerful fire with a cup of tea.' With a self-satisfied grunt, Mrs Maundy settles herself into the chair beside me. The springs creak. She sighs. 'It's so good to be able to put your feet up at the end of a hard day.' She glances at me out of the corner of her eyes. 'But I don't suppose you know what bliss it is. I mean, having nothing to do all day you wouldn't appreciate it.'

I remain silent, staring at the fire.

'Just think how lucky you are,' she adds. 'All you have to worry about is paying the rent. That apart. . . .' She waves her hand.

On the mantelpiece, occupying pride of place, is a photograph in a gilt frame of a bland, smooth-featured man, probably in his thirties. I grasp at this straw. 'Mr Maundy?'

'No,' she replies shortly. 'That is a friend of mine. He died during the war. I married Mr Maundy just after the war.' 'After' is spoken pointedly. 'He was in the Merchant Navy. His ship got torpedoed.'

I do not say anything. She seems irritated and speaks with a mixture of harshness and indifference.

'I've never been beyond these shores and never wanted to,' she says. 'I was happy to stay at home. But he – he was a great traveller.' Her eyes rest briefly and lovelessly on the photograph. Is she praising him? Or is she cursing him? I cannot make it out. Her tone is impenetrable. 'They finally got him though.' She speaks almost with triumph. 'Whoosh! Through the water it went.' Her arm dives towards the fire. 'Whoosh! A direct hit. And that was that.' She blinks reproachfully at me. 'You're not eating your cake. Is your stomach still upset?' She grins slyly at me.

I nibble at the edges of the yellow slice she has rested on my saucer. She watches me intently. Any moment now, I think. It will happen at any moment. The front door opens and closes with a bang. The house shudders.

'That will be Herbert,' she says absently.

I listen to Herbert's ponderous footsteps thudding on the carpet and ascending the stairs to his room.

'I wonder what it feels like to drown,' she says. 'To know you're going under with no hope of rescue – like my friend must have done. To have the water closing about you. Unable to breathe. Sinking deeper and deeper.' She is all harshness now. Herbert moves noisily overhead. 'Which is the worst way to die? By water? By fire?'

How mercilessly she taunts me.

'Are you afraid of dying?' She bites into her slice of cake and chews methodically.

'I try not to think about it too much.' My palms are moist. The thunder rolls nearer.

'Don't you now?' She arranges herself more comfortably. 'But you should prepare yourself. My friend wasn't prepared. But Mr Maundy was. I saw to that. And I tell you the same things I told him. I keep telling you. . . .'

'I know you do.' I answer, turning towards her. 'You torture me with it.'

'Torture you, do I?' She seems mildly astonished. She laughs. 'What an odd fellow you are. I try to help you and you call it torture.'

'Yes. You brought me down here in order to torture me at your ease. While putting your feet up. . . .' Again I have that strange feeling of dispassion. I jump up from the chair. The thunder rolls and crashes deafeningly about me, one with Herbert Maundy's resounding footfalls. 'You brought me down here to play cat and mouse with me. But I won't allow it.'

'Cat and mouse!' She shakes with laughter.

'If you know I can't pay my rent, why don't you say so straight out? Get it over with instead of. . . .'

'So,' she says, 'now we have it. From your own lips. I said it would all come out in the wash, didn't I?' She wags her finger at me. 'You've squandered all your money in the pub and now you can't pay your rent. You're begging for my charity.'

'Never! Never would I beg for your charity. That would be a fate worse than death by drowning and fire put together.'

'You ungrateful old man! After all I've done for you. . . .' She is shouting at me.

'Don't you dare shout at me.' I am standing by her chair. A raging, black cloud envelops me. 'You're quite right. I squandered my money. Every last penny of it. And I'll even tell you what I squandered it on. *Who* I squandered it on. I spent it all on a woman. . . .'

'You liar!' Mrs Maundy is not smiling now. She rises from her chair. 'What woman would so much as look at you? You – you with one foot already in the grave. . . .'

'I spent every last penny I possessed on a woman I picked up in the pub. On a woman of the streets. A common whore!'

She stares at me with speechless venom.

'I brought this common whore back to your house. Back to *your* respectable house! And . . . and I. . . .'

'Your brain is rotting,' she says. 'You lost your money. Your wallet. I found it out in the hall. Lying there. . . .'

She wants to make me believe it's a dream. She has invented another of her perverse games. But I will not be cheated. I cannot be cheated like this. 'Show me! But you can't show me. I won't be taken in by your tricks any more.'

'You're mad,' she says. 'Mad! I'm going to let them come and cart you away.'

She retreats as I advance on her. But she cannot go very far. Not in this small room crowded with furniture. She cowers against a table. I bring my face close to her. 'A common whore entered your house, Mrs Maundy. Smelling of rotting roses!'

Mrs Maundy has such a comical expression. She is babbling away. What a commotion there is on the stairs. I have never been able to cope with hysterical women. Herbert is bearing down straight towards me with those awful eyes of his starting out of his head. Mrs Maundy lies limp in my arms. Not me, Herbert. Not me. I'm not the one in need of attention. You are making a big mistake. It's your mother you should be tending, Herbert. But what is the good? He never sees what is in front of him. Why is he pinioning me like this? What have I done? All I can see is my Angel of Death with the dead blue-grey eyes. They are the colour of the pitiless sky itself. If Mrs Maundy would let me sleep, if only she would let me sleep, my nightmares would, I am sure, vanish into thin air.

Pieces

Living in Earls Court

I have had the dubious distinction of having lived in Earls Court twice: once (for which I should be excused) right at the beginning when I had only just arrived in England; then again right at the end (when I should have known better) just before I left for India. On both occasions departure was a cause for celebration. I was never happy in Earls Court. The account I shall give of it, therefore, cannot be free from the bias that unhappiness necessarily entails. I view Earls Court through the jaundiced eyes of an ingrained dislike; and where others might see a raffish charm I see only a kind of horror. However, my prejudice should not be interpreted as an implied distaste for London as a whole. That is not the case. I have also lived in Notting Hill Gate, Stockwell, Fulham and Ladbroke Grove. In none of these areas – including Earls Court – did I stay longer than a year. Thus the experiences derived from each tend to fuse into a single, indivisible history. On their own they are disjointed fragments. Earls Court is merely an episode – or rather, two episodes.

I was nineteen years old when I left Trinidad to come as a student to England. Coming as I did from the far outside, it was natural that I should think of London as existing in the round. Discrimination did of course develop later on. Ladbroke Grove, Notting Hill Gate, Earls Court ... I began to appreciate that they all harboured their own peculiar vibrations. But, at the time, London was simply London: the Big City of which I had always dreamt.

For a few days immediately after I arrived I stayed with my brother in a hotel in Blackheath. The hotel was inhabited chiefly by the middle-aged and solitary. Memories of Blackheath are tinged with the semi-magical quality which invests the week of my arrival: the impression of fantasy – of unreal things happening in an unreal world – was strong. There was a visit to the Observatory at Greenwich. A white line painted on the floor of a light-washed room: the meridian. I remember standing on a grassy hill and looking down at the silver sweep of the Thames knitted with a spidery fretwork of cranes and ships' masts. In a restaurant I ate my first rum-baba.

But the magic soon faded. The polite rituals of the hotel functioned in a void. I began to feel isolated in Blackheath. It seemed an infinity away from what I fondly imagined to be the centre of things. Where that was I had no clear idea. Neither could I say with any certainty what I expected to find when I got there. The pink glow kindling the sky nightly promised adventure. I wished to draw closer to the fiery source producing it. The Big City was beckoning.

Finally I saw a room advertised at a price I could just afford. I rang the number supplied. It turned out to be an Accommodation Agency. Was the room they had advertised still available? Unfortunately no. However – the lady's voice tinkled encouragingly at the other end of the line – they had several like it on their books. Why did I not come to their office?

The office, a cramped cubicle approached up a tortuous flight of stairs, was on the Earls Court Road. A wiry woman in a luminously red cardigan was in charge. I introduced myself.

'Ah! So you are the foreign gentleman who rang earlier.' Her voice had shed its telephonic twinkle. But it was not unfriendly. 'Come in and have a seat and we shall see what we can do for you. We have managed to fix up quite a few coloured people in our time.' She moved briskly to a paper-cluttered desk and sat down. 'Now you say you can't afford more than five pounds a week . . .'

'Maximum,' I said quickly.

'Quite, quite . . . mmm . . .' She thumbed through a box of index cards. 'Student?' she enquired absently after a while.

'Yes.'

'Studying what?'

I told her. The words sounded impossibly big and foolish.

'Really!' Extracting an index card she frowned thoughtfully at it. She reached for the telephone and dialled. 'Some of these landladies are a bit fussy when it comes to . . .' She reverted to her telephonic twinkle. 'Hello. Is that Mrs —— ? This is the —— Accommodation Agency here. I've got a young foreign student who is looking for a room. He seems a nice quiet fellow. What's that? Yes, I'm afraid he is. But . . . no, no. Not at all. Of course I understand.' The receiver clicked down. She considered me. 'Next time I think we'll say straight off that you come from India. It's better not to beat around the bush, don't you agree? Anyway some of them don't mind Indians so much.'

'But I don't come from India.'

'You don't?' She stared at me. 'But you look Indian.'

'Well, I am Indian. But I was born in the West Indies.'

'The West Indies!' She seemed vaguely aghast.

I understood. Sufficient unto any man the handicap of being straightforwardly Indian or straightforwardly West Indian. But to contrive somehow to combine the two was a challenge to reason. An Indian from the West Indies! I was guilty of a compound sin.

'We'll say you are Indian,' she said firmly. 'It's better not to confuse the issue. Don't you agree?' She beamed at me.

'Perhaps we'd better forget the whole thing,' I said.

'Don't give up so easily. We have fixed up a lot of coloured people in our time. Why not you?' She gazed defiantly at the box of index cards.

This was my initiation in the sub-world of 'racial prejudice'. I had read and heard about it at home: nearly everyone who had been to England had his own cautionary tale to tell. Now it was happening to me and I could not quite bring myself to believe in it. Of course I had noticed the slogans daubed on the walls of the tube stations, and morbidly deciphered the illiteracies displayed in the windows of newsagents. 'Room to Let: Regret no Kolored.' 'Room to Let: Europeen Gent. Only.' 'Room to let: Kolored Pipple Need Not Apply.' These signs depressed and amused. It seemed incredible that they should refer to me.

I was surprised to find myself categorised as 'coloured': in Trinidad the term is applied to people of mixed blood – usually black diluted with a dash of 'Europeen'. I have always thought it a detestable euphemism. Nevertheless, since it was one of the basic words in the vocabulary of the boarding-house culture, I had (albeit under protest) to learn to live with it.

I waited while the lady dialled number after number. '. . . I've got a young Indian student here who is looking for a room . . .' Her eyes were clouding with exhaustion. I stopped listening. Then, out of the blue: 'Yes. Yes. As I said, he seems a nice, quiet type. I shall send him around straight away. He's right here with me in the office.' She put the receiver down and regarded me with an air of triumph. 'I told you we could fix you up. Didn't I?'

The house to which I was directed was on one of those streets that lead off the Earls Court Road and blossom into the sudden respectability of a tree-shaded garden square. A roster of names, each with its attendant buzzer, festooned the door. This was bedsitter land with a vengeance. The entrance hall smelled dismally of a mixture of disinfectant and polish. Keys jangling from a giant ring at her waist, the housekeeper led me up several curving flights of red-carpeted stairs towards the twilit region of the top floor. With jailer-like neutrality, she ushered me into a charmless cell, obviously the product of sub-division of what must once have been an average-sized room. An insubstantial hardboard partition, plastered over with a flowery wallpaper, rose with grim commercial finality to the ceiling. The furnishing was spartan: a narrow bed; a dresser with a mirror; a solitary, soiled armchair; a coffee table emblematically ringed with the marks of countless hot cups. The floor was covered by a strip of grey, threadbare carpet. Daylight filtered through a small sash window. A gas fire, inserted into a scorched recess, completed the desolation. This was not how I imagined it would be. The harshness of that room repelled me. Was this the romance of the city? What kind of adventure could spring from a cell such as this? At five guineas a week (without breakfast) it was more than I could really afford. But the prospect of starting from scratch ('. . . I've got a young Indian student here . . .') was equally intimidating. Despairingly, I said I would take it. The Accommodation Agency duly extorted its tribute of a week's rent, and I moved in.

It was an introduction – which could have been gentler – into a new mode of existence. Since then I have lost count of the number of rooms in which I have slept. In Trinidad my geography was stable: I can recall no more than two or three rooms in the course of my nineteen years there. That cell in Earls Court initiated a nomadism which has persisted into the present and which shows no signs of abating. It has become second nature to me. Today, my attachment to Trinidad is sentimental; a child's attachment to the place where he grew up. It does not go beyond that because my real life lies elsewhere – though precisely where it is difficult to say. In London, the vestigial Trinidadian 'roots' I had arrived with underwent a gradual petrification. But the city, while exacting its price, did not confer a new identity: I do not consider myself a Londoner. On a conventional assessment this must be counted as a loss. Yet, on the other hand, it ought to be added that I am not bothered by it. I have no desire either to fabricate new 'roots' or rediscover old ones. Lack of acquaintance has diminished to vanishing point my knowledge of what it means and feels like to 'belong' to a community. This is why I regard with nervous suspicion all those who proclaim its virtues in poetry, prose and politics.

The three weeks I spent in that room are among the unhappiest I can remember. A dreadful anonymity descended. In the mornings I went to the nearby Wimpy Bar where I drank several cups of coffee and pretended to be absorbed in the newspaper. At midday I went to a dark, dingy pub frequented by elderly charladies who drank bottled Guinness. I would buy a pint of bitter and a plate of cheese and tomato sandwiches. In the evening I went to a coffee bar manned by Italians, where I bought more sandwiches and drank more coffee. Through the plate glass windows I would watch the life of Earls Court stream past. Then I would return to my cell and crawl into my narrow bed. I hardly ever saw my fellow inmates whose names decorated the front door. Two girls shared the room across the corridor. They would come in late, creaking furtively up the stairs and laughing softly. As they prepared for bed I could hear the surreptitious sounds of pop music from their record player – the house forbade anything of the sort after eleven o'clock. Next door – behind the partition – was a man who coughed terribly. Some nights, when he was expecially wracked, he would get up and pace the room, muttering to himself in between his spasms. Once I met the girls in the corridor but we passed without acknowledgment. Amazingly enough, I never set eyes on my cough-stricken neighbour.

The days slipped by in a haze of coffee, stale sandwiches and sickly beer. The visits I had planned – to palaces, museums, art galleries – were never made. I had become frightened of the city and my fright expressed itself in dulled curiosity and inertia. The glow lighting the sky nightly was transformed from a promise into a threat. I lost the desire to seek out its hidden source. My family to whom I had bid goodbye not that long ago seemed to belong to another life which had been snatched away from me. Hourly, Trinidad receded. I was being emptied; reduced to nothing in that room. How easy it is to be swallowed by the city! The legacy left by that time has not entirely vanished. Even now, I occasionally experience a thrill of fear when I suddenly come upon one of the dizzying vistas of anonymous urban housing and have to walk along streets that are like mirror reflections of each other. Though it was not what my innocence had envisaged, those three weeks were an adventure. But the adventure exists only in retrospect: at the time I was not even fully conscious of my misery.

Six years later – and under very different circumstances – I returned to Earls Court. Much had happened to me in the intervening period: I had completed an undistinguished four years at Oxford; I had acquired a wife; I had written my first novel. My boyhood was over. Something else had happened: my attitude to the city had altered. I had lost the desire to lay bare its secrets. Perhaps I had stopped believing there were any secrets to be laid bare. When I arrived in Earls Court for the second time it was my fourth change of address in two years. By then nomadism had become a habit. Shifting restlessly from one set of furnished rooms to another, I was living, in a sense, like a vagrant. The city was merely a convenient backdrop for my activities. While being in it I was not truly of it. No doubt writing and the private world it entails assisted in the process of withdrawal and detachment. I was leading an artifical and protected existence. Matters might have been different if I had been forced to earn my living in the ordinary way. As it was, I had little direct contact with the life lived around me. I observed, as it were, through glass.

Whether by day or by night, Earls Court knows no stillness; no moments of tranquillity. The big lorries thunder ceaselessly. On the Earls Court Road noise acquires a demonic quality, endowing the constant flow with an autonomous, impersonal character. Step out of your front door and the reverberating thunder breaks loose like a dammed wall of water obtaining release. The air is a soup of diesel oil and petrol fumes, rank and acrid to the taste. Have a window cleaned and within hours a mildewed sediment will spread like mould across the glass. It is the industrial equivalent of the encroaching jungle. Puny men, trapped in this tide, can meet sudden death. The drama unfolds with the rigidity of a sacrificial ritual: a screech of brakes; the peculiar thud of unyielding metal on soft human flesh; a pool of blood staining the asphalt; the chorus wail of a police siren. Early the next morning a truck of the Royal Borough will arrive and wash away the lingering traces of the sacrifice into the gutter. The God has been appeased.

The tube station is the soul of the place made visible. Around and about it Earls Court anchors itself. Out of it is disgorged and into it is ingested a steady stream of humanity. A multi-hued, multi-lingual crowd is always gathered near its entrance. Earls Court is nothing if not cosmopolitan. Long-haired students from the Continent weighted under rucksacks studded with the flags of their countries pore over street maps. Bearded Australians study the poster that invites them to join the Zambesi Club – Rhodesians, South Africans, New Zealanders and Canadians also welcome. West Indians – lithe black bucks dressed in the height of fashion – parade aimlessly. A shrunken veteran of the First World War, a hat upturned at his feet, scrapes at a violin. Another ferrety old man, half-asleep on a box, clutches in his lap a stack of weeklies from the 'underground' press. Waking with a start, he holds aloft *The Red Mole*; and then, just as abruptly, his hand falls and he relapses back into slumber. The flower sellers (who would buy flowers in Earls Court?) sprinkle water on their wilting exhibits. From the hamburger joint not many yards away throbs a delirium of pop music. Hippie-clad young men and women swagger in and out. Those of the tribe who congregate in Earls Court have a tough vacancy of expression: they represent the fag end of that particular dream of gentleness.

The elemental necessities are available in abundance. The Accommodation Agencies and the proliferating cheap hotels will always be able to provide you with a roof above your head; the gaudy constellation of cheap eating places will always provide you with food to fill your stomach; and, satisfying another need, the army of prostitutes – male as well as female – will always provide you with the cheap solace of their bodies. Watch the group of men, not all of whom are old and mackintoshed, assembled round the window of the newsagent and intently perusing the quaintly worded cards which are mixed in with blandishments to join overland trips to Australia and South Africa. 'Grounded Air Hostess Seeks New Position.' 'Chocolate Baby Teaches French. Very Strict.' 'Handsome Young Man Willing to Walk Dog.' Numbers are hastily jotted down on scraps of paper and the prospective client slips discreetly away in search of a telephone booth. With a quiet shuffle those at the rear shoulder forward. These havens of sexual delight are usually on the Warwick Road. I have often wandered along that bleak strip where, behind the drawn curtains of dank basements, passion is so easily bought and expended.

At dusk, on certain evenings, a fresh performer joins the circus. The hoarse orator of the World Socialist Party exhorts his handful of listeners to overthrow the exploiters and establish the universal brotherhood of man. In Earls Court his message falls on stony ground. In that chaos there are no allegiances. A man leans against a lamppost being sick. No one pays him any attention. Two women stagger along the pavement in the middle of the afternoon. One of them lies on the pavement and, lifting up her skirt, kicks her legs up in the air. Her companion, laughing uproariously, picks her up. They drift on and repeat the exhibition further down the road. No one pays them any attention. Late one evening I see a drunk approach the display window of the shop downstairs. He is carrying a brick in each hand. Calmly, deliberately, he takes aim. There is an explosion of shattering glass. The passers-by, their faces averted, hurry on. Like the appeal to universal brotherhood, the act of violence falls on stony ground.

Earls Court offers to its denizens the life of the city at its rawest and purest. It is uncompromisingly urban; a conglomeration of solitary individuals. Relinquishing responsibility, if offers frenzy. Therein lies its attraction. Nothing is permanent in Earls Court. The restaurants come and go with bewildering rapidity; the bedsitter population is notoriously ephemeral. Yet, the transience is superficial: it is the transience of a purgatorial clearing-house. The actors change but the play, revolving on its febrile treadmill, remains much the same.

One lunch time I went to the pub where six years before I used to sit and look at the charladies sipping their bottled Guinness. It had undergone a metamorphosis. Carpeted steps led to an upper bar where girls in hot-pants doled out the drinks. Sliding glass panels opened on to a terrace set out with tables shaded by colourful umbrellas. The charladies had disappeared tracelessly. I descended to the gloomy cavern of the lower bar. Strobe lights coruscated like demented fireflies in the interior recesses of the gloom. There was the heavy pound of rhythm and blues from scattered speakers. Groups of men, their faces indistinct, lowered their heads over glasses of beer. The garish designs of a watered-down op art decorated the walls. I bought my drink and settled in a corner. It was a weird, timeless world. The music stopped and the strobe lights were extinguished. Out of the hush drooled the West Indian voice of a disc jockey.

'And now specially for you cool cats out there something real hip. The beautiful Cheryl is gonna dance just for you.'

The groups of men surged forward into a solid phalanx and fenced in the wooden-floored circle where the beautiful Cheryl would perform. A spotlight was switched on. Then Cheryl herself appeared, a slight, pretty girl with protruding collar-bones. She was dressed in a shimmering bikini hung with silvery tassels and a pair of white boots that reached up above her knees. Moving awkwardly in her boots she came and stood limply, head bowed, in the middle of the circle: a drowned mermaid in the glare of the spotlight.

The voice of the disc jockey drooled again. 'Ready, Cheryl baby? Then let's swing it. Shake it up! Hey! Hey!'

An ear-splitting volley of music crashed forth and Cheryl, roused from her hibernatory stillness, pitched into her gyrations. She bobbed and weaved; she brandished her pale arms; she rotated her hips. The strobe lights flashed. A shine of sweat overspread her cheeks. She quivered orgasmically as the music climbed to a crescendo and, when it had passed, she rippled with the tremors of post-coital exhaustion and sank, eyes closed, on to the wooden boards of the arena. It had been a fine performance but she was not applauded. She rose to her feet and was once again a drowned mermaid in the glare of the spotlight. Ploughing a passage through her impassive masculine audience, she disappeared behind a door marked 'Staff Only'.

'That was way out, Cheryl baby. Thank you. And now we're gonna groove some more with the dynamic Shirley. She's gonna get you cats out there real hot under the collar. Hey! Hey!'

I did not wait to see the dynamic Shirley. Outside a fine rain was falling. The big lorries roared, tyres squelching on the wet roadway. I breathed in the soupy air blowing in chill gusts. In its metamorphosis that pub had conformed to the underlying spirit of Earls Court. A further revolution of the febrile treadmill: it was no more than that. Beautiful Cheryl and dynamic Shirley were part of the quick, passionate flux; souls resting awhile in the clearing-house. Eventually, they too would be swept away as the charladies had been swept away, leaving no trace. That was the iron law of Earls Court.

The usual crowd was gathered outside the tube station. His unfilled hat dampening in the rain, the veteran of the First World War scraped undaunted at his violin. Behind him, the collar of his donkey-jacket raised protectively, the agent of the underground press slept fitfully on his box.

Some months later I too was swept away. I could not work in Earls Court. Already I had fled once to a cottage in Suffolk where I stayed for six months. There I finished my second novel. On my return I found Earls Court even more intolerable. There being little to keep me, my urge to vagrancy reasserted itself. I obeyed the iron law and left. I write this in an Indian hill station. From the balcony of the hotel I can see the snow peaks of the Himalayas on clear days. Then the mists descend and they vanish completely. It is as if they had never been there; as if I were the victim of an illusion. At this distance, Earls Court too seems illusory. It is as if I had never been there; as if it had never existed. Alas, I know that that is not so.

Flying the Flag in Brixton

The landlord of the 'Coach and Horses' is a jolly man, proud of being the first black publican in this country. He appears to be on familiar, shoulder-slapping terms with all his customers, white and black.

'Good morning, Mom! Good morning, Pop! What's it to be? The usual?'

Mom and Pop, a retired English couple, nod. Although not unfriendly, they are not quite as effusive as their host. Having been served 'the usual', they move away from the bar. In the public bar a group of West Indians of employable age are gathered noisily around the pool-tables.

'Time for a little music,' the landlord says.

'Reggae?' I ask innocently.

He glares. 'No,' he says, calming himself. 'Something really dinky.'

The music of Bert Kaempfert oozes from the speakers. Perched now on a stool, he surveys his kingdom. He has lived in England for thirty-eight years. The last eleven of those have been spent in Brixton.

'This,' he declares in tones brooking no opposition, 'is the greatest country in the world.'

And Jamaica?

'A lovely place – for a holiday.'

Being prosperous he returns fairly often. A well-travelled man, he considers himself something of an expert on the quality of the services provided by various airlines. Indeed, it seems to be his favourite topic. His opinions are listened to with respect by those congregated at the bar.

'Air Jamaica is rubbish. Give me British Airways any day. BA is *our* airline. I believe in flying the flag.' Concorde fills him with patriotic zeal. 'The Americans are only jealous of *us*. That's why they're kicking up such a fuss about it.'

The sense of identification, so burlesque in its implications and vehemence, draws the line only at cricket. Air Jamaica might go to hell; the West Indian cricket team . . . well, that's a different matter. The paradox is part of the West Indian confusion. West Indians display an almost unrivalled hunger for absorption into societies other than their own. Emigration is an instinct; a reflex action. There was, it has been said, a revivalist atmosphere on the packed immigrant ships that crossed the Atlantic in the 1950s. Those who could, went. It was the thing to do. Nowadays it is the rich, the professional middle-class, who (because they possess desired skills) fly off like flocks of migratory birds to Canada and the USA. However, in the undiscriminating Fifties, it was the poor who came and settled in places like Brixton. Those who are here, despite everything, consider themselves to be relatively fortunate. Of course, the glamour has long since worn off and been replaced by the all too concrete and dour struggle for education, housing and employment. This has been accompanied by a sharpened sense of grievance. All the same, very few of those I met had any desire to return home other than for a holiday. ('Jamaica,' one man said to me, 'is a beautiful place. It's the most beautiful place in the world. But it's too small for me now. I couldn't live there any more.')

'Listen, mate,' the landlord says, 'I'm *English* now.'

I point out that some people – and not only those belonging to the anti-immigration lobby – might disagree.

The eyes bulge aggressively. 'Who would disagree? You mean Enoch Powell?' In his agitation, he lowered the volume of the dinky music. 'Listen. Enoch Powell don't bother me. Nobody's going to throw anybody out of here. Mind you, I would defend to the death Enoch Powell's right to say whatever he wants to say. This is a *democratic* country.'

A former policeman, who has lived in Brixton since 1946, agrees. 'The West Indians can say whatever they want as well. In the end, we all have to learn to live together.'

The landlord echoes the platitude.

But the Bangladeshi proprietor of one of Brixton's Indian restaurants takes an altogether gloomier view of the situation. The place, at lunch-time, is almost empty and I wonder how he manages to make a living. He sits at the table next to mine and begins to fold paper napkins into neat triangles – an activity, one suspects, born of habit rather than necessity. 'The outlook here isn't too good, especially with the younger blacks.' His gaze wanders mournfully over the unoccupied tables. He lowers his voice even though there is no one to overhear us. 'I sympathise with the English people. This is a small country. A poor country. What can they do with all these people?' I watch his deftly working fingers. 'You know something? If tomorrow they pass a law telling me I have to leave I would pack my bags and go. No fuss. No bother. It is always best for people to live in their own countries.' He looks at me with Asiatic resignation, a man obedient to the twists and turns of Fate.

The conversation depresses me. Seen through such eyes the tawdry streets of Brixton become a kind of no-man's-land; an unhappy hunting ground for lost souls, impossible causes. Human dereliction is everywhere in evidence. 'All black men are monkeys.' So reads the crudely chalked inscription on the walls of a public lavatory. Below it, the retort: 'All white men are devils'. Everywhere there is challenge and counter-challenge, assertion and counter-assertion, exhortation and appeal. Lambeth's twenty thousand homosexuals demand an end to discrimination. A sign executed in gashes of paint announces a campaign on behalf of the unemployed. Within the crumbling premises all is darkness and silence. Yet another daub on the façade of yet another crumbling building draws attention to (of all things) the Brixton-Bangladesh Cooperative. It is looked after by a lank-haired Yorkshireman probably still in his twenties. Rank upon rank of discarded overcoats, jackets, trousers, occupy the dim recesses. There is food as well – a haphazard collection of beans and lentils and fruit. On lamp-posts and walls an organisation calling itself Dominicans For Progress clamours against a hanging about to take place on their island. The Caribbean Peoples Solidarity Movement advertises a programme of films about black heroes. And, inevitably, the National Front invokes its own spectres and calls for support among the white population. It is strange to discover a part of London where there is little or no soccer-inspired graffiti. In Brixton the politics of protest reign unchallenged.

'The black people of the world,' writes J.A. Hunte (BA) in the glossy magazine produced by the Brixton Neighbourhood Community Association, 'are both racially and economically underprivileged and dispossessed; the white races, and especially their governments, bear the prime responsibility for this situation, and must accept their obligation for helping to remedy it.' This is the comfortingly familiar wail of black protest; of soulful grievance which threatens to become a way of life. Being a black man can be turned into a full-time profession. Something of the kind is already happening in places like Brixton. One expression of this tendency is the multiplicity of semi-official, semi-philanthropic bodies dealing with the 'problems' of the young, the old, the unemployed, the delinquent. Their existence conjures up visions of mass helplessness, of a population expected to sink rather than swim. The danger is that our expectations – like our prophecies – can often be self-fulfilling. No doubt these agencies perform a useful role. But, at the same time, they must also reinforce the (by now) near-instinctive assumption that to be black is to be, in some sense, disabled and thus in need of extra-special care and attention. One gets the impression that the area is regarded as a vast casualty ward.

This impression is strengthened by a visit to the Methodist Youth Centre where, on Friday evenings, there is a reggae session. Those who come are, without exception, black. They form a well-dressed but somewhat taciturn crowd. The hall is dark and smoky; the music is loud. But nobody dances with anybody else. Their relationship with the music is solitary and, it seems, entirely private. Occasionally, an individual breaks into a few jerky dance steps. The effect is eerie. 'This is the generation I fear most,' the Senior Youth Officer, himself a West Indian, observes with a respectful solemnity. 'They're not like their parents. They're not prepared to accept inferior living conditions.' He is full of gloomy reflections ('If you are poor and black in this area you may as well dig your own grave and jump into it') and even gloomier forebodings: 'blood-bath' is one of his favourite words. The 'under-privileged', the 'dispossessed', constitute in his eyes a perverse aristocracy towards whom he is submissive and deferential. 'They are angry,' he says, not without a certain bizarre, awe-struck relish. 'They are *very, very* angry. Such 'anger', recognised and sanctified by the tribe of social workers, can easily become its victim's most sacred possession; his birthright. He might be English in the sense that he has been born here. Most probably he will insist (like the publican) that this is *his* country now. But (unlike the publican) he will not regard British Airways as his airline: he has no flag to fly. While his elders frenetically seek absorption, he – no Uncle Tom! – frenetically seeks his 'rights'.

A few doors down from the Youth Centre is the 'local Community Bookshop', recently re-established after having been bombed a few years ago. The walls are emblazoned with colourful posters supporting the 'liberation' struggles of Angola, Mozambique, Palestine, Eritrea, Oman . . . At this end of the spectrum the search for 'rights', for 'justice' sinks into the maw of world revolution. The woman in charge refuses to talk; but her youthful assistant is slightly more forthcoming. He awaits the day when the oppressed English workers will make common cause with their oppressed black brothers to overthrow the exploiting capitalist bosses. The mind fogs. I buy a Frelimo poster and some of the works of Lenin and Chairman Mao and walk out into the wintry Brixton sunshine. A group of West Indians, coated and capped, loiter outside the betting shop amid a litter of discarded betting slips.

'Hey, Mister . . .' The accent is perfect Cockney.

A West Indian boy of about ten slides off the coping of a wall and comes loping towards me. On this cold day all he wears is a pair of short khaki trousers and a cotton shirt. His arms and legs are thin. His collar-bones protrude.

'Do you know where I can get this fixed?' He points towards a sash-window with a broken pane.

I hazard a number of guesses. But he quickly loses interest. Perhaps his request for help was no more than a conversation opener. He walks along beside me whistling – an urchin no different from those to be found in the streets of any West Indian town.

'Aren't you cold?'

He shrugs. 'Who, me? I don't feel the cold. I was born here.'

At a corner he suddenly bids me goodbye and races away up one of Brixton's bleak avenues of terraced housing. In its way, it was the queerest, most dislocating encounter of all.

Passports to Dependence

'You mustn't call them refugees,' the Administrator of the Plaster-down Camp scolded politely. 'It's one thing they have made very clear to me. They say they are English now. Part of England.'

The point was emphasised by Dr Patel. 'We Ugandan Asians are very bitter about the press labelling us refugees. We are not refugees. We have our legal rights in this country and Britain cannot tell her own citizens that they are refugees.'

At the Stradishall Reception Centre, Dr Patel's bitterness is echoed more aggressively by Mrs Mughal, a schoolteacher. 'We have got British passports and it is the obligation of the British Government to look after us. In fact, if it wasn't for the bloody quota system which they introduced we could have come here with our cash. Last year we decided to leave Uganda but when we went for our voucher they said we would have to wait in the queue for a year, two years ... Then Amin came in and we were thrown out without a penny. Now whose fault is that? It's the fault of the British Government. It is because of the quota voucher system that we are living like bloody refugees in this camp today.'

The anger and distress are untypical. Nevertheless, the outrage of Dr Patel and Mrs Mughal serves to highlight what – for the majority of those in the camps – is the crux of the matter: their possession of a British Passport. Their attitudes and behaviour, past and present, have been determined by it. It conferred on them an illusory security and a no less illusory 'identity'. The British Passport, like a deus ex machina, would rescue them. 'We always knew that one day we would have to come here.' That is what many of them tell you.

In the chilling space of ninety days, the Ugandan Asians have found themselves dispossessed and uprooted from the country where most of them were born. With pride rather than bitterness ('We always knew that one day we would have to come here'), they show photographs of a style of life that was so recently theirs: the pleasant suburban house with its garden; the excursion in the Volkswagen and the picnic by the Murchison Falls; the African 'ayah' tending the baby in its pram. Today, courtesy of their passports, they sit in remote reservations like the Plasterdown Camp on the windswept fringes of Dartmoor – jobless, moneyless, homeless. Sheathed in an abundance of warm, philanthropic clothing, they prepare to brave out the English winter.

'Do you ever get depressed when you think of what you have lost? Do you ever wonder why it should have come to this?' On the narrow cot lie the scattered photographs.

'Why think about the past? We were expecting it to happen – only not so suddenly. But we are very happy to be here now.'

'You have no regrets at all?'

The phlegmatic air deepens. 'We are very happy to be here. Everybody has been most kind and generous and helpful.'

The resigned cheerfulness is impenetrable. Perhaps there is no other way to cope with the startling transition from prosperous ease. It comes as a shock to the visitor who has prepared himself for solemnity and collective despair. Plasterdown has evolved a festive atmosphere. Children dart about gaily, dodging the washing strung out on lines. Groups of old men wearing scarves and overcoats stroll in the wintry sunshine – a few of them assert that the cold has actually improved their health. Some boys, preparing for their Ordinary Level examinations, relax around a table strewn with textbooks. 'England is better than Uganda,' one of them tells me. His companions echo the sentiment. Their faces reflect the happiness their words proclaim. The recent festivals of Divali and Eid had been celebrated with appropriate style. That evening the Muslims were giving a dinner at which the camp officials were to be the guests of honour. A few days before a Hindi version of *Romeo and Juliet* had been successfully performed. The following Saturday some volunteers were coming to the camp to hold an impromptu art class. A library and a youth club had been established. It was all very jolly.

The Asians also play a part in the running of the camp. They work at the switchboard, assist the Social Security and Resettlement Officers and have begun to issue their own clothing from the stores. Anyone who wishes can find something 'to do'. 'Immediately we find we are terribly free,' Diamond Meghji says, 'we rush down to the Administration and ask for some work.'

Officials and volunteer workers exude benevolence towards their charges. 'Anything the matter? No? Jolly good. Carry on.' On Sundays the camp is crowded with the cars of people who have come to take the refugees for drives and maybe out for tea somewhere. One such philanthropist, a beaming lady of middle-age, stops me as I am walking down a corridor. She carries with her a pile of comic-books. 'Do you speak English?' she asks. I murmur self-deprecating assent. 'Oh,' she says, 'I know how terrible it must be for you. To come from all that sunshine to *this*.' She gestures towards the misty desolation surrounding the camp. 'You must keep yourself well wrapped-up. And *do* take some of these – they'll help to pass the time.' She holds out to me one Superman and one Bat Man comic book. A puzzled hurt betrays itself when I decline the offer. 'We are trying to discourage the do-gooders,' the Camp Administrator says. 'Many of them, we've discovered, only come here out of morbid curiosity. They're a very mixed blessing.'

One such very mixed blessing was the matted-haired 'volunteer' who told me he had offered his services because of his admiration for Eastern philosophy. What, I asked, did the Ugandan Asians have to do with Eastern philosophy? He had not yet found out. Not long after his arrival a sudden attack of hepatitis had laid him low. He looked at me mournfully. 'I've spent most of my time here in bed. The refugees look after me. So far I haven't been able to do anything at all for *them*.' His was, perhaps, the saddest story of all. He was the most miserable person I met at Plasterdown.

Morale in the camp – the bed-ridden volunteer apart – remained astonishingly high even after five weeks. The Administrator ascribed the cheerfulness to initial euphoria. 'They're just glad to have escaped with their lives. The true nature of their situation hasn't actually begun to sink in. They haven't had time to think about things as yet. When that starts to happen . . .' He shrugged portentously. One of the refugees provided me with a somewhat novel explanation of the cheerfulness. 'We are happy because here in the camp nobody has any reason to be jealous of anybody else. In Uganda it was different. There the richer ones used to look down on the poorer ones. Now we all get the same £2.10 every week from the Social Security.' He laughed. 'So, you see, here we are all equal and everybody is happy.' The Church of England clergyman, the 'Entertainments Officer' at Stradishall, offers yet another explanation of the phenomenon. He resorts to a kind of cultural metaphysics. 'The Indian mentality is what you might call passive. Most of them are accustomed to living close to death, you see.' He gazed intently at me. 'They are fatalistic about misfortune. Life must go on – that kind of thing.' I, in my turn, gazed back intently at him. He seemed discomposed by this. 'Mind you,' he expanded, à propos of nothing I had said, 'I give my services free of charge. Nor am I trying to convert anybody.' Momentarily, we both relaxed. 'I've even organised a ruddy Hindu temple,' he went on. 'It's an example of practical Christianity at work.'

Any group of people which has a large stake in society will tend to search for means to protect interests. By any frame of reference, the Asian involvement in Uganda was profound.

'We grew up there. We were married there. We made our money there. Uganda was our *home*.' So says a former inspector of schools.

Dr Modhwadia is even more forthright than that. 'The Asians built up Uganda. We were the doctors. We were the lawyers. We ran the stores. We built up the cities. We even dug the drains. Without us there would have been nothing!'

Having created so much, there was correspondingly so much to defend.

A shopkeeper takes out from under his bed a crumpled copy of a Ugandan newspaper. He runs a finger down the long columns advertising the Asian businesses that have been seized and put up for sale to Africans. The finger pauses, circling the smudged newsprint. 'That's *my* business.' He indicates a name. 'And now I have not a penny. Not a penny!' He jabs at the frail paper. One suspects it is a ritual.

He is not alone.

Mr Ismail was an importer and exporter of bicycles.

Mr Patel had once owned a coffee factory.

Hansa Raj Padhiar was a commercial artist and interior decorator. A friend of his leaned towards me. 'If you wanted your home decorated,' he said, 'people would generally say, "Call Padhiar!" '

Mr Baloo, who stands at the window looking out at the moor, operated a trucking firm.

Diamond Meghji was the proprietor of two secondary schools.

The Asian involvement was enormous.

'I would say we led a privileged existence,' the inspector of schools concedes. Dr Patel agrees. 'Life in Uganda was very good for me – socially, climatically, in every way.' But did Dr Patel ever have any intention of defending that life if it should come under threat? The astonishing answer is that he did not. His possession of a British passport precluded any such thoughts. 'I wanted to remain a foreigner in Uganda so that I could move my family out at will.' In the face of danger the only solution that ever presented itself was flight. It was to be a surrender without even a token struggle; a surrender without terms. 'I am not interested in politics at all,' Dr Patel adds, his expression ripe with virtue. 'Nor were most of the Asians in Uganda. We decided to keep well out of it.'

Wasn't politics (I wondered aloud) to be counted among the traditional arts of self-defence? Didn't economic power find its logical extension in political power? To stand aloof – wasn't that an invitation to disaster? to pillage? Dr Patel smirks. He has, it turns out, scant regard for the handful of Asians who did try to play a political role. They were 'self-seekers'. He did, after all, have his British passport. Now, nestled in the breast-pocket of his jacket, it must have helped to keep him warm in this refugee camp on the fringes of Dartmoor.

'I just don't understand why we didn't get more involved in politics,' a bank clerk admits with belated incredulity. 'We could have tried harder and I just don't understand why we didn't. Just as we were the fathers of economics, so I think we could have become the fathers of politics.' He stares round the bed-crowded cubicle that has been his family's home for the last three weeks – and which may continue to be their home for a long time yet. Head-high screens shield them ineffectually from the public gaze. A strip of sacking masks the entrance. Suitcases and boxes are visible under the beds: inside them is the sum total of the family's worldly goods – mainly clothes. Wet undergarments steam on the radiator. On the window-sill above are scattered plastic cups, a shaving mirror and a collection of toothbrushes. Outside it is raining and a heavy, bluish mist conceals the distant hills. From the cubicle next door comes the ringing sound of children's voices. Footsteps clatter incessantly along the corridor. 'If we had tried harder perhaps we mightn't be here,' the bank clerk says. 'The people here in the camp are nice to us but I feel that is because they are taking pity on us. Sometimes I wonder what it would have been like if we could have come here with all our capital.' He cracks his knuckles and laughs. His father, who has been listening attentively, laughs too.

Others have other reasons.

'Asians stayed out of politics in Uganda because since independence Uganda has been ruled by dictators and so it was not possible to give your views.'

'If you talked politics it could affect your business. Since most of us were businessmen, we naturally stayed out of politics.'

'Most of us were not interested in politics because Uganda was so unstable. Things kept changing all the time.'

'You could get killed.'

They talk. You listen. Misconceived apathy, elevated to the status of wisdom, contributed to the existence of the conditions now adduced as justifications for their detachment. By the time Amin arrived on the scene it was indeed too late for them. They had already doomed themselves. Apathy had become an ingrained habit of mind. Having long since lost touch with the realities of their situation, they were incapable of effective action. Their British passports turned them all into would-be Houdinis.

'The first thing I am thinking is that I am a human being and the second thing I am thinking is that this is the time for people to forget about the boundaries of countries and to be known as universal men.'

I was reminded of the matted-haired enthusiast of Eastern philosophy. He would probably have agreed. But he had been struck down by hepatitis; and the speaker was a refugee.

Universal men often have a rough passage through this cruel world.

In the camp cinema a meeting is in progress. The Adult Education Programme is being discussed with a committee of 'hut representatives'. The Asians present listen with earnest attention as the Englishman in charge explains what the idea is. 'We shall be discussing English life, sport and local government. At a more advanced level we shall explore the English place in world culture – science, philosophy, etc. Is that understood?' Heads nod, pens scribble across note-pads. The bracken-covered hills of Dartmoor frame the view visible from the windows. At this time of year they are the colour of rust. Stony outcrops rise from the summits. 'What we want to do,' the Englishman says, 'is to give them the kind of confidence necessary to leave the camp.' He reverts to his audience. 'Are there any questions or complaints?' There were no questions and no complaints. The meeting breaks up and the Asians file out to spread the word.

The confidence necessary to leave the camp is not lacking. 'Literally,' a cinema manager says, 'our community likes to work. We can work as hard as any foreign company wants. Maybe that is why people are afraid of us – I mean the English people. I myself am cinematographically qualified and though I see that life will be hard, I shall work like a clock.' Dr Patel is equally optimistic. 'The technicians will get jobs in industry. It might be more difficult for the traders – they will have to take manual or unskilled jobs. But they are hardworking people and will make out.' Nothing, one is repeatedly told, is impossible for a hard worker. Some of this optimism, as Diamond Meghji points out, might be underpinned by more substantial expectations. 'A number of these people,' he confided in a low voice, 'made transfers of money to England some time ago. A few of those in this camp even own houses here.' Why then did they choose to stay there? Their problem is that they don't know exactly where the house is. Once they are settled, they will try to find out.'

Since it was set up in October, Plasterdown has received approximately eight hundred and fifty Asians. The rate of resettlement has been slow. Jobs and houses are scarce and the difficulty is compounded when the two have to be matched. Kishor Chotai, a watch-repairer, had been offered a job in Plymouth. But he could do nothing about it until he found somewhere to live. Still, Kishor Chotai is fortunate: he is young and has a marketable skill. But what sort of job do you find for a middle-aged man who ran a small grocery in Jinja? 'A few of them,' the Resettlement Officer grumbled with a hint of impatience, 'seem to expect to get exactly the same sort of work here. If they managed a cotton ginnery in Uganda, they seem to expect us to provide them with another one here.' These – the 'hard core' – contrast with the many who insist on their readiness to go anywhere and do anything.

The younger, willing nomads share the pessimism of the camp administration when discussion turns to the 'hard core'. 'I have seen old people,' Diamond Meghji says, 'who just can't cope with the timing of meals, the queueing, the arranging for social security and that sort of thing. It is all very confusing for them. These fellows just don't know when to go where. They just sit in their huts. I feel very sorry for them.' He is accompanied by his father and mother, neither of whom can speak English. The old man, looking at me, smiles gaily and murmurs something to his son. 'My father says his health is so much better in England.' His mother fares less well. She is suffering from eczema and lies on her bed, wrapped up in a grey blanket.

Dr Patel is resigned. 'The old folk will have to rely on Social Security funds. What else can they do?' He shrugs.

'I don't think some of the older ones will last the winter,' Mrs Mughal says. 'Those who do will become a burden to the Government. The old people should not have come here. They should have gone to India or Pakistan.'

India and Pakistan are for the old, the lost, the unemployable. But what about the young? The skilled?

'No! No! No!' Mr Mehta, an accountant, recoils at the suggestion that he might have gone to India. 'It is better to go ahead than to go backward. India is too poor. Here we will have more opportunities. Anyway, I am not Indian. I am *British Asian.*'

'The social conditions in India are quite different,' Dr Patel remarks serenely. 'I feel more secure here than I would there. The standard of living is of a different type. We have a right to resettle here and most of us would prefer to be here rather than in India.'

Mr Shah, an electrical engineer, is equally adamant. 'I would feel more at home in England that I would in India. I consider myself a more Westernised type of person.'

A more Westernised type of person. I look at him with an unbecoming, unprofessional irritation. Their passports, as ever, eliminate the need for further reflection. They turn their backs on India as, before, they had turned their backs on politics. Words like 'Westernised' and 'modern' and 'progressive' roll effortlessly off their tongues. They remind you that India refused to admit them – on the ground that being British citizens they were, therefore, Britain's responsibility. This was a most pleasing legalism. For, even if the electrical engineer could have got a good job in India he would not have chosen to go. 'I would always prefer to mix up with people in England. Get to know their ideas and ways of living.'

Mix up. It is another favoured expression. They all want to mix up.

Unhappily, a British passport cannot shield you from everything. Nor does being a more Westernised type of person. Nor, come to that, does the fervent desire to mix up. When Sultanali Rahemtulla went into Tavistock one day and asked the way to the library, the first person ignored him and the second one deliberately misled him: he found himself on the road leading back to the camp. In nearby Horrabridge, a group of refugees out on a stroll through the town was surrounded by a gang of youths on motor-cycles. 'They used bad words. Called us bastard Asians.' One day the wife of a local man sneaked into the camp and was discovered taking photographs of the lavatories – to show, with luck, how filthy and unclean 'Asians' were. Life wasn't always jolly.

But the cant, the hypocrisy, the shameful small-town hysteria engendered by their arrival in this country, has had no visible effect on them, prompted no second thoughts, Dr Patel, a man of philosophic temperament, dismisses it as a part of human nature. Mr Shah had read much about English 'prejudice' and hostility in the Ugandan press but he believes the reports were greatly exaggerated. 'The English people have been very helpful, very considerate and very cooperative. I think there are very few people who are racialists.'

'We will,' the inspector of schools admits, 'have to put up with a certain amount of displeasure of this kind. Anti-immigrant feeling is natural. But there are people who welcome you with open arms, treating you as their own brothers and sisters and letting you know that you are British now and not a separate group.'

A relentless imperviousness which is both their strength and their weakness protects them from hurt. And it does more than that: it makes them see 'kindness' and 'concern' where – perhaps – kindness and concern were not intended. The advertisement put out by the Leicester Council – this charitable tract was published in the Ugandan press – advising the refugees to stay away from Leicester is a case in point.

Mr Shah: 'I saw the Leicester advertisement. They are trying to provide facilities for their people and they are saying they can't provide full facilities for any more. It becomes the moral duty of the Asians to cooperate with them and stay away.'

Diamond Meghji: 'I wouldn't go to Leicester because my brother advised me to go where there are very few Asians.'

Mrs Mughal: 'They put in this advertisement for our good. Why shouldn't the Asians spread out? They should have that bloody understanding to spread out and mix up with other people. If I live in a place with few Asians, so much the better for me. I would like to integrate with this community because I am one of them.'

The desire to please, the desire to show that one is tractable and docile, shades away into an undignified perception of oneself. The 'integration' so enthusiastically advocated by the Asians themselves assumes their own undesirability. Spread out! Mix up! Disappear!

The Asians are going to be taught about the English place in world culture. Their habitual lack of introspection will cause them to neglect another and more important issue: what is a 'British Asian'? What is *his* place in English culture? I fear that the passport will intervene, as it has always done, to block thought; to hypnotise into paralysis. In the past, it has abetted the 'fatalism' that resulted in their expulsion from Uganda; at present it abets the illusion of being 'British'. England is, for the moment, the journey's end. Their presence in the camps is the ultimate flowering of their dependence.

The Road to Nowhere

When the Arts Council asked me if I would like to go on one of their Writers' Tours to Humberside, I was a little doubtful – for a start, I could not say with certainty where Humberside was. More importantly, it seemed such a strange place for me to parade myself and my work. Port of Spain, yes. Bombay, yes. London, yes. I could think of a dozen locations where such a manifestation might make sense. But *Humberside*? I stared perplexedly at my atlas. Could there be any real point of contact between Humberside and myself? I reproached myself for a timidity that verged on cowardice. Art, I reminded myself, ought to be universal in its appeal. Why make an exception of Humberside? Then, too, I thought of the financial help the Arts Council had given me in the past. To accept their invitation would, I felt, be one way of repaying their touching faith in me. Also, exposure to Humberside, whatever we made of each other, would be an 'experience'; even, perhaps, an interesting one.

I decided I would go.

Hull, in the middle of winter, is a sobering place. Chill winds, blowing off the North Sea, sweep unhindered through the town. A persistent drizzle nags. The Humber, its unfinished suspension bridge rearing into the mist, is a steely blur. Lymphatic faces peer from under dripping umbrellas. By seven in the evening, the town is largely deserted, abandoned to the wind and rain. Roaming in bands of three or four, platformed heels echoing through the emptiness, the young hurry along the glistening streets in search of diversion. In the bars of the Centre Hotel commercial travellers occupy the mock-leather armchairs, warming themselves with Scotch.

Until recently, the girls of Hull wore mini-skirts – fashions come late and change slowly in this part of the world. The town, stuck out on a limb, is on the way to nowhere. It lends itself to being by-passed. Once, though, Hull did get in the way – with disastrous consequences. It was bombed with particular severity during the last war. This (I was told) happened not because Hull was an important target, but was due to the unfortunate fact that it lay directly below the flight path of the German bombers. It was a convenient spot for the enemy aircraft to lighten their load before heading back across the North Sea. Being bombed is bad enough; but to be bombed for a reason like this is to heap insult on injury. The few other facts I managed to pick up were equally disheartening. I learnt that the population is declining; that the fishing industry is languishing; that the region boasts one of the highest rates of unemployment in the country; that enormous quantities of potatoes are grown in the bleak, table-flat countryside; that it is a good place to buy second-hand furniture; that it manufactures caravans by the score. Hull, as it has always done, looks to the sea for rescue – to its oil and its gas. Nevertheless, by the standards of the region, Hull is a big city, unpredictable and dangerous. In a village like Snaith it is held in reverential terror. They talk with awe of its street violence, of its motor-cycle gangs.

Cultural life has ground to a kind of standstill. To find a decent bookshop you have to travel up the motorway to York. The Humberside Theatre, which receives only the most grudging support from the city fathers, struggles to make ends meet. Now and then, the museum mounts an exhibition. In an alley of the old town the local branch of the Arts Council runs a tasteful, whitewashed showroom. They sell modernistic postcards, collections of indigenous verse, monographs on local history and cups of good coffee in pretty, earthenware cups. Its tiny, dedicated staff behave like a beleaguered garrison. Hull, astonishingly enough, does have a university. But it makes no impact at all on the life of the town. The students, immured in their halls of residence, are rarely seen. It is one of the quietest, most self-effacing institutions of its kind in the country. Compared to the University of Hull, a Buddhist monastery would be a model of social involvement.

Four of us had come to Hull to promote the cause of Culture. We were two poets and two novelists. The two poets were Patricia Beer and Edwin Brock; the two novelists, Gabriel Josipovici and myself. Only Patricia Beer had had any previous experience of these Writers' Tours – indeed, she was something of a veteran campaigner. The Arts Council provided us with a kindly shepherd and a charming shepherdess. One cold, drizzling Sunday evening, towards the end of January, we all came together in one of Hull's Italian restaurants. Our week's labours were set forth by our shepherdess: during the day we would go (usually separately) to schools; in the evenings we would give (usually together) public readings of our work. Over dinner I listened to spine-chilling tales of other Writers' Tours. I spent an apprehensive night, waking every hour or so and listening to the rain against the window.

Monday: To Snaith School in the morning. I share a car with Patricia and Edwin. Patricia can hardly wait to get to her assignment. Her zeal is alarming rather than infectious. We drop her off first. She leaps out of the car, her eyes bright with anticipation. Edwin is subdued; I am plunged in gloom. We arrive half an hour late at Snaith. The headmaster is displeased with us. 'Schools have these funny things called time-tables,' he says to my shepherdess. She reddens contritely. I find myself faced with, perhaps, fifty fifteen- and sixteen-year-olds. They stare at me blankly. I introduce myself. 'I was born in Trinidad, in the West Indies . . .'

'It's not easy to make them talk,' the English teacher whispers. I decide to read something. Even as I read I realise that I have chosen the wrong passage, that it is all going over their heads. However, it is too late to do anything about that. I press on to the bitter end.

'Are there any questions you wish to ask Mr Naipaul?' The teacher smiles hopefully. Feet shuffle. Dull eyes blink evasively.

'Mr Naipaul has come all the way from Trinidad to talk to you. You must have *some* questions you would like to ask him.' He leans towards me. 'Why don't you talk to them about football?'

'But I don't know anything about football.'

At last, at last, a hand is raised. The teacher beams at the questioner.

'Do you live in a mud hut?'

Laughter rolls around the classroom.

More hands are raised.

'Do you have elephants where you come from?'

'What kind of food do you eat in West India?'

'Do you wear ordinary clothes in West India?'

'Do they play football in West India?'

As I leave, the girls are gathered round a record-player, listening to pop music. My shepherdess awaits me. 'How was it?'

'Fine. Fine. We talked about elephants and football.'

In the evening, a reading at the Humberside Theatre. There are about thirty people present. Martin (our shepherd) and Sandy (our shepherdess) are quite pleased: it is a good turnout. Sandy meticulously sets up a display of our books. Penguin have been especially

lavish with my books. But Edwin is disgruntled. His publishers have
sent nothing at all. Someone asks if we enjoy being a circus.

Tuesday: To Hornsea School, some twenty or so miles out of Hull.
We are early. Martin and I kill time by strolling along the sea-front.
The discoloured North Sea hisses on the pebbly beach; the wind-
whipped rain stings. This morning I have about ten students to deal
with. They are supposed to be doing 'A' Level English Literature.
The teacher, it is clear, knows nothing about me. I introduce myself.
'I was born in Trinidad, in the West Indies . . .' Afterwards, I read one
of my more tragic short stories. They listen solemnly. Any questions?
The girls look as if I have made an improper suggestion. Finally, a boy
pipes up. His participation gives the occasion an aura of mild success.
Even so, I feel slightly foolish.

In the afternoon I go with Patricia to Kingston High School. The
entrance hall smells like a much-used gym. A plaque beneath a bust of
Amy Johnson, the aviator, proclaims her an ex-pupil of Kingston
High. We are greeted with the news that the heating system has
broken down. The English master has also had his own misfortunes –
not long before he had climbed up a ladder to replace a light bulb,
received an electric shock, fallen off the ladder and broken his leg.
Supporting himself on a cane, he hobbles up to welcome us. These are
bad omens. We are led into a chilly class-room. Some thirty students
confront us. I am becoming inured to the blankness, the apathy, of
these adolescent faces. The English teacher, not too steady on his feet,
pushes a chair towards Patricia. Smiling radiantly, she sits down.
Suddenly, she is spreadeagled on the floor – the chair had collapsed
under her. The students are amused. Patricia lies on her back, staring
up at the ceiling. She rejects all offers of help. 'I can manage! I can
manage!' With some effort, she manages to haul herself upright. I
study with admiration her swift recovery of composure and dignity.

Patricia is truly a veteran campaigner. She reads some short poems;
I read an extract from one of my novels. Any questions? None. Not a
single flicker of interest. A stray teacher, lurking at the back of the
room, wonders why poets don't use rhyme any more. Patricia
murmurs for a while about Eliot, Auden, Spender and Macleish. Has
anyone heard of them? No one has. The ignorance I have so far
encountered – and not simply of cultural matters, but of the world
lying beyond the borders of daily experience – has an almost mediaeval quality. I feel I could talk to them of men whose heads grow
beneath their shoulders and I would be believed. The darkness of

mind is really quite frightening. Only factory fodder is being churned out of these schools. Picture to yourself the homunculus who boarded the London-bound train from Hull. He could have been little older than sixteen. There he was, dressed in cloth-cap, overalls and clogs. A cigarette was clamped between his lips. In front of him was a can of beer. The *Sun* lay on his lap, open at the sports pages. His embryonic perfection was unnerving.

In the evening, to the Bell Hotel, Driffield. A dozen people, mainly elderly ladies, have come to hear us. Sandy is pleased. By the standards of Driffield this is a good audience. She meticulously sets up a display of our books. Halfway through the session, the heating is switched off. It becomes too cold to concentrate. We go to the bar. The poets are extremely popular; no one shows much interest in the novelists. Gabriel and I chat to each other. Edwin is surrounded by a band of ageing groupies. They hang breathlessly on his every word about the nature of poetic inspiration.

Wednesday: To Newland High School. A class of twenty girls. I read another of my tragic short stories. My audience is polite. Two or three girls ask questions. Even so, I am a little disappointed. I had been told that this school was more academically inclined than the others I had visited, but the level of general knowledge is no higher than elsewhere. Somewhere in the school, the rumour runs, there is a girl who might actually go to university. I did not meet her: she was too 'shy'.

In the evening we are the guests of the Adult Education Department of Hull University. The novelists and the poets go their separate ways. Having observed the mania for poetry among the cultural elite of Humberside, I wonder if Gabriel and I will attract anyone at all. The devoted Sandy sets up a display of our books. We do quite well – about forty students opt for us. Here there is a different kind of culture death: the students have been ruined by their academic training. Questions about 'technique' and 'symbolism' dominate the exchange after the reading. *What* one writes about, *why* one writes, seem irrelevancies.

The great excitement in our lives that day is the arrival of Josephine Falk (Literature Officer of the Arts Council) from London.

Thursday: To Market Weighton School, accompanied by Martin and Josephine. The drive is a long one. A heavy mist blots out the landscape. Josephine loses her temper when I tell her that I had bought a one-way rail ticket from London to Hull, instead of the economy return she had recommended. 'What's the point of my writing you all those letters if you don't read what I write?' I stare shamefacedly into the mist. Market Weighton is a country school. It has only about four hundred pupils. 'What can I assume they know?' I ask the English teacher. 'You can assume nothing at all,' he says. Most of the children are related to each other; most will be claimed by the land – it is an area of family-run smallholdings – when they leave school. But the children are nice, slightly more forthcoming than I was led to expect. They respond to the short story (a light-hearted one) I read. One or two of them even laugh in the right places. This isn't a bad session. If it were all like this, my week in Humberside just might be considered worthwhile.

Alas, even such mild optimism cannot be sustained for long. That evening, Edwin and I go to Hedon, to the Public Library, to give our reading. Present are two eleven-year-old boys, two eleven-year-old girls, an old age pensioner sheltering from the rain, a balding gentleman, our chairman, two cats and a dog. Sandy dutifully sets out the books. It is clear that the chairman knows not the first thing about either Edwin or myself. The boys and girls smirk and simper. Eventually, they walk out. The old age pensioner stares into the rainy night. The evening is a humiliating farce. Later on, I quarrel with Sandy. 'We've got to go on *trying*,' she says. It sounds like a *cri de coeur*. But why go on trying? We were achieving nothing. We were really no more than a circus, a collection of curious individuals. Humberside has no need of us. Football satisfied all the tribal desires of its people. The easy fulfilments of advanced industrial society had turned men into barbarians. Why inflict their indifference on us? I went on quarrelling. Diplomatic relations between Sandy and myself broke down.

Friday: To Bransholme High School. I request that volunteers alone attend. The teacher here is prepared for my coming. He has even drawn a map to show where Trinidad is. Fifteen students attend. One of them is actually reading a novel of mine. I am asked the usual questions; I give the usual answers.

The tour ends with a reading at the Station Hotel, Goole. About twenty people (most of them, I suspect, friends of the organiser) turn up. So inadequate is the heating, we have to keep our overcoats on. Loud pop music penetrates from the Saloon Bar downstairs. Faithful Sandy – nothing, it seems, will deter her – sets out the books. I read a passage that is meant to be funny and fail to raise a laugh. Two toughs burst in, nursing pints of beer. We try not to show our nervousness. Someone begins to twang an electric guitar. The toughs, too bored (or, maybe, too cold) to beat the place up, depart. Not long after, we too depart, hurrying along wet streets to the local kebab house where we are to have our farewell dinner.

'Dear Shiva,

Just a brief note to thank you for taking part in the Writers' Tour . . . You'll be pleased to hear that we sold twelve of your books, so there is interest in what you have to say, despite your fears to the contrary . . . !

Yours sincerely,
Sandy'

Twelve books! Well, maybe, it was worth it. But I have my doubts, Sandy. When I think of that homunculus, I despair.

On Cannibal Farm

One night, for reasons that will forever remain obscure, Carl Gustav Jung had a dream about Liverpool. He made heavy work of it. 'Liverpool,' he concluded, after considerable speculation, 'is "the pool of life". The "liver", according to an old view, is the seat of life – that which "makes to live".'

'Radio City Welcomes You To Liverpool.'

So announced the big, bright hoarding stretched across the exit gates at Lime Street Terminus.

Radio City is Liverpool's very much in-vogue commercial radio station, feeding its audience a twenty-four-hour diet of pop music, brisk chat, phone-ins – and quizzes.

– Can you name the highest spire in Britain?

– Er . . . the Post Office Tower?

– No, luv. Not the Post Office Tower. That's not a spire. A spire is something you find on top of churches. Think of a church . . .

– Er . . . St. Paul's?

– No, luv. Not St. Paul's. That's got a dome, not a spire . . .

Audience participation fades into rock'n'roll. Station 194 knows its business.

Radio City was welcoming me to Liverpool. It seemed appropriate that it should. The hoarding briefly provoked into life all the dated associations of my student days. Fifteen years ago, the Mersey was not a river. It was a sound, a style, a cultural revolution. This was my first visit to the legendary city.

Tourists still make the pilgrimage to the shabby, cobbled lane called Mathew Street, home of the Cavern club, the catacomb where the Beatles performed in the early days. But the club that now uses the name is not *the* Cavern. That was demolished some time ago, and the name (worth money) sold off. The site is now an empty plot. Some tourists, nothing deterred, take away as souvenirs the chunks of masonry that lie scattered about. Naturally enough, the new Cavern pays homage to the old. 'High above the door,' reads the marble plaque above the door of the new Cavern, 'is . . . a sculpted tribute to the Beatles by famous local sculptor Arthur Dooley. It shows the mother figure of Liverpool (who bears a striking resemblance to conventional renderings of the Virgin Mary) holding three cherubs representing John, George and Ringo – Paul has Wings and has gone off on his own . . .'

The legend of the Beatles, or, rather, of the era they helped to create, survives. 'The Beatles put Liverpool on the map,' I was told by more than one person. For many now in their middle thirties, the period represents a dream of freshness, of youth, of creative energy. Liverpool had not merely been put on the map. For a time, it must have appeared to occupy a position close to the centre of it; for a time, it must have seemed the cultural capital of a world-wide renaissance. The activities of the Liverpool poets (Adrian Henri is the best known) took place in this heightened atmosphere of self-awareness and self-importance. Liverpool was invested with a special élan, a special, almost mystical gravity. Not long ago that legend burst into acrimony over the issue as to whether or not the Beatles should be officially commemorataed by the city fathers. The myth-makers won the argument: Liverpool will soon be adorned with another sculpted tribute to the Fabulous Four. This nostalgia is part of the sadness of the city. Culturally, it is trapped in the grip of an arrested adolescence. It is not too difficult to find ageing leftovers of the early 1960s who, in return for a drink or two (or three), will parade their moth-eaten memories to you: men who, like the splendidly greased and spear-brandishing Masai 'warriors' of Kenya and Tanzania, have turned themselves into tourist attractions.

But the legend of Liverpool – that it is a very special place, that it harbours a vitality to be found virtually nowhere else – still persists. Indeed, it is clung on to with increasing desperation. Nowadays it finds its chief expression in the successes of Liverpool Football Club and the frenzied howlings of its supporters on the Kop. In few other places have I met so many people who churn out the inherited clichés about themselves with such zest. They talk incessantly of their independent spirit, their warm-heartedness, their fierce communal loyalty. 'Maybe it's why we're in so much trouble now,' you will be told, 'we're too independent-minded. We believe in sticking up for our rights.' Self-analysis does not go beyond the statement and restatement of cliché. And yet, there is something in it. The attachment of the ordinary people to their city is, for the most part, genuine and unaffected, deeper and more abiding than the delusions of grandeur spawned by the Beatle era. Liverpool does impart an identity and command a loyalty that is both impressive and touching. I think of the young waitress I met in a kebab restaurant; a small, pale-faced girl (she was a creature of the night) with cropped hair, one of a large family living in the Dingle. Her knowledge of the world was restricted. She may have been as far as Manchester once or twice. Beyond that, all was darkness and wild surmise. London (she had heard) was a vast and wicked town where most of the girls were little better than prostitutes. She wanted, she said, to be a film star.

'You'll probably have to leave Liverpool if you want to be a film star,' I said.

'Me? Leave Liverpool? Go away from me Mum and me Dad?' She looked at me with astonishment.

'Would you never think of leaving Liverpool? Not even to be a film star?'

'Never,' she said. The look of astonishment persisted. 'This is where I was born. This is where I belong.'

Her tribal simplicity was moving. But hers was not the Liverpool that had been put on the map; the Liverpool of legend. At the self-styled Liverpool School of Language Music Dream and Pun they talk differently.

'I really pick up the positive energy here,' said Charles Gilmour Alexander, a refugee from the desert wastes of London.

'The positive energy?'

Charles Gilmour Alexander was patient. He had worked out a theory of positive and negative energy. Apparently, when these two forces met – and in Liverpool they met as they did nowhere else – the result was explosive.

'Quite fantastic,' Charles Gilmour Alexander said. The positive energy he picked up in Liverpool was channelled into the making of ornate rocking horses. These concentrations of energy sell in London for two hundred and fifty pounds.

I tried to talk with his associate Peter Osborne O'Halligan. He pointed at the badge (badges are all the rage in Liverpool) he was wearing. 'I Am Mute' it declared. I thought it was a joke. But O'Halligan wasn't joking. He had vowed to remain silent for three months. This, happily, did not stop him from communicating with me by other means. He dropped a cyclostyled sheet into my lap. 'My operating at 0.00 decibels ... enables me to gain at least some awareness and understanding ... of spherical acoustic space.'

'I expect Peter figured he was beginning to talk too much bullshit,' Charles Gilmour Alexander said solemnly.

In a small auditorium at the back of the building, a science fiction 'opera' was being performed nightly. I looked in. In a corner of the room a drummer was drumming away concentratedly. A jeans-clad girl crawling about the scenery (I think she was a playwright) stared bad-temperedly in my direction.

'Is this man disturbing you?' she asked the drummer.

The drummer was non-committal.

'I have no time to talk to you,' she said even more bad-temperedly.

I went away.

That night I went to Falkland's Club. A punk rock band was the evening's main attraction. The girl singer (an Art School student I believe), hair shorn, face white and bloodless and with blackened holes for eyes, screamed agonisingly for half-an-hour or so. A drunken couple embraced in the middle of the floor. Liverpool's intellectual elite, trapped in adolescent arrest, takes it all very seriously. Intellectual surrender is confused with cultural revolution. At the Everyman Theatre, posters, dripping fake blood, protest against censorship, violence, injustice and brutality. Exiled Chilean groups come and play music at lunchtime. Punk, politics and poetry collapse into each other. The categories have been confused in Liverpool and they are like drowning men.

All the same, they say the 'scene' is coming alive again in Liverpool. O'Halligan, with the assistance of Jung, has calculated that the exact centre of the world is located where Mathew Street meets Temple Court, not many yards from the old Cavern out of which 'the four apostles' emerged. In the clubs and restaurants along Hardman Street the jeunesse dorée disport themselves nightly, dancing to punk and reggae. 'The Liverpool revival now is on,' exults a *Guardian* correspondent, 'it is a . . . sudden burst of energy . . .'

Poor Liverpool. The Beatles have a lot to answer for.

'Liverpool 8: home of the Mersey sound, the sound of guitars from a hundred basements and bedsitters. Liverpool's Left Bank or Greenwich Village, from Augustus John to the Mersey Poets, pubs crammed with painters, writers, musicians. Liverpool 8: the sound and the place, that went round the world in the 1960s . . .'

(*Handout – 1978 – by Liverpool Academy of Arts*)

In the early 1840s Herman Melville visited Liverpool as a boy sailor. An account of his experiences can be found in his novel *Redburn*. The Liverpool Melville saw, despite the horrors of its proletarian poverty ('it seemed hard to believe that such an array of misery could be furnished by any town in the world'), was at the height of its prosperity. The confidence and wealth of the city was symbolised by its port installations. '. . . I beheld long China walls of masonry; vast piers of stone; and a succession of granite-rimmed docks . . . The extent and solidity of these structures seemed equal to what I read of the old Pyramids of Egypt.' Today, those docks are silent; the vast warehouses are empty and crumbling. But the misery remains. Liverpool, its heart plucked out by postwar planning, has become one vast 'inner city'. It is in an area like Liverpool 8 that one begins to understand the terrible meaning of that term. Melville would have been no less shocked today than he was one hundred and thirty years ago.

I had arranged to meet my guide on the Rialto steps. The Rialto steps! Alas . . . the Rialto turned out to be an abandoned cinema now converted into an emporium of second-hand furniture.

'A sad and fascinating place,' my guide said. 'You ought to have a look inside.'

We roamed for a while among the upturned tables and chairs and dressing-tables. Not long before I had been in Hull, another area of high unemployment and social depression. There too the trade in second-hand furniture was in a flourishing state. Most of the debris gathered here would end up in America, to be sold as 'antiques'. We returned outside. An unsettling quiet reigned over the neighbourhood – and we were not much more than a mile from the centre of town. On nearby Upper Parliament Street most of the handsome terraced houses were given over to decay, their shattered windows boarded up, their basements lapped by a rising tide of refuse; a dereliction that was repeated in nearly all the surrounding streets. We walked past plots of wasteland which had been lying idle for many years, past abandoned shops and offices whose vandalised frontages were sealed by sheets of corrugated iron. Only a solicitor specialising in legal aid and a Greek delicatessen seemed to be open for business. Ahead of us loomed peeling, many-storeyed blocks of council housing.

'Many of the people who live in this area,' my guide said, 'are not merely unemployed. They are unemployable.' It was a district, she added, rich in mental disturbance.

We entered one of the blocks. A rash of graffiti covered the grimy walls; the light-fittings had been ripped out; rubbish was stuffed into available cavities and crevices. We met a group of middle-aged ladies on the way out to do their shopping.

'It's like this all the way up,' one of them said. 'All the way to the top.' She pointed at the graffiti, the wrecked light-fittings, the middens of rubbish. The block, in fact, was in a presentable state that morning – it had recently been cleaned. Usually, the rubbish was everywhere, overflowing from the badly designed chutes.

'Who does the wrecking?' my guide asked.

They did not know. The kids, of course. But they had never actually *seen* anyone. No sensible person left his flat after dark. Not even the lift – when it worked – was safe. They wanted to be moved, to get as far away as they could from the inner city horror. Knotty Ash would do. Decent folk, civilised folk, lived in Knotty Ash. We took the lightless, shuddering lift to the top of the block. Liverpool sloped away below us towards the silver glare of the Mersey and the dead docks; tract upon tract of desolation – from that height one had a panoramic view of the destroyed terraces, the council blocks, the barren wastelands between the buildings. Around and about us all the city's detritus – the black, the destitute, the depraved – had been dumped and conveniently forgotten. 'By night,' a caretaker said, 'a lot of the places around here are indistinguishable from brothels.' He spoke of drug-taking, child-molestation, alcoholism, the random, brutish violence of the young; he complained of bureaucratic neglect and insolence – not long before they had even halved his allocation of disinfectant!

We visited another block, this one only three or four storeys high, climbing dark, smelly stairs. A broken door signalled an abandoned flat. We pushed our way in. The place had been smashed and looted. Broken glass and ceiling plaster littered the floor. In the bathroom, the washbasin had been wrenched from the wall and taken away. The taps had been removed. Miraculously, the bathtub survived.

The tenants of these flats did not dare go away on holiday. They did not dare leave them untended for any length of time. We went down to the paved courtyard, surrounded on each side by a block similar to the one we had just been in. Not a tree. Not a flower. Not a blade of grass. Stray dogs snarled weakly at us. At the far end of the courtyard, a woman, wrapped up against the cold, was negotiating with a coal merchant. Crisp packets and sheets of newspaper, blown by the wind, scraped and skated across the concrete. Everywhere – shattered or boarded-up windows; leaking drainage pipes; patches of mossy wall. I stared at the stray dogs. Where was I? Was I really in one of the cities of the industrialised West?

'Do you know about defensible space?' my guide asked. We were standing in front of a two-storeyed modern terrace, each 'unit' of which was equipped with a small walled yard.

Did defensible space, I wondered, have anything to do with spherical acoustic space? 'No,' I said aloud. 'I'm afraid I don't.'

The idea, in fact, was quite a simple one: if, the theory went, you provided someone with a patch, a piece of territory, that he could regard as exclusively his, it would stimulate pride, protectiveness, endeavour and so on. He would want, in other words, to take care of his space, to defend it.

'These people,' my guide said, indicating the walled yards, 'were given defensible space.'

I stared at the arid plots of concrete, some flooded with pools of water from blocked gutters, some strewn with refuse from over-flowing dustbins, some stacked with junk. Nowhere did I see the tubs of flowers predicted by the theory.

'We try to do our best,' my guide said. 'Where do we go wrong?'

The question is not confined to Liverpool 8. What, for instance, had gone wrong at the 'Piggeries'? They are to be found a couple of miles or so north of Upper Parliament Street. The devastation that had overwhelmed the complex of multi-storey blocks, that had led, ultimately, to their complete abandonment, is shocking. Today, the site looks as if a civil war of Lebanese proportions had raged there; as if it had been hit by a fantastic outburst of negative energy. The wrecked playground, the burnt-out interiors, the screaming graffiti daubed across the very tops of the buildings, speak of deep-seated mental disturbance.

In Merseyside extremes rub against each other. Cross to the other side of the river, to the Wirral. You enter, almost immediately, a different country. Here are well-kept suburbs, picture-postcard villages, ponies grazing in large gardens, rolling pastures ornamented with cows. The Wirral is made uneasy by the steel, concrete and asphalt city across the water. It is both a little contemptuous and a little afraid of it. The Wirral turns away, voting Conservative and doing its shopping in Chester. It is a crude and startling contrast; it disturbs. After all the decades of reformist activity, it does not make sense.

*

'Kirkby!' The waitress shuddered. 'Why in heaven's name do you want to go to Kirkby? There's nothing in Kirkby.'

'I wouldn't say that. I believe many thousands of people live in Kirkby.'

'Kirkby's a dump. Nothing but vandals and graffiti. It's all violence out there. Nothing but violence and vandalism.'

'Why is it all violence and vandalism out there?'

'That's how the people in Kirkby are. They enjoy vandalising.'

'Maybe it's because there's so much unemployment in Kirkby.'

She scowled dismissively. 'That's the excuse they'll give you. But the people in Kirkby don't *want* to work. They prefer to live on the dole.'

All over Merseyside Kirkby (its rate of unemployment twice the national average, at twenty percent the highest in Western Europe) has a bad name. 'The people in Kirkby are *common*,' the wife of a motor-car worker told me, 'just plain *common*.' A good friend of hers, she said, had moved out to Kirkby for a while and then fled. But even she, after a relatively brief exposure to its miasmic airs, had become a little common. 'I could see the change in her straightaway.' Someone else will mention in a whisper that incest is a not infrequent occurrence in Kirkby – like unemployment, its incidence is well above the national average. Even those who insist (and, I believe, with some justice) that Merseyside has unfairly been given a bad name for industrial relations and who remain optimistic about the future of the region (in the sense that the outlook is no better – or worse – than anywhere else in the country), will pause at the mention of Kirkby and look grave. Distaste, hopelessness, will darken their countenances. Kirkby ... well ... yes ... there's Kirkby, of course ... you can't forget Kirkby ... nobody's trying to say that Merseyside doesn't have its warts ... not at all ... mind you, you mustn't only look at the bad ... you have to be positive. All the same, Kirkby remains. It is there. It cannot be wished away or explained away.

From Liverpool, the road out to Kirkby takes you along the bleak expanse of Scotland Road, a strip notorious in the past for its anti-social ways. Today, Scotland Road is an inner city desert: it was from such areas that people were uprooted and sent out to multiply and be fruitful in the 'overspill' new town of Kirkby – thereby (it is now claimed) destroying their sense of community and sowing the seeds of present disaster. After about twenty minutes' drive through a semi-urbanised countryside, a group of glacially white towers appears on the plain. It is the utter arbitrariness of their location on that featureless plain which first strikes one. They stand there like monuments raised by the planners to celebrate the inanity, the meaninglessness, of human existence. This is the Cantril Farm housing estate, fondly known to the local wits as Cannibal Farm. Those still in their thirties recall that in their childhood the area around Kirkby was 'real' countryside. There were farms, streams, trees, meadows.

Ahead of us, Kirkby proper took shape. Even from the motorway I could see the ripped roofs of abandoned houses, the rows of boarded-up windows, whole blocks lying empty – all the, by now, familiar symptoms of social decay. We explored the industrial estate, driving past factory compound after factory compound. Plessey, Kodak, Tate and Lyle ... Few people were about on that Wednesday mid-morning. Only the odd steaming chimney told of the industrial life that was quietly running its course. Outside the gates of the closed-down Bird's Eye factory (twelve hundred jobs lost) a group of three or four workers stood vigil, warming their hands over a fire. Kirkby existed only in order to feed these factories with labour. It was a kind of Bantustan.

At the Tower Hill housing estate, there were more wrecked multi-storey blocks. We climbed up and down the usual narrow stairways alive with the usual graffiti. We stood in the usual rubble-filled sitting-rooms. From the cramped balcony of an upper storey, I looked down on an expanse of bare asphalt. Directly below were the twisted remains of a tricycle. Here and there were sheets of rusting corrugated-iron. A young man, wrapped in an overcoat, hair long and tangled, wandered surlily towards the blank façade of a pub called, appropriately enough, the 'Tenterhook'. A few flats in one of the neighbouring blocks were still occupied – you could tell by the curtains drawn across the windows. My companion kept a watchful eye on his car. The 'kids' could sometimes display the rapacity of vultures: in some areas of Liverpool a car could be stripped in a quarter of an hour. We wandered down deserted lanes lined with peeling wooden cabins; adorned with spindly leafless saplings that would never be given the chance to grow.

'A kind of helplessness sets in,' my companion observed. 'They will complain for weeks about a broken lock or window. They develop a depressing dependence. More energy is used up in complaint than in action.'

Towering blocks flanked the commercial precinct at Cantril Farm.

Several of the shops had gone out of business -- they had been raided too often. The handful that had survived were screened behind folding metal shutters, drawn open just enough to allow access. An atmosphere of siege pervaded the precinct. A cold wind blew across the treeless undulations that passed for landscaping. Sheets of corrugated iron (Kirkby is rich in the stuff) and a mattress had been discarded in the dank 'adventure' playground. The more conventional type of playground was represented by a slide perched on a muddy mound. Drifts of waste paper and tins and bottles were washed up against walls.

What did it all mean? The wife of the motor-car worker would talk about 'common' people; the waitress would say it was how Kirkby liked to be; a nice middle-class lady blamed democracy; trade-unionists would blame unemployment; sociologists would talk about high-rise living and the break-up of communities. Society was running out of explanations. None of the explanations fitted; none could account for the rampant darkness of mind to which the devastations I had seen bore such eloquent witness. Those who worshipped punk rock worshipped that darkness. It signalled intellectual bankruptcy.

The man I spoke to at the Labour Club in Kirkby was gloomy. A whole generation was growing up without 'work experience'. There was hardly an eighteen-year-old in Kirkby who was in work. Given time, they would be not only unemployed but unemployable. Kirkby would not be released from its problems in the immediate future. New investment was in the offing. But new investment often meant new technology; new technology meant even fewer jobs. Machines were making men redundant. Nothing could be done about that. Progress was unstoppable. What was the solution? Earlier retirement? That would bring all the problems of leisure with it. Kirkby's problems were the problems of all industrial civilisation.

Terry sat on a table, swinging his legs. In the next room, beyond unbreakable glass windows, a five-a-side football match was in progress; in the room I was in, boys were playing darts and table-tennis. I was in a Boys Club in the Wavertree district. We were talking about vandalism. Had Terry ever 'vandalised' anything?

'Sure.'

'What?'

'A bus-stop. We smashed up the shelter.'

'Why?'

Terfy did not know why. He had just felt like it. It was something to do. He became thoughtful, struggling to put words together. He wanted (though he would not have known it) to articulate his sense of loss, his destitution. But he could not. I understood that, in the end, violence was the only form of self-expression he had at his disposal.

He would be leaving school in a year's time. I asked him what he planned to do.

'Go on the dole,' he said. He laughed. 'What else is there to do in Liverpool? Soon there won't be any factories or anything left here. There'll be nothing.'

I suggested that, perhaps, he was being a little too pessimistic.

He shrugged. 'What's so great about working in a factory anyway? Cooped up like a chicken all day. Clock in. Clock out. That's no life.'

I thought of the car-worker I had met. For fourteen years he had been an employee at the Ford plant at Halewood. He was determined that his son should not be condemned to the car factory – or any other kind of factory. 'I'm a great reader – four or five books a week. I *know* there's more to life than a bloody assembly-line. I've *seen* what happens to men in those factories. Pull this lever. Pull that lever. It kills the mind that kind of thing. You go home burnt out. Nothing to do but sit like you are dumb and watch the telly. You're good for nothing after that kind of labour.' He deliberately gave his son boring jobs to do about the house. 'When he complains, I say, "That's the sort of work I've had to do for fourteen years of my life. Imagine being bored, day in, day out, for fourteen years! Do you want *that* to happen to you?" He wanted his son to go to university, to leave the life of the factory behind. ('The boredom of the assembly line?' The multi-national executive smiled blandly. He had heard that story too many times before. 'What job isn't boring? Your job has its boring moments. My job has its boring moments. Clerks are bored. Typists are bored. We're all bored.')

At a plant like Ford, employing fourteen thousand workers, ninety percent of the labour force could be described as semi-skilled. They did not require 'O' Levels or 'A' Levels – only able bodies. Education counted for nothing on the assembly line. It was possible for a man to get hold of everything this society deemed desirable – colour television, annual holiday – without particular effort. Factories simplify life: the Amazonian tribesman exercises more skill in trapping an animal than does the man at Halewood putting together a motor-car.

Civilisation falls apart: it calls forth bad newspapers, bad television, bad schools, bad politics.

Terry was aware that education was useless. He laughed when I suggested that he might stay on at school a bit longer.

'What for? I've seen lads with "A" Levels and university degrees on the dole. I've seen them counting trees in the park – job creation, they call it.'

One-third of the boys who came to that Wavertree club were, for all practical purposes, illiterate – many literally so. Able bodies – that was all the factory required. Parents were apathetic, the organiser of the club said. They let their children run wild. They tried, without success, to involve the parents in the affairs of the club. Only once had they ever got anywhere – the time they had organised a five-a-side football competition.

'Around here,' Terry said, 'everybody wants to be a football star.'

In Wavertree, outside the factory, outside the football field, there was nothing.

The floodlights of Anfield glowed like over-bright moons against the night sky. Crowds streamed along the pavements. A mixture of snow and sleet blew against my face, a soft white rain picked up by the glare of the floodlights. I could hear the swelling roar of the Kop. This was my first football match and it was all rather intimidating. Within minutes of meeting anyone in Liverpool you will discover the team he supports – Liverpool or Everton. The good-natured rivalry between the two clubs is stressed: they don't maul each other as they do in neighbouring Manchester. 'You'll see people with Liverpool scarves and Everton scarves walking together after a match. Some families are split down the middle.' It is not always easy to remember that it is football which is being talked about.

For a novice like myself, the Kop was an unnerving sight – a restless, rippling sea of sunless faces, radiating frenzied loyalty. The middle-aged man sitting next to me followed the game with an endless stream of comment. 'Nice ball!' 'Shocking!' 'Send the bastard off!' He was taut with involvement. What did *he* wish for his son? Would he say to him, 'This is not enough. I *know* there's something more to life than this . . .'

Liverpool scored.

'Look at the Kop! Look at the Kop!'

My companion gazed with awe towards that turbulent sea of sunless faces.

There are those who worship the Kop as a manifestation of the Life Force. The Kop, you will be told, is *real*, a repository of folk wisdom and folk energy. Last year in Rome (before the European Cup Final) Adrian Henri recited poetry to them.

Did he know what he was celebrating?

The City by the Sea

The middle-class lady frowned.

'Bombay?' she said. 'There's nothing specially interesting about Bombay. It's just another big cosmopolitan city, like any other. Only more people. That's all.'

Below us, on a floodlit tennis court, an international tennis tournament was in progress. Pretty Indian girls in T-shirts and fashionably patched jeans dotted the wooden terraces erected for the occasion. The warm night was scented with a smell of dust. Lit-up skyscrapers loomed like mountain ranges. The match ended, the victorious Indian player shaking hands with his American opponent. Without warning, the spell was broken.

Out of nowhere, as if born of the musty night itself, a small army of sweepers invaded the court, meagre, stick-limbed men wielding short, soft brooms. Crouched on their haunches, their gaze anchored to the ground, they began brushing the playing surface. The middle-class lady did not look at this dwarfish, less-than-human crew. They were not supposed to be looked at: they were excluded from her vision of the cosmopolitan city. The sweepers, their job done, vanished as silently and as suddenly as they had come. Another match began; we left. Outside, established on the pavement, was a colony of five or six squatter huts. Within the low, dark interiors, fires burned. A smell of excrement tainted the smoky air. Ragged children crawled in the dust. Nearby, a group of dhoti-clad men lounged under a banyan tree. A beggar whined and was ignored. All about us the seething city hummed. The lady, lifting the border of her sari, looked at nothing.

I was seeing the city with the uncharitable eyes of the freshly arrived visitor. My responses on that first evening were raw, touched with a mild hysteria. Bombay, it is said, offers no 'foreplay'. It makes no concessions. Like New York, it plunges you straight in. I had arrived only hours before, in a dawn white with unseasonal rain. Even at that early hour a sea of urgent brown faces was to be seen pressed up against the glass doors of the terminal building. What were they waiting for? What did they want? There had been a moment of recoil; a dread of venturing out into the nightmare at which they hinted.

It was a long ride through the grey, humid morning to the city centre, through mile after mile of endlessly repeated suburban squalor – always, it seemed, the same squatter colonies (they spring up like mould on every available space), the same moss-blackened, uncared-for apartment blocks draped with washing, the same gaudy film posters adorned with fleshy, pink-faced women, the same rows of cramped shops, the same overwhelming sense of too many people spilling from crowded pavement into crowded street. At the traffic lights the beggars descended, thrusting their hands through the window, whining a litany of want, pointing now at their mouths, now at their bellies, now at the dirt-encrusted baby invariably attached to their hips. My driver was garrulous. Was it true that in London a man would be paid by the Government even if he did no work? A friend had told him that. If that was so, London must be a truly wonderful place. In Bombay, if a man did no work, he starved. 'Bombay no good, sahib. No good at all.' He fell silent for a while.

Then: 'I have nice girl cousin, sahib.'

'I'm glad to hear that.'

'College girl. Educated. Very modern.'

I waited.

'Eight hundred rupees one whole night, sahib. Modern girl.'

'Would you really sell your girl cousin to me?'

He laughed; and began to tell me of men who sold their wives, their daughters, their sisters. 'When life is hard, sahib, a man will do anything.'

On that first day, then, it seemed a city of terror, of despair. But I was wrong – or, at any rate, only partly right. It takes time to read Bombay. It takes time to understand that those moss-blackened apartment blocks are not slums, that they very probably are the homes of middle-class people and that the outer neglect is deceptive. It takes time to understand that those squatter huts occupying the pavement outside the stadium may contain transistor radios and gas cookers, that the men who live in them may have regular clerkly jobs and be earning three or four hundred rupees a month – a decent wage by Indian standards. It takes time to penetrate the veil of apparently hopeless dereliction and to see that the city still works reasonably well: buses run; trains run; electricity lights the roads and skyscrapers; water (more or less) flows; telephones (more or less) work. Bombay lives.

So it happens that, after an interval, the nightmare begins to fade and another idea of Bombay becomes possible. This is the vision of the city as it can be seen from Marine Drive, that lovely stretch of road, curving round a bay washed by the waters of the Arabian Sea, bordered to the north by the residential towers of Malabar Hill, home of businessmen and film-stars, and, to the south, by the towers of Nariman Point, reclaimed from the sea within the last ten years. To enhance the vision, go to the Taj Mahal Hotel. Sit in its marbled, air-conditioned lobby, which looks east, toward the Gateway of India, the harbour and the Indian mainland. Middle-class Bombay uses this lobby as a kind of grand piazza – a piazza locked away behind glass and protected from unseemly invasion by stern-faced Sikhs. Watch the carefully dressed families who come to parade, to examine the rich displays of jewellery and textiles, to read the advertisements for holidays in Goa. Or go, in the late afternoon, to the Gymkhana Club. Sit out on its long veranda with views of the towers, domes and spires of Victorian Bombay. Watch the young men playing rugger and the white-clad tennis players strolling to and from the courts. Or go, at lunch-time, to the restaurant attached to the Jehangir Art Gallery and observe the young journalists, secretaries and advertising executive who gather there. Gradually, the visitor begins to sense the liveliness, the glamour, of the city; he begins to appreciate – if not wholly to accept – some of the claims that are made for it.

That glamour, at its most extreme, slides into the dreams and fantasies spawned by the film world. Bombay, the centre of the prolific Indian film industry, churns out about eighty films a year. Nearly all are bad – so bad that they indicate a collective derangement of the intelligence. But this does not matter because, ultimately, it is not the films that count (in most of these films the actors simply play up their popular 'images') but the stars themselves. Magazines like *Stardust*, *Filmfare* and *Super* (to name only those published in English) are entirely devoted to chronicling their doings. The stars exist to embody all the lusts and longings of a deprived urban population. Film after bad film recycles elemental dreams of riches, of fair women, of virility, of humble virtue conquering arrogant vice.

The wealth accumulated by the more successful actors and actresses verges on the fabulous: some are paid a million or more rupees per film and a few are so versatile that they will have five or six films on hand at any one time. Their houses are palatial. At their parties, Scotch whisky, selling in India from thirty pounds a bottle, is rumoured to flow like water. They drive about in air-conditioned

Cadillacs and Mercedes Benzes – though one actor of left-wing persuasion contents himself with a red, chauffeur-driven Volkswagen.

Now and then they descend from their celestial mansions and display themselves to their devotees. One such manifestation occurred while I was there. Its heavily publicised purpose was to collect money for the victims of the cyclone which had struck the state of Andhra a week or two before. Dressed in specially made white suits, the stars toured the streets of the city on the backs of lorries. How much money was actually collected remains obscure. More memorable was the assault on two gossip columnists by one of the white-clad actors: he had been outraged by something they had written about him. It was *that* which made the headlines in the newspapers next day. The victims of the cyclone were forgotten.

The stars are the tutelary deities of Bombay – in a curious way the photographs that appear in the film magazines do echo the gaudy representations of the Hindu pantheon sold on every street corner. They are the guardians of the city's glamour and its promise. In a town where millions are compelled to eke out choked, near-impossible lives, they allow the imagination room to expand. They speak directly to the destitute. At all hours of the day Bombay's cinema houses are surrounded by gawking crowds of young men staring up at the glittering posters. Within, for a few rupees, they will be offered cloud-capped dreams. Bombay's cinemas are the opium dens of the masses.

Bombay, you will be told time and again, is like no other city in India. Indeed, its enthusiasts will point out, it is India's only 'real' city. Delhi is dismissed as too Punjabi-dominated, too obsessed by political intrigue and the niceties of the bureaucratic pecking order. Calcutta, despite its surviving pockets of English-influenced gentility, remains, at bottom, a Bengali preserve. Madras is of the orthodox Hindu South. Bombay, on the other hand, belongs to no one and everyone. Hindu, Muslim, Parsi, British – all have played a part in the creation of the city.

In the Indian sense of home, of what is quaintly referred to as a 'native place', Bombay is home to very few of its seven million people - with the possible exception of the Parsis who began migrating from Gujerat to the comforts of British rule in the seventeenth century. 'If a man tells you Bombay is his home,' I was told, 'that means he is without roots.' This lack of ancestral attachment adds yet another dimension to the glamour of the city. It undermines the constraints traditionally imposed by the varied and stifling communalisms – of family, caste, religion, region – which drive such deep and damaging fissures through all layers of Indian society and effectively destroy the free play of personality.

Bombay offers liberation. The individual can flower. He can, if he so wishes, cultivate his eccentricities. 'Here,' the journalist said, 'I can wear cheap rubber slippers to the office. I can dress how I like. Nobody cares. Nobody gives a damn. I couldn't do that in Allahabad.' A small victory, but, for him, one worth celebrating and savouring. In Bombay you can lead your own life. You can be anonymous. You can go up to your flat on the twentieth floor and lock yourself away. In Bombay, you can have a lover; you can have a mistress.

But, if the visitor has to be on guard against over-reacting to the outer dereliction of the city, he has also to guard against over-emphasising its modernity. Bombay is still of India. Its universality can be exaggerated. Everyone may belong to Bombay. But everyone – Parsi, Gujerati, Bohra, Goan, Maratha, Tamil, Sindhi – belongs in his own way. The city is a loose federation of communalisms, each of which tends to look after itself, each of which tends to mind its own business. The Parsis, running their own hospitals, schools and residential enclaves, are, perhaps, the most extreme example of communal self-sufficiency; but all the other communities, to a greater or lesser degree, follow the pattern.

Much of the life of the city is invisible. It runs underground, rarely surfacing, conducted through the parallel but non-communicating channels of the varied communalisms. Parsi politics (for example) touches only Parsis and is, in fact, known to few outsiders. It is entirely self-contained. One of the first things that strikes one about the city – and Bombay, it should be noted, crawls with journalists – is the absence of any overall community of news and intellectual exchange. 'Bombay', as such, is an administrative abstraction. A strike of thousands of government workers passes almost unnoticed: no one discusses the issues involved. Who, you ask, are those people marching down the street waving banners? What are they protesting about? Nobody is certain. Every event is isolated, as significant or insignificant as any other, appearing out of the blue and disappearing into the blue. Nothing joins up to make a coherent picture. In countries where journalism is a developed art, the newspapers tell a continuing story. The stranger finds himself, as it were, plunged into the middle of a long-running serial. After a while, however, he begins to pick up the strands of the plot. He becomes familiar with the issues and the main characters of the drama. This does not happen in Bombay. The city is permanently out of focus.

Universalism exists only in the upper reaches of Bombay society. It is in this tiny area that one finds the 'cosmopolitanism' referred to by the middle-class lady. This cosmopolitanism looks to the West for inspiration and sustenance; but it too must be treated with caution and not over-rated. The concern, for instance, with pollution and the environment is little more than a modish affectation, a direct, unadapted import. Bombay matrons will weep over the victims of thalidomide but lose interest when the talk turns to the one hundred thousand waifs at large in the city. A favourable review of an Indian film in a foreign newspaper will be presented as an immutable, eternal judgment, the final guarantee of its worth. The actress whose chief claim to fame in her own and the city's eyes is that she once played a part in an American film tells you how much she adores London, how, really, it is her true spiritual home. As it happens, she is not all that successful by the standards of the Indian cinema. This, her friends say admiringly, is because she is far too 'westernised', far too 'sophisticated' (in the American film she bared her breasts) for simple Indian audiences. As we talk, three white-haired poodles play about her feet – dogs, especially large, protein-consuming dogs, are very fashionable in Bombay just now.

'Where do you take them for walks?' I ask. The animals do not look well. They must suffer from the heat and the physical constrictions of life in a Bombay high-rise flat.

She looks shocked. '*I* don't take them for walks,' she replies. 'That's *her* job.' She points at a ragged maid-servant hovering in the background.

Thus dog-ownership is separated from its implications. It is carried on in a void. Her dog-keeping is purely imitative, a gesture of homage to London and its spacious parks.

A group of architecture students is on strike. Surrounded by slogans, they sprawl under a geodesic dome. They are on strike because, at the end of the their course, they will be awarded diplomas, not degrees. To justify their case, they tell the story of the professor of architecture who had a daughter of marriageable age. Two of the professor's students fell in love with the girl. One was reading for a diploma, the other for a degree. The degree student got the girl. I could get nothing more out of them. Architecture was irrelevant. They had no ideas, no plans. The geodesic dome implied nothing; it led nowhere. It was a misleading symbol of modernity.

Bombay is littered with misleading symbols of modernity. You soon learn not to be surprised at the girl who, looking as if she has stepped straight out of the pages of *Vogue* and doing what she calls an 'international' job, can speak quite calmly of the arranged marriage (correct caste guaranteed) that may be lying ahead of her. You learn not to be surprised that an Australian cabaret star, making the simplest of sexual jokes, can reduce a 'sophisticated' night-club audience to howls of laughter.

Bombay deceives at every level.

Over the last three years, on a hill-top in the suburb of Worli, a public garden has come into being. Previously, the hill was covered with the shacks of a shanty colony. Now there are terraced banks of flowers, well-tended lawns, an illuminated waterfall. The garden is not yet complete. In time there will be a lotus pool and a pavilion. In a city so choked for space, the creation of this garden is a small miracle. But it is worth a visit for another reason: it affords a visual summary of Bombay. To the west is the sea and the city of faery towers – the city of dreams. To the east are tightly-packed colonies of hutments. Beyond rise the chimneys of the textile mills, hazing the air with smoke – the city of labour and struggle. The Mill Area is another world. There are few connections between it and the middle-class town. Two hundred thousand people work in Bombay's textile industry – the mills are the largest employers of labour. Within them a stark industrial life is carried on. In vast sheds, swirling with cotton dust and humid as greenhouses (the humidity is deliberate – the cotton threads would break in a dry atmosphere), barebacked men day and night tend ranks of clattering machinery. One in every six of these men will eventually develop tuberculosis; most call it a day after five or six years. Clustered round the mills are the densely-populated tenements known as *chawls* – one of the distinctive features of the architecture of old Bombay – where the mill-hands live. Twenty or more men (the vast majority of the mill-hands are migrant workers who have left their families behind in the village) may share a cell in these chawls, sleeping in shifts. But the money is reasonably good (the average wage is around five hundred rupees a month) and the competition for jobs is fierce: when life is hard, men will do anything.

It was the mills which, in the latter half of the nineteenth century, brought industrial boom and the beginnings of population explosion to Bombay. Until then, the town had grown slowly, outstripped in importance by Calcutta and Madras. The Portuguese had been the first European overlords of the area. They, however, did not do a great deal with it – a fort or two remains, not much else. In 1660 the island (or, rather, the series of tiny islands out of which Bombay is compounded) passed into the possession of the English king Charles II as part of the dowry brought by his Portuguese bride Catherine of Braganza. Eight years later, in return for an annual rent of ten pounds, he leased it to the merchants of the East India Company. At that time the Company – still struggling to establish a secure foothold in India – had its main trading station further to the north, at Surat in Gujerat. There they were vulnerable not only to the exactions of the corrupt officials of the Mughal Empire but to the depredations of the Mughals' enemies – the Hindu Marathas. Sea-girthed Bombay offered escape from both these plagues.

The Company, unlike its Portuguese predecessors, was free of sectarian passion. Profitable, unharassed trade – that was its sole concern. By the end of the seventeenth century, Bombay had already acquired the features by which it can still be recognised. 'The people that live here,' wrote one of the Company's surgeons, 'are a mixture of most of the neighbouring countries, most of them fugitives and vagabonds, no account being here taken of them; others perhaps invited here by the liberty granted them in their several religions, which here are solemnised with variety of fopperies . . .' Across the sub-continent, in Calcutta and Madras, the British Raj soon hardened into the inflexible rituals and habits of imperial rule. That did not happen to quite the same extent in Bombay where the barriers to social contact between rulers and ruled were not as insurmountable as they were elsewhere. The influence of the westernised Parsis must have helped – in the 1830s Sir Jamsetjee Jeejeebhoy was entertaining Englishmen at his famous parties. So must have the pride of the Marathas, heirs to a powerful martial tradition – they would sit down as a matter of course in the presence of Englishmen. Such behaviour would have been unthinkable in Calcutta. But most important may have been the fact that everyone who lived in the city that offered refuge to all but was home to none was, to a certain degree, an adventurer. Everyone was on the make. Men came to Bombay to earn a living, to hustle. And that is why, after three hundred years, they still keep coming.

The migrants come, it has been estimated, at the rate of three hundred families a day. They come from everywhere, from Tamil Nadu (formerly Madras State), from Andhra Pradesh, from Kerala, from Mysore, from Assam in the distant north-east, from the hinterland of Maharashtra – of which Bombay happens to be the state capital. All India makes its claims on the cosmopolitan city. Six years ago the population of Bombay was six million; today it is seven and a half million; in 1990, at present rates of growth, it will have reached ten million; and by the year 2000 it will be fifteen or sixteen million. The migrants pour into an area that is just under 350 square kilometres in extent.

The statistics numb – as they always do in India. Every night one and a half million people sleep out on the city's streets and pavements. The number who live permanently on the pavements is put – con-servatively in my opinion – at one hundred thousand. Because Bombay is built on a series of narrow islands (they call it a linear city), the suburbs stretch northwards to the point of absurdity. It is possible to spend four or more hours a day in travelling to and from one's place of work. At rush hours the lemming-like crowds stampeding in and out of the Victoria Terminus are a frightening spectacle. Suburban trains carry nearly twice the number of passengers for which they are designed. As a result, three or four people are killed or seriously maimed every day, accidents which the newspapers do not even bother to report. The water supply is hopelessly inadequate. Improvements are being undertaken with the help of the World Bank but, by the time those have been completed, demand would once again have outstripped supply. Raw sewage washes into the sea. Nearly a third of the population is without sanitary facilities. Not surprisingly, millions are afflicted with energy-sapping gastric com-plaints.

Towards dusk the rats – there are supposed to be seventy million rats in Bombay, ten for every human being – and the cockroaches make their appearance, swarming about the Gateway of India and the broad promenade that borders the Worli Seaface. In the early evening, every yellow-lit window in every multi-storey block thrown wide open to the stagnant air rich with the smell of smoke and food, every transistor radio turned to full volume, every car horn blaring,

every voice raised to a shout, the human immensity rages with
something approaching frenzy. Bombay, while it remains awake,
knows no stillness, no solitude. Only late at night does an exhausted
peace descend as the yellow squares of light blink out, the cars
disappear from the roads and the blanketed bodies ranged along the
pavements assume all the abandoned attitudes of deep repose. Then,
on the Worli Seaface, you can hear the wash of the waves on the rocks.
For a few hours the city belongs to its seventy million rats and its as yet
uncounted cockroaches; for a few hours man is held at bay.

Bombay looks for rescue – but without any great conviction – to its
projected 'twin city' (New Bombay) which, it is hoped, will arise one
day on the mainland. The plans are both grandiose (they include the
construction of six-mile long bridges linking the island with the
mainland) and detailed (even the optimum distance between bus-
stops has been calculated). But the little that exists of the new city – a
down-at-heel shopping precinct, a block or two of flats, a cluster of
capital-intensive factories – still has about it the forlorn air of make-
believe. There is certainly no correspondence between what exists and
the fantasies of the planners – 'Entering the harbour one would see the
city on both sides, on the one side extending over the island, and on
the other rising above its shores into the hills beyond. In the harbour
and across the bridges one would see a constant and busy movement
. . . Citizens from all over the island . . . would cross to the Eastern
waterfront where would be located large, magnificent plazas . . .' It is a
dream that no one really believes in. The State government, in a burst
of enthusiasm, did promise to move to the new city but so far has
shown no signs of actually being prepared to do so. In any case, India,
under its new Janata rulers, is in the grip of a Gandhian resurgence
which seeks salvation in village regeneration. Metropolitan grandeur
is out of step with the humble mood of the times. While New Bombay
languishes for lack of interest and money, Old Bombay continues
to draw to itself the redundant humanity of unregenerated village
India.

The stress shows. It is there in the middle-class obsession with
housing: despite the space of high-rise building in the last ten years,
flats – and even single rooms – are not easy to come by. 'Would you
believe that I am forced to share one room with three other people?'
the young, smartly-dressed executive asked. 'I would like to get
married. But how can I? Where can I take my wife? It's intolerable.
It's no way to live.' He could not stay any length of time in that room.

To keep himself sane he walked. 'I just walk and walk and walk when I have nothing better to do.' The psychoanalyst adds his portion to the tale, telling of the fears of impotency that can arise from over-crowding and the lack of privacy it entails. In the squatter colonies drugs and cheap country liquor bring easy release at the weekends. That is the time for wife-beating and child-beating. In his dark, airless cell, the post office peon squats nervelessly. It is a public holiday, the Muslim festival of Muharram. He has no plans to make use of the day. His eyes are glazed with apathy; he can hardly summon up the energy to speak. Outside, on the crumbling landing, inches away from the spot where his wife crouches preparing his midday meal, the leaking drainage pipe has deposited a pool of fetid water. He will do nothing about that. He will do nothing about anything. He will not even complain. Occasionally, though, explosions do occur. Some years ago, the mobs of the Shiv Sena (the Army of Shiva), the vehicle of a revived Maratha nationalism which takes as its cult figure Sīvaji, the seventeenth century Maratha warrior-hero, rampaged through the streets of the city beating up South Indian migrants and smashing their shops and restaurants. The surprising thing is that such out-breaks do not occur more often.

The migrants, despite everything, keep coming. A visit to a typical area out of which Bombay sucks people helps to explain why. Ratnagiri lies (by road) some two hundred miles south of Bombay. The land, sea-edged, traversed by rivers and hills, is full of beauty. But it is a cruel beauty. A largely landless peasantry lives off a diet of rice, coconut and – when they can get it – dried fish. Malnutrition has led to an incapacity for sustained labour, mental and physical. Prawns are caught in the sea off Ratnagiri, but these, deep-frozen and put into pretty boxes, are all exported to the United States and Japan. The trade is controlled by a handful of Bombay entrepreneurs. Ratnagiri benefits only in the form of the semi-sweated labour employed in the packaging factories. No other industrial development worth the name has taken place in the entire district. Men must depend on what the land can give; and the land by itself can give very little. Those who can, leave.

In one village I visited virtually the only people left were those too old and too young to go anywhere. At the entrance to the village I came upon a scene that could have come straight out of one of Hollywood's Biblical epics. Perhaps a dozen men, emaciated, all but naked, sun-blackened torsoes glistening with sweat, were at work in the red depths of a neatly-terraced laterite pit, quarrying the rock, shaping the blocks which are the basic building material of the district. On that diet of rice and coconut, on that burning, cloudless morning, their labour must have seemed like a punishment inflicted by a malevolent god. At best, a man could hack nine blocks a day out of the rock. For that, he would earn about six rupees – just enough, perhaps, to feed him, to give him the energy he needed to hack another nine blocks the next day.

Uncultivated plots surrounded the huts. The topsoil was so thin that, in many places, the rock floor was exposed. To make this land produce anything, mud has to be brought in every year. Only one crop a year was possible because of the village's total dependence on the rains. If the monsoon played truant for a week or so that crop would be ruined. Everyone was locked into a deathly dance with the rains; the relationship between a man and his food was direct and brutal. I entered a lightless hut. Children rose out of the darkness, surrounding me. My host – legs and arms as thin as sticks – had four brothers. They were all away in Bombay working on construction sites. Without their remittances, the children would starve. It was as simple as that. The land did not produce enough, could not produce enough, to feed even those who were left behind; and, in Ratnagiri, there was nothing but the land. They counted as rich the man who had enough to eat all the year round. In every hut I went into, the story was the same: sons in Bombay, husbands in Bombay, brothers and sisters in Bombay. Without Bombay they would die.

In Bombay, it seems, there is always work, always some way of earning a few rupees, of keeping body and soul together. Consider this family living on the pavement, seeking shelter under a lean-to built up from scraps of polythene, sacking, cardboard and wood. Three years ago they migrated from a village near Poona, walking all the way. Husband and wife and children scour the streets and refuse dumps of the city collecting rags, paper, discarded cigarette packets – anything that can be recycled. Their gleanings bring in seven or eight rupees a day. On that they can just about manage. In their home district such a thing would not have been possible. Bombay allows them to survive. The family next door also comes from a village near Poona. They roam the railway tracks collecting charcoal. That too brings in seven or eight rupees a day. Bombay gives everyone a chance to live.

Sometimes it gives more than that: it is a place where miracles of a sort may happen. A year ago this shoe-shine boy, who now wanders about the Gateway of India in search of customers, left his family in Calcutta and came to Bombay. He cannot be much more than thirteen years old. Usually he makes anything from five to twenty rupees a day. Today, he tells me, he has earned nothing. However, he was not too worried. Some weeks before he had had an amazing stroke of good fortune. One of his customers, a Frenchman, had, rather strangely, taken him along as a 'guide' on a six-week tour of the country. They had been to Madras, Bangalore, Agra ... they had gone everywhere, flying from place to place. The Frenchman had paid him fifty rupees a day. He had been able to save, he said, about two thousand rupees. A friend of his (as youthful and solitary as he was and also in the shoe-shine trade) confirmed the story.

'He very bright fellow,' he said, nodding admiringly. He too, as it turned out, had his expectations. These were centred on a Dutchman who had promised to take him to Holland.

'He will go as houseboy,' said the waif from Calcutta.

'No, no. Not houseboy,' the other insisted. 'I go as *tourist*. I go to see the place as tourist.'

Bombay gives everyone a chance. A walk along any stretch of pavement will reveal a hundred minute specialisations of function, a hundred strategies for survival. You can hawk anything; water, nuts, cheap pens, toys, peacock feathers, religious bric-à-brac, plastic flowers, aphrodisiacs, quack medicines, lottery tickets, hard-luck stories – 'Ladies and Gentlemen,' says the handwritten appeal thrust into my hand by the teary-eyed, demurely dressed young girl, 'we are unfortunate people, we have been driven from our land by poverty. We ask donations from charitable and human people ...'; you can grind lenses, repair broken locks, stitch leather, sell cage-birds, charm snakes, read palms, interpret dreams, clean out the ears of passers-by; you can parade your dancing monkey, display your acrobatic skills, pick pockets. The will to live is capable of infinite articulation. When life is hard, a man will do anything.

The variety, the colour, of Bombay street life disguise its terrors. There are those who will deny that there are any terrors. The architect points to the photograph pinned on his office wall. It shows a man and a woman sitting down to their evening meal in a drainage pipe. 'Isn't it wonderful!' he exclaims. 'Look at them. Such formal poses. It's like a Mughal miniature painting!' You begin to protest. No! – he says. No!

They may be poor. But what is wrong with poverty? Had I seen Detroit? Glasgow? Frankfurt? The people in these places were no happier than that couple who lived in a drainage pipe. Affluence breeds ugliness; it is degrading. In that drainage pipe a new 'life-style' was being created. The photograph demonstrated the grandeur, the tenacity, of the human spirit.

Blessed are the hot, overcrowded cities of the Poor.

Mr Narayan shuffled into the hotel. He stood there, in the marbled lobby, staring uneasily about him, a small, very dark man dressed in white shirt and white trousers. About him milled the gorgeous, nocturnal pageant of middle-class Bombay.

'Is it,' he said, 'as cool as this in London?'

'Often it's cooler. Quite a bit cooler.'

'Then,' he said, 'they are right. London must be a paradise. All my friends say it's a kind of paradise over there. Is that true?'

'I think your friends exaggerate.'

'But to be so cool . . . where I live it is never cool. But you will soon see for yourself. You will see how the poor people of Bombay live.'

It was why he had come: to take me to his room, to show me how the poor people of Bombay lived. We went out into the warm night in search of a bus – he had responded with something like alarm to my suggestion that we take a taxi. Mr Narayan (he came from Andhra) was a typesetter. For several months now he had been unemployed and was living off the savings he had managed to accumulate. 'I have applied for how many jobs, sir, I cannot tell you. Typesetters are not greatly in demand at the moment.'

Our double-decker bus moved like a Juggernaut through crowded, noisy streets. Mr Narayan's fingers drummed nervously on the knees of his spotless white trousers. It was men like him – small men with small skills, for whom the life of the street represented not opportunity but the betrayal of possibility – it was men such as he who suffered most in Bombay. He took a sheaf of assorted documents out of his pocket and handed it to me – passport, health certificates, typesetting diploma, a letter from his previous employer stating that he had been a good and faithful worker. Mr Narayan's life was contained in those papers and he never separated himself from them. 'Now,' he said, 'I am concentrating all my efforts on going to the Gulf.'

The Gulf was, of course, the Persian Gulf. It is the new El Dorado for those with any kind of expertise; and India is a bottomless reservoir of the middle- to low-range skills required by the oil-rich desert sheikdoms. Engineers, plumbers, waiters, motor-mechanics – they all want to go to the Gulf for a few years and make a small fortune. Every week the Kuwaiti consul in Bombay issues nearly one hundred work permits. The Arab, as ubiquitous a figure in Bombay as he is in London, has come to rival the film star in popular mythology.

But Mr Narayan was afraid. The human traffic to the Gulf was controlled by a network of agents. It was these agents who located the going jobs, who fixed you up, and many were unscrupulous. The agent was asking Mr Narayan four thousand rupees for his services and he had no idea what to do. He knew of several men who had been swindled out of their life-savings. 'I will go mad if that happened to me, sir. I know it.' Fearful of committing his money, yet knowing of no other way to get to the Gulf, he lived in an agony of indecision. Meanwhile, day by day, his savings dwindled.

We got off the bus. The street was thick with people. Music poured from brightly-lit foodshops.

'This,' Mr Narayan announced solemnly, 'is red-light area.'

There were women everywhere, roaming the pavements, standing on corners, looking down from the balconies and windows of upper floors. Soon we were among Bombay's notorious 'cages'. In cell after iron-barred cell stood or squatted groups of prostitutes, the younger and more nubile dressed in short skirts, the older in grimy, if colourful, saris. In every nook and cranny overworked, ugly flesh was up for sale. Painted faces leered, pouted, simpered – or merely stared vacantly. A man could obtain animal relief in one of these pestilential dens for as little as three or four rupees.

A high proportion of the girls came from the South, from Mysore, where, apparently, there was still a lingering tradition of temple prostitution. Daughters were sacrificed by their families to the deva – the god. Many of these *devadasis* (slaves of the god), their lives effectively ruined, drifted to Bombay in due course, to a life of unvarnished prostitution. Others had been kidnapped or simply sold off by desperate fathers and husbands. Yet others had been lured into the trade by pimps who had promised to turn them into actresses: these men haunted the railway stations of Bombay, on the look-out for country girls coming to the city for the first time. For these, the dreams inspired by Bombay could melt swiftly into nightmare. A fortunate few might buy themselves freedom after five or six years;

some might even find husbands. But the majority worked until they dropped dead, killed off by disease.

The cages fell away behind us. We turned down a lane teeming with children. 'I will show you an aunt of mine,' Mr Narayan said. He led the way into an airless room, about ten foot square, on the ground floor of a tenement. A greying, wrinkled woman sat cross-legged on the floor. In front of her was a basin filled with loose tobacco and a bundle of tobacco leaves. Pictures of Hindu gods and goddesses lined the wall above her head. Cooking utensils were stacked neatly in a corner. The only item of furniture was a chest of drawers. Seven people lived in that room – the woman, her daughter, her son-in-law and her four grandchildren. The woman was making *bidis*, the hand-rolled cigarettes that are sold for next to nothing. She was able to roll one thousand bidis in twelve hours and worked seven days a week. In an average month she would earn about two hundred and fifty rupees. She had been rolling bidis for forty years. It was all she had ever done.

'Like a machine,' Mr Narayan whispered. 'Like a machine.'

The woman looked up at us and smiled. I watched the busy, expert fingers. They seemed to have a life of their own. Perhaps they were the only part of her that really lived. Age, Mr Narayan explained, was beginning to catch up with his aunt. In the room next door was a younger woman who could roll fifteen hundred bidis in eight hours. His aunt, to compensate, had begun to train her twelve-year-old granddaughter in the art – the girl had been taken out of school; her fingers were too valuable an asset to be wasted. Already the child could roll five hundred in a day. A vicious karma had closed in about her. I looked at the girl who, covered from head to toe by a blanket, lay fast asleep, stretched out like a corpse against the far wall of the cell.

Mr Narayan's room – it was in the same building – lay up a shaky, ladder-like flight of stairs. It was as tiny and airless as the one we had been into on the ground floor. But here there were definite signs of refinement – the name-plate on the door, the green-painted walls, the ceiling fan, the glass-fronted cabinet in which was stored the family's brassware, the row of books on a wooden shelf and, most surprising of all, the small tank full of brightly-coloured tropical fish. Mr Narayan's three children – two girls and a boy – lay asleep on the floor. A metal folding chair, obviously a highly prized possession, was presented with a flourish. I sat down and looked at the tropical fish.

'It is for *him* I got it,' Mr Narayan said, following my gaze. He pointed at his sleeping son. 'I thought it would be educative for him to have such a thing to look at.'

The boy was about seven years old. Mr Narayan centred all his remaining ambitions on him.

'It is really for his sake that I wish to go to the Gulf,' he said. 'No way else can I get the money for him to pursue his studies. If he has no education what will become of him? It makes me afraid to think of that.'

'What would you like your son to be when he grows up?'

'Maybe doctor. Maybe engineer. I am not sure. The choice will be his.'

The boy stirred restlessly, half-opening his eyes. Mr Narayan, reaching forward, caressed him. The boy slept again. He was being educated at a special 'convent' school which cost his father thirty-five rupees a month – a not insubstantial sum. Mr Narayan took down a leather schoolbag from the bookshelf and showed me an exercise book filled with drawings and Biblical maxims. I read and admired.

'One day my son will be a great man,' he said.

I wanted to believe him.

The outdoor sleepers had already taken up their positions for the night when Mr Narayan escorted me down the rickety stairs to the street. Bodies lined both sides of the roadway. In the cages the girls leaned sleepily against the bars, staring vacantly.

On Chowpatty beach the smell of excrement mingled with the smell of the sea. The pressure lamps of the foodstalls shone with flaring, painful brilliance. From afar came the cacophonous clatter of a temple. To the south curved Marine Drive. The faery towers of the dream city blazed with light. Indistinct figures squatted or walked along the water's edge. Nearby, a group of men and women sat in a circle, drumming and singing. Masseurs rose out of the darkness, soliciting custom. A statue of the elephant-headed god, Ganesh, grotesquely painted and ornamented, had been carved out of the sand. Offerings of money and flowers were strewn around the base. Strange city! It confounded hope and despair. One could never be sure where the one ended and the other began, so blurred was the boundary between realism and fantasy. 'Citizens from all over the island ... would cross to the Eastern waterfront where would be located large, magnificent plazas ... one day my son will be a great man ...' I listened to the drumming and singing.

Bombay lives because it denies its terrors.

A Dying State

The dark green plain, sliced through by a broad, orange-coloured arc of the Ganges, was dissected into shining rectangles by fields of rice which stretched as far as the eye could see. Scattered across that sodden verdancy were the brown-tiled roofs of huddled villages. Here and there, casting graceful reflections and breaking the monotony, were palm trees. But they were few and far between. For, over the centuries, the plain had been relentlessly surrendered to one of the chief obsessions of its inhabitants – the cultivation of rice. From the air, it was a vision of order, fruitfulness and peasant contentment. This was a deceptive first impression: I was looking down on Bihar, ancient but degenerate heartland of Hindu culture.

Bihar, home of at least sixty million Indians (it is the second most populous state in the Indian Union), is nowadays notorious for its squalor, its backwardness, its gross corruptions. It has become a byword for all that is most hopeless and terrible about the Indian condition: the sub-continent's heart of darkness. The mere mention of the name in the intellectual circles of Delhi or Bombay or Calcutta (even Calcutta!) calls forth shrugs of despair. In the drama of progress many Indians justifiably enjoy painting for visitors there is no place for Bihar. Bihar, it was often implied, had degenerated so far that it was now beyond the reach of the usual panaceas of social and economic reform. One of the seed-beds of the glorious past had decayed and the heirs of the men who had made that past had decayed with it and slipped beyond redemption. Best, perhaps, not to think about it. Let nature take its course. Bihar, it seemed, defied reason and alienated compassion.

It excelled in virtually all the negative indicators. It had the highest birth-rate, the highest level of illiteracy, the highest number of college dropouts. Its politics were the most caste-fettered. A model of political instability, Bihar, since 1947, had run through nearly two dozen Chief Ministers. With roughly thirty per cent of its population landless it had become a reservoir of the semi-slavery known as bonded labour. Brigandage was rife: dacoity was a favourite pastime of the college dropouts and of jobless graduates. Many were 'students'

by day and brigands by night. The educational system was disintegra-
ting. For one whole year the University of Patna had remained closed
after rival groups of students, organised on caste lines, had begun to
murder each other.

From one year to the next, Bihar generated more tales of atrocity
than any other region of India. Massacre had become almost a
commonplace in its more remote villages where caste warfare articu-
lated the struggle between the landed and the landless – or, as the
Marxist ideologues like to put it, between 'kulak' and 'serf'. Typically, it was Bihar which caused a furore in the New Delhi parliament
when news broke that the police, as a matter of course, had been
blinding scores of common criminals in their custody. It had been
estimated that probably fifty people are killed every day by politically
motivated acts of violence. The horror is obscured because many of
these incidents go unreported in both the local and national press.
'People ask how long Bihar can carry on as it is without the society
breaking down completely,' a civil servant who knew the state well
said to me. 'The answer is that the society has already broken down.'
Acts of God compound the Bihari tragedy. The people lurch between
the threat of drought and the threat of flood: too little or too much
water. In Bihar, famine is always just around the corner.

'You want to know if there is anything *good* that can be said about
Bihar?' The Punjabi editor of one of Patna's English-language newspapers was amused by my question. 'The truthful reply is no. I cannot
think of a single good thing to say.' His office, tidy and dark and cool,
kept at bay the over-heated glare and chaotic ugliness of the Patna
morning through which I had ventured to come and see him. He had
many problems trying to produce his paper. His staff, most of whom
were equipped with degrees in English, did not really know the
language and refused to accept that they did not know it. English was
a dying language in Bihar. 'To be frank with you,' he said, 'this
so-called paper of which I'm editor is fit only for toilet paper. I'm quite
ashamed of it. But what can I do with these people? What can anyone
do with them?'

He lived the life of an exile in Patna. It had proved almost
impossible for him to create a social life in that debilitated environment. If, for instance, he invited a Bihari to his home, it was more
than likely that the invitation would not be reciprocated; and if by
some chance it was, his host's womenfolk would be carefully locked

away from his gaze. The Bihari suffered from an eerie lethargy. Such energy as there was came from imported individuals like himself. The locals who were desperate enough and ambitious enough often emigrated to other states: Bihar was a major exporter of raw labour power. 'What we are faced with,' he said, 'is a human problem, a *personality* problem. How do you solve the personality problems of sixty million people?' And he too had shrugged despairingly.

The businessman who had come from Delhi to set up a factory making pump machinery for tube wells was equally discouraged. He reckoned that roughly twenty-five per cent of his original investment had been eaten up by bribes to politicians and bureaucrats. 'You have to grease palms at every stage. To push even the littlest piece of paper up the ladder costs you money.' He had not yet come across an honest politician or bureaucrat. Yet he was a realist. He was not against bribery as such. To do business anywhere in India, bribes usually had to be paid. What upset him, what he found 'unfair', was that after paying your bribe nothing much happened. 'That is the astonishing thing. That is what I still can't get over. *Nothing* happens. They just wake up enough to hold out their hands for the envelope and then go straight back to sleep.'

Like the editor, he was perplexed by the Bihari character. They signally lacked what he called a work ethic. Mostly, they were apparently quite content to take home the two or three hundred rupees a month they earned for doing next to nothing. The idea of working harder or earning more did not appear to have any appeal. Without notice, his employees would disappear for days at a time – to attend the wedding or funeral of some distant relation; or to take part in some lengthy and obscure religious ritual. He had concluded that the Bihari was almost devoid of ambition in the conventional sense. At any rate, ambition was not associated with productive, disciplined labour. Its place was taken by a fatuous greed. If his factory managed to produce anything at all that was only because half of his work-force had been recruited from non-Biharis.

After autumnal Delhi, the Patna air was disagreeably vaporous and clammy. My taxi-driver was an unshaven, sullen-faced man, mouth bloodily discoloured by over-indulgence in *pan*. We proceeded slowly, carefully dodging the cows which reclined by preference in the middle of the road, showing not the slightest tremor of anxiety at our approach, serenely contemplating their ramshackle world. 'That tranquil, far-off gaze [of the Indian cow],' wrote a businesslike

American observer in the 1920s, 'is, indeed, often remarked and acclaimed by the passing traveller as an outward sign of an inner sense of surrounding love ... after examining the facts, one is driven to conclude that the expression in the eyes ... is due partly to low vitality.' We crawled along dusty, pot-holed lanes crowded with pedestrians and cycle rickshaws and lined with the stalls of petty merchants. Ceaselessly, the driver honked his horn. I stared at the meagre limbs of the rickshaw wallahs, haunches angled off their saddles, effortfully pumping the pedals of their cumbrous vehicles as they toiled their human cargoes homeward. India, even today, offers a still more elemental mode of public transport: in Calcutta I saw people being carried about in hand-pulled rickshaws.

We were halted by a religious procession. Gaudily coloured idols, bedecked with tinsel and garlands of marigolds, were riding on the open tray of a lorry. A shabbily uniformed band walked behind the lorry, their trumpets and drums filling the steamy air with strident discordancy. Patna, as I was to discover, was a pious town, much given to exhibitions of Hinduism's polytheistic zeal. Hardly a day passed without my seeing processions similar to this one. Dusk was falling when I got to the hotel.

The hotel, owned by a state-controlled corporation devoted to the development of tourism, was a gloomy place, so dimly lit that it was painful to the eyes: the electricity was running at about half-power. After filling in many forms, I looked for the bar.

'Bar is closed,' said the receptionist.

'What time does it open?'

'Bar is closed permanently.' He spoke, I felt, with some satisfaction.

The bar had been shut up during the Janata era, a victim of Morarji Desai's prohibitionist fervour. Despite Janata's demise and Indira Gandhi's more tolerant attitude towards the consumption of alcohol, no steps had yet been taken to reopen it. If I wantd anything to drink, anything either hard or soft in a bottle, I would, the receptionist explained with intensifying satisfaction, have to send 'outside' for it. Indeed, he pointed out, if I wanted cigarettes I would have to send 'outside'; if I wanted matches I would have to send 'outside'.

'What about food? Do I have to send outside for that as well?'

He laughed. 'Food you can have inside,' he said. 'Restaurant is in operation. But if you want anything else ...' He spread his hands resignedly. 'If you wish, I'll send a boy right away. Of course he'll require a little extra ... it is not, properly speaking, his job, you understand.'

I was beginning to understand. It was not in the staff's interest to provide too many facilities within the hotel. Sending 'outside' was a much more rewarding exercise. Desai's attempt at moral revolution had coincided neatly with self-interest.

As I stood there meditating on these matters, the lights went out altogether. A peon was summoned. He arrived, bearing a lighted candle, and escorted me to my room. After about an hour, the lights came on again, spreading their painful glimmer. I went down to the restaurant. Young men in red trousers and black jackets lounged listlessly. The only diners apart from myself were a taciturn Bihari family and a Japanese woman of middle age – come to Bihar, I assumed, to see Buddhism's sacred places. During dinner the lights went out again. Candles flamed into life.

'Does the electricity go on and off like this all the time?' I asked my red-coated attendant.

'Every day, sahib.'

'Why?'

'Power shortage, sahib.'

'Why is there a power shortage?'

He simpered inanely and shrugged.

The shortage of power in a state that accounts for more than half of India's coal production had ceased to be strange. It had become one more unalterable fact of life to be endured. Later, I discovered one cause of the shortfall: the private contractors licensed to transport coal from the nationalised mines had fallen into the habit of siphoning off substantial quantities into the black market. Bihar was as powerless before the doings of men as it was before the doings of nature.

I watched the wavering reflections of the candles in the panes of the windows and doors; I listened to the murmur of voices penetrating from the lightless road. The Bihari family departed. So did the Japanese woman. I called for my bill. My waiter bent over me, whispering the amount into my ear.

'But where's the actual bill?'

He looked embarrassed; he signalled over one of his colleagues.

'You have a problem, sahib?' asked the newcomer politely. He was dressed in a less flunkeyish style than the others and seemed to be in a position of some authority.

'I would like my bill.'

My original attendant skulked away, vanishing into the candle-lit gloom.

'Naturally, sahib, we'll provide a bill if you want one ...' He hesitated, his soft eyes exploring my face. 'May I be frank with you, sahib?'

'By all means.'

He explained succinctly the system of petty embezzlement engaged in by himself and the rest of the staff. The loot, he explained, was shared out equally among them. It was all very democratic, all very cooperative. 'Sahib,' he murmured, assuming a piteous expression, 'we cannot live on what they pay us. If we tried to do that, we would all starve.'

He paused. I watched the reflections.

'Do you really require the bill, sahib?'

'Forget it.' I felt weary, infected by a sudden apathy.

He smiled. 'I can see you're a good man, sahib. I'll invite you to my house. You will see how I – a *chef de rang*, sahib . . . a *chef de rang*! – you will see how I live, in what conditions I must raise my children. Would you like to visit my humble home, sahib?'

I said I would. The *chef de rang* led me through the candle-lit gloom to my room. 'Take care to lock your door, sahib. Patna has many bad, anti-social characters.'

I promised I would take every care. Bowing solicitously, he retreated. Sleep did not come easily in the overheated darkness.

One sultry evening I am led by the *chef de rang* down a meandering, muddy lane. He goes before me, lighting my way with a torch whose beam traces the outlines of fetid pools. We leap across a gutter. He says, 'We're here. Welcome to my house.' A young woman appears in the doorway. She draws the edge of her sari forward so that it veils the lower half of her face. Twittering, she scuttles off into the darkness. 'That is my wife,' says the *chef de rang*. 'She is shy. You must excuse her. It is not our custom for women to talk to strange men.' He takes me into a white-washed room about ten foot square, roofed with corrugated iron. The lingering warmth of the day continues to soak through the metal. 'Sometimes,' he says, 'in the hot weather season the heat is so great that the skin of the children is blistered by it.'

Most of the space is taken up by a bed. On it his three children, two girls and a boy, lie sleeping. He switches on the ceiling fan, the only noticeable item of luxury I can see in the room. Gaudy icons decorate the walls: gods and goddesses with faces tinted mauve, pink and blue; multi-armed, elephant-nosed, monkey-faced divinities. On a shelf there is a shaving mirror, some tattered Hindi paperbacks and a collection of medicines. A folding table is set out before me. He covers it with a white cloth, arranges a knive, fork and spoon and offers me a napkin. All of these refinements are stamped with the monogram of the hotel. His wife, head lowered, brings in a bowl of curried chicken and scuttles out. The *chef de rang* squats on the bed, using his fingers, swallowing with noisy relish.

'You think,' he says when we have finished eating, 'that I am a wicked man to cheat my employers.'

'I haven't said that.'

'Will you please tell me how a man can live on 450 rupees [about twenty-five pounds] a month?' His rent alone consumed one hundred rupees. How could he survive on what was left? How could he feed his family? It was not possible for him to live honestly on what he earned.

Yet the *chef de rang* could consider himself a fortunate man. By the standards of Bihar his salary was almost princely. If the most humble post in the hotel where he worked fell vacant there would be literally thousands of applicants for the job.

'If I did not cheat a little, sahib, my children might not be alive today. The Ganga would have taken their bodies a long time ago. When big men cheat, sahib, they take lakhs, they take crores. What do I take? Ten rupees here, five rupees there – so I can put food in the mouths of my children. It makes me sick at heart to do it, sahib.' He pauses, massaging the region of his heart. 'There are some who do worse things. Some sell the bodies of their daughters, their wives. Our mentality is no good, sahib. No good at all. I do not care for my own country or countrymen.'

His confession is becoming oppressive. What prompts it? The hope of a handout? Sympathy? It is likely that he himself does not know. He has probably lost touch with his own motives. The *chef de rang* is obscurely ready for any eventuality – compassion, money ... anything.

'We have thought of sterilisation. Even that we have thought of.' He falls silent, staring at his sleeping children.

'What stopped you?'

'I have only one boy child. He may sicken and die tomorrow. Who can say? Girl children do not really belong to their father. Boy children look after you in your old age. They alone can perform certain rites. What would happen to me if this one son of mine should die? I have bad dreams about that, sahib. It worries me a great deal.'

I sit in the hot cell, looking at the gods and goddesses, listening to his complaints and the chorus of the frogs; I sit there until the power fails and I begin to sweat. The beam of his torch guides me back through the malodorous darkness to my room.

'Peaceful Exam At Hajipur,' announced the headline in the newspaper. 'The Intermediate examinations in Vaishali District,' said the accompanying report, 'were being conducted peacefully at RN College and Jamunilal College centres ... Strict police arrangements have been made to maintain law and order on the campus ...' Elsewhere was reported the tragic end of a 'notorious criminal' who had been mysteriously drowned in a river, a misadventure the police were at a loss to explain. As if to compensate for that, the body of a murdered policeman had been found lying beside the railway tracks in Forbesganj. I read on, confining myself to the same page. Saharsa District had, for many days past, been cut off by floods from all other parts of the state and the rest of the country. The District had no prospect of immediate relief. In Nawada there had taken place a protest march by teachers who wished to voice their opposition to the rampant corruption of the District's education office. A 'sugar famine' was raging in the town of Khagani. In the Kolhan region, noted one of the more cryptic dispatches, the people were 'in distress' – no cause was specified. A small item repeated allegations about the mass torture and killings of Adivasis – the tribal folk who make up about ten per cent of Bihar's population. In Araria a gang of bandits had attacked the house of a local high school teacher. Electricity flowed in the district of East Champaran for only one or two hours a day. This meant, among other things, an acute shortage of drinking water. 'Moreover,' continued the item, 'the Public Health Department and the local municipality have not yet installed any power-generating set specifically for water supply in the town. It has become nobody's concern here.' Between Bagaha and Narkatiaganj train services had been 'paralysed' because of mass casual leave. The residents of Khagaria had not received promised flood relief and, like the people of Kolhan, were in distress.

But in Bihar that morning there was some good news too. Bhagalpur University announced its intention to establish a diploma course in Gandhian Thought.

In the creation of Hindu culture, Bihar occupies a pre-eminent place. On its rich flood plains north and south of the Ganges arose some of the earliest kingdoms and tribal republics of Northern India. In a small republic in the foothills of what is now Nepal, the future Buddha was born. It was the towns of Bihar that first heard his preaching; whose princes offered their patronage. It was on its soil his Enlightenment occurred. Nearly contemporary with him was Mahavira, the founder of Jainism. The third century BC saw the ascendancy of Chandragupta Maurya who helped to drive back the armies of Alexander the Great beyond the Indus. Chandragupta created the first Indian empire with its capital at Pataliputra – present-day Patna. One of his ministers, Kautilya, is credited with the authorship of the *Arthasastra*, the most comprehensive Hindu treatise on statecraft.

Chandragupta's grandson, Asoka, a convert to Buddhism and non-violence, was to become the most famous of India's *chakravartins* – universal rulers. During his reign missionaries were sent out to spread the Buddhist gospel not only throughout his Indian dominions but to Ceylon, Nepal, Burma and Central Asia. For Indians, he remains the ideal of the philosopher-king. From the fourth to the sixth centuries AD, the Gupta emperors held sway, presiding over a period regarded by many as the classic age of Hindu civilisation. They helped endow the famous university at Nalanda to which scholars came from all over Asia. Nor was Nalanda the only well-known seat of higher learning. 'Bihar,' one of its more distinguished native sons (Rajendra Prasad, former President of India) has written with justifiable chauvinism, 'radiated for centuries not only to all parts of India but also to distant regions of Asia, religion, philosophy, arts and all that stands for culture and civilised life.' It was no exaggeration to say, he concluded, that the history of India was, for nearly a millennium, the history of Bihar writ large.

But the glories he celebrates ended more than a thousand years ago. Maybe enough had been done; maybe no more could reasonably be expected of any people. With the decline of the Guptas, the region we now know as Bihar (the name was conferred by Muslim invaders who were struck by the number of monasteries – *viharas* – they saw) faded,

politically, intellectually and spiritually, into a dark age: a darkness
from which it has never emerged. Neglected even by the chroniclers,
it became a marginal land, a supine tract of territory in the shadow of
Bengal to the east and Delhi to the north-west, criss-crossed by
ravenous armies, squabbled over by petty feudatories who wielded
ephemeral power over the downtrodden 'human herds' chained to
the cultivation of rice, locked into the eternal struggle with flood and
drought, famine and pestilence.

Severe injuries were inflicted by the successive waves of Muslim
invaders whose incursions became endemic during the course of the
eleventh century. Hindu temples and Buddhist monasteries were
destroyed. Scholars and monks were subjected to wholesale
slaughter. Libraries were burnt. The great centres of learning,
including Nalanda, were extinguished. No culture can withstand
such assault. Bihar must have gone into a state of shock. No other
major religion – with the possible exception of Persian Zoroastrianism – has been so ravaged by Islam as has Hinduism. The effect on
the Hindu character has been profound, long-lasting and damaging.
The Hindu heartland became a catacomb. If Bihar had shouldered a
disproportionate share of the creative burden of Indian civilisation
for a thousand years, it was now its fate to shoulder a disproportionate share of the sterile burden of Hindu defeat for another
thousand.

The Muslim invasions swept away the last traces of Buddhism. With
its denial of the fundamental importance of caste, it had, to a certain
degree, functioned as a protestant movement within the Hindu fold.
With this check removed, Bihar began to succumb to the grip of an
ever-tightening Brahminical doctrinairism, one of the symptoms of
the cultural exhaustion that had set in. Unchallenged, the Brahminical interpreters of Hinduism would seek to bind and fetter their
religion and its adherents. The centre of this 'reaction' was a territory
north of the Ganges (anciently known as Mithila) which had
somehow managed to maintain a semblance of autonomy – at any
rate, it did so until Moghul times. Significantly enough, it was an
area that had traditionally prided itself on its 'purity', a prejudice
dating back to its relatively early penetration by the Aryans.

So pure did the Maithalis consider themselves that a crossing to the
southern bank of the Ganges was regarded as a defilement and
required the performance of cleansing rites. This was the severe,

neurotic atmosphere that would determine the tenor of Bihari Hinduism in the dawning age of defeat and ossification. Mithila's Brahmins had nothing new to say. That was not their ambition. Their energies would be expended on composing endless commentaries on the sacred texts, elaborating rites, describing duties, prescribing expiations. They shackled the ancient religion, anchoring men even more securely in the airless cells of caste and karmic fate. Under their tutelage, caste endogamy was more strictly enforced. So was the hereditary aspect of the professions. Every act was hedged in by regulations and taboos. The fear of defilement became universal. Castes and sub-castes multiplied like cancerous cells. In Bihar, Hinduism made for itself a maximum security jail.

The havoc caste can wreak has been nowhere better demonstrated than in the relentless degradation imposed over the centuries on the millions of untouchables. No other tyranny has ever surpassed it in cruelty. To the pariah, the temples were forbidden; instruction of any kind was forbidden; the free use of the public highways was forbidden. He was not allowed to have in his possession – or to recite – the sacred scriptures. He had to live apart from other men and draw his water from separate wells. He was condemned to the most squalid tasks. His mere shadow was polluting and its heedless deployment could lead to his murder. Those more fortunate could sleep with a clear conscience because to suffer thus was his *karma*, his punishment for wrongs committed during the whirl of many lifetimes. The untouchable was a felon preordained by fate and the extremity of his condition was an ethical necessity. At the other end of the scale, crowning the sublunar Hindu chain of being, was the Brahmin, the earthly god. Such was the nature of the system that came to full flower in Bihar.

Hindu education in Bihar – a monopoly, needless to say, of the Brahmins – was mainly religious and ritualistic and imparted only to the chosen few. The picture that emerges is one of a people increasingly mired in superstition of the grossest kind, in proliferating caste taboos, in all the neuroses connected with defilement remorselessly channelled through their Brahminical preceptors. The traveller, Tavernier, visited Patna in 1666. His stay coincided with an eclipse of the sun. 'It was a prodigious thing to see,' he wrote, 'the multitudes of people, men, women and children rushing to the Ganges to wash themselves. . .' This lemming-like stampede was, of course, prompted by the ever-present fear of pollution, of a karmic short-circuiting. At the beginning of the nineteenth century, the Abbé Dubois gloomily observed: 'I do not believe that the Brahmins of modern times are in any degree more learned than their ancestors of the time of Lycurgus and Pythagoras. During this long space of time many barbarous races have emerged from the darkness of ignorance, have attained the summit of civilisation, and have extended their intellectual researches . . . yet all this time the Hindus have been perfectly stationary . . .'

Bihar did not simply remain stationary. The level of culture, of civilisation, had been regressing for centuries. In southern India, anti-Brahminical sentiment could take shape as a kind of racial self-assertion – Dravidian against 'Ayran'. This was not possible in Bihar. With cultural decline there went a growing economic wretchedness as – especially after the middle of the last century – population began to increase. Land, mirroring caste, was ceaselessly divided and sub-divided, resulting in miserable patrimonies barely sufficient for subsistence. (Bihar, primordial land of the agricultural instinct, had to wait until 1953 for its first Agricultural College.) The numbers of landless rose steadily. What little industry there was was decayed. The mills of Lancashire ruined the cottage trade in textiles. German advances in synthetics laid waste the indigo plantations. Hundreds of thousands were forced out of the region, compelled to seek what work they could find in the jute mills of Bengal and the tea plantations of Assam. Many would ship themselves overseas as indentured labourers, ending up in remote places like Trinidad – the island of my birth.

Speaking of this period, a Bihari historian adds this revealing lament: 'Moreover,' he says, 'it forced many high-caste Hindus and the descendants of respectable Muslims to accept menial service in the households of middle-class people for paltry remuneration.' Bihar limped into the twentieth century under-educated, over-populated, poorly fed, intellectually and spiritually denuded; enfeebled in almost every way. Caste remains a basic reality to the Bihari, as fundamental to his sense of himself as are his arms and legs. It determines everything he does. His perceptions, his feelings, his loyalties, his treasons, his tortures, his massacres, his nightmares, are all moulded by caste. Deprived of it, he flounders. After generations of conditioning, it is his only lifeline; the only compass he has. Thus it is that students, politicians, police, banditry and peasantry organise and kill on caste lines. There is nothing else they can do because they know no other way of conducting themselves. Each and every one is a victim of a tragedy that started a thousand years ago; of a series of assaults coming at first from the outside and then brought to fruition from within.

Patna ... a town without the faintest traces of charm, a sprawling caravanserai of dusty roads and fenny lanes; a junk-heap of peeling, crumbling buildings, of squatter colonies earthed in tracts of mossy mud; a swarming hive of *pan*-chewing, meagre-limbed men. Stagnant, black-watered gutters reek. Inches away from these sewers people squat, arms limply hanging, oblivious of the stench, staring as vacantly as the wandering holy cows. I watch the interminable procession of cycle rickshaws. Where are they all rolling to and for what purpose? A cacophony of drums and trumpets unsettles the moist, motionless air. Another pageant of piety; yet another shimmering divinity escorted by its chanting devotees.

At dusk, there is a thunderstorm. The sky is cracked open by shafts of orange lightning. Big drops of warm rain fall, disturbing the dust which exudes its rich store of miasmic vapours. Late at night packs of starved, hairless mongrels roam restlessly, rootling and snarling round the embers of cooking fires. Along every roadside bodies lie sprawled in sleep. The disorder, the dirt, the ugliness is overwhelming. How do men manage to live in a place like this? How is it that they do not all go mad?

With a friend I drive out to a far suburb of Patna – he wants to take me to an untouchable village recently scarred by a massacre of its menfolk. A light rain begins to fall. I stare at the glistening lines of buffaloes trundling along the verges, at the shaggy crowns of the palm trees, black against the sky of light grey. The rain stops, the sun comes out in its full force, the earth steams. A rainbow appears and disappears. The car can go no farther. To get to the village we must walk. The suburban lanes through which we pass are quagmires. We pick our way through slimy, ankle-deep mud, skirt mossy pools. On the more treacherous stretches we have to climb up on to the tiny stoops of houses and shops or leap from one strategically placed stone to another. This fetid swamp is a main thoroughfare. We give up, deciding to walk along the railway embankment instead. At the foot of the embankment lies the *dhoti*-clad corpse of a man, a pool of his dried blood staining the earth. He has probably been hit by a train. The body lies in the sun, abandoned like any animal's, unregarded by the passers-by. Soon, in this heat, it will begin to smell.

Leaving the railway, we follow a network of rutted, shadeless tracks snaking across the paddy fields. Here and there portions of track are flooded and we have to wade up to our knees in slippery ooze. Men, women and children, bent under loads of grass and firewood, lope under the merciless sun, heading for villages that could be miles away. They have been loping like this across fields like these forever. We discover we cannot reach our destination: it is marooned by flood water. We find a tree and lie down in its shade. Rice. Nothing but rice. The acres of luminous green stretch to all corners of the horizon. I sit in the shade and watch kingfishers swoop. In the watery fields, egrets contemplate their own perfect reflections. A young boy wearing a ragged loin cloth and carrying a staff comes up and stares at us. Behind him, a buffalo wallows in a mud pool. Flies buzz about our faces. The warm wind brings with it an odour of excrement. In the far distance I can see the tiled roofs of the village of massacre. I am glad I don't have to go there after all. The shepherd boy, one stick-like leg propped against the other, leans on his staff and stares. My companion talks of revolution; of kulak and serf.

It was through the Governor's kindness I met Sharma. Sharma considered himself and was considered by others something of a scholar: he had shared in the authorship of several booklets devoted to the history of Bihar. I was not sure that I wanted to be 'guided' but refusal would have seemed impolite. When I met Sharma, doubt turned into anxiety. He wore his Brahminic caste like a badge. Powdered discs of orange and yellow adorned the middle of his forehead, the lobes of his ears, the base of his neck. His light-brown eyes oozed a remote and mysterious self-absorption.

'Shiva!' he exclaimed. 'Where did you get such a name, sir? That is name of one of *our* Hindu gods.' He was proprietorial about the matter and regarded me with a faint air of amusement and a more definite one of condescension and scorn. 'Is that the full name, sir? It is most irregular.'

Reluctantly, I supplied the fuller version of my name.

He began to laugh. 'It makes no sense at all. No sense at all.' I had made Sharma's day; fired his Hindu wit. 'Yours is not proper Hindu name. It is all mixed up. You should be able to tell everything from a man's name – his village, his caste . . . everything. From yours one can tell nothing.'

I understood then that someone like myself could never be

entirely real to someone like him. I was beyond his friendship, beyond his enmity, beyond – even – his scorn.

'Mr Sharma is *very* high caste Brahmin,' one of his colleagues put in. 'Tip-top quality Brahmin.'

Those discs of orange and red tattooing his forehead, his ears and his neck seemed to glow a little more brightly each time I caught sight of them. Sharma was pleased by this public affirmation of his status. He relented somewhat. 'I will work out excellent sight-seeing programme for you,' he said.

Together we visited the Patna Museum, an unkempt, fusty mausoleum stocked with many fine specimens of Hindu and Buddhist art. These treasures had not been arranged with an eye to either instruction or delight. They were, for the most part, merely thrown together, stony relics of distant creation, bleakly lined up in rows in dusty rooms. Ragged guards dozed under ceiling fans. Occasionally, we encountered groups of peasants standing silently before some half-mutilated divinity. On what strange impulse had they wandered into this place? I stopped before a Buddha.

'The English do not understand about BC,' Sharma said.

'How do you mean, Mr Sharma?'

'I mean,' he said fingering the smooth, dusty torso, 'they believe all history starts with them. But that is not so. For English people there is no history before Julius Caesar. That is *fact*. For us, on the other hand, history has been going on for thousands and thousands of years. We understand BC very well.' He smiled ironically at me, his sour breath playing on my face.

We entered a room lined with glass cases arrayed with often superb terracotta and bronze figurines. Sharma drew my attention to a female figure with a bouffant hairstyle and clad in a short, skirtlike garment.

'You will observe how *modern* she is,' he said. 'You people in the West think you invented all these styles. But India knew about the mini-skirt three thousand years ago! Westerners always think themselves the originators of *everything*. We Hindus laugh.' Sharma smiled his ironic smile; I inhaled his rancid breath.

One moist afternoon we drove out to the outskirts of the town, to a small park whose centrepiece was an archaeological reminiscence of the ancient capital of Pataliputra. Sharma led me along mossy paths winding through groves of palms and mango trees. We came to a pond covered with lotus. A solitary, truncated column protruded above the surface of the water – the remains of a hall of the Mauryan period. Two peasant girls wandered about the slopes of the pond, cutting bundles of rushes. The park, except for us and for them, was deserted.

'Asoka himself might have walked here,' Sharma said. His voice was startlingly loud in the stillness.

Contemporary Bihar was a replica of that ruin: the living who surrounded me were the all but drowned and truncated remnants of the dead civilisation.

Sharma took me to a pavilion. In it was displayed a rescued pillar. It lay there on its side like an embalmed corpse.

'Feel how smooth,' Sharma said.

I ran my hand over the stone. It was indeed extremely smooth.

'How long was Rome capital of the world?' Sharma asked. I shrugged.

'Only for a few hundred years,' he answered dreamily. 'But Patiliputra was imperial capital for much, much longer than that. It was imperial capital for thousands of years. Yet you people in the West call Rome the Eternal City. We Hindus laugh.'

Once again Sharma smiled his ironic smile; once again his rancid breath, the breath of dead ages, played over my face.

Sometimes we Hindus have to weep.

The Sanjay Factor

The package group of German tourists, cameras dangling from their necks, did not have to wait long for India to reveal itself. Within a minute or two of disembarking, they were given an opportunity to relish its ancient misery. There, next to the entrance of the terminal of Delhi Airport, was a perfect tableau. Perhaps a dozen men, women and children were breaking and carrying stones. The pick-axes of the nearly naked, sweat-drenched men rose and fell in effortful spasms; the women and children collected the rubble, filling small baskets which they took away on their heads. Their skins were burned black by the sun. Hair was bronzed by malnutrition. Their wasted bodies seemed to be melting away in the heat.

What they were doing appeared less like work and more like some divinely ordained punishment. Theirs was a sterile expenditure of all but depleted human energy. Several of the Germans paused, staring at the tableau, fingering their cameras. The labourers also paused. Some among them raised their heads, returning the scrutiny of their audience. They began murmuring to one another, but whether their unlooked-for animation expressed resentment, amusement or bewilderment was not easy to say. The Germans, made suddenly uneasy, hesitated. Then they shuffled forward, abandoning the tableau to the dazzle of the Delhi morning.

Suffering India: India of the begging-bowl; of countless Oxfam and War on Want appeals. India: object of universal charity and universal despair. A generation after Independence, poverty and disease remained inalienable attributes of the country – like the Himalayas, the Ganges and the ashrams to which well-heeled Westerners repair in search of spiritual recreation. Suitably enough, the woman ahead of me in the Immigration queue presented for inspection a UN passport: she was a representative of one of its welfare agencies. A decrepit taxi trundled me through the city's broad, tree-lined avenues. Bungalows, somewhat the worse for wear after the assaults of the monsoon, occupied spacious, bushy gardens. I noted the tower of yet another five-star hotel recently erected. Lamp-posts were adorned with posters displaying the austere countenance of Indira Gandhi. The accompanying slogan appealed for unity in face of the country's many problems. Interspersed with these representations of the Mother were icons of her recently-deceased Son, Sanjay. His photograph was superimposed on a map of India. Rays of unspecified hope emanated from the edges of the map.

In the marbled, air-conditioned lobby of my hotel richly-apparelled women paraded. A wedding reception was in progress. Bobby, a notice board proclaimed in letters of white plastic, was marrying Radha. An efficient bell-boy accompanied me up to my room. Here, he said, I would lack for nothing my heart desired. Twenty-four-hour room service. Twenty-four-hour coffe-shop. A discothèque. A choice of restaurants, offering Indian and 'international' cuisine. In the bathroom there flowed from one of the taps chilled, filtered water. If the electricity supply failed, I was not to worry. The hotel was equipped with its own generator. Shivering with the artificial chill, I went to bed. He spoke no lies. Everything in that hotel worked exactly as he said it would. Owned and run by a Punjabi family, it symbolised an aspect of the country about which one seldom hears. In its way, it represented an India no less real than the India of famine and flood.

Late that afternoon I sat in a friend's garden in one of the southern suburbs of the sprawling city, watching the twilight thicken, enveloped by the humid warmth of the dying day. Gaudy bee-eaters darted through the dusk. Out on the road a pack of pariah dogs snarled and fought with each other. Ten years before, on my first ever visit to India, I had also sat in this garden. Then too I had watched the bee-eaters and been disturbed by the warfare of the pariah dogs. On the surface, everything seemed much the same. Even my hosts and their friends seemed unchanged. And yet, during the previous decade, India had had a more diversified and alarming history than during the previous twenty years. It had fought a successful war with Pakistan and helped to set free Bangladesh; it had lived through the Emergency, the failure of the Janata coalition, the return of Indira Gandhi and, most recently, the death of her younger son and heir apparent, Sanjay. The sense of sameness was simultaneously true and illusory.

Spread all about us were the buildings of the technical college where my friend, a mathematician and physicist, taught and researched. He could, had he so wished it, have lived the lucrative life of an exile in Britain or France or the United States. But he had chosen to stay in India, to be a teacher. Like so many educated Indians he oscillated between pride and disparagement when he talked about his country. Hundreds of students crowded the halls of residence scattered around the campus. I was reminded that India now had at its disposal the third largest scientific and technical 'cadre' in the world, surpassing China and exceeded only by the United States and Soviet Union. In the league table of industrial output India ranked tenth. The country could make almost everything – after a fashion. It manufactured motor-cars, aeroplanes, pharmaceuticals, machine tools, heavy earth-moving machines. Satellites had been launched with the aid of Russian rocketry. And, as the whole world knew, it had exploded a nuclear bomb.

In Bombay I was to see young, locally-trained engineers designing machines for the surprisingly complex business of making medicinal capsules. Their innovations had earned international recognition. The equally young businessmen who owned and managed the enter-prise occupied offices of modern design decorated with abstract works of contemporary art. They spoke the up-to-date commercial language of 'motivation', 'incentive' and 'productivity'. They had nothing in common with the hallowed Indian *bania*, that big-bellied figure of caricature, sitting cross-legged in his cramped hole of a shop counting his profits. 'We work hard and play hard,' I was told – and the remark was made without the slightest trace of irony. It was also in Bombay that I had spent a happy afternoon at the Tata Institute of Fundamen-tal Research, a haven of scientific intellect on the Bombay seashore, many of whose residents could, like my friend who taught in the technical college, have been working abroad and winning high honours. 'I think it is wonderful,' said a mathematician who worked there, 'that we should have a place like this in India.' It was com-forting to be part, however modestly, of the world current of scientific enterprise and discovery – and for India's most gifted minds to know that there was a place for them in their own country. In the fierce afternoon sun we had strolled along the edge of the sea, watching the scatter of spray among the rocks. Across the bay, hazed by mist, the ivory-coloured towers of Bombay shimmered.

'India,' remarked a journalist present in that Delhi garden, 'works quite well for about a hundred and fifty million people.' Of course, he was quick to concede, that left about five hundred million of its citizens unaccounted for. Still, the capacity to provide decent living conditions for a hundred and fifty million people was no mean achievement. Especially so when it was remembered that India had had next to no industrial and technical capacity at the time of Independence in 1947. In 1978 forty-nine per cent of the population was classed as living below the 'poverty line'. Being below the poverty line in India means that you are unable to spend 2.50 rupees – about fifteen pence – on basic needs. Roughly five million such 'poor' people are added every year to the population. 'You have to ignore such things,' the journalist continued. 'If you let yourself worry about statistics in a country like India you'll go mad. You'll give up. You'll do nothing. What you must do is look at the youth. They are now very, very, impatient, fed up with the status quo.' The Young, those who took India's Independence for granted and were not interested in old battles, had had enough of empty talk and posturing. Their eyes were focused on the present and the future. The Youth were demanding *action*. They wanted to see *results*. They were tired of listening to promises. It was a vocabulary to which, over the next few weeks, I would grow accustomed: a vocabulary vague and militant.

Indian youth – and the journalist gave as an example his own teenage children – were increasingly 'Americanised' in behaviour, appearance and outlook. Their *dynamism* – another word to which I was to grow accustomed – astonished him. For them it was a matter of honour to wear faded jeans and become acquainted instantly with the latest crazes of the New World. But keeping up with the times is not always easy. The routes of cultural exchange can be circuitous. 'For many people in Bombay,' reports one of the newer glossy magazines of that city, 'the first time they heard The Clash, the Pretenders or Cheap Trick was over the piped music system at the Taj Mahal Hotel ... The Western pop channel ... plays records purchased recently abroad by hotel employees out on tour. As a result, the restaurants always play the latest music most of which is never released in India ... A little thing perhaps, but for many rock fans in the City, it remains one of the few ways of keeping in touch with new releases abroad.' It is an odd dynamism that leads its devotees to lounge away at some expense idle hours in the restaurants of a five-star hotel. In poor countries the role of the 'international' hotel in promoting cross-cultural fertilisation should not be overlooked. They are one of the main carriers of imagined modernity.

More was involved, however, than this hunger for the latest. These Americanised youth were striving to create 'social mobility'. They wanted to get India 'on the move'. The supine India of flood and famine, of endemic want and disease – India of the begging bowl – had become repellent to them. (But how, one wonders, does sitting around in faded jeans and listening to rock music promote those ideals?) To understand the appeal of Sanjay Gandhi – the journalist called it the Sanjay phenomenon – one had first to understand this revolt of Youth. Sanjay's enemies had represented him as engaging in cynical acts of corruption and violence executed for narrowly personal ends. But it had not been like that. Sanjay was more, much more, than the spoilt unscrupulous son of an autocratic, unscrupulous mother. His had been the voice of youthful impatience; he had represented a dynamic vision of the future. With one bound, Sanjay seemed to say, India could snap its fetters and break free.

That evening I was taken to a discothèque in Delhi's newest five-star hotel, a palace of marble and softly splashing fountains. Turbanned attendants patrolled the air-conditioned lobby. All the latest from America's record industry was being pounded out by the sophisticated sound system. The dance floor, of glass, was illumined from below by flickering, multi-coloured lights. At intervals a gentle rain of bubbles would float down from the ceiling, expiring in soapy explosions among the dancers' heads. On this Saturday night the place was full – we were admitted only because one of the women in our party had a 'contact'. Sikhs, bright turbans bobbing, gyrated awkwardly but contentedly. The girls, dressed predominantly in Western modes, moved with a more practised fluency. Everyone oozed self-consciousness: they were watching themselves and each other being 'modern'. I was seeing (so I was told) India's new rich, the beneficiaries of what was described as the contractor economy.

I fell into conversation with an architect and his over-scented, sallow-complexioned wife. They talked of their recent trip to London, abusing and disowning the immigrants who had given Indians as a whole such a bad name in England. It emerged that they had been given a fairly rough time by the Immigration officers on arrival at Heathrow.

'You can't blame the officers,' the woman remarked charitably, wounded self-esteem obviously assuaged by the passage of time. 'If all they generally see are those villagers with their filthy bundles and none of whom can speak a word of English – how can you blame them if they think *all* of us are like that?' Still, the trip that had started off so discouragingly had ended in triumph. Battered racial self-esteem had been restored in the most unlikely of places: the Brent Cross Shopping

Centre in the bleak reaches of north London. They had gone there to buy a watch. The sales-staff, to begin with, had treated them with an off-putting casualness. Yet again their honour was under threat.

'So,' the architect confided, 'I said to my wife – "You make sure you buy the most expensive watch in this shop. Tell them you're only interested in Cartier." ' Immediately their intention became known, the attitude of the staff underwent a magical transformation. They were not merely polite but deferential, only too anxious to please. He was called 'sir', his wife, 'madam'.

'You see,' the woman concluded, 'only the very rich can afford to buy such things. Ordinary English people can't afford Cartier. They *had* to respect us.'

I watched a fresh rain of bubbles waft down from the ceiling.

The thirst for respect is real. But, like Hinduism itself, its manifestations can range from the sophisticated, to the foolish, to the downright absurd. It can give rise to temptations of all kinds. Self-conscious, hurting India wants, in a sense, to abolish itself as it has traditionally known itself; it wants to look at itself with borrowed eyes and be pleased with what it sees.

Revolutionary lust is shared by the 'right' – to which end of the political spectrum Sanjay has usually been consigned – and by the extreme 'left' – those young men and women who do not go to discothèques and do not seek self-respect by buying Cartier watches but, instead, disappear into the jungles and villages to become Naxalites (an indigenous form of Maoism) and to baptise with the blood of exploiters the near-mystical rebirth of which they dream. 'We are going to be ruled by the *lowest*,' a would-be Naxalite screamed ecstatically at me as we walked along a railway track in Bihar, flayed by a relentless sun. 'We shall smash everything. You have no idea what a cruel, callous society this is. Outsiders like you have no idea! Every day thousands are destroyed by it. It has ruined *me*! It has messed *me* up. Nothing will be spared. And, after we have destroyed, we shall build afresh.' He gazed fiercely at me, savouring the melodramatic aura with which he had enveloped himself. But the same man, on another occasion, looked strangely at me when I suggested that he and his friends should convert and channel their 'anger' into some concretely useful activity – they could for instance, teach the Bihari villages the elementary codes of sanitation. 'Bourgeois window-dressing,' he said. 'Only when the political consciousness is raised can you bother with things like sanitation.' In the mean time he was a busy man, he had been commissioned to write many heated articles for the Bombay and Delhi magazines. The simple rules of hygiene would have to await the coming of the Revolution.

Sanjay too, in his own way, had been messed up by the society. He too had wished to tear down and start afresh.

'Yes,' a smartly-dressed clerk said to me, 'I was a supporter of Sanjay from the first.'

'Why did he appeal to you so much?'

His response was catechetical in its fluency. 'Because Sanjay was a *doer*. Not a *talker*.'

A doer. Yet another of the terms spawned by that new Indian vocabulary associated with Sanjay.

I asked if he could tell me in a sentence what kind of hopes Sanjay had implanted in him. He thought for a while.

'Sanjay,' he said finally, staring at me with utmost seriousness, 'was going to make India *ultra* modern.'

Sanjay's death let loose a flood of hyperbole. The Minister of Agriculture described it as the greatest catastrophe that had befallen India for a hundred years – thus ranking the event above the assassination of Mahatma Gandhi. A rising sun had vanished, said another. Sanjay's death, someone else elaborated, was like sunset at sunrise. The *Times of India* believed that Sanjay had harked back to an order of great antiquity. He was the young ruler on horse-back, dispensing justice as he rode along. The *Hindustan Times* was unrestrained in its grief. 'We knew,' it said, 'he would impose discipline on a people who, while lacking it themselves, fully subscribed to the ideal of a disciplined society. We knew he would not be bound by any isms, save pragmatism, and bring a sense of down to earth realism in pressing for result-oriented programmes ... Sanjay Gandhi – India will mourn you for no one within living memory has left so great a void in our lives as you have done and we cannot find anyone who can fill it! Your death is like the death of a son in every Indian family.' Indira Gandhi also invoked the image of the universal son. Although Sanjay, she said, had always been a tremendous personal source of strength to her, he was not merely her son. Sanjay had regarded himself as the son of Mother India. The poor, the 'weaker sections', had always been particularly dear to Sanjay. As she spoke, she wept. But Sanjay, it seemed, could be all things to all men. His compassion for the weaker sections did not in any way diminish or interfere with his sympathy for the strong. This aspect of Sanjay was brought out by an Indian foreign correspondent working in Washington. Sanjay's predilection for private enterprise, he wrote, and his unbending antipathy to communism, had begun to stimulate optimism in American business circles; circles too long denied free access to the Indian market. These circles were now hoping that the 'Sanjay factor' in Indian politics would be kept alive and nourished. If that was done, a time was foreseen when business opportunities would 'burgeon to a satisfactory degree'.

His cremation, a national spectacle, was attended by scores of thousands. Trains, buses and aircraft were chartered to transport the faithful from all corners of the country. Mrs Gandhi wore a white sari. Her furrowed, handsome face, withdrawn into austere acceptance, encapsulated the essence of a sorrow at once maternal and national as the flames leapt up from the pyre. Sanjay's ashes were scattered over India's holy places – just as, a generation before, had been scattered the ashes of the Mahatma; and, more recently, the ashes of his grandfather, Jawaharlal Nehru. An eternal flame was lit in his memory. Schools and roads were renamed. A football competition was organised in his honour. A Sanjay Gandhi Memorial Trust Fund was established, with Indira Gandhi as its chairman. The trust fund, it was announced, would devote special attention to those concerns Sanjay had made peculiarly his own – afforestation, reform of the dowry system and – it went almost without saying – slum clearance and family planning.

But the hyperbole was underpinned by undeniable fact. A big hole *had* been torn in India's political fabric. Sanjay's death had left a void which would be difficult, if not impossible, to fill. Until the moment when his light aircraft had plunged into some trees not far from his mother's house, India's political future had seemed decided. Alarmingly so. There could be no real doubt that Sanjay, in due course, would have been propelled into supremacy. His enemies, although as numerous and as vociferous as his friends, appeared impotent in the face of the 'Sanjay phenomenon'. Incoherent, riven by faction, the Opposition was unable to offer any credible resistance. They might complain about dynasticism, nepotism and 'spoilt brats'. But they did not carry conviction. There was Kanti Desai, son of Morarji Desai, first Prime Minister of the Janata coalition. A committee of investigation had recommended the prosecution not only of Kanti but of his wife. The 'Suresh-Sushma' case was no less troublesome. Suresh, a married man of mature years, son of former Minister of Defence Jagjivan Ram, was discovered delicately involved in a government car with a pretty student – Sushma. There were scandals surrounding the wife of Charan Singh (second Prime Minister of the Janata coalition) and some of his sons-in-law. Dynasticism, nepotism and spoilt brats were to be found in virtually every corner of Indian political life. The accusations of enemies such as these could only have a hypocritical and hollow ring.

Sanjay, temporarily disgraced by the 'excesses of the Emergency', had, with determination and cleverness, fought his way out of the wilderness. His performance, his single-mindedness, his tenacity, commanded admiration. Now, with Janata itself in disgrace, with a fresh crop of courtiers in search of a court and a prince (Indian politics must never be judged in ideological terms: its workings are strictly feudal), Sanjay's derelictions could be reinterpreted. Without too much discomfort, the demon of yesteryear could be transformed into the saviour of his people. Indian politics, amounting as it does to little more than rival forms of vassalage, lends itself to the most abrupt reversals. He who would search for profundity is doomed to labour in vain. There are no 'movements', only personalities engaged in endless and ultimately meaningless conflict.

When compared to the warring Janata gerontocracy, Sanjay could be portrayed as the embodiment of youthful 'dynamism' and purpose. His very 'excesses' could be used to enhance his appeal. Excess, in fact, was turned into a manifesto. The means, the style, became the thing, overwhelming the 'ends' and, in so doing, it abolished rational discourse. 'Talking' became a subversive activity. In the Sanjayite creed it was regarded as a cardinal sin. Sanjay was projected as the man of Passion; a prophet possessed by a Vision. If his opponents accused him of dictatorial tendences, so much the better. They, for their part, threatened only anarchy and garrulous futility. Sanjay was by no means universally loved, but the fear he inspired was an essential part of his appeal. Take it away and there would be nothing left – just, perhaps, a semi-literate Indian street-boy blessed with a famous name and a powerful mother. In fearing him, his enemies helped to create him. Gradually an aura of inevitability had come to attach itself to him.

Sanjay, not long before his death, had been made one of the General Secretaries of the Congress (I) – the 'Indira Congress', a rump of the defeated and fractured post-Emergency Congress which Mother and

Son had fashioned into the vehicle of their restoration. The very innocuousness of this title, its neutral bureaucratic ring, served to emphasise his power. It was a political euphemism that fooled no one. Recent happenings told a different story. In the lately elected (January 1980) lower house of the Parliament – the Lok Sabha – there were no less than one hundred representatives, most of them young, most of them unknowns, who owed their elevation and, consequently, their primary loyalty not to the Indira Congress or even to Indira Gandhi but to Sanjay. They were *his* vassals. He had lifted them up out of obscurity and, if he so wished, he could cast them down again. They even adopted a distinctive style of dress – white *kurta*, white baggy trousers, sandals – in imitation of their creator, so further underlining their separation from the orthodox mass of the party and their personal devotion to Sanjay.

Theirs was a message, a style, no one could mistake. In Parliament they formed a noisy, uncouth, contemptuous bloc, shouting down Opposition speakers, ostentatiously disregarding parliamentary procedures and etiquette. Ascendant, dynamic Youth was going to let nothing stand in its way. Many had received their basic training during the Janata era when the Mother and the Son were being called to account for the 'excesses of the Emergency'. Then they had crowded into court-rooms, upset and hurled tables and chairs, and screamed abuse at the judges. Indira Gandhi, upholder of law and order, had not complained.

In the states, apart from the Communist-dominated legislatures of West Bengal and Kerala, Sanjay had, in recent elections and manoeuvrings, masterminded the overthrow of administrations hostile to the Indira Congress. Most of the freshly-installed Chief Ministers were no less loyal and no less personally obligated to Sanjay than the caucus he had introduced earlier in the year into the Lok Sabha; no less his creatures. They might have paid lip service to the Mother, but they knew they owed their positions to the Son. In June 1980 he had been offered the Chief Ministership of Uttar Pradesh, the most populous (home of at least ninety million Indians) and politically influential state in the Indian Union. Almost every member of the State legislature had signed a petition urging Mrs Gandhi to set up Sanjay as their overlord. 'No person,' proclaimed the author of this petition, one Devendra Pande, 'howsoever great can ignore the wishes and aspirations of the people.' Sanjay, Pande averred, was India's 'only hope'. Bold words indeed to address to Mrs Gandhi. Who was 'greater' than she? How, while she remained active, could her son be India's 'only hope'?

'But who dare not sign it?' murmured one cowed, elderly member of the Uttar Pradesh legislature. The petition had the ring of an ultimatum. Its swaggering boldness reveals the confidence of the Sanjayites. He, obviously, had ceased to be simply his mother's son; ceased to be a mere parasitic accretion clinging to the hem of her sari: he had acquired a power base of his own and an autonomy that might even have begun to intimidate his mother. As it was, Mrs Gandhi demurred, partly, perhaps, out of pique. But it is also likely that she was reluctant to see Sanjay lose himself in the mire of provincial politics. It is possible that Sanjay himself was not interested in the job: that he was, so to speak, only teasing his enemies. The point, nevertheless, had been made. Pande, the organiser of the petition, was an authentic Sanjay type, a good specimen of the new breed he had injected into the political scene. He was young (only just turned thirty), fiercely idolatrous and a conspicuous 'doer'. In December 1978 he had hijacked an Indian Airlines aircraft to protest against the arrest of Mrs Gandhi. About a year before that, gripped by the same obsession, he had tried to take over the Lucknow station of All India Radio.

Then suddenly, unbelievably, the 'meteor' vanished, tumbling precipitately out of the heavens, brought to a fiery end by yet one more act of illegal daredevilry, performed this time in the skies above his mother's house. It was absurd. It was senseless. But there it was. All the same, it was a curiously appropriate climax to a career which had based itself on bending and breaking the rules; which had been conjured out of thin air. Not even Sanjay, it turned out, could defy the laws of gravity.

Weeks afterward one could still see small groups of his bemused, white-clad followers hanging forlornly around the twenty-four-hour restaurant of New Delhi's Taj Mahal hotel. For a while, their prospects had been dazzling; they were the men of the future. Now there was only darkness and uncertainty. The anonymity out of which so many of them had been plucked was once more closing in around them. They were paying the penalty of a too-eager vassalage. These abruptly pathetic, white-clad figures showed up the courtly super-ficialities of Indian politics. 'Doers' to a man, idolaters by instinct, they had nothing to sustain them now that their prince had vanished.

Delhi's rumour factories were hard at work. I listened to descriptions of an insomniac Mrs Gandhi walking distractedly in her garden at all hours of the night. She had developed, I was assured, a heart condition. Visitors had seen her swallowing many types of pill, red, green, blue, yellow. The will to govern, it was suggested, had died within her. Some astrologers were predicting her imminent political demise. Inevitably, typically, Delhi also speculated about the 'succession'. Yet again, there was exposed to view the debased nature of Indian politics, its sham 'modernity'. Yet again there was nothing to grapple with but courtly intrigue. Would Sanjay's mantle fall on Rajiv, his elder brother? Or would it be seized by the dead man's pretty widow, Maneka – ambitious daughter, it was alleged, of an even more ambitious mother? It seemed that the 'Sanjay factor' was not easily transmissible, hardly a cause for surprise when one recalls that Sanjay and the 'Sanjay factor' were synonomous. Strictly speaking, there was nothing to transmit. With Sanjay the medium was the message. The mild-mannered Rajiv had the ancestry but he lacked the style. Maneka might have a touch of the style but she lacked the ancestry. Without Sanjay, she became what she was – an over-ambitious parvenu. The *Hindustan Times* was not all that far from the truth when it cried out in its sycophantic show of grief, '. . . no one has left so great a void in our lives . . . and we cannot find anyone else who can fill it!'

Sanjay Gandhi was thirty-four years old when his light aircraft, the gift of an industrialist crony, crashed. When the State of the Emergency was proclaimed in June 1975, he was mainly known to the Indian public as a failed manufacturer of the 'People's Car', the Maruti. Sanjay had won the project licence over the heads of more likely bidders. A great deal of money had been made available to him. Many acres of valuable real-estate had been appropriated – the existing residents were expelled – for the site of the would-be factory. But no Marutis had ever rolled off the assembly lines. Sanjay's shaky educational background did not help. 'He cannot design a car engine,' one of his critics had mocked, 'and without an engine a car, unfortunately, cannot run.' Until June 1975 Sanjay was associated with failure, corruption and self-indulgence. Suddenly, he underwent a metamorphosis, surfacing as a man with a vision and a programme for the salvation of India. It was all rather remarkable. Nehru's legacy, under the guardianship of his daughter, had rotted away almost beyond recognition.

*

Kamal Nath was one of the new breed of men Sanjay had brought with him into the Lok Sabha after the 1980 General Election. He had all the characteristics of the type – youth, an idolatrous disposition, a 'dynamic' impatience with old-fashioned rules – and liked sophisticated gadgetry: video machines, cassette recorders and the like. He would, I suppose, approve of being called a 'technocrat'. Nath, product of an industrialist background, also had other qualifications for his new role. He was rich, he was well-travelled and he knew at first hand the needs and frustrations of Indian big business. For years he had been a confidant of Sanjay. They had attended the same exclusive public school up in the hills of Dehra Dun and had remained close friends. 'In that school,' one of its former pupils told me, 'you eventually come to believe that the world owed you a living, that other people were privileged to have you around. Nothing specific was said. It was just part of the atmosphere of the place.' He remembered Sanjay as a 'forceful character', someone who exploited rather than lived up to his distinguished background.

In the new order that Sanjay had threatened, Nath would have been a figure of consequence. But now, in common with the rest of those who had merged their destinies with his, he was someone of uncertain political future. For the time being, at any rate, he continued bravely unrepentant, cherishing and embellishing the legend of his hero. The driveway of his Delhi house was crowded with petitioners when I arrived. There was nothing particularly unusual in this: in India such throngs of favour-seekers gather round the presence of every political personality, even those of relatively humble status. Each member of Parliament conducts, in effect, a miniature court. A minion escorted me through the bustle to an inner sanctum. Nath, suave in manner and handsome, was dressed in the white garb of the Sanjayites. The walls of the high-ceilinged room were decorated with photographs of Sanjay and Mrs Gandhi – and a big map of India. An air-conditioner emitted a soft technocratic hum.

'Nobody ever motivated me as Sanjay did,' he said. 'For me, he was the greatest propelling force.' From the earliest days of their acquaintance, he had detected in Sanjay a 'vision' that promised to make India what it could and should be. India, Nath said, was a rich country inhabited by poor people. Sanjay, alive to that fact, had plotted the economic uplift of the country. The phrases rolled smoothly, effortlessly, in the air-conditioned room. I could sense their visceral appeal.

A rich nation inhabited by poor people.

How alluringly different that was from the usual view of India as a poor country inhabited by a few rich people! It was an arresting slogan (not an *idea* – Sanjay didn't deal in those), one that stood India on its head and hinted at a different set of solutions. For those receptive to its subliminal message it would open up vistas of alluring possibility and temptation. India's poverty could be re-interpreted not as something dismally intrinsic, a defining condition of the society that imposed limits on what could plausibly be desired, but as a kind of villainous illusion – a malfunction, a distortion – that hid the true face of the country from itself. It conferred legitimacy on those who lusted after video machines, cassette recorders, Cartier watches and the like; those who felt ashamed of their country and themselves could become shameless in the pursuit of their aims. It removed moral restraint and it banished the common decencies.

To put the Sanjayite attitude simply, India seemed to be poor because it had too many poor people. What was needed to release India from its degraded torpor was not social reform, not Red revolution or any other species of 'ism', but a massive 'technocratic' assault on ugliness. It was not poverty as such that had to be understood and controlled but the teeming masses, the filthy, under-nourished, uneducated millions, breeding like rabbits in their huts and slums, who were devouring the birthright of the real India waiting to be born and disfiguring the landscape. Out had come, as we all know, the bulldozers – and the knives of those arch-technocrats, the sterilisers.

'With Sanjay,' Nath said, 'there was no empty rhetoric. He was a doer. Just plain and simple *doing things*. All of Sanjay's people were dynamic. All were doers. We all had lots of hopes and visions for the future . . .' That was what had made it so exciting to be in politics while Sanjay was around: 'things' got 'done' with a minimum of idle talk.

I asked him to spell out the 'vision' more clearly for me. But Nath hardly seemed to hear the question.

'One thing you have to understand about Sanjay Gandhi,' he went on, raising his voice and waving his white-clad arms, 'is that first and foremost he was a *tremendous* and *fanatical* nationalist.' It was an aspect of the man that had never been properly appreciated. That nationalism was already evident during the earliest days of their friendship. Nath provided an example. Back in school, he recalled, all the boys were crazed on foreign knick-knacks. At the start of each term, they would show off their latest imported gimmickry. This, apparently, would make Sanjay furious. 'What are you getting so excited about?' demanded the grandson of Jawaharlal Nehru. 'You can have these things right here in India if you want to. What's so special?'

His enemies had accused Sanjay of ignorance and philistinism. They had claimed that comic books peddling stories about the Wild West had been the staple literary diet of the Saviour of India. Nothing, Nath insisted, could be further from the truth. That was a slander invented and spread by so-called intellectuals (i.e. 'talkers') who were jealous and afraid of him. 'He could,' Nath said, getting excited again, 'talk to you on Kampuchea. He could talk to you on the Guinea Islands. [The geographical reference is obscure.] Sanjay could tell you how many different types of dams there were, how many different types of irrigation systems. He could . . . he could talk to you on *anything*.' All this 'talking' sounded a little untypical of the man, but I refrained from comment. Maybe, in the new India, Sanjay would have been the only one allowed to talk. Nath's white-clad arms flailed; his voice rang with passion. Sanjay was 'the greatest human information bank' Nath had ever encountered. It was an appropriate technocratic accolade.

All kinds of classes of people had supported Sanjay. He had mesmerised everyone with whom he came into contact. Everyone, Nath was anxious to make clear, who was not a phony. Those who were genuine and sincere invariably attached themselves to Sanjay. The phonies, however, ran for their lives. They were mostly the so-called intellectuals earlier derided by Nath. Sanjay, by-passing this effete crowd of talkers and grumblers, had reached out to the hearts of the 'have-nots', of the Youth – those, in other words, who had the greatest stake in the future. He had offered them (Nath was no mean rhetorician) a 'constructive nation-building programme'. Until his irruption on to the political stage, there had just been drift, a pervasive hopelessness. Overnight, Sanjay had altered that. He caused the air to crackle with electricity. One measure of his mag-netism was that not a single disciple had ever deserted him. (This was not entirely accurate. Nath failed to mention a man called Sunder, one of Sanjay's underworld cronies. Sunder, for some reason, objected to Sanjay's schemes of forcible sterilisation. He fell into the hands of the police and managed to get himself drowned while under their care. Some considered it murder and Sanjay was charged with complicity.)

Scores, conversely, had abandoned Mrs Gandhi to her fate during her time of trouble. Without the backing of Sanjay's loyalists, she may have perished. Now the loyalists like himself felt 'rudderless' – still, naturally, full of hopes and visions, still committed doers, but alas . . . alas . . . Nath looked at me sadly. Truly, it was cruel to be orphaned at so tender a political age: what greater sadness than to be a committed doer with nothing to do? Rajiv, Nath was sure, possessed all the qualities required of a leader, 'competence, dynamism, nationalis- ticness', he – Nath – supported him . . . but his gestures and his voice had lost their enthusiasm. It was strange that this fervent technocrat, this believer in super-modernity, could still only think in the courtly terms of dynastic succession. It represents a confusion beyond the reach of reason.

A precise articulation of the Sanjayite programme was impossible to come by. Was he, as his mother had said, the Son of India, the tender-hearted protector of the powerless? Or was he, as he so often seemed to be, their deadly enemy? 'Sanjay,' a small time businessman said to me, 'had pain in his heart for the poor people of India.' And, indeed, Sanjay could abruptly alter his camouflage. In May 1980, addressing a provincial rally, he accused the Janata government of having sold gold to enrich a group of 'capitalists'. The 'entire capitalist press' was hostile to him, he went on, because they wished to protect their 'vested interests'. Neither he nor the Indira Congress, he vowed, would ever be intimidated by the capitalist lobby. Peculiar sentiments to come from an ostentatious devotee of free enterprise in all its forms. Peculiar sentiments to fall from the lips of a man from whom so much was expected by American business circles.

Sanjay, despite his odd excursions into demagoguery, never really went much beyond 'the four-point programme' he had outlined during the period of the Emergency.

Plant a tree.

Plan your family.

Marry without dowry.

Let each one teach one.

Even an admirer and promoter of the Sanjay cult like Khushwant Singh (one of India's best-known journalists and men of letters) had to concede as much. Sanjay, he wrote, had no erudition, no serious political philosophy. 'You can't expect economic planning from him. He has very simple yardsticks . . .' So, he was not after all the greatest human information bank. Yet, drawbacks such as these were no barrier to Singh in his espousal of the cause. They, in fact, were not perceived as drawbacks at all but contributed to the primal fascination Sanjay exercised over him. Betraying his caste, he turned himself into a propagandist for the Sanjayite uprising against the talkers. 'Sanjay phobia,' Singh declared, echoing disciples like Kamal Nath, 'is a phenomenon of the self-styled intellectual and the so-called educated élite of our metropolitan cities: it has not infected the simple-minded honest villager or the factory worker'.

Trying to elicit information of any kind from Sanjay was a virtually impossible task – as Singh himself discovered when he tried to interview him.

Had he been, Singh asked, close to his grandfather?

'As close,' Sanjay replied, 'as other people are to their grand-fathers.'

Had he been close to his father?

'Yes – like any son is to his father.'

What kind of relationship did he have with his mother and brother?

'. . . my relationship is no different than that of anyone else with his mother or brother.'

What books had influenced him?

'I cannot think of any.'

What did he enjoy reading most? Poetry? History? Biography?

'No, none of those. My reading is of a different kind.'

Technical? Books on engineering?

'Yes, that sort of thing.'

The man marked by destiny does not have to justify himself or his ways to ordinary mortals. He can be as rude and as brat-like as he pleases; he is a sphinx acting out of deep recesses of compulsion which are beyond scrutiny. You tremble and obey. Words define and enclose; taciturnity can suggest boundless possibility. It is better, Sanjay is reported to have said, to be feared than to be respected. That was why – explained this man with pain in his heart for the poor people of India – 'when I tell anybody to do something they damn well do it.' What Sanjay should have said was that it was easier to inspire fear than it was to inspire respect: that was his first major discovery and it conditioned everything he did. It is not surprising that Sanjay was said to not much care for his illustrious grandfather, a man respected rather than feared: he felt that Nehru had been too soft, that he had spoiled the Indian people.

But then in India fear and respect tend to go hand in hand. The association between the two, sanctioned by religious practice and imagery, is old and deep and tantalising. The goddess Kali, blood-thirsty and potent, simultaneously provoking terror and reverence, commands the worship of millions of Hindus. Her temples are slaughter-houses, her priests are butchers. During the Emergency one of India's most eminent painters paid devotional tribute to Mrs Gandhi by assimilating her to Kali. Later, playing his part in the struggle for succession after Sanjay's death, Khushwant Singh would compare his widow, Maneka, to Durga – a sunnier manifestation of Kali. Exploiting the licentious atmosphere of the Emergency, Sanjay, anonymous, sullen, self-created, would, in conjunction with his mother, become the personification of abstract power, thrusting aside with contempt the alien and effete niceties of the Nehruan heritage. Mother and Son, Kali and Rudra, reverted to a more elemental approach, one that was truer to the Indian soil that the Westminster-style constitutionalism imported by Nehru.

Khushwant Singh, after initial hesitation, began to applaud. Democracy, he decided, was unsuited to the Indian temperament. The only way India would ever function properly and make progress was under the leadership of one dominant character – 'one man, a *strong* man, surrounded by technocrats.' He supported Sanjay because he, Singh, (but, no doubt, Sanjay too) 'recognised the reality of India'. The institutions handed down by Nehru had long since degenerated. Parliament, for instance, was a farce, no more than a noisy college debating society where nothing of substance was achieved. Excess lay at the heart of the political and intellectual retrogression Singh was advocating. Just plain and simple excess, as Kamal Nath might have said. Singh captures the mood well. 'There's no way of clearing slums in this country except by force,' he said to me. 'If you went through the normal legal processes you could spend the rest of your life. So what do you do? You just *bulldoze* them. Same with sterilisation. You just take them and forcibly *do* it.'

In the newspeak sanctioned by the Emergency excess was trans-lated as 'action'. Action – just plain and simple doing things – was tirelessly contrasted to 'talk'. 'Work More, Talk Less' was one of the slogans spawned by the Emergency. Referring to the unfriendly, Marxist-ruled state of West Bengal, Sanjay was scathing. 'The whole atmosphere in that state is political,' he observed. 'In every field of activity they concentrate more on politics than on the work that is to be done.' Bengal was crawling with so-called intellectuals and insincere phonies. Sanjay, no less than the British, hated *babu*-dom. 'He appealed,' Singh tellingly observed, 'to all those young boys who had not passed their examinations. He became an ideal for them of what you could achieve.'

Sanjay's appeal to the young boys who had not passed their examinations is comprehensible. But what was his message for the 'simple-minded' villager who, after all, makes up three-quarters of the population? How did their interests and his coincide? It is not immediately obvious what 'slum clearance' – so prominent a part of the Sanjayite 'vision' – had to do with him. If slums (squatter colonies) were exceptional and adventitious blots on the Indian landscape then bulldozing them might make sense: they are eyesores and it would be nice to be rid of them. But in India the conditions that lead to the spread of squatter colonies are not exceptional and adventitious. They arise out of the poverty of the land and its people. The flight from the countryside is a flight from despair. To bulldoze the squatter colonies that result is to attack the symptons, not the disease. Sanjayite slum clearance meant, in fact, only the physical removal of the men and hovels from the cities, a banishment to the fringes of consciousness. Looked at from the point of view of the *pukka* townsman, they are indeed merely eyesores. He wants to be surrounded by objects bright and beautiful which reflect his idea of India and himself, which make him feel less ashamed.

I remember a conversation I had with a fanatical Sanjayite (he had a white-collar job in one of Delhi's five-star hotels) about the squatter colonies. 'Those people have no *right* to be here,' he said.

'But why ever not?' I asked, slightly astonished by his vehemence. 'Aren't they like you citizens of India?'

He became somewhat hot under his white collar. 'But what do they come here to do? There's nothing here for them. Why can't they stay in the villages where they *belong*?'

The argument that they might be forced out of the villages by sheer want was of no consequence to him. A rich country inhabited by poor people will always be tempted to repudiate its pariahs – as happens in the United States. The doctrine of 'action' was the cloak under which the townsman hid his fury as he set out on the totalitarian path of beautification. Sanjay's new India was a cruel fantasy born of the city and its sensibilities – a shame that turned away from compassion and became pitiless. Sanjay was a purveyor of urban values, prejudices and needs. His vision of modernity, cradled in the five-star hotels of the big cities, had no reference to anything else.

Occasionally, even Khushwant Singh had 'dark thoughts' about what might happen to India under Sanjay's rule. But he was a 'man of passion' and one of his first passions was to see his country rich and powerful and respected among the nations. 'I saw all his warts. He did many things I didn't like when he and his mother came back to power – like ordering the arrest of a police officer who had once prosecuted him. Sometimes I had nightmares. I would wonder if I had backed the wrong horse . . .'

Nevertheless, he persevered. What did the wrongful arrest of one police officer matter in the grand scheme of things? The siren roar of the bulldozers, the self-sacrificing squads of sterilisers, smothered his qualms. Despite the nightmares, despite the dark thoughts, he felt he owed it to the future of his country to support Sanjay Gandhi.

To obtain an experience of over-population, one need travel no farther than the old city of Delhi. By day or by night you can hardly move or breathe in the narrow lanes choked with pedestrians, bell-clanging bicyclists and clamorous, meagre-bodied rickshaw wallahs. Merchants squat in cramped cubicles festooned with ornaments of brass and silver, gold and copper. Clouds of steam ascend from food-filled cauldrons stirred by bare-backed attendants. School children, crouching in tiny cages, stare impassively as they are pedalled to and fro by straining cyclists. You pause to watch a young man pounding silver-leaf destined for the adornment of confectionery. But you cannot linger for long amid the eddying surge of humanity. Ceaselessly you are being pushed and shoved, shouted at and rammed. Beggars appear out of nowhere, exhibiting their deformities, pursuing you with energy. Emaciated children tug at your trousers and hold out cupped palms. The air is charged with vague hysteria.

The Jama Masjid mosque rises grandly out of the chaos and the heat, its domes precise against the autumnal sky. In the distance, the battlements of the Red Fort glow in the heat haze. Still, despite the terrible over-crowding, the inhabitants of Old Delhi cannot be described as squatters: families have been settled there for centuries. The ancestors of these people would have been witness to some of the great events of Indian history – the invasion of Nadir Shah, the seizure of the Peacock Throne and its removal to Persia; some would have fought in the mid-nineteenth-century Mutiny (Indians call it the War of Independence) against the British. Old Delhi is a museum of Mogul grandeur and decadence. It is, as Indians put it, the 'native place' of most of those who live there. An Indian's attachment to his native place is profound. Nevertheless, hardly anyone denies that living conditions are almost intolerable. As far back as 1926 the British had drawn up detailed plans for improvement, plans inherited and reconfirmed by Independent India. The proposals recognised both the historical importance of the old city and the residential rights of those who lived there. Nothing, however, had been done.

When, in June 1975, the State of Emergency was declared, Inder Mohan was doing social work mainly among the Muslims of the old city – a Hindu consciously holding out to the traditional enemy a hand of friendship and help. By July, his beat was flooded with rumours of demolition and expulsion. It was said that 'they' – the suddenly emergent Sanjay and his supporters – were planning to send in bulldozers to raze the shops and stalls clustered about the Jama Masjid and, maybe, to carry out other as yet unspecified acts of destruction. Alarm gripped the populace. Mohan sought an interview with Mrs Gandhi – and was candidly told that it was not she who was taking decisions about Delhi but her son. Mohan arranged an interview with Sanjay. Redevelopment, Mohan said, could be carried out more slowly, more rationally and without violence. Sanjay listened civilly. Now and then, as Mohan talked, he smiled. At length, he remarked that he was familiar with all of Mohan's arguments. His mind, however, was made up. The people, whatever Mohan or anyone else felt, would go where he wanted them to go. 'People like you,' Sanjay said, 'should do whatever we tell you to do.' He rose, folding his arms in the Indian gesture of farewell. Two days later, just after midnight, Mohan was arrested. He was thrown into jail under the Defence of India rules.

Thrusting aside the long-winded processes of the law, the bulldozers invaded not only the vicinity of the Jama Masjid, but extended their depredations throughout the old city and into the squatter colonies of New Delhi. It has been estimated that at least seven hundred and fifty thousand people were expelled from the capital while the Emergency lasted. They and their belongings were piled on to trucks, carted out to the far reaches of the sprawling city and there dumped on waste ground. In the heavy rains of the monsoon the land flooded; there was no drinking water; there were no sanitary arrangements; mosquitoes plagued the refugees; there was no transport into the city, the only place where work was to be had. At the Turkman Gate in the old town the people resisted. The police moved in on them with *lathis* – long, heavy staves – and guns. Twelve demonstrators are known to have been killed, but the actual figure, certainly higher, remains unknown. Women were raped. Houses were looted. This was 'slum clearance' and 'beautification' with a vengeance. Nor was that all. While the bulldozers were on the rampage, the sterilisation squads were hard at work, seizing their 'quotas' at random, picking up their clientele from the lanes and tea-houses, carrying them off to hastily organised 'clinics'. The screams of the victims aggravated the atmosphere of terror: 'birth-control' had also arrived with a vengeance. Many would be permanently maimed, scarred physically and mentally by the experience. Some would even die, poisoned by infection. Perhaps mercifully no figures have ever been published as testimony to the pain Sanjay carried in his heart for the poor people of India. All that remains are the victims and the stories they have to tell.

Four years later I stood with Mohan on a 'slum-cleared' site not far from the Turkman Gate. He showed me the rubble of brick pediments and stone pillars. The place, now that it had been neatened up, resembled an archaeological dig.

'Look,' he said. 'Solid brick ... stone ... have you ever seen a "squatter's hut" built out of such materials?' Many of the houses pulled down by the bulldozers were centuries old. They had been occupied by generations of the same family.'

Sanjay had not been able to complete his programme of expulsion and demolition. He had hoped to tear down all the houses in the (still intact) nearby lanes and so open up a depopulated swathe of territory extending to the steps of the Jama Masjid. On the spot where Mohan and I stood on that burning Delhi morning, he had planned to raise a building of fifty storeys, one of whose claims to fame would have been that it was taller than the headquarters of the United Nations in New York. This extravaganza of glass and steel – I saw a photograph of the model – was to have been the 'biggest commercial and office complex in the country'. Its underground car-park would have had space sufficient to accommodate 1,453 cars – space, that is, to accommodate 1,452 more cars than Sanjay's Maruti plant had managed to produce. Sanjay, it was clear, was going to make India not simply modern: he was, as the white-collared hotel clerk had told me, going to make it *ultra* modern. Indian poverty was an illusion. The poor, mere unaesthetic accretions, could be gathered up and banished to the wastes of the countryside. Doubtless they would form – when required – a useful pool of cheap, submissive labour. By day, the sterilised hordes would have been permitted to come into the city and help build his many-storeyed tower of progress.

Mohan stopped to exchange greetings with a group of Muslim men. I asked one of them what was his opinion of Sanjay.

'It is not good to speak ill of the dead,' he said gravely.

'That is true,' intervened another with equal gravity. 'It is not good to do that. But this I would say: he who has been a devil in life cannot be with the angels in Paradise.'

One afternoon I visited a model resettlement colony, a showpiece of the new order on which money and effort had been lavished. A spindly grove of eucalyptus trees bordered the approach road – a memorial to Sanjay's policy of afforestation. The colony was tidily arranged on a grid pattern. Brick-paved lanes ran between the houses. At the top and bottom of each lane was a square of sun-burnt grass fenced in by low iron railings painted black. At intervals, there were communal, ochre-coloured lavatory blocks. A school and a dispensary were in operation. It (still) being India, cows grazed on what had been intended as a playground. The interiors of the little houses were dark, spartan in lay-out and furnishing, and blisteringly hot under the roofs of corrugated-iron. How could anyone quarrel with these paved lanes, eucalyptus trees, tiny squares and lavatories? Yet, they were disturbing. The residents of the colony were no longer persons. They had been reduced to a sum of catalogued needs; become the objects of technocratic engineering. They were voiceless, faceless, powerless. But even more disturbing was the reflection that I was reacting like a sentimental democrat, out of touch with the urgency symbolised by the totalitarian, semi-militaristic ideal of redemption.

I had to remind myself that in the elections of January 1980 the majority of those who lived here had voted for the return of Indira Gandhi and, by extension, Sanjay. Maybe, there was no other way. Their votes seemed to say that India had run out of options.

But the meteor had burnt itself out, disappearing from the Indian sky as suddenly as it had appeared. Sanjay's enemies – those who, while he had lived, had been powerless to stop his advance – could now disparage him and all that he had claimed to stand for with impunity.

'That boy never made the grade anywhere,' a well-known lawyer and former Janata luminary said to me. 'He was a complete rotter. That's all he ever was.' A moral monster and a psychopath, Sanjay had not known the difference between right and wrong. He had never had any mass appeal, either actual or potential. He had used money and a famous name to buy the loyalty of a few depraved young men. That, in a nutshell, was the Sanjay story.

Yet, had it not been for the intervention of freakish fate, the 'Sanjay phenomenon' would, in all probability, have swept the country. With the demise of its creator, it could now be blandly scaled down by its enemies to a minor aberration: an episode not worth discussing with any degree of seriousness. Possibly they did so out of sheer relief; possibly the shock of his death, the unexpectedness of their reprieve, might have made his entire career seem incredible and, therefore, unreal. They had been having a bad dream – and, having woken up, could laugh at themselves and at the absurd demons that had so frightened them. They were either reluctant or unable to analyse the matter any further. It was another triumph for inanity: the inanity of a politics that had begun with the Emergency and a sado-masochistic attraction to its 'excesses'; that had then proceeded to overthrow its authors and instal in their place a quaint Prime Minister of Gandhian persuasion who drank his own urine every morning and indulged in romantic notions about village virtue; that had then voted back into power the Mother and the Son; and now the Son was dead and nobody was sure about anything. What would Mrs Gandhi be? Would she be Kali? Or would she assume the sunnier manifestation of Durga? Once more the fatal shallowness of Indian politics had been exposed.

Even Sanjay's disciples were doing their best to play down the extremist image he had cultivated. Sanjay, Kamal Nath insisted, bore no responsibility for anything untoward that had occurred. It was the Mother, not the Son, who had got the 'slums' bulldozed. How could Sanjay be held responsible for that? He had not been a government functionary at the time. '*She* did it . . . *she* alone could have done it.' Sanjay may have 'suggested' the idea to her – but then, any other party worker could have done the same. It was an odd and paradoxical attitude, one which made no sense, that contradicted nearly everthing else he had previously said or implied. Nath did not seem to understand – or, at any rate, no longer found it convenient to understand – that Sanjay, shorn of his extremism, was like Samson without his hair.

The sociologist I spoke to at Delhi University saw it differently. He did not underestimate the political appeal of Sanjay Gandhi or try to expurgate him. Personally and politically he had recoiled from the man. 'Yet ... yet ... I have to admit it. Sanjay did express a certain dark side of the Indian personality. I recognise that darkness in myself.'

What was it, that darkness?

'Sometimes,' he said, speaking slowly, 'when you look around you, when you see the decay and pointlessness, when you see, year after year, this grotesque beggarly mass endlessly reproducing itself like some ... like some kind of vegetable gone out of control ... suddenly there can come an overwhelming hatred. Crush the brutes! Stamp them out! It's a racial self-disgust, a racial contempt some of us develop towards ourselves. That is the darkness I speak about. I detested Sanjay Gandhi but I fear I understood him – better, perhaps, than he understood himself.' Nehru, he suggested, had had that arrogance accompanied by contempt for his own kind. It had expressed itself, in the main, by a notoriously short temper. These characteristics, he suspected, had been passed down to his daughter. But the authentic, visceral contempt, unmediated by compassion and intelligence, had come to fullest flower in the grandson.

Reading the attempts that have been made at writing the history of India, of Hindustan, is a disconcerting and debilitating experience for a Hindu. What happens is that less than half-way through the texts, at around the seventh or eighth century AD, the creative history suddenly runs out like sand between the fingers. There is only invasion, conquest; Hindu withdrawal and ossification. Hindustan fades away behind waves of Turks, Afghans and Persians. The Hindu – unsanitary, caste-bound, cow-worshipping, idolatrous, underfed, diseased, drained of vigour – has been pilloried for centuries. He is the child, as has been said, of a wounded civilisation. Sanjay's methods – or, rather, their magnetic quality – evoked a vitality long ago lost; it held out a debased promise of release from a condition and tradition shot through with defeat and despair and shame.

Bubbly

I knew she was extremely rich; I knew she was held in awe by those whose lives she controlled; and I knew she was approaching a vigorous, undaunted middle-age. So much Mr Chaudhuri – the astrologer who had effected the introduction – had told me. Her voice crackled faintly on the bad telephone line.

'I should be delighted to meet you,' she said. 'Mr Chaudhuri has told me so much about you. You sound a most interesting person.'

I laughed lightly, but volunteered no comment.

'Have you ever seen an Indian country house?' she asked.

I said I had not.

'Then, in that case, you positively *must* come. I'll send a car and a driver to pick you up.'

I put the receiver down and looked at Mr Chaudhuri. He was standing next to me, smiling and rubbing his hands.

'So,' he said, 'it is all fixed up.'

'I'm afraid so.'

He shook his head. 'Nothing to be afraid of. She is a most extraordinary lady. You will not regret it.'

Mr Chaudhuri was a darkly handsome, happy and prosperous man. Of late, his business had been booming to such an extent that he had been able to alter his rates from 180 rupees for a forty-five-minute consultation to 180 rupees for a thirty-minute consultation. 'You can tell these Germans *anything*,' Mr Chaudhuri said, 'and charge them *anything*.' (Germany seems to provide the bulk of India's well-heeled tourists.) He had, so to speak, adopted me. Exactly why, I was not sure. But, I had no reason to complain. Astrologers get around in India and Mr Chaudhuri seemed to know everyone of consequence. He talked familiarly of cabinet ministers and industrialists and film stars: all seemed to have need of his services.

'What did you tell the lady about me?' I asked.

Mr Chaudhuri giggled but would not say. I had first encountered him in a heavily curtained cubicle he rented in the basement of the hotel where I was staying. He was sitting on a low stool, surrounded by magazines and newspapers. On a bookshelf behind him were arrayed his celestial charts, treatises and almanacs. He had taken my right hand. 'Oh God!' he exclaimed, kneading the tender flesh. This outburst, naturally enough, had aroused both curiosity and alarm. However, all was well. It so happened, Mr Chaudhuri explained when he had calmed down, that mine was one of the most astonishing palms he had ever had to interpret. Its configurations heralded a future resplendent with honour and fame. So impressive was his perspicacity that we became friends. He had insinuated me into the presence of one of his cabinet ministers; he had manoeuvred my way an industrialist or two; and now there was this woman, a legend in Delhi's high society, fabled for her riches, who, at his prompting, had invited me to her country house. Could anyone expect more from his astrologer?

Car and driver arrived at precisely the appointed hour. The chauffeur oozed an odd mixture of deference and hauteur as he hurried before me, opening and closing doors.

'I hope I did not keep you waiting, sahib.'

'Not at all. It was I who kept you.'

My answer appeared to pain him. 'Of course not, sahib. If I waited for you that is my job.'

He ushered me into the car. Was the sahib perfectly comfortable? Would he like the windows down? Half up? Closed?

'What do you think would be best?' I asked.

He offered the shadow of a smile. 'That is not for me to say, sahib.'

Eventually, it was decided that I should have them rolled up half way. We set off, moving smoothly along empty avenues. It was easy – traversing these broad roads lined with lovely old trees, catching glimpses of mansions protected by solid walls, circling roundabouts planted with beds of flowers, looking out into a cool night bathed in a blue electric glow . . . it was easy to put aside the poverty of India, to slip into the mood required by a country house evening. The sensation of opulence was enhanced by our transition to a multi-laned highway. On our right, necklaces of multi-coloured lights patterned the runways of Delhi's airport. Then we were out of the city, driving along narrower roads bordered by dusty trees and invisible fields, flashing past bullock carts piled high with hay. After about an hour, we slowed at a pair of heavy, wrought-iron gates supported on stone pillars surmounted by illuminated globes. A guard inspected us. He saluted. The gates swung open. We entered a broad drive flanked with shrubs and palm trees. Landscaped grounds stretched away into a leafy darkness punctuated by carefully dispersed spotlights.

I was let off at a flight of steps leading to the main entrance of a large house of modernistic design. To my left, on a lower terrace, was a swimming pool. This was screened on one side by a hedge of illuminated shrubbery which cast an eerily perfect reflection of itself in the still water. Beyond this oddly unsettling aquatic fantasia was another house similar in design to the one outside which I had been deposited. It too might have been an eerily perfect reflection. The front door opened, framing a strangely attired figure. I saw an elderly man of dwarfish stature – he was some inches less than five foot – with creased Mongoloid features. He wore a loose crimson robe, a furry hat whose edges were twisted upward like the eaves of a pagoda and a pair of outsized leather boots the tips of which narrowed to a wrinkled apex. It was difficult to decide what to make of this apparition; how to react. My sense of hallucination deepened as, standing there in the lighted doorway, he wordlessly beckoned me within.

As I entered, he presented the guest book. I signed my name. This ritual completed, he led me into a spacious reception room. Immediately on my left was gathered a group of perhaps half a dozen men dressed in white kurta pyjamas, occupying a cluster of sofas and armchairs arrayed around a low, glass-topped table. They were talking in low voices. My irruption caused their conversation to die away altogether. Assuming they were fellow guests, I began to move in their direction. However, my crimson-robed manikin nudged me away from them, guiding me across the room to another, but untenanted, cluster of sofas and armchairs. This ritual completed, he went away. I sank into yielding foam. The room was heavy with silence, the voices across from me not having been reactivated. Only the subdued hum of the air-conditioners disturbed the sepulchral gravity. Another attendant appeared. This one, perhaps in deliberate contrast to the former, was a tall, fine-featured Rajput. He was dressed in white – white starched tunic, close-fitting white trousers, white turban cascading in a stylish flourish down to the nape of his neck. He carried a silver tray. Bending low, he elicited my choice of drink. Within half a minute a generous measure of Scotch had been set down on a silver coaster on the immaculately polished glass table in front of me. Gliding behind the sofa where I was sitting, he put on a record: discothèque pop. I noticed the strange group of men was not drinking anything. Their manner suggested unease and patient submission. Obviously, they were not guests like myself. I examined my surroundings more closely. Every surface was spotless; every ornament that could glitter glittered. A tapestry of abstract design covered one wall. Around the rails of a balcony overlooking the room were draped garlands of marigold. I sipped my Scotch, awaiting developments.

Voices sounded. An elderly man in a navy-blue blazer and a plump, sari-clad woman, pale neck and arms glinting with jewellery, entered the room. The manikin guided them over to where I was sitting.

'Where's Bubbly?' asked the woman. 'Bubbly' was the name by which our hostess was familiarly known.

I said I had yet to set eyes on her.

'Bubbly!' shouted the woman. 'Where are you hiding yourself?'

An answering cry came from a distant room. It summoned her to its presence. The woman disappeared, leaving in her wake a trail of sweet perfume. Silver tray clutched at his side, the Rajput bent low over the man with the blazer. A whisky and soda was requested. We introduced ourselves. He was, he revealed, in business; the chairman of 'two, three companies'.

'What do your companies trade in?'

'We manufacture things, you can say.' He stared vaguely, taking his drink from the hovering Rajput. He appeared not to want to talk about his business activities. 'Actually,' he said after a short silence, 'my number one love is flying. Before I took up business I used to be a fighter pilot.' He paused. 'I was given the highest award after the last war with Pakistan.'

I congratulated him.

'The *highest* award.' He patted his right leg. 'There's metal everywhere inside of there. Got shot up during the bombing of Karachi. You must remember the bombing of Karachi.' He took a gulp of whisky.

How could I say I did not?

'I also served with the RAF during World War II,' he expanded. 'I bombed France. I bombed Germany. I bombed Holland. I bombed everywhere.' A nostalgic smile overspread his face as he caressed his injured leg.

A hoarse voice resonated through the room. The enigmatic group of men stood up. Our hostess had arrived.

'You must think I'm very rude,' she began, making straight for me. 'But I have delegations of people coming to see me all the time. It's difficult to turn them away. Many have travelled a great distance just to come and see me. Being rich is hard work . . .' She spoke breathlessly, her round, dark eyes darting about the room. She was of medium height and voluptuous build – a voluptuousness which, here and there, had begun to melt into mere fleshiness. Coarse, extravagantly black hair flailed like a horse's tail as she restlessly tossed and twisted her head, taking in the scene. She was dressed in the conventional Punjabi style – clinging trousers, smock, loose-hanging scarf. Her full, furrowed lips were painted scarlet; her cheeks were rouged; her eyes were lined with kohl. She clapped her hands. The Rajput and the manikin came hurrying up to her. 'Drinks! Drinks for my guests!' She seized my nearly-empty glass, placing it on the Rajput's tray. She addressed the room. 'You can have French wine, champagne . . . anything . . . anything . . . Lama! Lama! . . .' She grasped the manikin by the shoulder. 'Bring food . . . *khanna* . . .' The grinning Lama scurried off. She looked at me. 'Mr Chaudhuri has already told me all about you. He's a most remarkable man in his way . . . what did he tell you about me?'

'That you were a most remarkable woman in your way.'

Her hoarse laughter resounded; her hair flailed. 'That is good. I like that very much.' She signalled to the enigmatic group of men, still standing in poses of submission. 'Tonight you see me in my role as patroness of the arts. Those men you see over there are singers, dancers and musicians. Unknowns who have been brought to my attention. If they are talented, I may be able to do something for them.'

'Do you patronise the arts a great deal?'

'The rich have their duties . . .'

'I suppose so.'

'Especially in a country like India. I do a lot of social work. Half of my time is devoted to helping the villages around here. I'm very keen on birth control – you might say it is one of my passions.' She adjusted her scarf. 'Most people believe I'm a hard, unscrupulous woman. Would you say that is all I am? Would you wipe me out when the revolution comes?'

'Are you expecting a revolution?'

She laughed and moved off towards the troupe of unknowns, chattering at them in Punjabi.

The war hero had drifted away, his place taken by a bony, black American girl whose skull was draped by a beaded curtain of pendent ringlets. I discovered that she lived in Sweden, was a dress designer and travelled regularly to India in search of fabrics. The sofa opposite was occupied by a big, barrel-shaped man costumed in the traditional regalia of a Congress Party wallah – peaked white cap, white tunic and close-fitting white trousers. Two minions were perched deferentially on either side of him. The Congress man boomed his name.

'I expect you have heard of me,' he said.

I hesitated.

'Surely you have heard of him,' one of the minions put in, gazing reproachfully at me.

Then I remembered: he was one of those politicians now considered closest to Indira Gandhi; a man of consequence, suddenly reaping the rewards of an Alsatian-like fidelity to his mistress – a fidelity which had never once wavered even during her darkest days. Without prompting, he embarked on a catalogue of his more memorable exploits. His egocentricity was so unabashed, so childlike in its naïveté, that it was almost captivating. I heard how he had been detained during the Janata era, how nobly he had conducted himself while in captivity, how 'the people', outraged, had taken to the streets in their thousands to protest against the injustice of his incarceration.

'I was never afraid,' he said.

'Correct,' the second minion said. 'Fear was never known to him during that time.'

'Never!' confirmed the first minion.

Lama was circulating kebabs. The great man paused while he helped himself, washing it all down with draughts of whisky. 'In fact,' he said, resuming his narrative, massaging his belly, 'in fact it was police who were afraid. Can you imagine such a thing? Why should police be afraid of me?' He spluttered with amusement.

'Police were quaking in their boots,' the second minion said.

He talked about his involvement in the recent outbreak of communal rioting between Muslims and Hindus – how he had gone to one of the affected towns and how, single-handedly, he had restored the errant citizenry to their senses.

'Who gets hurt in riots?' he asked, raising his arms.

'Yes,' said the first minion, looking sternly at the Swedish resident and myself. '*Who*? That is the question you must both ask yourselves.'

'It is the poor who get hurt,' answered the great man, smiling contentedly at his wisdom. 'Not Hindus or Muslims or Christians – but poor people. That is what I told them. Poor people, I told them, have only one true religion – their tummy.'

Lama circulated more kebabs; the Rajput poured more drinks. The great man chewed, swallowed, gurgled and massaged his belly.

'That is so,' the second minion said. 'Tummy is *only* religion of poor people.' He too, perhaps empathising with their misery, began to massage his belly.

Bubbly was clapping, calling us to attention: the evening's entertainment was about to begin. Lama and the Rajput guided us upstairs to a terrace festooned with garlands of marigolds.

Rugs were spread on the floor of the terrace. A dance, performed by a teenage boy, opened the evening's entertainment. Bubbly, crouched beside me, clapped softly, body swaying to the rhythms the boy tapped out with his feet. He moved with confidence and grace, smiling girlishly at us. There were oohs and aahs of appreciation. While he danced, more food, more drink, was offered.

'Do you like my house?' Bubbly asked, eyes fixed on the dancer.

I said I did.

It was, she pointed out, simplicity itself. 'I told the architect to give me four walls, four windows and a roof. And that is what he did. Isn't that what a house is supposed to be?'

I enquired about the other house I had seen beyond the swimming pool.

That, she said, belonged to her husband. It had occurred to them that having separate houses was the best way to preserve their marriage. 'If he wishes, he can have a bird in there and I don't have to know about it. I can have a lover in here and he doesn't have to know about it. It is a good arrangement.'

It suddenly struck me that she was not altogether sober. This was something of a mystery. I had not seen her drinking all that much – only, every now and again, swallowing tiny crystalline pellets stored in a bottle kept by Lama.

'You know,' she said, 'I was always stinking, stinking rich. Our family were zemindars. We were stinking, stinking rich ...'

The boy finished his dance. Everyone applauded: he was adjudged a promising prospect. Bubbly, propelling herself with her hands, sped across the floor to congratulate him. A sequence of love songs – ghazals – followed. Bubbly exclaimed, clapped her hands, sighed.

'The singer is serenading me,' she explained, crouching down once more beside me.

'What is he saying?'

'He says my face is pale like the moon, my cheeks are like peaches, my teeth are like pearls and my lips are the colour of pomegranates. He says all men pine for me as I wander through my walled garden, green after the monsoon, feeding my peacocks . . . it is not so good in English . . .' She pounded the floor. 'Lama! Lama!' Lama came running. He supplied her with another pellet. She drank it down with wine. She took off across the room, propelling herself with her hands, clapping, shouting encouragement at the singer, flailing her hair. 'Yah! Yah! Yah!' She came back. 'Stinking, stinking rich,' she murmured to herself, gulping more wine, swallowing another crystal. 'Stinking, stinking rich . . .' Energised, she circumnavigated the terrace. 'Yah! Yah! Yah!' She came back. 'What they sing is to me like Shakespeare, Shelley, Keating, Kant and Hegel all rolled into one.' She grasped a clump of her hair and stared cock-eyed at it. 'Only Mr Chaudhuri knows what a great romantic I am. Only Mr Chaudhuri knows the secrets of my soul . . .' She resumed her roaming, clapping, shouting, flailing her hair.

I noticed that one of the great man's minions had cradled his head on the lap of the American girl.

'Yah! Yah! Yah! . . . Lama! Lama!' Another crystal. More wine.

The entertainment ceased. She was back beside me. 'Stinking, stinking rich . . .' She stared at me with reddened eyes. There was something wild about her now. Her head lolled. 'Mr Chaudhuri told me you were very passionate, very full of emotion. Is that true?'

I cannot remember what I answered.

'If you stay with me this one night you can kiss these lips like pomegranates, you can stroke these cheeks soft as peaches. Let us wake together in my walled garden and listen to the song of the peacocks at dawn.'

'You have peacocks?'

'Hundreds.' Her head lolled. The guests were making their way downstairs. The Rajput watched us. 'I'm frightened,' she said. 'I cannot stand straight. I shall fall if I stand. I feel as if I'm falling into a black hole, as if I'm dying . . . Lama! Lama!' He came running. The Rajput watched. I too went downstairs.

'What are you doing in India?' asked the wife of the war hero, on our way back to Delhi.

'Collecting material for some articles,' I said.

'What kind of materials are you interested in? Cottons? Silks?'

'Cottons,' I said.

Funeral of a Pope

Of grief, there was little outward sign. True, the wall-posters (many already defaced) were up – this is a form of communication the Italians seem to share with the Chinese. The Communists, anxious to proclaim their peaceful coexistence with the Faith, had bordered their condolences in ostentatious black; the Catholic Action group had theirs done in blue; even the cooperative farmers were moved to public utterance. 'I Coltivatori Diretti Italiani ricordano con immensa riconoscenza gli incontri, le parole, i gesti d'amore del Pontefice, grande profeta di pace . . .' But Rome in August is an almost dead town. Italians treat their holidays with utmost seriousness and it was painfully apparent that not even the death of a Pope was going to persuade them to hang around. The few restaurants that remained open on the Via Veneto were empty – ranks of tables covered with pink cloths tended by surly waiters. Those prostitutes who, in normal times, would cruise along it in their Fiats had vanished to the sea-side along with the rest of the citizenry. 'La dolce vita!' demanded the American photographer who had come to cover the funeral. 'Where is la dolce vita?' The waiter to whom the question was put shrugged unhelpfully. Tourists too were surprisingly thin on the ground, kept at bay by the terrorist threat. However, rumour had it that the terrorists were also on holiday and offered no immediate challenge to the hundreds of armed policemen and soldiers patrolling the streets. Their gay uniforms lent a welcome touch of colour, a welcome touch of melodrama, to the dead city.

The expressions of grief were, at best, formal, prompted by courtesy rather than feeling. A Pope had died, but his death seemed, somehow, a distant bureaucratic event, arousing not sorrow but controlled curiosity. A Pope had died. Not a man, not a personality, but an abstraction, a being no less impersonal and mysterious than those blank tiers of Vatican masonry rising behind St. Peter's. In the end, it has to be admitted, Pope Paul was not greatly loved. John XXIII remained a lively memory, pre-empting affection. Paul had never had the advantage of the comparison. Not even his death could change that. It was all a little sad. On Friday, the day before the funeral, the great square of St. Peter's was crowded with pilgrims and sightseers, but not overly so – certainly the crowds were not as big as I had assumed they would be. A reasonably ordered, spacious queue, well-equipped with Japanese and their cameras, filed along the sides of the square towards the Church where the body, removed from its coffin, lay in state, a body already many days dead and whose state of putrefaction was giving rise to ghoulish speculation. Indeed, the city's English-language press was obsessed by the subject. On that Friday in Rome they had been full of it. Papal decomposition, it emerged, had always been something of a problem. It was claimed that the body had begun to turn green, that it had become so 'high' that special fans had had to be installed, the air in the vicinity irradiated with powerful perfumes. I was told that the Swiss Guard was having a rough time – but my source was Irish, inebriated and, therefore, not entirely to be trusted. And yet to me, an outsider, a man trained to the unapproachable, gun-guarded pomp hedging in the bodies of public figures, to me it was strange, comforting and moving that this body, whatever its stage of disintegration, should be so freely exposed, so casually accessible to my profane gaze. We filed in, shuffling along the marbled aisles, mothers shushing their noisy children, Japanese gawking, a hundred cameras being readied for action. 'Avanti! Avanti!' chivvied a weary-looking, blue-suited functionary. In side chapels groups of nuns prayed, oblivious of the shuffling throng. 'Avanti! Avanti!' The window above the altar glowed orange; the halberds of the Swiss Guard flashed as they caught the light. A single candle burned by the body, very small, very pale, very dead. Its hands were crossed demurely, the face – as had been said – full of calm repose. Perfume sweetened the air; I thought I heard the whirr of fans, but the sound was muted and I could not be sure. Cameras clicked and flashed. The Swiss guard stared. I was struck by their youth. 'Avanti! Avanti!' I hurried out into the square. A youth, hanging outside the window of a motor-car, was singing at the top of his voice. The car roared out of sight down the Via della Conciliazione.

In his will, Paul had said, concerning the funeral, 'Let it be pious and simple'. The English press described with relish the elaborate security precautions – the sharp-shooters to be stationed on the roof of the colonnade, the circling helicopters – that were being planned for the funeral. Somebody in Naples won the lottery using the numbers derived from the date of the death. There were, it appeared, other complications and confusions. Certain embassies were offended because they had not been *officially* informed of the death. The Vatican, sensitive to the distinction that it draws between itself and the Italian State, was creating difficulties for a number of ambassadors whose countries did not have a separate representative appointed to the Holy See. Seating arrangements were a little confused. The simple service requested by the Pope was, according to one newspaper, going to be the most elaborate affair of its kind in the two-thousand-year history of the Church. Why hadn't Archbishop Coggan come? – one Irishman wanted to know. Had he fallen out with the Pope? No, no, replied another Irishman: Coggan was busy doing the Lambeth Walk. When the laughter had subsided, another litro was ordered. In any case, it was pointed out, the Vatican wasn't really all that interested in the Church of England. Ecumenism was, at bottom, directed at the Eastern Orthodox Churches. The Monophysite doctrine was briefly expounded.

But it was time to go to the English College, the stronghold, since the Reformation, of English Catholicism in Rome, breeding-ground of martyrs and saints. However, old enmities were in abeyance and the College, in true ecumenical spirit, had opened its doors to Michael Ramsey, ex-Archbishop of Canterbury, the Bishop of London, a Canadian representative of the World Council of Churches and Archbishop Sepaku, the Anglican Primate of Tanzania. We went past the Martyrs' Chapel, mounting shallow flights of stone stairs, designed for measured ecclesiastical tread, to a room on one of the upper floors. The young Anglican who greeted us became embarrassed when I asked for more information about the English College. The English College? Ah! Well ... you see, we are not the people to ask about that ... we're not ... well, I hope you'll understand ... *They* have very kindly offered it to us ... very kindly indeed ... if you want more information ... ha! ha! ... there are a number of people I could put you in touch with ... Michael Ramsey sat under a white-curtained window, the afternoon light flooding over him, white, whiskery brows beetling. 'I represent no one,' he says, 'I hold no ecclesiastical office.' But he could not resist coming to Rome for the funeral. 'I loved Paul. My memories of him go back over twelve years.' Paul had taught men to treat one another with love and knowledge. 'I revere Pope Paul.' He loved and revered him as a man of God, one who possessed 'that deep humility that comes from walking with God.'

The Bishop of London apologised for the absence of Archbishop

Coggan. He was preoccupied with the Lambeth Conference. His own attitude to Pope Paul was one of deep affection and reverence. 'I count it a great privilege to be here to represent Archbishop Coggan and therefore the Church of England.' They were extremely grateful for the mark Paul had left on the ecumenical movement. He sat down. The Primate of Canada spoke next. Meeting the Pope had been a memorable experience. Working with him in the cause of unity had been a great privilege. He sat down. The Archbishop of Tanzania felt that he had nothing to add and remained silent, lost in solemn reverie. 'Archbishop Sepaku met the Pope in an African situation,' the young Anglican priest observed somewhat mysteriously. What kind of Pope would Ramsey like to see elected? Ramsey laughed. 'Let me make it clear that I represent no one but myself. I'm on the shelf so to speak.' Speaking purely personally, he would like the new Pope to be genuinely keen on Christian unity. But he was not interested in superficial solutions. It was not going to be easy. There were many problems. What kind of problems? Papal infallibility for one; the Virgin Mary for another. There were many problems ... The Canadian Primate hoped that the new Pope would hold the Church together, the Bishop of London talked about the ordination of women and hoped that there would be no backbiting 'between those who decided to go one way and those who decided to go another, between those who do one thing and those who do another ...' Sepaku remained silent, staring out at the Roman afternoon, perhaps being lulled into somnolence by the Bishop of London's metronomic cadences. Ramsey, brows flaring white in the sun, mouth working, played with the ring Pope Paul had given him.

By early Saturday afternoon the streets round St. Peter's had been closed to traffic. Busloads of armed policemen and soldiers, some in brown uniforms, some in blue uniforms, some in green uniforms, some in black and white uniforms, established their occupation. The square filled slowly – even at the height of the service it was to be no more than two-thirds full. A helicopter circled periodically. The atmosphere was relaxed, bordering on the jovial, the crowd moving freely, laughing, smoking, taking photographs, eating ice-cream. VIPs massed blackly on either side of the improvised altar; the hoi polloi down in the square were less than funereal in their attire – jeans, shorts, bright dresses. When, at 5.30, the bells began to peal sombrely, the pigeons rose up, flapping restlessly about the square. Out of the tall central doors they came, the Cross borne aloft. Two by two the Cardinals bent low and kissed the coffin. The powerful Public Address crackled across the square, carrying its message in Italian, English, French and German, aggravating the restlessness of the pigeons. I looked but did not see the marksmen who were supposed to be stationed on the roof of the colonnade. An old woman, dressed in black, dabbed her eyes with a handkerchief: it was the only expression of private grief I was to witness. Later I was told that even those who had lined the balconies of the Vatican had remained dry-eyed. The service went on a long time; the helicopter circled; the crowd processed, moving in and out of the square, drifting down the Via della Conciliazione to buy a beer, an ice-cream, a sandwich, from one of the bars. A beautiful young woman came and stood next to me, dressed in the briefest of shorts and leading a dog. She looked, grew bored and went away. The cardinals, tall white hats precise against the façade of the Church, resembled nothing so much as a statuesque chorus-line. One had to admire the stamina of these old men – though, apparently, the effort proved too much in the end for a frail Chinese cardinal. Gradually, the sun sunk behind the great dome, shadow invaded the square. 'Now that the day is setting,' Paul wrote in his will, 'and everything ends and disappears of this stupendous and dramatic temporal, earthly scene, how can I thank you again, O Lord, for the natural gift of life, and the gift, even greater, of faith and of grace, in which, at the end my surviving being is uniquely sheltered?' A small wind stirred the pages of the Bible which had been placed on the coffin. Faith, grace – I had seen so little of either. As the coffin was hoisted on to the shoulders of the bearers to be taken back into the darkness beyond the tall doors, ('for the last time' the Public Address intoned) the crowd applauded. The applause – so it seemed to me – was polite, not enthusiastic. Twilight deepened over the emptying square. Within half an hour the workmen of the municipality were taking down the barriers. Soon the traffic was flowing again. The dramatic, temporal earthly scene quickly reasserted itself.

Legacy of a Revolution

Poised atop his tall, traffic-besieged column, companioned by a lion, the Marquês de Pombal, eighteenth-century strong man of Portugal, gazes southward down the elegantly graded slope of the Avenida da Liberdade – the imposing thoroughfare slicing through the heart of central Lisbon – to the broad, glinting Tagus framed, on its farther shore, by a line of misty hills. He is looking towards his own creation, the Baixa or lower quarter of the city, a dour, militaristic grid of streets adorned with a regimented architecture of precise, virtually prefabricated symmetry: the new Lisbon he had planned – following the disastrous earthquake and tidal wave which had struck the city on All Saints Day 1755 – to give expression to the rigorous rationalism of the Enlightenment then flourishing in the more advanced lands across the Pyrenees. It has been estimated that between fifteen and twenty thousand people were killed in the Lisbon earthquake; many of them, on so sacred a day, trapped in the city's crowded churches. Voltaire was not slow in providing an ironic commentary on the event: his ingenuous Candide happens to be in Lisbon when the catastrophe strikes.

Pombal had spent many years abroad. He had been Portuguese ambassador in London and Vienna. During his travels, he had absorbed many of the more advanced ideas and hostilities of his day. In 1750 he was recalled home and appointed a Minister. The earthquake was, in a sense, his great opportunity. When the king asked him what was to be done, his reply was brusque. 'Bury the dead and feed the living,' he replied. Pombal buried the dead, fed the living and razed the ravaged city. In the affected area he levelled even those buildings which had remained intact: he would start anew. The ruthless energy he displayed secured his ascendancy.

From then on for roughly the next twenty-five years it was Pombal who ruled Portugal; who, seizing his chance, used it to impose his visions of 'progress' on Western Europe's most fallen, most backward society. The reconstruction of Lisbon was only the most visible aspect of his programme. Suspicious of their power and, in particular, of their near-monopoly on education, he expelled the Jesuits – a move that was to encourage the eventual dissolution of the Order; he humiliated the feudal aristocracy, setting up a royal despotism which modelled itself on the practices of Europe's more 'progressive' monarchs; he subverted the powers of the Inquisition; he reorganised the University at Coimbra, sweeping away the traditional pietistic curiculum, founding instead schools of mathematics and natural science; he abolished slavery – though not, let it be said, in Brazil; he sought – without great success – to promote an industrial revolution and to weaken the commercial stranglehold of the long-settled English merchants.

He was one of the great figures of the period, an embodiment of its impatience and its optimism. His type remains familiar in our own century – the intolerant moderniser seeking to rescue his country from dereliction and decay. It seemed appropriate that, on his pedestal, he should be escorted by a lion and look towards the Baixa – that Enlightenment dream of order, of rationality, of unclouded light; of a new dawn. Pombal was, in some ways, the exact opposite of his twentieth-century successor – the reclusive Dr Antonio de Oliveira Salazar – whose distrust of international influence was so deep-seated that he even discouraged the formation of a Boy Scout movement in Portugal. The Marquês struggled to kick and drag his society into the world of the late eighteenth century. Salazar locked the doors against the ideological incursions of the twentieth and did his best, with the help of his secret police, to lose the key.

To the east of the Baixa rises the Alfama, Lisbon's mediaeval Moorish quarter. Strangely, it was unharmed by the earthquake; and survived the subsequent tidal inundation. Nor was it affected by Pombal's city-planning. What he can see of it today from the summit of his column is probably much the same as he would have seen two hundred years ago. Only the television aerials might puzzle him. Westward, in the direction of the open sea, Lisbon sprawls along the northern shore of the Tagus. A vertiginous suspension bridge looms triumphally over the river. When it was opened in 1966, a grateful nation dedicated it to Dr Salazar. But then times changed. Portugal decided it wasn't so grateful to its dictator after all. Now it is dedicated to the Revolution of 1974 which overthrew all that Dr Salazar had ever symbolised. With the Portuguese fondness for dates it was rechristened Ponte 25 Abril, commemorating the day despotism was said to have ended for ever. On the distant side of the bridge, dimmed by the haze, robed arms spanned out like some prodigious bird of prey, rears the giant effigy of Christ the King. Beyond the Ponte 25 Abril – the sun-bleached splendours of Belém, imbued with evocations, ancient and modern, of vanished grandeur, of Empires gained and lost ... Belém with its rattling commuter trains, its slogan-daubed walls, its dreary suburban slopes climbing away from the water. Further along the shoreline, the Tagus by now lost in the Atlantic ocean, are the resort towns of Estoril and Cascais, Lisbon's Sunday retreats. Along this shoreline, turquoise waves hiss and foam among the rocks; sand-dunes drift across the highway. In high summer, the pine groves and wind-blown grass smoulder. Ash spreads like a greyish snowfall up the barren slopes yellow with gorse. Along the roadside, stalls offer for sale sheepskins, blankets, all kinds of trinkets. The wind slices off the sea. At Cabo da Roca, Eurasia's western-most projection, tourists buzz about the gift-shop. 'Portugal Is For Lovers' say the tote-bags and T-shirts. The stele marking the site strikes a more poetic note. It is inscribed with a quotation plucked from the work of Luis de Camões. 'Aqui ... Onde a Terra se Acaba ... E O Mar Começa ...' Here the earth ends ... here the ocean begins ... The wind scythes through the grass. Buffeted tourists flee to the warmth of the shop.

Pombal gazes south. Northwards, behind his back, towards the airport, wide avenues sweep between featureless banks of apartment blocks, circle round bleak housing estates that have sprung up within the last twenty years; and pass within the shadow of shanty towns, promontories of rural restlessness trespassing close to the heart of the city. Maize grows in gardens; chickens scuttle along muddy lanes; bare-footed girls fill water buckets at a communal pipe; peasant faces stare from windows and ramshackle verandas.

But Pombal and his lion see nothing of this.

Lisbon, I had been told, was sometimes compared with San Francisco. It had not occurred to me to compare the two places – despite the fact that I knew San Francisco fairly well, having once spent several months there. The similarities were listed: the proximity to the ocean; the Ponte 25 Abril – an admittedly somewhat less elegant replica of the Golden Gate; the fog or mist that now and again creeps over the water; the survival of trams; the hilliness – Lisbon, like Rome, is alleged to have been built on seven hills; the abiding fear of earthquakes. Even the increasing prevalence of homosexuality had been cited. After that catalogue, I could appreciate the temptation to draw the parallel. But the similarities having been listed, there, so to speak, all similarity ended. At bottom, the coincidences were no more than arresting curiosities, offered up as a kind of joke at Lisbon's expense.

'You have to come to the Third World,' an acquaintance had remarked sourly. It was a point of view prompted by exasperation. But there was also truth in the statement. Portugal remains, despite everything, the poorest country in Europe. It tends to be either at or near the bottom of just about every index of 'development' – agricultural yield, industrial production, per capita income, etc, etc. As late as 1960, for instance, only about 35 per cent of the population had received a primary education. Under the Salazar régime, university education was the preserve of the wealthy, the state offering virtually no scholarships or any kind of assistance to those who were not well-off. In 1967 this élite made up less than 0·5 per cent of the population. One in every four or five Portuguese was probably an illiterate. The situation has improved since then, but Portugal must harbour among its population the highest proportion of illiterates in Western Europe. Exactly what that proportion is remains a matter of dispute. There are those who would claim – on grounds more emotional than factual – that the problem has been eradicated. When one reflects on all of this, San Francisco seems very far away.

Portugal, when the Revolution arrived in 1974, was 'European' merely in a geographical sense; an essentially agrarian society governed by feudal attitudes, riven to its foundations by class privilege, vaingloriously battling to preserve her 'overseas provinces' in Africa and maintain the long outmoded doctrine of her 'civilising mission'. 'Authority and liberty,' Salazar had said, 'are two incompatible ideas . . . Liberty diminishes in proportion as man progresses and becomes civilised.' The atmosphere on the eve of the Revolution must have been surreal.

Symptoms of backwardness are to be found in the beggars who frequent the open-air cafés of Lisbon, in the cripples seeking alms near church entrances, in the roughly typed hard-luck stories which, occasionally, are flourished in one's face (the same technique of drawing attention to personal suffering is used in India), in the shanty towns teeming with refugees from the countryside, in the thousands who transform themselves into 'guest workers' and take themselves off to France and Germany in search of work. As happens all over the Third World, you get nowhere without 'influence', without knowing the 'right people' and being able to exploit a system of relationships based on family ties, on favours given in the expectation that, in due course, some return will be made. He who naïvely confronts the Portuguese bureaucracy is, they say, doomed to futile expenditures of energy. A Sisyphean labour can ensure.

Portugal, in 1974, resembled, to a certain extent, a country that had just been granted an unexpected and dubious Independence: panic-stricken, skill and capital immediately fled abroad to more congenial havens – chiefly Brazil. And, after seven years of turbulent democracy, the rich remain anxious and fearful of further change. Some, when they let themselves go, assume the outraged demeanour of expatriates complaining about the spoiled natives. 'You know,' one affluent woman said to me, 'nobody wants to work any more. You cannot fire anybody any more.' Her lovely face contracted with indignation. 'Why,' she exclaimed, 'after these women have their babies, they have to be given so many hours off for each breast.' I looked flabbergasted. 'It is true,' she cried. 'It is there in the labour regulations. For each breast, so many hours. That is what we have come to in Portugal.' I could have been in almost any newly indepen-dent African state listening in to vulgar Club conversation.

VOTA APU ... SOCIALISMO EM LIBERDADE ... CONTRA D'FASCISMO, CONTRA A MISERIA ... REPRESSA NAO! VIVA REFORMA AGRARIA ... The charged atmosphere of the 1974 Revolution lives on, to some extent, in the slogans defacing the walls of Lisbon. These slogans are one of the first things to draw the attention of the freshly arrived visitor. Daubed on virtually every available surface, they assume, after a while, the appearance of a disfiguring lichenous growth. The Left makes most of the running in this wall war. Apart from the occasional swastika, I saw few overtly 'fascist' proclamations and symbols: these, in fact, are a much commoner sight in London. The Communists seem to be the masters of the art. Some of their efforts are quite elaborate pictorial compositions, showing the 'people' – the *povo* – heroically advancing towards lurid skylines serrated by the roofs of factories and smoking chimneys.

In the euphorically blurred period that had followed the stirring events of April 1974, the Communists had swiftly shown themselves to be the best organised political party in the country – virtually the *only* party. Throughout the years of suppression the Party, though invisible, had managed to maintain itself and preserve a coherent identity. It was a seed frozen into impotence by the Salazarian ice-age but with its capacity for germination still intact. The Communists emerged from their hibernation united around their exiled leader Alvaro Cunhal: who, on his return home, was given a hero's welcome by an ecstatic Lisbon. He was even made a Minister. For a while, it was not entirely inconceivable that the country might fall into the Party's waiting, well-prepared hands. Anything seemed possible in a Portugal suddenly loosed from its leading strings, suddenly on course for the previously unutterable and unthinkable – voluntary relinquishment of its cherished 'overseas provinces' in Africa and the long martyrdom they had entailed.

Angola, Mozambique and Guinea were indeed surrendered one by one. After five hundred years, the Portuguese Empire was dead. But the Communists did not seize power. Cunhal's hero's welcome did not signal love of his doctrines. It was a celebration; a festa. He was a symbol, not a saviour. In the seven years that have since gone by the Party has declined steadily in popularity: in the last elections they received a modest 13 per cent of the vote. The Revolution's novelty, its excitement, has, inevitably, been dulled with the passage of time. Portugal, meandering through a succession of ephemeral coalitions, has gradually drifted rightward, towards what one might describe as the conservative-centre. 'The revolution is screwed,' lamented a Canadian folk-singer of unspecified leftist persuasion and a long-time resident. 'If tomorrow Salazar should be raised from the dead, these people would fall at his feet. They don't care for freedom any more.' That is too bitter and uncharitable a judgment. There is no evidence that surviving Salazarist nostalgia is anything more than idle fantasy. Too much has happened in Portugal, too much has been overturned, for so naïve a reversion to occur.

Whatever the discontents, the fruits of democracy remain real. One Saturday evening I went out to Belém to have a look at a lavish festa sponsored by the Communist Party: the colourful posters advertising the event – to be held over three days – were freely displayed all over Lisbon. It seemed at a glance that the whole city was wending its way to the fairground. The nearby streets were jammed with cars, buses, trams. Serpentine queues fermented about the turnstiles. It was a long time since I had seen such swarms of people. On distant stages bands performed. Red, blue, yellow and green flags fluttered from tall poles. Scattered loudspeakers broadcast snatches of music and exhortation. Dust rose from the beaten earth, fogging the noisy, fluorescent night.

Young men and women danced among the eddying multitudes, holding aloft flags adorned with the hammer and sickle.

'Sixty Years of Struggle' proclaimed the banners. I wandered in and out of booths – the Communist Party of Cape Verde sent fraternal greetings to their Portuguese comrades; so did the Angolans, the Poles, the Cubans, the Italians; so too did *Pravda*. Militant internationalism scented the Lisbon air that evening. By no means all – or even a majority – of these people were Communists. For most, no doubt, it was a night out, one unmarred by ideological commitment. Yet, whatever their motives, each, by his mere presence, was an emblem of the new Portugal. Salazar ('We are opposed to all forms of internationalism, Communism, Socialism, syndicalism . . .' he had once proudly declared) . . . Salazar, so apprehensive of the Boy Scout movement, had been well and truly buried.

Nevertheless, those who mourn the past, who suffer from acute withdrawal symptons, are not necessarily wicked men hellbent on destroying the achievements of the last seven years and restoring dictatorship. That is an unjust assumption. The lunatics aside, most will concede that such a restoration is not possible. Their sense of loss, their *saudade* (a visceral Portuguese concept, not easy to render into English, combining the notions of nostalgia, yearning, deprivation: it finds its purest expression in the *fado*, those sombre love-songs which, over the last two hundred years, have become the distinctive folk music of Portugal), is rooted in a feeling, cloudy but none the less real, that the country has lost its 'soul'; that it no longer has a reason to be. 'We have lost our way,' a former ambassador mourned. 'We Portuguese have lost our sense of ourselves. We no longer know why we exist.'

The Revolution of 1974, he went on, had gone even deeper, had been, in its special way, even more devastating than the French and Russian revolutions. Those revolutions might have changed profoundly the structure of their societies but they did not harm their essence. The upheavals in France and Russia, he argued, had enhanced their national destinies: France, under Napoleon, dominated Europe; Russia, under the Communists, had transformed itself into the standard-bearer of a new idea of civilisation – one, it went without saying, he abhorred . . . but that was not the point.

In Portugal it had not been like that. Their Revolution had severed the ties linking them to their past. What was Portugal without its African territories? Where now was its 'civilising mission'? It was nothing! A cork floating aimlessly on the ocean of history! Overnight, it had shrunk into marginality; a poor, small, shabby country on the fringes of Europe, whose highest ambition was entry into the consumer paradise of the Common Market. Theirs, he concluded, was a tragic fate.

In Belém, a bluish mist hangs over the river. The tide is out, stranding its sixteenth-century watch-tower, exposing its mossy, barnacled base. Seaweed drapes the rocks. I make the pilgrimage to its summit and look down on the Tagus. The Ponte 25 Abril rises dreamily out of the blue mist. Christ the King is barely visible in the milky haze obscuring the far shore.

Along these shores Portugal had embarked on its great maritime adventure – when, in 1415, crusading piety fusing with the desire for gold, the armada was assembled that would seize Ceuta in North Africa from the Moors. The success of this expedition would give birth to the 'civilising mission,' to the lust for overseas expansion and the conquest of new worlds. In the far south of Portugal, on the windy promontory of Sagres, that dour and obsessed prince, Henry the Navigator, would, in the years to come, brood over his charts, collating rumours of unknown lands, enticing to his presence the most knowledgeable and skilled mariners and navigators of the time.

Under his guidance Madeira was discovered and settled; as were the Azores and Canary Islands. It was at his instigation that frail Portuguese ships began their explorations of the African coast and initiated the European trade in slaves. When he died in 1460, the Cape of Good Hope was still to be rounded, the sea-route to India and the Far East yet to be revealed. But the momentum had been established. Within forty years of his death, Vasco da Gama would be dropping anchor off Calicut – the voyage transmuted into legend in *Os Lusiadas* (the Lusiads), the national epic composed by Portugal's most celebrated poet, Luis de Camões.

On his return from India, da Gama had offered prayers of thanks in Belém, at the Church of Our Lady. King Manuel, carried away by the scale of the discoveries, conferred on himself the title of 'Lord of the Conquest, Navigation and Commerce of Ethiopia, Arabia, Persia and India'. In 1502, on the Belém beach where da Gama had embarked on his voyage, he ordered the erection of what was to become one of the masterpieces of Portuguese architecture – the Jeronimos Monastery. Nothing better reflects the self-assurance and magnificent optimism of Portugal's heroic age. Half a millennium later it stands there, facing the river, its greying, ivoried façade glowing in the white heat of noon.

Not far away is the modern monument raised to the pioneering glories of the Navigator Prince. He holds himself erect at the stylised prow of a ship, gazing out across the water. Angled behind him, faces lifted to the sky, are some of those he had gathered about him at Sagres. Etched into the brick pavement of the surrounding plaza is a map of the world. Meticulously, it charts the explorations of the Portuguese along the coasts of the continents. How small Portugal! How immense the scope of its endeavour!

I stare at the Jeronimos Monastery glowing in the sunshine. Gone were the lords of Ethiopia, Arabia, Persia, India . . . Africa. REPRESSA NAO! proclaimed the walls of Belém . . . VIVA REFORMA AGRARIA! The commuter trains sweep past. Below me, the muddy fringes of the Tagus nuzzle the mossy rocks and stir the tentacles of blackened seaweed.

The Aryan Dream

The house, as is usual in Persia, was hidden behind high walls. Its style was vaguely Iberian – façade washed in white, red-tiled roof, a ground-floor veranda framed by arches. The proportions were those of a small palace. A swimming pool gleamed in a corner of the twilit garden. My host, a lawyer, was rumoured to have made his money only within the last ten years; the house, a tangible expression of that success, was less than a year old. Northwards the lights of Teheran were spread like a rash up the lower slopes of the Elburz mountains. Snow streaked the higher summits. Beyond that black mountain wall lay the Caspian, sea of sturgeon and caviar. A majordomo waited on the pillared porch. I was led through a hall adorned with Persian miniatures, across a parquet floor strewn with rugs of intricate design. My host and his wife were in the library. A bell summoned a manservant. He approached soft-footedly and, bending low over me, took my drink order. I gazed at the books.

'Over five thousand volumes,' my host said.

The books were ranged on two floors, the upper, bordered by a wrought-iron balcony, housing, my host explained, his collection of Persiana; the lower, books of a more general nature. A spiral staircase connected the two. The house, in fact, had been designed around the library.

'We ran out of space,' my host's wife said. 'In the end we decided that the only thing to do was to build a new house.'

A girl of about fifteen – the daughter of the house – appeared. She put on a jazz record. Both she and her brother attended American boarding schools. My gaze strayed to the group of terracotta animal figures arrayed on a sideboard.

'3000 BC,' my host said.

Other guests began to arrive. Abdol and Manny; Ali and Layla; Xerxes and Fatima. The women glittered with jewels, sparkling on fingers, necks, bosoms. Their fat husbands were more casually dressed, T-shirts sleekly stretched over bulging stomachs. A servant passed round caviar on thin slices of toast.

My host's wife fingered Manny's soft white dress.

'It's exquisite, Manny. Really fabulous. Where did you find it?'

'I picked it up the other day in a little shop in Soho.'

'Is it Indian?'

'Afghan, I think. Abdol insisted I buy it. "That's *you*, Manny," he said. You know what Abdol's like.'

But now it was Manny's turn to praise. 'What a beautiful emerald that is! I don't think I've seen you wearing it before.'

'I got it on our last trip to New York. I can't resist Saks. Every time I'm in New York I just *have* to buy something at Saks.'

'I know the feeling,' Manny said. 'Abdol and I were in Chicago not long ago.'

'What was Chicago like?'

'Very windy,' Manny said.

'They say it's a windy city,' my host's wife confirmed. 'Did you buy anything there?'

'I picked up quite a nice diamond . . . but, you know, I prefer to get my jewels in Paris.'

'It's *ages* since we've been to Paris,' my host's wife said. 'Darius is getting lazy in his old age.'

'So is Abdol,' Manny said. 'Lazy and fat. Last year I literally had to drag him to that health farm in Sussex.'

'Darius won't hear me talk about health farms.' My host's wife looked martyred.

Manny smiled sweetly at me. 'Do you know Paris well?'

'Not very.'

'Do you know,' Manny said, 'I spend sleepless nights worrying that Paris might change, that one day they might pull down Notre Dame and build a supermarket. I must see Notre Dame at least once a year. I would die if I didn't.'

The ladies drifted away. More caviar was passed around. Dinner was announced. Two candle-lit tables had been set up in the dining room. A manservant filled our crystal goblets with a rosé wine. I was sitting next to Layla, a pretty, scented creature. She smiled at me. 'Do you come from Tahiti?' she asked.

'What makes you think that?'

'Ali and I were there a few weeks ago.'

The line of deduction was not easy to follow. 'What were you doing in Tahiti?'

'Ali *loves* islands. We've been to Jamaica, Barbados, Mauritius, the Seychelles, Fiji . . . Ali's really into islands.'

I looked at Ali (he was sitting at the other table), the man who loved islands. He was masticating slowly, majestically, his eyes half-closed, sunk in satiated repose.

'If you don't come from Tahiti, where do you come from?' Layla asked.

'I come from Trinidad.'

'Is that an island?'

'I'm afraid so.'

The news excited Layla. 'Ali! Ali! This man comes from a place called Trinidad. An island! Have you heard of it?'

Ali blinked. He studied me with inert, saurian voracity. Would he devour me on the spot?

'I must write it down,' Layla said. She called for a pen. The manservant offered his. Layla stared critically, disapprovingly, at the instrument – an expensive Parker ballpoint.

'Look.' She showed it to my host's wife.

My host's wife shrugged. 'What can one do?'

'I would keep my eyes on that fellow,' Xerxes said.

The pen was passed around the company. Obviously, the man was getting above himself. A peasant with a Parker. What next?

Liqueurs were served in the library. I had cognac mixed with Grand Marnier.

'O Cyrus, Great King, King of Kings, Achaemenian King! I, the Shahanshah of Iran, offer thee salutations from myself and my nation ... Cyrus! We have today gathered at thy eternal resting place to say to thee: rest in peace, for we are awake, and will forever stay awake to guard thy proud heritage.'
(His Imperial Majesty Mohammad Reza Shah Pahlavi, Shahanshah Aryamehr – King of Kings, Light of the Aryans – commemorating the 2,500th anniversary of the Persian Empire. 13 October 1971)

Not far from Teheran Airport is the Shahyad Tower. Built in 1961 to celebrate the Shah's 'White Revolution', its hyperbolic bulk dominates the western skyline of the city. 'It seems,' says a guidebook, slipping with ease into the spirit of the thing, 'that when the Shahyad Tower was inaugurated, the message was: the base is solid, the impetus is given, the nation is heading towards its new destiny ... the future can but lie higher!'

The Tower exemplifies that monumentalism – the impersonal

assertion of resplendent personal power – so characteristic of all despotism. In this respect, as in others, the Shah, an authentically archaic figure, models himself on his Achaemenian predecessors, looking towards the tomb of Cyrus on the plain of Parsagadae and the surviving splendours of Persepolis, the royal seal of Darius destroyed by Alexander the Great. 'Since my childhood,' he told a visiting Indian journalist, 'I knew that it was my destiny to become a king and to rule over a people and a land whose ancient and magnificent culture, great prophets and famous kings I have deeply venerated.' It is not easy to escape the Shah's kingly presumptions; his tendentious archaism. The official Persian calendar now dates itself from the founding of the Achaemenid Empire. Virtually every city and town in the country is embellished with an imposing stela enunciating the principles of the White Revolution. Imperial graffiti whiten the slopes of the brown hills outside Isfahan, the bold Persian characters spelling out the antiquity and glory of the Empire. Even the strictly functional works of the régime – a dam, a steelmill, a bridge – tend to have about them a monumental air, symbolism overriding purpose.

But it is the Shahyad Tower which captures in its purest form the spirit of the White Revolution. A slow-moving walkway conducts you into its dark heart. Within, the spectator is submerged in a totalitarian fusion of sound and image. On giant screens and against a background of unceasing martial music, cinematic cameos flash on and off. Goose-stepping soldiery prance. A turbulent river rushes down a gorge. Costumed peasants dance. A man walks dreamily across the desert towards the setting sun. Fighter aircraft streak across the sky. The Shah salutes. Out of a misty perspective looms the tomb of Cyrus. Oil refineries gush fire – 'the gas torches of the oil refineries,' my guidebook points out, 'can be seen as recalling the ancient (Zoroastrian) fire altars, the chimneys of Abadan, the colonnades of Persepolis.' Tanks roll. Blocks of molten iron hiss and spurt steam. More peasants dance. The Shah salutes ... Virile image succeeds virile image. Everywhere in that darkness – movement, colour, sound. In illuminated tanks swim the fish of Iran's rivers and seas; fountains splash in blue-tiled basins; an emblematic engine revolves on a pedestal. And, set in a central niche is a replica of a Zoroastrian fire altar, kept burning night and day. I watch an old man staring intently at the flame – fuelled, I would suppose, by piped gas. What does he make of this curious – and disturbing – act of homage to the religion swept aside by the Islamic Conquest in the seventh century? In another room are displayed bowls and other antique objects, some going back to the fourth millenium BC. The display seems designed to stress the longevity and continuity of Iranian civilisation. It is brought startlingly up to date by a large painting depicting the coronation of the present Shah. Winged figures hover protectively about the idealised, near god-like figure. Heaven and Earth pay obeisance to the King of Kings.

Outside, the dusty afternoon is yellow, warm and noisy. To the north, the higher summits of the Elburz mountains are streaked with snow. A steady stream of traffic flows along the roads that hem in the concrete island on which the Tower stands. Flags flutter – the German flag and the Iranian flag: the President of the Federal Republic is coming to pay his respects, to salute the Shahanshah. After the German President, the Senegalese President will come; after the Senegalese President, Margaret Thatcher . . . Everybody, sooner or later, fetches up in Teheran. A trade agreement or two may be signed. But this procession of important foreigners satisfies another need: it enhances self-esteem, re-enacting the scenes portrayed on the stair-ways of Persepolis. There, in exquisite relief, file the client peoples of an Empire that once extended from the borders of the Aegean through Egypt and Syria and Mesopotamia to the Indus Valley and the plains of Central Asia. Iran has been born again. The Achaemenian past is being recreated in modern dress.

'Until a few years ago,' the civil servant said, 'we Persians used to be treated like dogs. Nobody gave a damn about us. The Russians and British did as they liked, carving up our country as it suited them. Now, no one can afford to ignore us. We're in the ascendant and the West is in decline.' It was one of the Shah's favourite themes – the decline of the West, its softness and moral laxity. 'Westerners resent us – the British especially,' the civil servant continued. 'They can't stomach the fact that they have to come to our Shah on their hands and knees and beg for money.' He was old enough to remember how it used to be – the old people suffering from trachoma, the desperate men going from door to door begging for work, the malnutrition. How insolently foreigners behaved in those days! All of that had changed. Persian dignity had been restored: it would not be lost again. The long sleep was over. As if to emphasise the point, a squadron of fighter aircraft roared overhead, their vapour trails scarring the blue sky.

But the elimination of unemployment, trachoma and malnutrition is only half the story. The Shah's dreams go far beyond such mundane achievements. His evocation of antique glories is linked to a strong sense of divinely ordained mission, to a transcendent vision of his role and his destiny. 'Since my childhood, nay ever since my birth,' he told the Indian journalist already referred to, 'I have been living under the protective wing of Almighty God.' God's concern for his well-being has manifested itself on several critical occasions: the subject is treated at some length in his autobiography, *Mission For My Country*. When still a child, he fell dangerously ill. One night Ali, the son-in-law of the Prophet, appeared to him in a dream and offered him a bowl of some unspecified liquid. The Crown Prince drank. Recovery was swift. Some years later he was riding in the Elburz mountains when his horse suddenly threw him. He pitched head-first towards a jagged rock but, as he fell, Abbas, 'one of our saints', caught him up in his arms, saving him from certain death. On another occasion, while walking in the street with his guardian, 'I clearly saw before me a man with a halo around his head ... As we passed one another I knew him at once. He was the Imam, or descendant of Mohammed ... who is expected to come again and save the world.' The incident could not help but reinforce the Crown Prince's conviction of divine election. God, clearly, was on his side. Here he is (as Shah) discussing these wondrous happenings with the Indian journalist.

Q: ... sophisticated moderners may dismiss your spiritual experiences and visions as mere hallucinations.

A: If these were simple illusions and hallucinations, how can one explain the stupendous inner strength and confidence that these happenings built up in me, the faith and power that helped me overcome diseases, dangers and perils.

Q: Well, I suppose there are people who have a highly developed and mysterious faculty for recalling the past and peering into the future ... You are probably one of them.

A: I do have my mystical side.

Q: I somehow think our countries will give the world its future prophet or messiah.

A: Yes, and I only hope our twelfth Imam will come soon to guide the world.

We have come a long, long way from unemployment, trachoma and malnutrition. The Shahyad Tower arises out of an archaic Messianic dream, the mystical adoration of the kingly self and kingly power.

*

The story is told of the lady – the wife of a man who had speculated wisely in real estate – who wished to decorate her house in the style of the Louis XIV period. But then she was advised by a cruel friend that the style of Louis XXX was much more chic. So she went to Paris and began asking around in the shops for Louis XXX furniture. 'That,' the man who told the joke said, 'sums up the *nouveaus riches* of our country. Ignorant and West-mad.' National grandeur roots itself in a crass materialism: the sick West rushes in to fill the Iranian vacuum. Teheran is rife with rags-to-riches stories – tales of street-corner hawkers who have become millionaires, of building contractors who have become multi-millionaires, of chauffeurs who have become property tycoons. The Shah himself is, of course, something of an arriviste: the Pahlavi dynasty – the creation of his rough, semi-literate soldier father – is barely fifty years old. (To mark the anniversary, Iran's mountaineers have been ordered to scale fifty peaks.) His chief worshippers are to be found among the 'West-mad' élite. He is their Shah. They are his people.

The money is new. Very new. Nearly all of it has been conjured up within the last ten years, the ten glorious years of OPEC. It is these new rich who give Teheran its flashy glamour, whose buying power, whose taste, is reflected in the shops crammed with costly foreign goods; whose cars flood the broad avenues and make a journey at any time of the day a torment; whose lusts are catered for in opulent brothels where mere entry might cost fifty thousand ryals – almost four hundred pounds; who fill to capacity the Iran Air jumbos flying West – last year two hundred thousand Iranians visited London, spending (on average, nearly two thousand pounds a head) more, much more, than the typical Japanese and American tourist; whose sons and daughters wear faded jeans, chew gum, play guitars and speak bad English in rank American accents; for whom the 'International' channel of National Iranian Radio and Television fills its broadcasting hours with 'I Love Lucy' type programmes and whose presenters are brought over direct from the United States – 'Good evening. This is Teheran. Here is the noos . . .' And everywhere, there are the spivs, the young men in tight trousers who call you 'Meestah' and who, in the late afternoon, loiter outside the cinemas, gawking at the near-naked, lasciviously posed women festooning the posters advertising Western films. 'They get very weird ideas about us,' an English secretary complained, 'after seeing all those pornographic films. They think we're just waiting to be laid. It's terrible.' Thus it is that the West, imperfectly understood, its complexity almost entirely eluding those who wish to immerse themselves in it, is reduced to caricature. It becomes not a liberation, but a kind of highly infectious disease.

Teheran's boom-town atmosphere is oppressive. Fifteen years ago the city had a population of about three million. Today, it is approaching five million. This seems to cause neither alarm nor misgiving: Iranians are proud of their burgeoning megalopolis. They regard it as indispensable, a necessary attribute of modernity. One can almost literally see the city taking shape day by day. Everywhere cranes rise into the sky. Everywhere there are excavators at work, gouging holes out of the earth, spewing up clouds of dust. To combat the menace of the traffic a Metro is being constructed – by the French – at a cost of untold millions: whatever Iran wants, Iran gets. Dense clusters of apartment blocks are being built on the outskirts of the city to meet the housing shortage. But, despite the spate of building, the cost of accommodation remains exorbitant. A perfectly ordinary two-bedroomed flat can easily cost five hundred pounds a month. Often, a man must have more than one job if he is to meet his commitments. Landlords are reaping a rich harvest. As in all boom towns, little attention is paid to engineering proprieties. For Teheran, this negligence spells future catastrophe. The city is in a high-risk earthquake zone. On the fateful day of its destruction, it will be a death-trap. The flimsy towers of concrete and steel will collapse like packs of cards.

However, no one gives much thought to earthquakes: the present will do. So, the population continues to grow, money continues to be made, money continues to be spent. Unemployment (it is claimed) is virtually unknown. The factories that line the western reaches of the city have to compete with each other for labour: an unskilled worker can earn one thousand ryals a day – about eight pounds. So acute is the scarcity of labour – and skill – that one million foreign workers have had to be brought in, mainly Turks, Indians and Pakistanis. These factories are devoted to the assembly of consumer goods. They cannot satisfy the hunger for their products. The 150,000 washing machines (all parts imported from Italy) turned out every year by the Arj works comes nowhere near meeting existing domestic demand. At the Paykan car plant the story is much the same: they make four hundred Hillman-type cars a week but the waiting lists grow longer. By 1985, it is officially hoped, one in two Iranian families will own a car, three million television sets will be produced annually, per capita income will be 4,500 dollars.

The showpiece worker I met at the Paykan factory was a true child of the White Revolution. He had come to Teheran from Isfahan where, traditionally, his family had traded in brass. The new world of the assembly line excited and fascinated him. 'I *like* working in factory,' he said. He was not in the least bored by the repetitious nature of his job; nor did he have any nostalgia for the craftsman's life he had abandoned. ('I am going crazy,' a Shirazi carpet-weaver told me, 'crazy after forty years of tying these knots. This is bad work for the brain. It has made me stupid, all these knots.') My car worker was earning four hundred dollars a month, a wage swelled by the occasional bonus. On top of that, the company provided him with subsidised food, free medical care, virtually free housing – and, even, holidays abroad. 'We are better than the Japanese in looking after our workers,' a company official exulted.

The same official took me to see the man's apartment on the Company's nearby housing estate. We were welcomed by the man's plump wife who, obviously, was well-prepared for the visit. The official piloted me into the kitchen.

'Look,' he said, 'refridgerator.'

'Look,' he said, 'gas cooker. With automatic timer.'

'Look,' he said. 'Hoover vacuum cleaner.'

We went upstairs to the sitting-room. He drew my attention to the pile carpet, the Scandinavian-style suite, the colour television set, the telephone, the framed paintings of European landscapes decorating the walls. A low table was set out with colourful confectionery and bowls of almonds and pistachios. But most surprising was the leather-bound, gold-tooled volume of *Hamlet*.

'Who is reading Shakespeare?'

The woman giggled; the official picked up the book.

'No Eshakespeare,' he said. 'Look.' He drew back the cover: it was a musical cigarette box.

Agriculture has suffered because the farmers cannot always compete with the wages offered in the factories and on the building sites. Some land has actually gone out of use. Many of the villages round and about Teheran are half-deserted. Neglected orchards line the roadsides. It is a rare sight to see anyone actually at work in the fields. One of the consequences is that Iran has to import more and more of its food, a situation aggravated by the all-round increase in consumption. Subsidies are used to keep prices down – meat, for example, brought in from France, is generously subsidised; so is wheat, sugar and vegatable oil. The chances are that if you order tea in a restaurant you will be provided with a cup of boiling water, an English teabag and an English packet of dried milk.

The motorway out of Isfahan sweeps through the bare hills daubed with imperial graffiti out to the Aryamehr steelworks. This is one of the major monuments of the White Revolution, a counterpart, in its own way, to the Shahyad Tower. The giant complex, a gaunt fretwork of chimneys, girders, globes, tubes and towers, rises up out of the brown land like a mirage. My guide was a lecturer in the training school run by the works – one of those Iranians, possessed of skill, lured back from abroad by the government. We wandered through enormous sheds, cathedrals of iron, echoing with the clamour of machinery. Steel manufacture conveys all the elemental excitement, the machismo, of the brute processes underlying industrial civilisation: it cannot be bettered as a symbol of progress and power. From catwalks we looked down at cauldrons brimming with molten ore, at glowing pillars of iron shooting out of furnaces and rushing along rollers, at explosions of gushing steam.

'There was nothing here a few years ago,' my guide said, 'just a few farmers scratching a living. Now – all this. It is like magic to me.' The Russians had built the plant in exchange for supplies of natural gas. A few of their technicians lingered on to make sure that everything went smoothly. 'In time we will not need them,' my guide said, 'in time we Iranians will be running all this for ourselves.' When would that time come? Five years? Ten years? He laughed at my efforts to pin him down. Naturally, there were many difficulties to be overcome. But there had been progress. When the plant was first set up they had had some trouble in recruiting workers. 'The people were so afraid, you know.' Afraid of what? Afraid of the machinery, the heat, the scale and sheer violence of the industrial process. Now the people were no longer afraid. Wasn't that progress? 'For me it's just like being in America. No difference.' He told of the town, built to accommodate the workforce, equipped with drive-in cinema, golf course, swimming pools, tennis courts. Just like America. That was what really mattered. Symbolism overrode function: the motor-car factories continued to import the high-grade steel they needed from Europe and Japan. The place was a monument, the creation of a revolution that dealt in images. Aryamehr *was* a kind of mirage. It connected with nothing.

It did not connect with the cheerful Indian I ran into one afternoon. He was working (illegally) in a smallish, family-run hotel. He had come to Iran 'touristing', but had found the pickings so good he had stayed on: indeed, the owner of the hotel (at which he had originally turned up as a bona fide client) had become so dependent on his electrical know-how that he would not hear of his leaving. 'I am making too much money,' he said happily, 'too much money. These people can do nothing for themselves. They look down on me because I am a poor Hindustani, but if a light bulb goes wrong they cannot fix it. They call me. If the air-conditioning stops working, again it is me they call. They can do nothing at all for themselves." He wagged his head in gleeful despair. 'I cannot respect these people. Too much money has made them stupid. They do not know what to do with themselves.' He cited as a typical example of Iranian idleness and decadence the son of the hotel owner. 'That boy cannot sit still. He's always travelling somewhere, wasting his father's money. Europe, UK, America. Always travelling somewhere. He says he is studying. But what can he be studying? If you ask him something, he knows nothing. He is always only boasting of fucking the foreign girls. No, I cannot respect these people.'

The son of the hotel owner called himself a student. In few other countries had I seen such an ostentatious passion for learning. In Shiraz the parks were crowded with young men strolling up and down or squatting in secluded nooks conning textbooks, lips silently moving as they learned by rote. Even by night they were to be seen, stationed like sentries along the pavements, sprawled on rugs spread under the street-lamps. Yet, on the whole, Iranian students leave so much to be desired. They are of such poor quality that universities in this country are increasingly reluctant to grant them admission, to take their paper qualifications at face value; even in America – where the Shah *buys* the cooperation of one or two major universities – they are becoming disenchanted. 'Most of my students don't seem to know *why* they are doing what they are doing,' an expatriate academic observed. 'The most assiduous ones collect information with the same kind of zeal squirrels show in gathering nuts. They don't seem able to give it a shape, to make something out of it.' Many of his post-graduate students had the greatest difficulty in thinking up theses. 'They come to me and ask for a subject. I always refuse – on principle.

My feeling is that if a man is doing "research", he shouldn't need me to tell him what's worthwhile.'

An American technician who had been in the country for some years was sunk in gloom. He had little faith in his Iranian assistant, a man armed with all the paper qualifications. 'Put that guy in front of a machine and he goes dumb. Doesn't know what to do. But you should see the fancy digital watch he wears. Never stops playing with it. The guy isn't stupid – he's quite good mathematically. But to translate that mathematics into practice . . .' He sighed. 'I can't figure it out. If all the foreigners cleared out tomorrow, there'd be ruins everywhere. This place would be a twentieth-century Persepolis.'

The comparison was more apt than he might have known. Persepolis and Parsagadae do not reflect a flowering of Iranian skill: they are the creations of the artisans and craftsmen of Mesopotamia and the Hellenised regions of the Empire who were imported to express in stone the new-found glory of their lately nomadic Persian conquerors. The Shahyad Tower (its audio-visual magic engineered by Italians) belongs to a hallowed tradition.

Over a century ago Frederick Engels diagnosed the Persian disease. He was writing about military matters, but his observations came close to being a metaphorical description of the Persian condition. 'In Persia,' he wrote in 1857, 'the European system of military organisation has been engrafted upon Asiatic barbarity' – with disastrous results in the field. 'Oriental ignorance, impatience, prejudice and the vicissitudes of fortune and favour inherent to Eastern courts' guaranteed failure. Military revolution required cultural evolution and the latter had not taken place. He compares the situation in Persia with that then prevailing in China, 'the rotting semi-civilisation of the oldest State in the world,' which, however, was meeting the European challenge 'with its own resources'. Because of that, present Chinese despair could be balanced against future hope. Dissolution could be seen as the necessary prelude to re-creation. From the rotting body of the old Chinese Empire would arise 'a new era for all Asia'. On the other hand, 'a Sultan or Shah is too apt to consider his army equal to anything as soon as the men can defile in parade, wheel, deploy . . .' Only grief would follow this false dawn of modernity. He hoped the day would eventually arrive when the Persians would realise 'that European dress and parade drill is no talisman in itself'. The day Engels hoped for has not yet come: image continues to be confused with substance; messianic dreams abolish introspection and self-analysis. Perhaps Persia is paying the price for having escaped – by the skin of its teeth – a full-blown phase of Western imperial domination. That might have forced the introspection and self-analysis now so sadly absent. Blessings come in many disguises.

There are Iranians who understand the hollowness of the White Revolution – such as the well-heeled but melancholy businessman I met at a party. 'Industrial revolution? What industrial revolution? Listen. The other day I was looking at a catalogue from South Korea. I suddenly thought – why, we couldn't even make the goddamned catalogue. We couldn't even make the staples that hold the pages together. All this talk about industry and so on is a fraud. What's going to happen to us when the oil runs out in twenty-five years? Are we going to live off pistachios and carpets? The Shah is spending *fifty billion* dollars on nuclear reactors. Who's going to run them? Iranians? But forget that. What are we going to do with these reactors? The Shah says he is going to make electricity with them. Fine. But what is he going to *make* with that electricity? What's Iran going to make that the world will want?' He stared at me sombrely. 'An oil-less Iran is going to be worse off than Bangladesh. At least they still know how to grow food for themselves. We would have forgotten even how to do that.'

He raised his brandy-filled glass. 'Cheers!'

The White Revolution is founded on affluence, on consumption. A kept workforce profits from a kept 'industrial' revolution. The normal process of development – sacrifice now, satisfaction later – has been thrown aside. 'We're running before we have learned how to walk,' a pessimistic economist conceded. 'The balloon's bound to burst. What a bang that's going to be!'

The posters decorating the railings outside the modernistic Rudaki Hall advertise a Mozart opera. At the Museum of Contemporary Art there is an exhibition of incomprehensible works by artists with difficult Central European names – though far and away the most eye-catching exhibit is a group of wall-sized photographs of the Imperial Family. Down south in Shiraz a theatre director tells me of his plans to stage some obscure and relentlessly avant-garde Polish play. But what about Iranian plays? Weren't there any? He looks embarrassed and begins to talk about Brecht and universality. Sometimes Iran's Westernising aspirations take unusual forms. Questioned about the use of torture in Iranian prisons by *Le Monde*, the Shah had this to say: 'Why should we not employ the same methods as you Europeans? We have learned sophisticated methods of torture from you. You use psychological methods to extract the truth; we do the same.' Mozart and torture – Iran has so much to learn from the West.

Too much truth has been extracted from Iran. Intellectual life is dead. That death is symbolised by the knots of soldiery, bayonetted rifles at the ready, who keep guard outside the gates of Teheran University, by the censored, sycophantic newspapers, by the paid ideologues (some foreign) of the régime who compare the Shah to Napoleon and call him the saviour of mankind. 'I don't like that word "intellectual",' the lady with courtly connections confessed, 'because that usually means anti-establishment.' The archaic fantasies of the Oriental despot end in fear (The lecturer was scared as a rabbit. 'I cannot talk to you,' he said, 'please go. If you want me to tell you something about mediæval Islamic philosophy, that is different. It is all I am qualified to talk about'); they end in brutality ('A few weeks ago,' an American academic said, 'the police entered the campus and started clubbing every student they could lay their hands on. There was blood in the corridor outside my office. You read about these things in the newspapers, but to actually see it . . .' He covered his face with his hands); they end in lies ('We are developing a new kind of civilisation,' the philosopher said, 'one that develops the spiritual dimension of man. This civilisation will replace the sick civilisation of the West').

The poet was depressed. 'It's bad. Very bad. I sometimes think it can't possibly get any worse, that we can't sink any lower than we have already done.' He had given up trying to write. The atmosphere did not lend itself to creation. Who, in any case, would publish his work? Who, outside a tiny coterie of friends, would read it? Writers cannot survive without an audience and in Iran there was no audience left. The new élite wanted to believe that they were part of Europe, that only a ghastly accident of geography had placed them in Asia. 'Everything you see in this country is false. There is no truth left. We lie not only to one another but to ourselves. Iran is one big lie.' He was just standing still, doing nothing – trying to preserve his mental balance, to keep sane.

Yet (he went on) Iran was no trumped-up country. It wasn't like Kuwait or, even, Saudi Arabia. Thousands of years of civilisation could not be abolished just like that. 'They're cramming this so-called Western culture down our throats, force-feeding us with all kinds of rubbish and bad dreams. But I know in my heart that our people won't accept it. Maybe this generation is lost. But in the end we'll reject the bad dream. We'll come back to ourselves.' He warmed to his theme. 'We're not Arabs from the desert. We are Iranians – *Aryans*. The Arabs may have conquered us and given us their religion, but it was *we* who civilised them.'

I had been in Iran long enough not to be surprised at this sudden eruption of national fervour; it was often there, just below the surface, tempering the decadence and the West-mad inanity.

'We are a people with thousands of years of civilisation behind us, do not forget that.' Iranians were possessed of a profound sense of their identity, of who and what they were. Nothing – not even the current West-madness – could destroy that. Iran had always absorbed its conquerors. It had absorbed Alexander's Greeks, the Arabs and the Mongols. Ultimately, it would absorb the West too.

I felt he was whistling in the dark.

'Do you know what I do when I want to remember what it is to be Iranian? I go out into the desert and look at the Towers of Silence [the towers in which the Zoroastrians exposed their dead]. It seems to me that it is Zoroastrianism which is closest to the spirit of our land and our people.' He smiled. 'You must not misunderstand me. I am a good Muslim. But, I am also a good Iranian.'

He was part of the Iranian confusion. Aryanism and Islam – these two strands of the Persian past coexist uneasily, tending to contradict rather than to complement each other. Their juxtaposition leads to a kind of cultural schizophrenia. Iranians, you will be assured again and again, are not Arabs. Islamic, yes; Arab, no. A hundred times no. And, it will be further pointed out, the Iranian brand of Islam – they are Shi'ites, followers of Ali, the Prophet's son-in-law – is quite different from the Sunni orthodoxy that dominates the Arab world. 'Our Islam,' an enthusiastic and patriotic girl told me, 'is very humanist. We do not put women in veils and chop off people's hands. We are not like the Arabs. Our religion has advanced. *Their* Islam has hardly developed.' The Shah, in his autobiography, is no less anxious to emphasise the distinction. 'Certainly,' he writes, 'no one can doubt that our culture is more akin to that of the West than is ... that of our neighbours the Arabs. Iran was an early home of the Aryans from whom most Americans and Europeans are descended, and we are racially quite separate from the Semitic stock of the Arabs ...'

An Aryan people practising a Semitic religion: the schizophrenia to which this paradox gives rise is met with everywhere. It will be found in the names of people. You will meet Xerxes, Darius and Cyrus; and you will meet Ali, Abdul and Fatima. It will be found in the Aryan-conscious Shah whose visions are derived from Islamic eschatology. It was to be found in the poet, a 'good' Muslim, who yet remained vulnerable to the appeal of the Zoroastrian past. Iran's sense of its destiny, of its role in history, is fed by Aryanism, not Islam. The former, morally neutral, is the modernising, westernising force. A dangerous tension now exists between the two incompatible modes of feeling, a tension expressed in the struggle between the Shah and the *mullahs* which, not long ago, exploded into open violence. But Aryanism is itself a Janus-headed ideal. It can look not only West but East. 'I want,' the Shah has said, 'a renascent Aryan brotherhood of Iran, India, Pakistan and Afghanistan ... Hindus, Muslims, Buddhists – all can come together in a common Aryan brotherhood.' Hindus, Muslims, Buddhists and – looking towards our Aryan brothers in the West – Catholics, Protestants, Mormons, Druids ... Aryanism compounds the confusion of loyalty.'

Inside the Shahyad Tower the old man stares intently at the flame burning in the Zoroastrian fire-altar. Poor old man. Poor Iran. Thirteen hundred years after the Islamic Conquest the country is in a bigger mess than ever.

Victim of Ramadan

The idea was simple enough and, on the face if it, harmless: to spend a few days in Fez and write a short piece about it. Idly, I set off for Morocco. But I would not have gone if, beforehand, I had received this letter which I found awaiting me on my return to London. '... I want [the New York editor wrote to me] ... that sense of place which the great travel writers of the past so wonderfully evoked and which I hope to restore, albeit in a more modern idiom ... photographically, I see this as a dramatic, riveting story which should provide wonderful contrast to a piece such as the English Lake Country or trekking through New Zealand. In words and pictures, the redolence of spices, the ceaseless counterpoint of languages in the market; the silence of the Arab mosque, the clamorous and enveloping crowds of the street – all that should be conveyed by both words and pictures ...' Really, there was no need for me or anyone else to have actually been sent to Fez. The dramatic and riveting story could and should have been composed in Manhattan. It would have been far more convincing, far more convenient and much cheaper.

Nor, perhaps, would I have gone if I had known it was the holy month of Ramadan and been forewarned of the privations and dangers to which I would be exposing myself during this season of austerity and exacerbated religious sensibility. In Morocco, as I was soon to discover, the dietary strictures of Ramadan are enforced on the Faithful by state power: Muslims caught eating, drinking or smoking between the hours of sunrise and sunset can be jailed for six months. But, as Royal Air Maroc bore me swiftly over the brown coast of Christian Spain, traversed the wrinkled neck of the Mediterranean and swooped low over the beaches of Islamic North Africa, I had no conception of what lay ahead. Tribulation began almost immediately: while waiting for my luggage to be disgorged from the aircraft a policeman bore down on me, grasped my arm and ordered me to extinguish the cigarette I was smoking. Other, more obvious foreigners were smoking too but they were not troubled by his zeal. It was my misfortune to look as if I ought to have been a Muslim and, therefore, to be treated like one. Argument was useless – and, possibly, full of potential peril. Most Moroccans had never heard of Hindus; and the few who had seemed to think that my ancient religion were merely an eccentric form of Islam.

At my hotel I was told that the restaurant would not be open until 8.30 in deference to the nutritional needs of the staff who would be eating for the first time that day. I went into the bar. The barman looked askance at me. Out on the terrace I could see French and German tourists drinking tall icy glasses of beer. I ordered a Scotch. He frowned at me. I showed him my room key, showed him my passport. The waiters watched and whispered. Reluctantly, I was served.

As I crossed the market square of the Grand Socco, my shoulder bag lightly brushed the arm of a young man. It was nearing noon and extremely hot. He stopped, turning back towards me, his face sullen with rage as he pointed at his arm. I apologised. He did not, however, seem to want a peaceful solution, but continued to advance on me. I apologised a second time – a little more profusely. This appeared to mollify him slightly. Muttering curses, he went on his way. 'It is Ramadan,' I was assured again and again whenever I sought from my Morocccan acquaintances an explanation for some display of enigmatic brutishness. Under the blazing sun, men deprived of food and drink operate on short fuses. The Faithful become unpredictable, liable to explode at any moment, to reach for their knives. Ramadan may bring men closer to Allah and Paradise but not, it would seem, to tolerance and compassion. It is a scarifying – not a softening – experience; it must entrench the association of religious purity with suffering and violence.

Ramadan alters the rhythms of life. By day, lethargy reigns, all effort directed towards the conservation of energy. Inert bodies lie sprawled in parks and pools of shade. In field and factory men slow down, waiting for the sun to disappear. After dusk and the break of the fast they return to life. At night the streets of downtown Tangier swarmed with sated and voluble promenaders. Hordes of men crowded bright cafés and restaurants, drinking sweet coffee and mineral water. The atmosphere would become almost festive. Until the small hours of the morning there poured through the open windows of my un-air-conditioned room the babble and roar of human activity – for there was a second meal to be eaten at two or three o'clock in the morning. In Fez, almost the whole town, it seemed, would migrate by car and bus to the resort oasis of Sidi Harazem. There, under a nearly full moon floating above the encircling hills, the smoke of kebab fires hazed the air, plump Berber tribeswomen sang and danced in concrete pavilions, pious beggars recited sutras from the Koran. In the swimming baths which have been built there, bikini-clad women splashed unaffectedly in close proximity to strange men – a reminder of the comparative mildness of Morocco's Islamic régime; a mildness which, I sensed, may be under threat. Over all of them, on chanting beggars as well as bikini-clad girls, there arched the enforced rhythms of Ramadan, regulating metabolism and mood. Islam, especially during this holy month, is an unescapable reality clamped down on everyone and everything. The unstable cycle of torpor and release, of denial and satiety, induces a kind of claustrophobia. I recall seeing from a train a peasant clad in coarse robes making his obeisance towards Mecca in a bleak, sunburnt field. When the world becomes a mosque, there is nowhere to seek refuge.

The package tourists who sweep in and out of towns like Fez are a fortunate breed. Sealed off by their air-conditioned coaches from the dusty anarchy through which they move, protected from its assaults and treacheries by their well-trained handlers, they are immune from reality. They come, they take their photographs, they go away. It is a splendid way to travel. I returned from Fez to Tangier, exhausted, after four days. During that time, I had been harried by cheating merchants, felled by a bad stomach and threatened with grievous bodily harm by my guide because I refused to allow his rapacity. The congested alleys and lanes of the medina had quickly lost their charm. I recoiled from the ceaseless counterpoint of language in the marketplace and the clamorous, enveloping crowds. I brought back with me on the long train ride not the redolence of spices but the stench of animal droppings, of heaps of rotting vegetables, of dripping, uncured hides destined for the tanneries. The cloying sourness of the medina seemed to cling to my clothes, to exude from the pores of my skin. Mostly, though, as the train crawled through sunlit, semi-arid dereliction, there hovered before me the feral cunning that had darkened the face of my guide as he sought to terrorise me. It had been a pitiless performance. I thought I would rest for a day or two in Tangier before setting out in search of further adventure.

The hotel I chose was pleasant and sedate – washed in white and

green-shuttered. From its terraced garden, planted with bougainvillaea and oleander, pines and palms, there was a view of the town and,
beyond, the Mediterranean. When there was no mist I could see the
mountains of Christian Spain. They were a comforting sight.

Even my guide book, which usually made mountains out of molehills,
admitted that there was nothing much to see in Tangier. I had seen
what there was to see – the Kasbah, the medina, a palace, a few heavy
old guns. Freed from guilt, I felt I could stick to the hotel. Within its
high walls my alien status was accepted and I could do much as I
pleased. Grateful for the opportunity to recuperate from Fez, I sat by
the swimming pool and watched the sunbathers. My attention came to
rest on two men with dark glasses and a little girl. This was not only
because the child was making a nuisance of herself. I was intrigued by
the language they were speaking, not French or Spanish or German or
Dutch. From what exotic corner of Europe did that guttural sing-song
emanate? With a slow start of surprise, I found myself able to pick up
the occasional English word. Gradually, it dawned on me that they
were, in fact, speaking English; that they were from Liverpool. When
the older of the two men, both of whom seemed mildly drunk,
knocked over his glass of beer into an ashtray filled with stubs, the girl
shrieked with joy. She held the ashtray close to his lips.

'Drink it! Drink it!'

The man demurred, but without force. She insisted, joy turning to
rage.

'I want you to drink it! I want to see you drink it!' The high-pitched
voice cut like a knife through the peace of the afternoon.

I could only wonder at the childish desire to inflict public
humiliation.

Later, I went down to the palm-lined sea front. The sun was low,
colouring the tops of the apartment blocks whose roofs bristled with
television antennae. In Tangier they consider themselves triply
blessed: they can receive, in addition to the local service, Spanish and
Gibraltar television. I rested on a decaying concrete bench facing the
sea, my skin irritated by the prickly heat of late afternoon. Armed
policemen paraded in pairs, on the lookout for any signs of impiety.
The day's fast was drawing to an end and the vendors of kebabs were
stoking their fires. Young French and German vagrants, bohemianly
rough, struggled by under the weight of backpacks. There wandered
by a barefooted girl of European provenance. She was wrapped,

sarong-style, in a strip of green cloth, exposing shoulders flayed by over-exposure to the sun. Meandering at a snail's pace along the corridor of palms, she murmured to herself, frequently stopping to stare vacantly about her, plucking distractedly at the pages of what looked like a passport. Hers was a stylish delinquency, a studied throwback to vanquished hippiedom. A ragged youth circled about me. He offered hashish, he offered boys, he offered girls. Night was falling. I walked uphill through nearly empty streets: at this hour of impending release Tangier retired indoors. As I neared the hotel, a gun boomed through the dusk, muezzins wailed. Another day of abstinence was over. Fearlessly, I lit a cigarette.

The Liverpudlians dominated breakfast, the shrieks of the little girl now joined to the penetrating voice of her American mother – who was dilating on her feminist views. At the table next to mine a demure English couple exchanged scandalised whispers.

'They drink like fish,' the lady said. 'They make a real spectacle of themselves. When they get drunk, they even begin to sing . . .'

After breakfast I went out on the terrace overlooking the garden. The morning was clouded and humid; the town was quiescent. A sea mist obscured the mountains of Spain. Tranquillity was shattered by the arrival of the Liverpudlians. They were quarrelling about money.

'I try to ask a straight question,' the American was saying, 'and I get bullshit.'

'Calm yourself,' urged the man who had almost been compelled to drink out of the ashtray.

The American would not calm herself. 'I don't like this fucking space at all, let me tell you. This trip is my bag. I want to know what's going for what . . . I'm not that spaced out. But this whole scene's too far out . . . too fucking far out. I can't relate to it. It bugs my head, man . . .'

The little girl shrieked. He of the ashtray started to sob, laying his head on the shoulder of his friend.

On the street below, a group of veiled women walked slowly downhill, carrying clanking milk churns.

'I don't want to be bugged,' the American shouted. 'I wanna keep my head straight, relate to my own space. I don't want no fucking MCP to lay some heavy sexist trip on me . . .'

The veiled women disappeared around a corner. But I could still hear the clanking of their milk churns.

*

'You know,' the writer said, 'I believe in the Islamic *identité*.'

He was Moroccan, he lived in Paris, but returned home four or five times a year so that he could keep in touch with his 'roots'. We were sitting in an open-air restaurant in the small, white-washed town of Asilah on the Atlantic coast of Morocco, about an hour's drive from Tangier. The restaurant lay in the shadow of a fifteenth-century Portuguese fort. Atlantic waves exploded against the remnants of a sea-wall. Asilah had had a turbulent past. Octavius had deported its people to Spain because they had supported Mark Antony. In 1578 King Sebastian of Portugal had landed here in a disastrous attempt to conquer Morocco. It had formed part of the Spanish zone during Morocco's colonial period and was restored to it only in 1956 when the country regained its independence. (The Spanish still hold the enclave of Ceuta.) It seemed a peculiar place to be talking about *identité*.

'The strict enforcement of Ramadan might seem harsh to you,' he said, 'but it helps to remind the people of who and what they are. Ramadan brings us back to ourselves. It renews our sense of being Muslim.'

I suggested that *identité*, in the sense in which he understood it, strangled rather than liberated men: that it took no account of the historical process and was a sad and overheated reaction to Western dominance.

He laughed. 'We are dealing with eternal truth,' he said. France was a decaying country, a cemetery. Would I deny that the West was riddled with moral and spiritual disorder?

Disagreement was silenced by the memory of the American woman. Between him and her, I felt lost.

The mountains of Spain beckoned: it would be pleasant, I thought, to traverse the Mediterranean, to escape Ramadan for a few hours. I decided to make a day trip to Algeciras. There was confusion on the dock. My first attempt to board the ferry was repulsed: my exit card had not been properly stamped. I returned to the long, slow-moving queue.

A German voice spoke close to my ear. 'Is it possible to ask where to get one of those?' He pointed at my exit card. I told him; he ran off.

Some minutes later, the voice spoke again. This time it was tinged with panic. 'Why do they all have blue cards? I do not have a blue card. What does the blue card mean? Is it possible for you to explain?'

It was not possible for me to explain because I myself was not in possession of a blue card. Looking around, I saw what he meant. Blue cards everywhere. We both ran off. It seemed likely that I might miss the ferry.

'Writer?' the immigration officer asked. 'What do you write?'

'Books . . .' I hazarded.

'Books? You are a writer of books? What kind of books? Please tell.'

I could not grasp what this might have to do with a day trip to Algeciras. Nor did it seem the appropriate place or time to embark on a literary discussion.

'I write stories,' I said.

'You are a journalist, perhaps?' He scrutinised my face, comparing it with the photograph in the passport. With deliberation, he studied the official record of my travels.

'You are a great voyager,' he said. It was not intended as a compliment. 'What have you been doing in Morocco?'

'Nothing,' I replied truthfully. 'Tourist,' I added, also with considerable truth.

He scowled, grudgingly applied his stamp and flung the passport unceremoniously in my direction. I headed for the good ship *Ibn Batouta*.

'Passport . . .'

By the gaping jaws of the ferry I submitted to another cross-examination. The officer fingered my shoulder bag.

'Open . . . open . . .'

I opened it up. He examined my guide book, thumbed the novel (*A Passage to India*) I was reading, sniffed my cigarettes, explored every pocket and niche of the bag. At last, I was allowed on board. But already I was exhausted. My day trip between Islam and Christianity, between Africa and Europe, had gone sour on me.

The white huddle of Tangier receded. A sign above the bar declared that it was forbidden to serve alcohol to Muslims. Not wishing to provoke a jihad, I contented myself with coffee. Going up on deck, I stared at the corrugated Spanish coast. In the distance loomed the rectangular, misty mass of Gibraltar. Dolphins frolicked close to the bows of the ship. To cross from the Spanish enclave of Ceuta into Morocco was, by all accounts, a murderous business; to cross from the British enclave of Gibraltar into Spain could, by all accounts, be a murderous business; and, as I was now discovering, to cross from Tangier to Algeciras was no joy ride – not, at least, for those who called themselves writers. How much nicer to be a dolphin.

'That is the Rock.' I turned to find a wizened American dowager, incandescently clad in an emerald green trouser suit, standing beside me. 'That is what the Brits call Gibraltar,' she added.

I thanked her for the information.

'Where are you going to in Spain?' she asked.

'Only as far as Algeciras.' I pronounced it with a 'g'.

'Al*h*eciras,' she corrected. 'It's a Spanish name, you know.'

I thanked her for the information and sidled away. How much nicer to be a dolphin.

The Spanish let me in. There was little to do in Algeciras. I drank some wine in a café not far from the ferry terminal, deafened by a churning cement-mixer. At five, I returned to the ferry terminal. The Spanish let me out. Morocco, however, had other ideas. The boatride was a nightmare. Orders to submit to immigration control were ceaselessly relayed on the Public Address system. Islamic righteousness had turned it into a prison ship.

'You're a writer . . . what do you write? . . . are you a journalist? . . . what have you been doing in Morocco . . . you need a visa to enter our country . . .'

'But I have a visa.'

'It is expired. It is suitable for only one entry. You cannot enter Morocco. You will return to Spain.'

'But I have all my luggage in a Tangier hotel . . . I have a plane ticket, a passage booked . . .'

Silence.

'Let me at least make a phone call.'

'Stand back!' Oriental despotism had spoken and I was shoved away.

'It is Ramadan,' said a Belgian lady who lived in Tangier – and who had befriended me. It was from her, with the mountains of North Africa hard and high in the afternoon light, that I learned of the death of the Shah of Iran.

'Such a shame,' she said, 'that only Sadat should have had the courage to attend his funeral.'

I had been to Iran; I had written about the Shah; I had judged harshly. But now I could sympathise. He must have known about that *identité* which, one day, would eat Iranians alive. Against that hard and high North African skyline, he became a little easier to understand.

That *identité* had proved itself locust-like in its voracity: it was even trying to eat me up. I was sad that only Sadat had had the courage to attend his funeral.

We docked; the passengers disembarked. 'Hope to see you again,' intoned the Public Address. On came the cleaners. The Belgian lady promised to get in touch with my Moroccan acquaintances, but she was nervous and would commit neither names nor addresses to writing. Two hours later, I began my third crossing of the Mediterranean. If the Spanish were surprised to see me back so soon, they did not show it. At two o'clock in the morning I set out to look for a hotel. Ragged and luggageless, I did not rate my chances very high. But the four-star Reina Christina took me in without a murmur. How dreadful it was to wake up the next morning. Unshaven, my head swimming with fatigue, my clothes crumpled, I considered my position. I decided I would call on the British Consulate. They were courteous but completely unhelpful.

'It is your problem,' I was told. The man smiled charmingly and shrugged. It was Ramadan. The Moroccans were always difficult during Ramadan. They could exercise no influence over them.

I wandered around the streets of Algeciras, unable to face the Moroccan consulate, feeling and looking like a tramp, reflecting wistfully on the failure of the Christian Reconquest of Spain to extend itself to the shores of North Africa. I drank glasses of Fundador and cups of black coffee. Resolution returned and I went in search of the Moroccans. I submitted to the same old questions, filled out forms in triplicate, tried to remember the names of my grandfathers and grandmothers, had to decide who in London I could use as 'references'. When I lit a cigarette, officials screamed at me and pointed at the portrait of King Hassan. In the end, I was given a visa valid for five days. It occurred to me that I should avoid the ferry and take the hydrofoil which goes from Tarifa. Late that afternoon, I crossed the Mediterranean for the fourth time.

Policemen in brown robes and yellow slippers shepherded us off the hydrofoil, barking orders. I had begun to detest these underdeveloped Moroccan faces, trapped, it seemed to me, in a perpetual adolescence; a perpetual puberty.

My passport was seized and put away. 'Stand aside!'

I was too stunned to protest. I was made to wait until all the other passengers were processed. Files were searched. Eventually, it was agreed that I could re-enter Morocco. I found a taxi.

At the gate of the dock a policeman halted us.

'Where's passport ... where's luggage ... where you stay in Tangier ... where's airplane ticket ... what you do here? Eh? Eh?' In due course, I was allowed to proceed.

'I seen you in Tangier,' the taxi-driver said. 'I seen you walking around. Tourist?'

I did not answer. The world was becoming too small, too dangerous. Early the next morning, I went to the airport.

More shouting. More barked orders. My luggage was searched once, twice, a third time. I appeared to be running a gauntlet. The immigration officer demanded that I write down the titles of my books.

'What magazine you write for? You journalist? Give name of magazine ... give name ...'

But I did not give any names. To lie seemed the safest course. I continued down the gauntlet. Just when I thought I had made it to the relative safety of the departure lounge, a policeman waved me aside. I was taken away into a room full of other policemen. My mouth went dry. I realized that anything could happen among the lesser breeds without the Law. My shoulder bag was opened up; my books were leafed through; hands crept up my trouser legs, were inserted into my shirt.

'You like hashish ...' said one of the grinning policemen.

'Where you keep the hashish?' asked another with an adolescent leer. 'Where? Suppose we find a little hashish on you ... what then? Moroccan jail not good, no?'

Miraculously, I got out of there. Half an hour later, high over Spain, my mouth was still dry.

Two days afterwards, I had a nightmare: I was dreaming I was in Libya.

The Bush Negroes of Surinam

Bush Negro country is forbidding – even from the air. At five or six thousand feet, broken only by the dark ribbons of the meandering rivers and creeks, the Amazonian jungles of Surinam look like broccoli gone mad. At that height the outlines of massive rock outcrops can be glimpsed in the depths of the rivers. Jungle and rapid-fomenting rocks: together they had guaranteed the safety and isolation of these men who had fled the slave plantations of Holland's only South American colony. The white men, however, have never quite been able to stop pursuing them. Originally, they did so as missionaries – and still do. Latterly, and with increasing frequency, they have begun to come among them as tourists. I was sharing the small, propeller-driven Surinam Airways plane with a noisy party of Dutch travellers, skins shining with insect repellent, in search of an adventurous weekend in the Bush. The little plane droned on, shuddering through the cloudy vapours exhaled by the jungle below us. We were heavily loaded with medicines, food and equipment for the mission hospital at Stoelman's Island on the Marowijne River. From Stoelman's Island I would make my way up the Tapanahony River, a tributary stream of the Marowijne, to the village of Drietabbetje, the residence of the paramount chief of the Ndjuka tribe of Bush Negroes.

Suddenly, the Dutch tourists became even more voluble, pointing and gesticulating. I looked and saw a tiny opening in the forest, a bald, circular patch. Then I say another ... and another. The little bald patches, criss-crossed by the whitened trunks of felled trees, were scattered like an attack of mange across the green face of the wilderness.

'Bush Negro gardens,' Rudi (my guide) said. 'Soon,' he went on, 'you see real Bush Negroes. You see ... [he grinned] ... you see women wearing nothing on their chests ... soon you see *real* Bush Negro.' He made it sound as though we were approaching the lair of some exotic and elusive species of wild animal; as though these gardens were its tell-tale spoor. Rudi was a young, fashionably dressed town black, a fervent Catholic (he always wore a silver cross), who worked in his spare time for one of the missions. In some ways, although he knew the Interior well, the Bush Negro was no less foreign to him than he was to me, a figure arousing both awe and superstitious dread. 'These people are not Christians,' he had whispered to me earlier, fondling his Cross. 'They are *pagan*. They do not believe in God. They make much *black-magic* and *ju-ju*.' But, at the same time, he could be passionate in their defence. 'The Bush Negroes,' he had declared, 'they are the true people of Surinam. They fought to be free. They refused to be slaves.' Urban, Roman Catholic Rudi was torn by this unresolved ambivalence of sentiment. Admiration and dread warred for control of him.

The plane dipped, tracing a bend of the dark-watered Marowijne, falling towards more hilly country. We passed low over a village. The huts were crowded together higgledy-piggledy, many roofed not with thatch but with corrugated iron, a sign of the creeping modernity spreading through the bush. Soon we were bumping down the grassy airstrip on Stoelman's Island.

Surinam was discovered by the Europeans at the beginning of the sixteenth century. For the next hundred and fifty years, the French, the English and the Dutch struggled with each other for the control of the territory. Eventually, the Dutch got it for good in 1667 – in exchange for New York ('a place much cried up of late,' a contemporary wrote), which the English had taken from the Netherlands in 1664. At the time the bargain must have seemed a good one to the Dutch: fortunes were being made out of tropical produce and it must have been clear that New York was an unsuitable place to grow sugar-cane and tobacco.

The Dutch had got hold of a country peculiarly suited to their genius. Surinam's river-dissected littoral is flat and constantly threatened with inundation by the sea. It was, in many ways, a tropical version of the homeland. Today, flying over the coast, you can see the remains of plantations once won from the sea and now returned to it. Its new owners applied themselves with zest. Plantations of sugar-cane, coffee, cotton, indigo and tobacco, all worked, naturally, by slave labour (blacks outnumbered the whites fifteen to one), sprang up along the banks of the rivers. By the middle of the eighteenth century, Surinam was a prosperous place. In Paramaribo elegant houses, built of the finest timber, were adorned with paintings, gilding and crystal chandeliers. The town's European inhabitants denied themselves nothing. They dressed in velvets, diamonds and silver lace. Some wore buckles of solid gold on their belts. The most exquisite china appeared on their dinner tables; food was exotic and abundant. Canopied barges, rowed by crews of sweat-shining blacks, plied the broad rivers (the only real means of getting about), often carrying on board a small orchestra to help pass the time.

Surinamese life was oriental in its splendour and despotism. Its flavour is caught by John Gabriel Stedman, a Scottish soldier of fortune who went out to Surinam in 1772, an officer in one of the mercenary armies dispatched by Holland to help quell the – by then – endemically mutinous slaves. In the book he wrote describing his experiences, he gives a vivid account of a typical planter's day. 'Our lord' rises at six in the morning and presents himself on the piazza at the front of his house. There, attended by six at least of his hand-somest slaves, male and female, he takes his coffee and his pipe. The overseer – always, in slave societies, an archetypal figure of evil – arrives and makes his report on the night's happenings; the slaves accused of dereliction of duty are driven before their master. Some are tied to the rafters, some are suspended from trees. Then the floggings begin, administered with long hempen ropes by the overseer's black subordinates. The levee ends and 'our lord' readies himself for the day's other business. Dressed in finest Holland trousers, silk stock-ings and morocco slippers, his jacket of finest Indian silk negligently unbuttoned, he may now take a stroll or ride out on horseback to survey his dominions. If he walks a boy will shade him with an umbrella; another slave will be ready to refresh him with Madeira when he shows the slightest sign of fatigue. If he is not in the mood for such business-like pursuits, he may go for a cruise in his barge serenaded by his musicians. Towards lunch-time, he returns to the house and dresses a second time. One boy puts on his stockings and shoes, another tends to his hair, a third keeps off the mosquitoes. His table will be lavishly arrayed with bacon, ham, beef, fowls, pigeons, bottles of Rhenish and Madeira. Afterwards, he retires to his hammock where he is fanned to sleep by a couple of his female attendants. Towards three o'clock he wakes and eats again. At six the overseer arrives with his second report, climaxed by another round of floggings. The evening is spent playing cards, smoking and drinking punch. When he grows weary he retires to his hammock where, more likely than not, 'he passes the night in the arms of one of his sable sultanas' – for 'our lord', it goes virtually without saying, maintains a well-stocked harem. At one of the plantations Stedman visited master and mistress were served at table by naked male and female attendants.

If the lords are bad, the ladies are worse. They too give way to their 'unbounded passions' and exhibit 'a most relentless barbarity'. Many of the grossest acts of sadism reported by Stedman were carried out by women. He tells, for instance, of the lady who, on reviewing a batch of newly acquired slaves, singled out a pretty young girl of about fifteen and immediately ordered her disfigurement. There and then the girl was branded on the forehead, cheeks and mouth; and had her Achilles tendon cut. The same lady is reported to have drowned a black child because its crying disturbed her; its protesting mother was whipped. Taking a walk one morning he saw a black girl being flogged across the breasts, a punishment that seemed to give the girl's mistress a 'peculiar satisfaction'. Obviously, sexual jealousy had its part to play in the numerous acts of insane feminine cruelty that litter Stedman's pages: the Dutch planters in Surinam gave free play to their lusts, resembling, in this respect, the Portuguese rather than the English. The results are visibly apparent today. But sexual promiscuity, as the experience of it in Surinam shows, did not make for mildness of rule. 'As for old men being broken upon the rack,' an acquaintance casually remarked to Stedman as they were watching a public hanging, 'and young women roasted alive chained to stakes, there can be nothing more common in this colony.' Surinam was versed in all the refinements of torture – live Negroes were torn apart by horses; others had slivers of metal inserted under their nails; others were chained to furnaces. 'The Colony of Surinam,' Stedman wrote in the preface to his book, 'is reeking and dyed with the blood of African Negroes.' He was not exaggerating. Or if he was – pardonably so. Even in the slave islands of the British West Indies (no utopias of race relations by any stretch of the imagination) Surinam was regarded with something approaching horror. It was said that, when English slave-owners really wanted to frighten their blacks, they would threaten to sell them to a Surinam planter. Possibly, one must seek the explanation in the prolonged servile wars that raged in the territory, wars that went on, in one form or another, for nearly sixty years. Fear breeds cruelty. Cruelty breeds rebellion. Rebellion breeds fear. That, if one may use the term, is the ineluctable *karma* of all slave societies. In Surinam, that *karma* came close to ripeness.

The outboard motor roars steadily. Whiskers of warm, white water stream at the front of the boat. Up front, precariously balanced on the very lip of the boat, squats a man with a long pole, our navigator, silent and watchful, his eyes fixed on the water: the Tapanahony is an obstacle course of rocks, submerged reefs, sudden shallows and turbulences. Its negotiation requires delicate skill, long experience and courage. In some ways, the conquest of the rivers can be seen as one of the major accomplishments of the Bush Negroes. Indeed, they often refer to themselves as 'river people', rejecting, as inaccurate and somewhat undignified, the epithet 'bush'. The rivers are more than highways of communication and sources of food. They have been absorbed into ritual and myth; become part of the imaginative life of the people.

Ndjuka oral tradition tells of the time when, the numbers of escaped slaves having grown large, their leaders met and decided that they should leave the vicinity of the plantations, move deeper into the interior and settle down as a tribe. They prayed to their old gods for help and guidance; and from Africa, in response to their prayers, there came three semi-divine beings – Balai, who knew the secrets of the air, Aduwanman who knew the secrets of the soil, and Ajenge who knew the secrets of the waters. They led the fugitives away from the plantations and up the Marowijne River, their magic neutralising the hazards of swamps and mountains, jungles and rapids, until they reached the spot where the Marowijne divides itself into the Lawa and Tapanahony tributaries. Here there was a disagreement. One group, the followers of Aduwanman, wished to continue waging war against the white man; the other wished only to live in peace and be left alone. The former, because they remained warlike, chose the 'warm' waters of the Lawa; the latter, because they wished for peace, chose the 'cool' waters of the Tapanahony. At a certain creek, those who had gone up the Tapanahony heard the call of a bird familiar to them in Africa, 'ju . . . ka . . . ju . . . ka . . .' So it was that the tribe, taking its name from the call of the bird, came to be called Ndjuka. The other group, true to its war-like spirit, came into conflict with an Amerindian tribe known as the Aluku whom they defeated in battle and drove away. Their tribe came to be called the Aluku as a consequence of this. History as myth; myth as history: the Bush Negroes are truly the possessors of rivers like the Tapanahony and Marowijne. The rivers flow with their memories.

Occasionally, our navigator signals, his arms articulating a precise semaphore. In response, we bear now left, now right, skirting dangers not always apparent to naïve eyes. The enclosing walls of forest are lit up by the sun. Here and there are groves of palms. Their slim, columnar boles, the childlike simplicity of their leafage, inject an odd touch of theatricality. On board, apart from Rudi and myself, is a young Surinamese medical assistant making one of his regular tours of inspection through the villages. We pass a tiny settlement, a derelict assemblage of yellowing huts. The place looks abandoned – its occupants are probably away camping in their gardens which are always established several kilometres from the village. This peculiar separation of village and provision plot dates back to the earliest days. It started as a security measure: the runaways wished to ensure that the discovery and destruction of their settlements did not automatically lead to the discovery and destruction of their food supplies. The custom has persisted, despite attempts to persuade them that there is no longer any necessity for it. Neither has it been easy to persuade them to grow 'long-term' crops – for instance, oranges – to improve what is, in fact, an extremely poor diet based on cassava and rice. Guerilla tactics have hardened into 'tradition', into 'culture'.

Ahead of us lies broken water. A line of purple-brown rocks is stretched like a barrage across the width of the river. The restless water sparkles, gushing over the crowns of the rocks in small, swift cascades, foaming through narrow gaps, coiling itself into conflicting currents. We move cautiously into the turbulence, slowing our speed. Our navigator rises, probing the water with his pole. The noise of the engine dies away altogether. I stare at the rocks which are overgrown with spiky plants bearing pretty lilac-coloured blooms. We scrape across a submerged reef. For a second or two, the boat, unbalanced, teeters dangerously. Water slops over the sides, we seem to be on the verge of capsizing. I think of the piranha that live in these rivers. Already I have seen one or two people with missing fingers and toes. I think too of the stories I have been told about the Bush Negroes not rescuing people who have gone overboard in the belief that they 'belong' to the river. However, the boat rights itself; the immediate threat of being sacrificed to the hungry waters passes. The engine comes to life again and we shoot at sudden speed one of the cascades, the boat pushing itself up the watery face. And then it's all right. The turbulence falls away behind us; our navigator squats once more in the bows. Our two boatmen must do this nearly every day of their lives. But no one could be certain of success. The river has its moods. Sometimes the judgments are wrong, sometimes concentration strays, sometimes bravura throws aside commonsense. Then boats are smashed to pieces. Men drown. The Tapanahony usually gets the sacrifices it requires.

A village appears on our left: we shall be stopping here – the medical assistant has a number of children to tend to. It looks a sizeable place. Many of the huts are roofed with corrugated iron. Naked children splash at the water's edge. With the forest as backdrop, they form an idyllic tableau of savage innocence. We moor by a flight of rotting wooden steps. Some women are scrubbing cooking-pots. They work on their knees, diligently, concentratedly, scrubbing the metal until it shines like new. The lives of Bush Negro women seem to revolve around this interminable cleaning and burnishing of their kitchenware. There is something obsessive about it. Morning, noon and dusk you will see them down on their knees at the river's edge. Pots and bowls and enamel basins are more than merely utilitarian objects, individual collections going far beyond the call of necessity. They are symbols of wealth. A dream of food, of plenty, of full bellies. Their rebel forebears must have been haunted by visions of fired fields, a recurring nightmare now sublimated into fetishism. Every hut is arrayed with glittering displays of these pots and bowls and enamel basins.

We walk up a track to the village. A few huts are decorated in traditional Ndjuka style, adorned with geometrical designs rendered in red, blue, white, yellow and black. (The Saramacca, the other major Bush Negro tribe, use no paint at all.) Only women, children and old men seem to be about. The men are clearing the forest, establishing their gardens – which, afterwards, the women will cultivate, for agriculture, as in tribal Africa, is woman's work. But that is not the only reason for the atmosphere of desertion and depression. Many of the able-bodied have gone off to Paramaribo in search of work. Urban migration has robbed many of these villages of half their young people, and the townward tide is gathering momentum. One-third of the Bush Negro population (roughly estimated at between seventy-five and eighty thousand) have now left the Interior. Some (the fortunate ones) drive bulldozers for the American-owned bauxite company at Paranam; some work on the roads being driven through the bush; many become domestic servants and street-sweepers – street-sweepinng is virtually a Bush Negro monopoly. Those who have nothing better to do turn to crime and prostitution. They crowd into the decaying suburbs of Paramaribo. I had seen a hundred or more of them crammed into a disused abattoir, still heavy with the rank odours of past butcheries, encamped like refugees among their bundles and boxes. This village betrays many of the symptoms of urban-derived blight – decaying huts, a compound littered with leaves, tin-cans and bottles, the colourful advertisements for cigarettes ('Come To Marlboro Country') and beer that decorate a number of doorways. A woman, her face eaten away by leprosy, buzzes about me, begging for tobacco. The medical assistant weighs the babies that are brought to him, examines eyes and ears, doles out vitamin pills, gives vaccinations. After about an hour we return to the boat.

There is a woman down with fever at the second village. Her hut, even in the middle of the afternoon, is dark and airless. The wall facing the entrance is covered with rows of pots and pans and ranks of gleaming cutlery. Her husband is away, working – she is not sure where – on some government road-building project. She crouches on a low wooden stool, hugging her trembling body. She seems very ill. It is probable that she will have to be sent to the hospital at Stoelman's Island. I return outside and walk through the unkempt compound to the river bank. Here the usual ritualistic scouring and scrubbing of kitchenware is going on. Others are washing clothes, beating lengths of cloth on the rocks. A woman, knee-deep in the water, is fishing. She stands there motionless, catching nothing – and maybe not really expecting to catch anything. The jungle is fast running out of food. It is no longer possible, as it was in the old days, to rely on its largesse. Often men can hunt for days and come back empty-handed. Close by is a gigantic silk cotton tree, sacred in Africa and sacred too in Surinam. Its elephantine branches spread out far above my head. Raw, vegetative power – I can understand why it is worshipped. The sky is clouding over when the medical assistant returns.

The rainstorm catches us on the river. Yellow streaks of lightning flash through the clouds, the thunder is ominously close. Enveloped in driving whiteness, we could be drifting on the ocean. Luckily, our next port of call is not too far away. We scramble up a muddy bank. Many of the huts here flaunt political posters supplied by the National Party, the main element in the coalition that governs the country. The Bush Negroes are by no means a negligible factor in Surinamese political life. At election time, cargoes of 'presents' are sent up the rivers by men in search of votes. 'The Bush Negroes?' a defeated candidate answered sourly. 'They sell themselves to the highest bidder. They don't seem to have any *ideology* at all.' There is an organisation that calls itself the Bush Negro Party, but it gets no support from the Bush Negroes. Ever since they had been granted the vote in 1963 – exactly one hundred years after the abolition of slavery in Surinam – they had voted for the (predominantly black) National Party. I knew something of the methods employed by this party's propagandists. During the last election the Bush Negroes had been told that if they should decide to vote for any of the Opposition parties (largely identified with the Hindustanis – as Indians are called in Surinam) they would be re-enslaved. They might, it was further suggested, even be killed off because the Hindustanis, commercial-minded as ever, were longing to use their skins in the manufacture of shoes and ladies' handbags. Whether or not any of this was believed, it is difficult to say: certainly, Bush Negro history must lend itself to paranoiac fantasising. Whatever the reasons, the Opposition candidates were heavily defeated in the river constituencies.

Gradually, the rain eases, the thunder recedes. When the sun comes out again, the afternoon steams. We move on upriver. Shortly after four o'clock we reach the portage near the Gran Holo Falls. The boat will have to be hauled over rails to the next navigable stretch. Here the river tumbles down a series of rocky terraces. Boatmen not wanting to be delayed at the portage sometimes shoot these cascades on the downriver journey. The atmosphere at the portage is sociable: it is a natural resting place and rendezvous. We meet two boatmen heating soup on a primus stove. They have been nearly three days on the river, coming from Albina, a town about thirty miles from the mouth of the Marowijne, carrying a cargo of cement and corrugated iron – someone in Drietabbetje has decided to build himself a thoroughly modern house. It has been an exhausting trip. The mosquitoes on the Marowijne had been so terrible that they could hardly get any sleep; twice they had nearly been wrecked. Together they will earn about seven hundred Surinam guilders (about £200) for their pains. Not bad for a week's work, I suggest. They disagree. Had I forgotten the exorbitant price of fuel? If the cargo was lost, they would be paid nothing; they could fall sick; they could drown. No. It was a dog's life on the river.

Beyond the portage, the character of the river changes. It becomes more pastoral, more populated. The rocks, overspread with lilac-blossomed plants, create a chain of water-gardens. We wind among miniature waterfalls, clear, pebbled pools, rippling cascades. Canoes slip slowly beneath banks shaded by drooping branches festooned with creepers. Children play on little sand beaches. Women, carrying towers of pots and bowls on their heads, walk in Indian file along forest paths, coming from or returning to villages hidden away in green glades. Whether by accident or design, the Ndjuka appeared to have found themselves a truly sylvan retreat. It is almost dusk when, at a bend in the river, we come in sight of Dreitabbetje. The handsome, two-storeyed house of the Paramount Chief dominates the village. On the opposite side of the river are the buildings of the mission station, including a school. A lanky Dutch nurse stands on a lawn waiting to welcome us.

As befits the residence of a Paramount Chief, Dreitabbetje (it has a population of about six hundred) is something of a metropolis. It has electricity, a couple of small shops selling tinned goods, beer and Coca-cola and an impressive wooden jetty. That night we cross the river and take a stroll. The village is full of the odour of woodsmoke. Now and again the electricity falters, plunging the place into thick darkness. The nurse, like nearly everyone else, remarks on the poverty of the diet. Too much cassava. Too much rice. Too little meat. They keep no cattle, no pigs, no goats. Some do have chickens but they never eat them; neither do they eat the eggs: these are used in certain of their rituals. The nurse has heard rumours of the projected tourist invasion of the Interior. She reacts to the prospect with proprietorial anger. After eight or nine years' service in the bush one senses that she considers this to be 'her' river, that these are 'her' people: it is an occupational hazard. She does not want to see them 'spoilt', to have them exposed to the corruptions of the outside world. But I fear it is already too late. A man standing at the door of a modern house invites us in. We enter a room about ten feet square, hot under its corrugated-iron roof, furnished with aluminium-framed chairs. A table is arrayed with bottles of beer, a bottle of wine, a bottle of rum, some garishly coloured soft drinks and – startlingly – a dusty bottle of champagne. Next to his drinks cabinet is a Japanese-made 'music centre', forbiddingly decorated with controls of all kinds. That, however, is not his only source of music. He also has an orthodox gramophone, its sound channelled through a giant speaker made to resemble the radiator grille of a motor-car – this strange-looking contraption turns out to be his own handiwork. Our host, dressed in tight trousers, a shirt embroidered with US Army insignia and wearing platformed heels, is as contemporary as his room. He dreams of the day when the government will blast away some of the more dangerous rock outcrops in the river to ease communication with the outside world. Sitting on his aluminium-framed chairs, drinking his beer, listening to Stevie Wonder booming through the radiator grille, I have to keep reminding myself that I am in the middle of the jungle, that I am in the house of a descendant of a runaway slave.

Mist swirls on the river, blurring the outlines of the forest. A ghostly canoe glides upstream. As the eastern sky begins to glow sullenly pink, bands of pale light fall across the colourless water. Somewhere an outboard motor growls into life. I shiver in the damp, lukewarm air and think of electricity, of Stevie Wonder, of rock outcrops being blasted, of the advertisements for detergent and the National Party, of the boatmen with their cargo of cement and corrugated iron . . .

In more senses than one, a new day had begun on the Tapanahony.

From earliest memory slaves had been running away from the Surinam plantations and seeking refuge in the forests. Vast, little-known and dangerous to Europeans, the forests were a ready-made sanctuary. They must have been a standing invitation to escape. It was so easy to disappear, so easy to evade recapture and put oneself beyond the reach of white men. The mountainous interior of Jamaica excepted, such escape was not possible in the West Indian islands. Literally, the slaves there had nowhere to run to.

At first, they were regarded as little more than a nuisance. Gradually, however, as their numbers grew and they acquired firearms, they ceased to be a nuisance: they became a menace. The earliest runaways were, for the most part, settled on the upper reaches of the Coppename and Saramacca rivers – it was from this last river that the Saramaccan tribe eventually took its name. In 1730, hoping by a show of ferocity to dampen the ardour of the rebels and to discourage those who might be thinking of joining them, eleven rebel captives were publicly put to death in Paramaribo. One man was hanged on a gibbet, suspended from an iron hook anchored in his rib-cage. Two were roasted to death on a slow fire. Two were decapitated. Six were broken on the rack. The hoped-for effect was not achieved. On the contrary, the situation worsened. It began to look as if the entire colony would be engulfed in flames. The authorities decided to sue for peace. In 1749, after prolonged negotiation, a treaty was signed. The Saramaccans were granted autonomy and promised annual tributes of arms and liquor; in return they promised to keep their settlements at a discreet distance from the towns and plantations and not to harbour any future runaways who might seek refuge among them. Adoe, the rebel chief, was given a large cane with a silver pommel engraved with the arms of the colony: these canes continue to be associated with the paramount chieftaincy of the Bush Negro tribes.

But by 1757 the situation was threatening to get out of hand once more. Not only were the Saramaccans continuing to burn and plunder (the promised tribute had not arrived) but now a new storm centre of revolt had begun to take shape in an area to the south-east of Paramaribo. The leader of this rebellion was called Araby. Interestingly, he had actually been born in the forest and so had never known slavery. Once again the authorities sued for peace. In 1761, a treaty similar to that worked out with the Saramaccans was signed with him on the Auca plantation. This group, as a result, was christened the Aucas. Today they are more familiarly known by the name they gave themselves – the Ndjuka. Araby, civil but distrustful, was not content with the Christian oath sworn by the Dutchmen. He had, he said, too often seen such oaths disregarded. Some more potent formula was necessary. In genuine African style all were required to give of their blood. This was mixed with earth in a calabash and, after a libation had been offered to the ancestors, black and white drank, the ritual accompanied by the frenzied chanting of an obeah man. It must have been an odd little scene. Araby was presented with his cane engraved with the arms of the colony.

Meanwhile, a second peace signed with the Saramaccans had also proved abortive – and for the same reason. In the end, though, Dutch persistence was rewarded. A third – and this time lasting – peace was worked out with the Saramaccans in 1762. All seemed set fair. The elated governor invited the leading rebel captains to Paramaribo where they were treated with appropriate ceremony and regard, being paraded through the streets in his carriage and entertained at his table. 'They are already become overbearing and even indolent,' it was observed, 'brandishing their silver-headed canes in defiance of the inhabitants, and forcing from them liquors, and very often money, and reminding them how cruelly their ancestors had murdered their parents . . .' Confidence revived, planter society giving itself up to its usual round of riot and debauchery. Surinam, Stedman tells us, resembled a large and beautiful garden. It was a land flowing with milk and honey. Even so, his ears remained 'deafened with the clang of the whip, and the shrieks of the Negroes'. Surinam could not escape its *karma*. Soon, the plantations were going up in flames yet again. The slave populations of entire estates were fleeing into the bush; and down the rivers there floated the mangled bodies of their masters, mistresses and overseers – more food for the piranha.

The names given to the village-fortresses established by these latest rebels stressed their implacable resolve: Boucoo – 'I shall moulder before I shall be taken'; Gado Saby – 'God alone knows me'; Boosy Cray – 'The woods weep for me'. Their leaders were driven by fanatical hatreds; a fanaticism that reminds one – far-fetched as the comparison may seem – of those young Khmer Rouge cadres who, not long ago, emerged from the Cambodian forests bent on slaughter and destruction. Several of Surinam's eighteenth-century rebel chieftains were gripped by the same annihilating frenzy. Unlike the Khmer Rouge, however, they could lay claim to no revolutionary aims. These were not noble men fighting for a cause. Only backward-looking sentimentality can cast them in that kind of congenial role. Possessed by obsessive *personal* hatreds, they wanted revenge; they wanted blood. They were frightening men, the deranged creations of a deranged society. There is 'Joli Coeur', raiding the plantation where he had been a slave and – while his followers, dressed in looted laces, velvets and cocked hats, danced and feasted – confronting the estate manager, a Jew called Schults. 'O Joli Coeur,' cried Schults, 'remember the dainties I gave you from my own table, when you were only a child, and my favourite, my darling, among so many others ...' 'I remember it perfectly well,' Joli Coeur is said to have replied, '... but recollect how you ravished my poor mother and flogged my father for coming to her assistance. Recollect this ...' With one blow of a hatchet he decapitated his victim, kicked the head about like a football, sliced the skin from the slain man's back and spread it over one of his cannon to keep the priming dry. There is 'Baron', a favourite of his Swedish master, able to read and write and trained as a mason. But the manumission he had been promised never came. The Swede, going back on his word, sold him to a Jew. Baron, refusing to work, was publicly flogged under the gallows. So he fled to the forest, screaming revenge 'against all Europeans without exception'.

But the most notorious of all was Boni (or Bonny), famed not only for his bloodlust but for his remarkable military skills. He was of the Aluku tribe – they who in going up the Marowijne had chosen the warm, warlike waters of the Lawa tributary. No white man ever set eyes on Boni – at least, no white man who saw him ever lived to tell about it. However, it seems to be generally accepted that he was a mulatto, his mother having been seduced by her master whose outraged wife cut off one of her breasts. The pregnant woman fled to the forest where Boni, like Araby before him, was born.

Copper-complexioned and red-haired, Boni, it is said, was tormented from childhood by the physical difference between himself and those surrounding him, a torment aggravated by their taunts and the obvious mutilation his mother had suffered. The Ndjuka tradition credits him with magical powers, claiming that he was tutored by Aduwanman, the semi-divine being who knew the secrets of the soil, and who had flown from Africa to lead the runaways to safety. What is certain is that he raised and trained a tough, ruthless guerilla army which spread its reign of terror far and wide: Boni had vowed that he would drive all the whites out of the Surinam. But Boni – 'the relentless mulatto' – was no kinder to the blacks. A captive rebel woman spoke of the severe discipline he maintained – she was present when he had had two of his soldiers slashed to death with sabres merely for saying a few favourable words about the Europeans. He trusted no one with arms until they had served a number of years as his personal *slaves* and shown their complete loyalty and devotion to him. Others added their testimony. On one occasion a solitary, near-demented black was captured in the woods. The man told his story in Paramaribo where he was taken to be tried. He spoke of his birth in Africa, of being made a slave by his own countrymen and being shipped out to Surinam. His overseer treated him so harshly '. . . that I deserted and joined the rebels in the woods. Here again I was condemned to be a slave to Bonny, their chief, who treated me with even more severity than I had experienced from the Europeans, till I was once more forced to elope, determined to shun mankind forever . . .' Boni's was a private war, an attempt to settle an account that could never be settled. He hated the whole world. Ultimately he was defeated (but at great cost) by the mercenary armies sent against him. His followers were driven across the border into French Guiana where they have remained.

A Ndjuka myth describes his end. Boni, the Ndjuka say, tried time and again to persuade them to join him, but they remained stubbornly faithful to the treaty they had made with the Dutch. Desperate, he insulted their ancestors. That was too much. Even Aduwanman turned against him then. The wise men got together and fashioned an ape that could turn itself into a beautiful woman. Boni was overcome with desire when he saw the ape-woman. She said she would only give herself to him if he revealed the source of his magical powers. Boni did so. As he reached for her, she resumed her ape form and escaped to the Ndjuka. After a last bitter struggle Boni was killed. The Ndjuka cut off his head which they planned to give to the Dutch. But, while they were negotiating a rapid on the Marowijne, the head jumped out of the boat and disappeared in the water. That rapid still bears his name.

Boni's was the last of the great servile rebellions. By the end of the eighteenth century Surinam had been effectively partitioned between Dutch and rebel spheres of influence. Both sides, depending on the point of view adopted, could be considered victors: the whites remained in Surinam; the runaways remained free. Passion exhausted, the fugitives retreated up the rivers made treacherous by rapids and into the forests. There, they sought to reconstruct their broken lives.

It was as much a psychological as a physical retreat. Rejecting the world of towns and plantations, holding fast to their memories of Africa, conservative to the core, they fell out of Surinamese history. But to say (as is usually said) that they recreated 'Africa' in the jungles of Surinam is not strictly accurate. True, their religious beliefs, their arts, their crafts, their style of dress – all of these speak of Africa. Nowhere else in the New World did blacks retain such strong links with the homeland. Nowhere else was Africa remembered and venerated to such a degree. But their lives had been *broken*. They could not help but recreate what might be called a 'synoptic' Africa; an Everyman's Africa, half authentic and half fabricated. It could not be otherwise. The slaves, after all, came from different tribes, spoke different languages, had subtly differing religious beliefs and practices. They were, by the very nature of things, an artificial community, men and women thrown together by a common misfortune – enslavement. In the end, then, however 'African' they might seem to be, they belong to the New World. They are one of its genuine creations. Their clan and tribal structure are pure products of their slave past – slaves coming from the same plantation formed a 'clan'; clans joined together to make 'tribes'. Their language (excepting that used for religious purposes) was a patois compounded out of a mixture of African dialects, Portuguese, Spanish, French, English and Dutch; their most powerful myths arise out of their historical experience of the white man. The Amerindians taught them the preparation of the poisonous cassava and how to shoot fish with the bow and arrow; they taught them how to build canoes; they may even have passed on some of their cults associated with the spirits of the rivers and the forests.

For two hundred years town black and bush black went their separate ways, distrustful and contemptuous of each other. To the town black, the Bush Negro became as remote – as unreal – as the blank-faced, wandering tribes of Amerindians who, now and then, appeared in the towns offering for sale hammocks, trinkets and the colourful birds they had caught in the deep forest. By some curious refraction of perception the Bush Negro too became aboriginal (my guide Rudi regarded them as such – 'they have *always* been here,' he said to me), one more mysterious exhalation of the South American jungles – no different from the Amerindian. Between Bush Negro and town black there was little or no sense of a shared past; there was no confluence of sympathy, no point of contact. Both literally and in the imagination, the Bush Negro was consigned to the wild places. All those women with bared breasts, all that black magic and ju-ju was, to say the least, embarrassing to the Christian convert, the creature of European civilisation. He turned his back on it. At best, they were a source of 'ethnic' objects d'art, providing the culture-conscious with hand-painted paddles, carved trays, incised calabashes and the like. Voteless until 1963, the Bush Negroes, like the Amerindians, mattered to no one except the missionaries and the anthropologists. Town black and bush black became not merely separated societies, different kinds of people; they had, it could be said without too much exaggeration, been transformed into distinct races. After two hundred years of racial isolation, the Bush Negroes, their features undiluted by miscegenation, *look* different. Surinamese have no difficulty in spotting a Bush Negro even though he may have lived a long time in Paramaribo and dresses and behaves like everybody else.

Disregard and contempt: and yet, the town black knows the Bush Negro had fought for his freedom; had spurned the white man; had preserved 'Africa' in the jungle. Today, these are fashionable attributes among politically conscious blacks all over the New World. 'I stretch forth my hands to Africa/ To restore my dignity/ And as I learn my history/ I see how much they did steal from me . . .' – so runs part of the chorus of a popular (and not untypical) reggae song. Black power. Black dignity. Disregard and contempt pass effortlessly into semi-mystical rediscovery of the Bush Negro and through him of an 'Africa' that never quite was. Not long ago, two 'Afro-Americans' (so they insisted on referring to themselves), scientists attached to Washington's Howard University, came out to the jungles of Surinam to do some research. They made a film; a film in which it was soon made apparent that scientific curiosity was not the sole motive of their expedition. It was also a spiritual quest: they had come to pay homage to their racial and cultural origins. One saw them, dressed in loincloths, standing in the river, being washed clean of centuries of sin by a Saramaccan high priest. The New World can play some cruel jokes.

Nowadays it is becoming increasingly modish to build weekend huts in the middle of the bush. To these come Paramaribo's middle-class radicals, anxious to learn, anxious to imbibe the wisdom of the bush folk. The preservation of Bush Negro culture and tradition has become a revolutionary virtue. One afternoon, in a semi-urbanised Bush Negro village not far from Paramaribo, I met a schoolteacher, a man who readily described himself as a Marxist. He was not only – and predictably – hostile to Christianity and the work of the missions along the rivers, but was also opposed to government attempts to grant individual land titles to the villagers – land belongs, by custom, to the tribe, not to the individual. He dismissed the government policy as 'bourgeois'. More fundamentally, he disagreed with the proposal because, he said, it was not in accord with the old ways, the ways of the ancestors. Marxist radicalism and tribal conservatism has fused, become one and the same thing.

It is all a little late in the day.

Seventy-five kilometres to the west of Tapanahony, on the upper Surinam River, lies Djoemoe, the residence of the paramount chief of the Saramacca tribe. Here – the same forest, the same rocks covered with lilac bloom, the same mission station, the same lanky Dutch nurses. Granman Abakoni, heir of Araby, received us in the office that occupied the ground floor of his government-built house. He was not sure how old he was but, by his own reckoning, he could not be much less than eighty. Between his legs he balanced his silver-pommelled cane of state. He wore a military-style cap and navy-blue jacket with braiding and brass buttons. His legs were daubed with clay – he had just been taking part in a religious ceremony, praying for one of his village captains who had fallen ill. The plastic-covered armchair on which he sat was soiled and torn. He was in sombre mood, talking about the desertion of the villages, about the young men and women who were leaving, heading wherever there was work to be had and money to be made. They were not only going to Paramaribo. Many were moving across the border to French Guiana, to Cayenne. Wages were very high in Cayenne. Much higher than in Surinam itself. The Saramaccans were being scattered everywhere. In Paramaribo they talked a great deal about the Interior, but they did next to nothing: not once since they had elected him had their representative showed his face among them. His wife came in. She bent low over him, whispering. He rose shakily from his chair, supporting himself on his cane. It was the middle of the afternoon, he explained. He was an old man. He needed his rest.

He received us on his upstairs veranda later that evening. The night was cool. Below us, beyond a couple of coconut palms, was the black river, only made visible by the beams of electric light thrown across it. Street-lamps glowed blue among the houses and the huts. Many of the houses were perfectly modern brick cabins – their architecture that of any low-cost housing scheme. Loud music flowed from someone's gramophone: a party was going on in the village directly opposite. The Chief, dressed in a pair of crisp blue pyjamas, creaked back and forth on a rocking chair. Behind him was the sitting-room, the doors of which were thrown wide open. It was quaintly and haphazardly furnished. I saw a mirrored wardrobe, a cuckoo clock, several Chinese and Indian calendars and, occupying pride of place, a large colour photograph of Queen Juliana and Prince Bernhardt, hung somewhat awry.

He resumed where he had left off. So much had altered on the river. The young had lost their respect for the old. 'Before you would tell a man to go and he would go. Now he *comes* when you tell him to go.' Stealing too was on the increase. Why, just the other day three women had stolen a boat and fled upriver to Paramaribo. Such a thing had never happened before. The world he had known as a boy was falling apart in front of his very eyes. Every day a little bit more seemed to crumble away. He stopped speaking and listened to the music from the village opposite sweeping across the water.

'If I were young,' he said suddenly, 'I too would leave. But I would not go to Paramaribo, Cayenne or Holland.'

Where would he go?

'I would go to Africa! I would go and help to build Africa and make it a great place. But I am an old man and Africa needs young men. What use could I be to them?'

Some years before he had gone with the other paramount chiefs on a tour of Ghana, Dahomey and Togo – a trip paid for by the government.

'Sometimes,' he said, 'I think we were sent to Surinam as a punishment.' He became thoughtful. 'We must have offended the ancestors. So they punished us by sending us here. Now we are offending them again. How will they punish us this time?'

The cuckoo clock called the hour. His wife appeared, bent low and whispered. The chief, nodding obediently, struggled to his feet. It was time for the old man to go to bed.

We crossed the river. The party was in full swing. There, in a sandy clearing, bordered by jungle, naked electric bulbs glaring, shining bodies swaying to the amplified rhythms of reggae, the old ways, the ways of the ancestors, were finally being buried.

The Rise of the Rastaman

On sunny Saturday afternoons on the Portobello Road, the blacks with the tangled braids of hair – called 'dreadlocks' – look alluring and picturesque. They blend into the lively scene which still evokes memories of the Sixties; they are an accepted part of the masquerade. Venture, however, a street or two to the north, to All Saints Road, and the innocuous quality disappears. One strays into a realm in which the masquerade of racial assertion, of ostentatious Blackness, is suddenly stripped of its eccentric and theatrical charm, assuming an altogether harsher aspect. Being Black on All Saints Road is no joke.

Whether by night or by day, it takes courage to enter the Apollo public house. Near the entrance cluster knots of dreadlocked blacks. If you look a promising prospect, you will, in all probability, be surrounded. The litany of illicit commerce will be hummed into your ears. Fending off the hawkers and the pimps, summoning resolution, you force a passage into the pub. Within, the odour of ganja (marijuana) is unmistakable. The smoke of the holy herb – nowadays claimed as an essential ingredient of West Indian 'culture' – hangs in a motionless mist. The landlord seems somewhat taken aback to receive an order for a real drink: the consumption of alcohol, it appears, is not the main preoccupation of this establishment. Someone feeds the juke-box. The numbing, pseudo-portentous rhythm of the reggae pulses through the ganja mist. In one corner I notice a white girl, reading one of the many 'black' publications now available in London. Elsewhere, a roughly dressed white youth, hunched into an oversized combat jacket, is striking a bargain with a dreadlock who, quite openly, holds up for his inspection a plastic bag that must contain at least a pound of marijuana. On the tables are scattered signs of holy herb usage – the broken stubs of unsmoked cigarettes pillaged for their tobacco. The seating lining the walls is torn and ripped, bumpy with outcrops of eviscerated foam rubber.

'So, man, what can I do for you?' A hand falls on my shoulder. The accent is cinematic American hoodlum.

Resinous sticks of hashish are displayed.

'The best, my friend. From Pakistan.'

Isn't he, I ask, afraid of getting into trouble with the law? No . . . he has no fear of that. The police wouldn't dare come in there and make trouble. They knew what would happen if they attempted anything so foolish. I discover that he has already served a two-year prison sentence for burglary. A frame-up.

We are joined by one of his comrades. His stock of hashish is still to be cut into strips. He heats the blade of a penknife on the flame of a cigarette lighter and settles down to his task. Each strip will fetch five pounds. He will have about twenty such and would hope to sell them all that day: he conducts most of his business in the pub. As he works, he sips orange juice from a carton. Never touches alcohol. Never! He comes, I gather, from Jamaica.

'Would you call yourself a Rastafarian?'

He does not cease his labour. 'I prefer to call myself dreadlock.'

'What's the difference?'

But he is not inclined to pursue the point. I ask if he has been to prison. He smiles enigmatically. 'Babylon is prison, man. Babylon is one big prison.'

'I take it, then, you're longing for the day of repatriation to Africa?'

He throws me a vague glance, sipping at his orange juice. I assume this to mean that, for the foreseeable future, Africa will have to wait; that the Portobello and its environs are not about to be robbed of his presence. I watch the heated penknife blade slice easily through the block of hashish. The Babylonian captivity, at a hundred pounds a day, is sweetness itself, not to be lightly surrendered.

A third young man insinuates himself. He is lean and clean-shaven. Amphetamines are his speciality. His approach is more aggressive, tinged with suspicion and hostility.

'Are *you* a Rastafarian?'

The amphetamine salesman gazes levelly at me. 'All black men are Rasta.'

'How do you mean?'

No further enlightenment is volunteered. He wants to trade, not talk. Warily, I breathe in the cloying ganja mist. The reggae throbs.

'The true Rastafarian,' Lord Scarman wrote in his report on the Brixton disorders (or 'uprising' as it has come to be known in certain circles), 'is deeply religious, essentially humble and sad . . . The dreadlocks, the headgear and the colours, which he affects, are a daily reminder to him of Africa and a witness to the world of his belief that his exiled people must return there.'

The *true* Rastafarian. For more than a month, in Jamaica and in London, I had been pursuing this Holy Grail of authenticity. In that West London pub, I had reached the end of a wretched road.

Jamaica seemed the logical place to begin my search. After all, it was there that the cult of Ras Tafari had first seen the light of day towards the end of the 1920s; and, prophets not always being without honour in their own country, it is there that the movement – if it can be so described – has achieved its most widespread recognition and been accorded a respect that frequently verges on the idolatrous. The funeral of the reggae singer and sage, Bob Marley, demonstrated the extent to which Rastafarianism had penetrated the national life. It was transformed into an affair of State. Orations were delivered by both the newly elected, capitalist-minded Prime Minister, Edward Seaga, and by the socialist leader of the Opposition, Michael Manley. The assembled multitudes smoked their ganja, grieved and grooved – and were not molested by the police. The only comparable event in the history of Rastafarianism was the visit to the island, in 1966, of the Ethiopian emperor, Haile Selassie, King of Kings, Conquering Lion of the Tribe of Judah, the god in human form destined to redeem his abused brethren, whose divine wrath would one day wreak its vengeance on iniquitous Babylon.

The messianic hopes generated among the common people by that jet-fuelled Epiphany startled middle-class Jamaica. Selassie must have been thunder-struck. Fifteen years later, the funeral of Marley aroused no such reaction: by then, there were very few middle-class Jamaicans left to be shocked. The cult, for a delirious moment, was all but invested with the dignity of a state religion. This was hardly surprising. For some time the historians and sociologists and political scientists of the University of the West Indies had been hard at work. Their language was impressive and passionate – and, in its way, as befuddling as the inarticulate gropings of Rastafarian doctrine. One of them (a director of the University's Adult Education Programme, a former Chairman of the Institute of Jamaica, a former Cultural Adviser to a former Prime Minister) was writing sentences like this: 'The prophetic vision of the Rastafarian assumes a particular significance in the religious sphere of Jamaican existence, second only to the political vision which receives special reinforcement from institutional control of coercive power but with which the Rastafarian phenomenon shares the prime concern of decolonisation.'

The politicians were also making their contributions to the raising of consciousness. In one of his election campaigns, Michael Manley, advocate of a socialism simultaneously democratic and scientific, revealed that he was in possession of a rod endowed with a mystical potency, allegedly given to him by the Emperor of Ethiopia. His rivals were not slow in responding to this challenge. They too, it emerged, possessed rods of similar potency. One question dominated that campaign: which rod was the real one? Between the visit of Haile Selassie and the funeral of Bob Marley a great deal had happened; a great deal had come to fruition in Jamaica. Most portentously, the Rastaman had crawled out of the shadows of nightmare and been crowned a king: a phoenix risen from the ashes of the Black Power era.

It is barely an hour's flight from Miami to Kingston. The transition from the First to the Third World is brief and dramatic. After the fair-ground, electric splendour of the former, Jamaica's unlit mountainous interior looked bleak and uninviting, a desolation now and then relieved by the dim glow of scattered human settlement. I had last visited the island some twelve years before and I was no longer certain about my reception – or about what I would find. In 1970, to the far south of the Caribbean Sea, Trinidad, that most innocent land of the calypso and the humming bird, was recovering from the recent shock of a mutiny by its fledgling army, some of whose officers had been inspired by Black Power ideology. In Canada, West Indian students, aflame with militancy, were making a nuisance of themselves. One of their more memorable feats, I seem to recall, was an assault on a computer centre. At the Jamaican campus of the University of the West Indies, some of the staff were proving as troublesome as the students. A Guyanese historian, Walter Rodney (subsequently assassinated in his homeland – of whose government he was somewhat critical), was preaching the undiluted gospel of Black Power (Africans had invented everything worth inventing) on the campus and in the slums – more fashionably designated the 'ghetto'. He was critical of the 'local lackeys of imperialism' and was predicting a new phase in the 'epochal march forward of the Black Humanity of Jamaica'. The Jamaican government became alarmed and he was deported. His case was to become a *cause célèbre* in the region. Ugly storms were brewing nearly everywhere. I was glad to get back to London.

During the following decade, Jamaica's Black Humanity marched with epochal vengeance. As Michael Manley's experiments in democratic socialism fell apart, as the dream of Third World leadership unravelled, as the shelves in the shops became emptier, Jamaica was inundated by a tide of violence amounting to civil war as the 'ghetto' supporters of the two main political parties took to the streets and alleys of Kingston with their guns. The rival rods were of no use. In that period, the Jamaican showed what a cold-blooded killer he could be. The distinctions between political activity, the rapid growth of black consciousness and criminality were lost in the mêlée. Caribbean blacks were finding a style that transcended the clenched fist and the cry of 'Power! Power!' They were discovering the splendour of the gun. This atmosphere was celebrated in a well-received film, *The Harder They Come*. The sleeve of the record spawned by the film is revealing:

'Shanty Town – Jamaica – where the best grass in the world sells for two dollars an ounce in the street, where shooting a film can he held up when an actor is shot (two have died since it was completed), where people sing in church till they have an orgasm (thank you, lord) . . . Reggae was born and grew in these slums . . . Crime runs through the life of Shanty Town like the incessant rhythms of the sound systems, feeding on the ganja herbs that flourish on the banks of the rivers of Babylon . . .'

A new Jamaican, a new Caribbean man, had been born. He was not at all familiar to me. Gone was the genial, straw-hatted calypso type singing about rum and Coca-cola and mothers and daughters compromising their virtue for the Yankee dollar. (If you did drink rum and Coca-cola, you called it Cuba Libre.) In his place had come the ganja-fed troubadours who sang about shooting sheriffs in self-defence; about rampaging 'rude boys' a-looting and a-shooting. The Caribbean black had undergone a sea change. He was beginning to acquire a style and a mystique peculiarly his own. With the collapse of Black Power during the course of the Seventies, that mystique, that style, now in search of a fresh resting-place, would discover the Rastaman. His was a style that brought together and transcended all styles of black rebellion. Above all, with the international success of singers like Bob Marley, he made it glamorous to be oppressed.

1960 was a significant year for the Rastafarians. It was in that year that a team of researchers from the University of the West Indies issued a hastily compiled report on the sect. It was not the first time the

Rastafarians had been the objects of serious study. Previous efforts, however, had been academic in intent and had had a confined circulation. In the Fifties it was still possible to treat eccentrics – even black ones – as eccentrics and there let matters rest. The University report was aimed not only at the general public but, more speci- fically, at the Jamaican government. Its recommendations aroused considerable controversy. Interestingly, the idea for the project had come from a number of prominent Rastafarian brethren made anxious by certain alarming incidents and a consequent spate of bad publicity. The publication of the University report marked an impor- tant stage in the Rastafarian quest for sympathy, popular acceptance and legitimacy. Suddenly, after a generation in the wilderness, the cult had an audience. Suddenly, it had to be taken seriously. Rasta- farianism had arrived. Still, the Sixties were in their infancy. The report, though friendly in tone, was not fervent. Detachment was possible. It would take another fifteen years or so for the cultists to be hailed (by one of the authors of the report) as the 'protagonists of many of the universal ideals that have informed man's activity time out of mind'.

The brethren had good reason to be anxious. Trouble was brewing. Some two years before the University report came to the rescue, the Rastafarians had begun to adopt a more challenging posture and to focus attention upon themselves. In 1958 they organ- ised a month-long 'convention' in one of the slum districts of King- ston. It was an arresting cultural manifestation. There was much drumming, dancing and chanting. Ganja was smoked in quantity. A rumour spread that, as part of the celebration, a policeman was to be decapitated, his head to be used as a sacrificial 'peace offering'. Nothing of the kind occurred. But the convention was not devoid of accompanying drama. There was, for instance, the attempt to 'capture' Kingston. Early one morning, scores of cultists gathered in one of the city's parks. They carried tall poles crowned with banners coloured black and green and red. Kingston, they announced, had been 'captured'. When the police arrived to disperse them, one of the leaders, arms upraised, intoned, 'Touch not the Lord's anointed.' A sociologist, becoming excited, uttered this prophecy in a local news- paper: 'In the long run,' he said, 'the type of Prince Emmanuel [one of the organisers of the convention] may have more to do with the West Indian future than the type of Lord Hailes . . .' Lord Hailes was the then Governor-General of the West Indian Federation which was soon to be dissolved. The sentiments of the sociologist ought not to be misunderstood: he was burying Lord Hailes.

One of the visitors to the convention was a black clergyman, the Reverend Claudius Henry. Henry may or may not have been a Rastafarian. But, whatever he was, his links with the movement were undeniably close. In 1959 he created, in the slums of West Kingston, his very own organisation. This he called the African Reform Church, referring to himself as a Black Moses. The Black Moses soon set about living up to his name. His first step was to have printed the following card or 'ticket':

'Pioneering Israel's scattered Children of African Origin back home to Africa, this year 1959, deadline date Oct. 5th, this new Government is God's Righteous Kingdom of Everlasting Peace on Earth, Creation's Second Birth. Holder of this Certificate is requested to visit the Headquarters at 78 Rosalie Ave ... August 1st 1959 ... Please Reserve this Certificate for removal. No passport will be necessary for those returning home to Africa. Bring this Certificate with you on August 1st for Identification. We are sincerely, The Seventh Emmanuel's Brethren gathering Israel's Scattered Children for removal, with our leader, God's Appointed and Anointed Prophet, Rev. C.V. Henry, R.B. Given this 2nd day of March 1959, in the year of the reign of His Imperial Majesty, 1st Emperor of Ethiopia, God's Elect, Haile Selassie. King of King and Lord of Lords. Israel's Returned Messiah.'

Some fifteen thousand of these Certificates were bought at a shilling each. On the appointed day, the purchasers – some of whom had sold all their possessions – arrived at the headquarters in Rosalie Avenue. But there were no ships and no planes to take them away to Africa. Henry was arrested – and allowed bail. The news spread that he planned to 'take over' the island; and, indeed, when the police raided the headquarters of the Black Moses, they unearthed a large quantity of arms and ammunition. Eventually, he would be tried and condemned for treason. Even worse was to follow. Henry's son, Ronald, arrived from New York and took to the hills with a band of Rastafarian guerillas. They meant business. Two British soldiers died in an ambush. Graves were found containing the bodies of some of Ronald's own followers – the youthful revolution already beginning to eat its children. A state of emergency was declared. Events like these formed the background to the University report.

The University report provided what historical background it could; set out – so far as it was possible to do that – the Rastafarian creed; and, addressing itself to the Jamaican government, made a number of recommendations. Taking note of the brethren's avowed desire for repatriation (some zealots rejected the very notion of Jamaican citizenship) and conceding the existence of indestructible 'religious and emotional' ties with Africa, the authors suggested that a mission should be sent out to explore the possibilities of emigration to the motherland. 'Jamaica,' they wrote, 'now facilitates the settlement of emigrants in England; from a racial point of view, emigration to Africa seems more appropriate.' The island, they added encouragingly, was already overpopulated and could never expect to provide work for all its inhabitants. Moreover, the Ethiopian Emperor had indicated a willingness to be hospitable. Out of his private estates, he had bequeathed several hundred acres of land to 'Black people of the West', a token of his gratitude for the support they had given him and his country during the dark days of Occupation by Mussolini's legions. The authors do not seem to have been deterred either by the paucity of the land on offer or by the conditions laid down by the Ethiopians. They had made it clear that they had no desire for a 'mass migration'. Even more chillingly, they wanted the settlers to be of 'pioneer calibre'. The emigrants had to have definite skills and thus be able to pass on to their backward brothers and sisters the rudiments of sanitation, carpentry, plumbing, masonry and all the rest. Repatriation was going to be a tough business.

The report further advocated the setting up of a branch of the Ethiopian Orthodox Coptic Church in Jamaica; exhorted the government to allow the brethren untrammelled liberty to express themselves and communicate their views; and urged the police to learn to distinguish between 'true' and false Rastafarians, a plea to be echoed by Lord Scarman twenty years later in a much colder climate: 'It is his [the true Rastafarian's] great difficulty that young hooligans have aped the outward signs of his faith without accepting its discipline or adopting his religious approach to life.' The staying power of that myth, that Holy Grail of Rastafarian authenticity, has to be admired.

Ras Tafari (Haile Selassie) is the living god.

Ethiopia (sometimes construed as 'Africa' in a more general sense) is the black man's home.

Because Ethiopia is the black man's home, from which he has been cruelly separated by enslavement, repatriation to his origins is a necessity. His repatriation is not merely necessary but inevitable; it has been foretold by Biblical prophecy.

White men are evil. Their treatment of the black man is adequate proof of this.

These are the four doctrinal assertions which the authors of the 1960 report decided were common to all Rastafarians. A later observer expands the number to six, including in his list the propositions that White is inferior to Black and that the latter would one day rule the world.

No theology is more fluid, more elusive. There is no church; there are no scriptures; there is no ordained leadership. Each Rastafarian has his own version of the thing. You become a Rastaman by declaring yourself to be such – or, simply, by beginning to look like one. There are those who call themselves Rastafarian and who abhor ganja. Some reject the divinity of Selassie. The brethren can be 'clean-faced' or dreadlocked. Many are socialist and many are not. Some are primitivist in outlook, some drive around in sports cars and travel between continents by jet plane. There are brethren for whom African repatriation seems more of a threat than a promise. Many appear to be neither deeply religious, nor humble nor sad. Quite a number of the brethren I have encountered are not – to disagree once again with Lord Scarman – 'scrupulous' in their observance of the law. Each Rastafarian is free to invent his own version of the creed. Each ordains himself. In that chaos of attitudes and posturings, the true cannot be separated from the false.

At one extreme, Rastafarianism sinks into the morass of the 'rude boy' mentality. At another, as a result of infiltration by the sons and daughters of the Jamaican middle class, it is attenuated in a fairyland of quasi-mystical philosophising about love and peace and oneness. The idea of Babylon – realm of exile and oppression – loses its visceral simplicity. It is reinterpreted as a 'system', breeding-ground of depersonalising, alienating and soul-destroying tendencies. 'Rasta is about *livity*,' one of its middle-class practitioners said to me. What, I inquired, was 'livity'? He had some trouble explaining. Rasta, he seemed to imply, was rooted in the life-giving forces animating the universe – with which forces blacks had a unique relationship. They were grounded in the 'livity of the livity'. Seeing my bewilderment, he fell silent and took several consoling inhalations of the holy herb. He blew gentle puffs of the smoke across the placid countenance of his baby son who lay in a cradle. The child's hands reached up to grapple playfully with father's pendent dreadlocks. 'I-n-I,' he went on, using the Rasta circumlocution for 'we', 'believe in clean earth, clean sky. I-n-I don't like fertilisers and such things. I-n-I want to live natural.' He was an exemplar; a herald of a spiritual revolution that was destined to save the world. Another middle-class Rastafarian I met discoursed somewhat abstrusely about the Yin and the Yang and speculated on the links that might exist between Rasta and Hindu philosophy. Rasta, he said, had a history going back hundreds of years.

In a recent film – *Countryman* – the Rastaman is portrayed as a kind of super-wizard, capable of bending the powers of nature to his will. Sun and storm are at his command. The two whites he has rescued from a crashed aircraft – helpless children of Babylonian civilisation and entirely dependent on him for their survival – gaze at him in unflagging wonderment. In the mirror of their childlike wonder, the Rastaman achieves his apotheosis. But it is an apotheosis entirely detached from reality. Seduced by the attention and respect showered upon it, Rastafarianism has become a masquerade exploiting images devoid of substance.

'Princes shall come out of Egypt; Ethiopia shall soon stretch out her hands unto God.' (Psalm 68)

'And I saw a strong angel proclaiming with a loud voice, Who is worthy to open the book, and loose the seals thereof? . . . And one of the elders saith unto me, Weep not: behold, the Lion of the Tribe of Juda, the Root of David, hath prevailed to open the book, and to loose the seven seals thereof.' (Revelation 5)

In 1930 Ras Tafari ascended the Ethiopian throne and took to himself the name Haile Selassie, 'Power of the Trinity'. He took other titles as well: King of Kings, Lord of Lords, Conquering Lion of the Tribe of Juda. An ocean away, in the distant colonial outpost of Jamaica, this event was to have the most bizarre repercussions. Independently of each other, certain religious maniacs began to subject their Bibles to close scrutiny. Could this Ras Tafari, this Haile Selassie, be the Saviour whose coming had allegedly been foretold by the inspired Jamaican apostle of black liberation, Marcus Garvey? 'Look to Africa,' Garvey is supposed to have said to his disciples, 'where a black king shall be crowned, for the day of deliverance is near.'

They looked to Africa and saw a radiant King who claimed he was descended from Solomon and the Queen of Sheba; whose lavish coronation ceremonies had drawn the attention of the world upon himself and his country. They studied their Bibles. In scattered passages (Rastafarians, though enamoured of the Bible, use it very selectively) they found the confirmation they desired. The good news was announced. Haile Selassie was not merely King of Kings and Lord of Lords but none other than God Himself in human form.

They, the blacks, were the true children of Israel, the Chosen People long denied their earthly Zion. But their hour of deliverance was at hand. The most prominent exponent of the doctrine to emerge was one Leonard Howell. He was fairly candid, preaching hatred of whites and asserting the superiority of blacks. Blacks, he said, should exact vengeance for the crimes that had been committed against them. He denied the legitimacy of the colonial dispensation in Jamaica and advised his audiences to ready themselves for the return to Africa. Nearly all the familiar elements of Rastafarian doctrine and behaviour are discernible in the Howellite crusade – although the violence he openly espoused is an embarrassment to his more sophisticated successors who prefer to equate the primary impulses of the movement with 'peace' and 'love' and 'brotherhood'.

But behind Howell and the other contemporary preachers looms the curious figure of Marcus Garvey – yet another would-be black Moses. Despite the fact that Garvey was a secular, not a religious, leader, it is possible that without him there might have been no Rastafarian cult. It might, at any rate, have assumed quite other characteristics and not found so fertile a soil for its message. For it was Garvey – hailed as a prophet and often referred to as the John the Baptist of the movement – who, in the slums of Kingston, created the expectant, hectic atmosphere in which messianic fantasies of racial redemption could take root. The Rastafarian movement is, at one and the same time, a culmination and a subversive caricature of his life's work.

In 1897, Marcus Garvey was 'ushered into a world of sin, the flesh and the devil'. Made increasingly restless by his aggravated racial awareness, he embarked on an extended pilgrimage, travelling in the West Indies, South and Central America and through much of Western Europe. Everywhere, he realised, was hell if you were a black man. 'I asked: "Where is the black man's Government? Where is his King and Kingdom?"'

It was in London that his sense of mission became clearly defined; where, as he put it, the 'doom' of race leadership descended upon him. Fired by his vision of a regenerated black race, of a glorious Negro Empire in Africa, he returned to Jamaica. There, in 1914, he founded the Universal Negro Improvement Association with its motto, 'One God, One Aim, One Destiny'. Two years later, he went to the United States. By 1919, branches of the UNIA had been set up in several American cities and Garvey was boasting of a membership of two million. The following year he was laying claim to four million, a figure soon to be inflated to six million. Yet, however overblown the estimates of membership, there can be no doubting the fact that Garvey and the UNIA had made a major impact.

Garvey's vision of himself and his organisation was grandiose. The line separating fantasy from reality was never easy to draw. He represented, he said, *all* black men; all 400 million of them. At the first 'International Convention of the Negro Peoples of the World' held in New York in 1920, the UNIA conjured up a dazzling array of hierarchs endowing each with an impressive salary. There were, for instance, His Highness, the Potentate (12,000 dollars per annum), His Excellency, the Provisional President of Africa (10,000 dollars), His Excellency, the Leader of the American Negroes (10,000 dollars), His Highness, the Supreme Deputy Potentate (6,000 dollars), His Excellency, the Leader of the Eastern Province of the West Indies, South and Central America (6,000 dollars). Everyone was given a splendid uniform. Garvey himself was elected Provisional President of Africa. 'Subsequent experience,' he wrote with sad hindsight, 'proved that all the majority of these men wanted were the offices with the titles and the privilege to draw large salaries.' No wonder, as the disappointments and betrayals crowded in one after the other, he so often castigated the Negro as his own greatest enemy.

Garvey did, however, make two major attempts to realise his dreams. The more famous of these two disasters was his attempt to form a shipping company – the Black Star Line – which, it was hoped, would engage in trade with Africa. The venture was also intended as an exercise in 'racial self-reliance'. One ship struck a reef on its maiden voyage. The captain Garvey had hired turned out to be a drunkard. The 'captain' of a second ship had false credentials – and, Garvey insisted, was another drunkard. 'Think of it,' Garvey exclaimed, 'a ship at sea with nobody in the engine room, no engineer. Do you wonder the cylinder covers blew off and piston rods were broken? Do you wonder the Kanawha became a wreck so many times?' A third ship, for which down payments had been made, never materialised: the company had been swindled by one of its brokers.

In 1922, the Americans accused Garvey of fraud. He was found guilty and sentenced to five years' imprisonment – later softened to deportation. And yet, despite the catastrophes that had attended its brief existence, the Black Star Line was to find new life as a symbol. Today, Garvey and his ships are a recurring theme in Rastafarian iconography, second only to portraits of the emperor. Kwame Nkrumah inserted a black star into the Ghanaian flag.

Garvey's other disaster was his scheme to send out colonists to Liberia, 'a natural home for Negroes'. To begin with, all had augured well. The UNIA, at its own expense, was to establish four colonies in the republic. Garvey submitted plans for the 'cities' he hoped to see rise in the West African bush. These blueprints made provision for everything from water filtration plants to vague but wonderful 'Colleges of Arts and Sciences'. The Liberians, more down to earth, provided a list of patent medicines the colonists should bring out with them. These included Sloan's Liniment, Dr Jayne's Household Remedies and Redman's Ready Relief. It was a peculiar curtain-raiser to a programme of racial salvation. Suddenly, the Liberian government changed its mind. The land promised to Garvey was given instead to the Firestone Rubber Company. When the first group of emigrants arrived, they were served with deportation orders. 'I would not,' Garvey wrote, 'exchange two five-cent cigars – even though not a smoker – for all the Colored or Negro political leaders, or rather mis-leaders. . . . The fraternity is crafty, heartless and corrupt.' Garvey died in London in 1940. He was not allowed to rest in peace. Some twenty-five years later, none of his ideals any nearer realisation, his remains were disinterred and repatriated to Jamaica. He was declared a National Hero. The failures were all but forgotten. Only the symbolism, the fantasy of being black without tears, mattered by then. Garvey, like the Rastafarianism he had helped to make possible, had long been put out of reach of rational scrutiny.

Racial pain and longing lay at the heart of Garveyism. He saw history as a battleground of competing races, each one striving for self-realisation and supremacy over the others. Those who were not equipped for that struggle would inevitably go under. It did not take a great deal of perspicacity to see that the Negro had fallen to the bottom of the heap and was an endangered species. Without a god and a kingdom of their own, the blacks were doomed to extinction. Garvey rejected liberal ideals of 'integration'. Blacks could have no future in white-ruled societies, no matter how well-disposed these might be. The UNIA proclaimed its opposition to miscegenation which, in its opinion, was tantamount to race suicide. It believed in 'the purity of the Negro race and the purity of the white race'. It is hardly surprising, therefore, that Garvey was openly sympathetic to the aims – if not the methods – of the Ku Klux Klan. His enemies went so far as to accuse him of being a member of that organisation. Garvey denied the charge. But he did not deny that he had had a meeting with the Klan's Imperial Wizard. Jamaica's National Hero declined to attack the Klan because he had 'no proof . . . that the Ku Klux Klan had any other desire than to preserve their race from suicide through miscegenation and to keep it pure, which to me is not a crime but a commendable desire . . .' In the West, blacks were strangers in a strange land. They could never be happy because their hearts were perpetually sad; they were captives who, one day, must be restored to the land of their fathers, realm of prophets and saints, God's crowning glory. A note of what might be described as race-weariness creeps into the vision of salvation. 'Our desire is . . . but to lay down our burden and rest our weary backs and feet by the banks of the Niger and sing our songs and chant our hymns to the God of Ethiopia.' Strange this Awakened Negro of Garvey's fancies – longing for rest, for the cessation of struggle; pining for solitude. The politics of racial redemption loses itself in a mystical yearning. We are on the threshold of the original Rastafarian delirium.

The day was coming, Garvey said, when the God of Africa would speak with a voice of thunder. Down would come crashing the pillars of a corrupt and unjust world. In that fateful hour, Ethiopia would be restored to her ancient splendour. The Negro had been denied access to his real history, cheated out of glory by the lies of white men, who were so terrified of him that they had conspired to rob him even of his past. He must now rediscover the truth about himself – that he is the descendant of the 'greatest and proudest race that ever peopled the earth'. For while others had lived in savagery, rudely clothed in animal skins, trembling with fear in lightless caves, Africa had, for uncounted centuries, been the seat of all learning and wisdom. In those far-off times, black men had walked hand in hand with the gods, being their favoured children. Generously, they had brought civilisation to Asia and Europe. But then, Africa had sinned, becoming drunk with power and success. The Negro had fallen into a long and terrible slumber. Now, however, he was shaking himself into wakefulness while the Caucasians, bloated with sin, were sinking under the weight of their iniquities. The resurgent black would bring to its fullest realisation the power and genius of Man. '. . . the Negro shall put the world to wonder in the revelation of God through the race.'

By 1933, the Howellite sect was selling photographs of the lately-crowned Haile Selassie at a shilling each, describing them as passports to Ethiopia. Howell was sent to jail for two years. Gradually, his followers came to be known as 'Ras Tafaris'. On his release from prison, he formed the Ethiopian Salvation Society. A ruinous estate – Pinnacle – was acquired by the Society. Taking some sixteen thousand disciples with him, Howell settled down there. At Pinnacle, Rastafarianism acquired its most distinctive 'cultural' attributes. Ganja was the commune's main cash crop and its usage among the brethren became an accepted practice. The Bible, as usual, lent its support ('. . . and thou shalt eat the herb of the field . . .' Genesis 3:18), the brethren ignoring the fact that this dietary injunction was part of the punishment inflicted on the disobedient Adam. It was also at Pinnacle that the hairstyle known as dreadlocks first came into fashion among Howell's bodyguards. This too was justified by Biblical reference ('They shall not make baldness upon their head, neither shall they shave off the corner of their beard . . .' Leviticus 21:5), although the initial inspiration came from a less sublime source: the brethren were much taken with photographs of nomadic African tribesmen published in the *National Geographic* magazine. Towards the end of the 1940s dreadlocks could be seen roaming the streets of the capital. These sightings were to become much more common when, in 1954, the police broke up the Pinnacle commune, thereby releasing large numbers of its now homeless denizens into the slums of West Kingston. Rastafarianism had come to town. Its architecture was complete.

He was the most ferocious-looking Rastaman I had yet set eyes upon, a monument of a black man. Coal-black locks, thick and wild and spidery, framed a broad, beaten face. Behind mutilated lips lurked an arbitrary collection of twisted, yellowing teeth. A pair of bulging eyes rolled at me with torpid interest. Speech, when it eventually came, was mangled, creeping out of his throat in a subterranean growl that was barely comprehensible. He reeked of ganja. But, however unprepossessing, he was well known in Rastafarian circles, a blend of teacher and high priest. His claims to fame were substantial. He was one of the senior brethren who had instigated the 1960 University report; he had twice travelled to Ethiopia; he it was who had controlled the frenzied crowds gathered at the airport during Haile Selassie's visit to the island in 1966 – to him alone would the rabble listen, to him alone would it concede authority; and – his crowning glory – it was he who had first recognised the genius of Bob Marley, become a guru to him in the early days of 'struggle', and even composed a song for him. I shall refer to him as the Elder. Accompanying the Elder was an acolyte whose dreadlocks, by comparison, were embryonic. The acolyte was a journalist by trade: he wrote a column about mainly musical matters for the *Gleaner*, Jamaica's major newspaper. He too, therefore, was not to be lightly treated.

'We do not call ourselves Rastafari*an*,' the acolyte remarked primly, glancing at the incoherent Elder. 'Nor do we like that word Rastafari*anism* either.'

'So what do I call you?'

The acolyte looked at the Elder. They exchanged knowing smiles. 'You may call us Rastafar*I*.'

'This 'I' language is one of the Rasta conceits. Most common is the 'I-n-I' doing service for 'we'. But there are scores of others: 'I-thiopia' (Ethiopia), 'I-vine' (divine), 'I-tal' (vital – a term applied to the vegetarian cuisine of some cultists), 'I-story' (history), and so on. It is a harmless affectation, but that, of course, has not deterred fanciful interpretations of its significance. There are those who see in it a profound self-assertion. Some go even further and talk about the birth of a new and revolutionary language. It is hard, nevertheless, to understand how talking about 'I-bages' instead of cabbages contributes to that process.

I was to be corrected again.

'RastafarI have no beliefs,' the acolyte said. 'RastafarI do not *believe* anything. The I-dren [brethren] *know*.' The I-dren knew, for instance, that they were living in the Last Days.

Later that evening, we went to the 'ghetto', driving through unlit, litter-hazed alleys. I was escorted into a compound inhabited by two or three families. Under an open-sided shed lit by a feeble bulb some children were playing a dice game. A row of hens slept on the rafters. Reggae pulsed from a transistor radio. We sat outside in the warm and windless dark. A pipe with a long stem and an oversized bowl was produced. Piously, it was filled with ganja. At the first inhalation, the Elder choked and coughed and spluttered. The hens up on the rafters were disturbed and stirred restlessly. In the still air, the smoke of the holy herb was overpowering, ascending in clouds which did not disperse. The Elder began to speak – about the Falkland Islands, about Richard Nixon, about Enoch Powell. He spoke about the First World War, the Second World War, the coming Third World War. He spoke about Hitler and about the Queen. It was impossible to grasp the logical structure of this discourse.

'Your English Queen know all about Rasta,' he said. Had she not been to Addis Ababa, holiest of cities? Had she not spoken with His Imperial Majesty? What did I think they had talked about? Was I not aware that at the coronation of His Imperial Majesty the Duke of Gloucester had been sent by George V to return to its rightful owner the golden sceptre of the House of Judah which had been seized from Ethiopia by Rome and from Rome by Britain?

He laughed. 'Your Royal Family know *all* about Rasta. They know *who* His Imperial Majesty is.' He rolled his reddened eyes at me. 'Now you have come all the way from England to find out about Rasta. You should ask the Queen!' He turned to his spell-bound audience. 'This man has come all the way from England to see us. We always knew that one day the world would come to seek us out. We predicted that one day Rasta would cover the world like an ocean.'

The smell of ganja hangs around. It inheres to clothing, to skin; it resists dissolution. All morning, as the acolyte's Volkswagen laboured up the slopes of Jamaica's hill country, its fumes billowed like storm clouds. Behind me, the Elder spluttered and gagged and banged his chest. 'Rastafari,' a female disciple of the cult had written, 'has arrived at the spiritual plane of consciousness by smoking the herb, and by continuing to smoke it, I & I can bring I-self back to that special place where I & I can find peace and spiritual silence and insight into I & I Christ Consciousness.' Ganja was not only beneficial to the spirit. It enhanced physical and mental performance. Because it altered perception, it allowed the brethren to develop a 'Black viewpoint on life'. This was all extremely interesting. But the road was narrow and the countryside precipitous. I could not help wondering about the effect such intensive consumption might have on the acolyte's driving skills; I could only hope that he had not yet reached an advanced state of spiritual peace. There was another reason for worry. The holy herb, my informant had warned, did not always promote serenity. It could, in unpropitious circumstances, provoke paranoia.

For the moment, there was no sign of that. The acolyte seemed happy enough to explain to me that the Roman Catholic Church was the instrument of the Anti-Christ and to describe how the Pope and his Cardinals performed the rites of the Black Mass behind the high walls of the Vatican. Towards noon, the north coast of the island appeared far below us. We entered the parish of St Ann, an area vibrant with mystical import for the brethren. Its sacred soil had nurtured both Marcus Garvey and Bob Marley. A dirt track took us to the hovel of a poor brother, an emaciated, copper-complexioned dreadlock approaching middle age. He bowed from the waist when I was introduced by the Elder. 'Greeting, my lord,' he murmured. A faded portrait of Selassie decorated the entrance, its frame covered with freshly picked flowers. On the walls – some curious mathematics of salvation? – were involved algebraic equations. 'If You Don't Love Jah [God],' proclaimed a scrawled exhortation, 'You Can't Love Rasta.' Pride of place, however, was given to a panoramic photograph of Addis Ababa. Silently, the woman of the house prepared an Ital lunch. The voice of Bob Marley quavered through the sparsely furnished room; the ganja fumes thickened into a fog. In the unkempt yard, I discovered a circular brick enclosure, roofless, doorless and with gaping spaces where there should have been windows. Out host had intended it for a place of worship. But he had run out of money and it was unlikely that it would ever be completed. Amid the rubble his wife grew a few vegetables.

'I want to go to Africa,' she said, as we sat together on the temple's crumbling threshold, staring at a starved dog heaving its ribs in a patch of shade. 'This place is not our home. We are strangers here.'

'You were born here. You know nothing else. You must feel some attachment to this land.'

She shrugged. 'This place is not our home,' she repeated, her gaze remaining fixed on the panting dog. Suddenly, she looked up at me. She was smiling. 'When I leave Jamaica, I won't behave like Lot's wife. You'll never catch *me* looking back.'

*

'Everything's gonna be all right.' So runs the refrain to a well-known reggae song. Why everything's gonna be all right is not clear. But, of course, clarity is not the point. The pseudo-portentousness of the beat is everything. Rastafarianism – as style, as imagery – has spread on the wings of its music. 'Music is an integral part of Pan-Afro Caribbean peoples' way of life,' says the *Voice of Rasta* (a north London publication), '... I and I have made a lot of sacrifices and compromises, but music and dance is something I and I won't sacrifice to please babilan.' Such theology as is espoused by the London-based brethren derives almost entirely from the lyrics of Bob Marley. They have a dim perception of the Caribbean, most of them having either been born here or brought here at an early age. Victims of a double displacement, they have come to see themselves as, and be treated as, merely Black. It is the saddest of denudations.

The Rastafarian creed – with its notions of Babylonian captivity and martyrdom, its racial emphasis, and its alluring denials of the Western world and Western achievements ('I don't see what it have to admire in all this space exploration,' a Notting Hill youth said to me. 'We Africans have been all over the universe. Thousands of years ago we were voyaging among the stars') – is ideally suited to the circumstances. It makes it possible to be merely Black. No further effort is required of its disciples. The medium is the message. 'Soul' eats up intellect; rhythm replaces struggle.

His existence confirmed by the slack-jawed wonderment of his Babylonian audience, the Rastaman is not required to justify either himself or his caricature of faith. Rastafarianism does not bring its devotees closer to self-comprehension. If anything, it has led them further away from any understanding of themselves or their condition. At best, it gives the black a congenial image of himself. At its worst, it stimulates lethal visions of grandeur. Rastafarianism transforms Blackness – being a Negro in a White Man's world – into a cultic experience; a quasi-apocalyptic ecstasy of empty assertion. Allegory displaces reality. As Marcus Garvey said – the Negro does not know how to stop hurting himself.

Two Colonies

Over the years my relationship with the Caribbean has suffered a progressive deterioration. Nearly eighteen years have gone by since I first left Trinidad. I have lived more than half of my life away from the island. Inevitably, I have changed a great deal during that interval; and, of course, so too has the region. In some ways, I would say, it has changed even more than I have done. Much that was familiar and congenial and comprehensible has been swept away. On my sporadic visits, I walk the steaming streets of Port of Spain uneasefully, not quite an outsider but no longer a native. I do not know what to make of myself; what my status is. A wall has arisen between me and what was once so familiar. The perils and temptations bred by Independence have descended on nearly all the islands. A political condition which was still a novelty when I sailed out of Port of Spain harbour one cloudy August afternoon in 1964 has now become a settled fact of life – often a chilling fact of life.

On my visits to the Caribbean, I feel like someone going back to have a look at a house in which, formerly, he has lived and with which intimate remembrances are linked. I go and look only to discover that no one remembers who I am, that my past connection with the place is of no account to the strangers who now live there. I turn away, book myself into a hotel for a night or two and make sure that my return ticket is safe. I have been by-passed by events. The assumptions of affinity I took away with me in 1964 have ceased to be tenable. The evolutions and convolutions of 'black consciousness' (I am, when all is said and done, of Indian ancestry) have nothing, as such, to do with me. I recoil from the degraded ideologies that would re-classify me as 'black'. A new marginality has been thrust upon people like myself by the assorted wog-doms that have come into being during the last twenty-five years – those penitential states of mind that are equated with 'liberation'. Marginality is sad. But, in my case, it is a sadness beyond my control.

'So where you come from?' asked a sullen Port of Spain waitress.

'Me?' I reflected briefly. 'I don't come from anywhere in particular,' I said.

*

Independence had come to most. But not to all.

'Welcome to Puerto Rico, USA' said the handout in my hotel room. I was being greeted by the Puerto Rican Manufacturers Association. They were confident I would enjoy my stay in their 'Caribbean island paradise'. Manufacturing and a stable political climate, I was informed, had transformed the island into one of the foremost industrial centres of the Western world.

It was an odd introduction to an island paradise. Through plate glass doors I stared out at hibiscus, at oleanders, at wind-ruffled coconut palms, at a turquoise sea breaking over a line of rocks. Americans in colourful caps and gaily checked trousers sped about the well-kept grounds in golf-carts. But, as the handout from the Manufacturers Association had said, Puerto Rico was not be confused with other beach-ringed Caribbean paradises. I had come to an island which had managed to escape many of the maelstroms of Caribbean post-colonial history; whose failure to wrest an independent existence for itself appeared to have paid handsome dividends. Puerto Rico is an anomalous sort of place: not quite a colony and not quite a state of the American Union; at one and the same time proudly 'autonomous' and hopelessly dependent. In English the paradox is expressed by the enigmatic term 'Commonwealth'. In Spanish the island's puzzling condition is rendered as 'Estado Libre Asociado' – free associated state. Puerto Rico's hybrid status is admirably expressed by this mildly oxymoronic description. The islanders are American citizens. As such, no restrictions are imposed on movement to and from the United States (the million or more Puerto Ricans who live on the mainland show just how popular a privilege this is); and, as a quid pro quo, they can be drafted for military service. On the other hand, they do not pay Federal taxes and cannot vote in Federal elections.

The blur has existed ever since the Americans – chary of imperialism in the old-fashioned sense of the word – took over from the Spanish in 1898. But the perplexity was not a wholly novel one for the Puerto Ricans. 'Status' had been the one abiding political question for the last one hundred and fifty years. It was the dominant theme during the dying decades of Spanish control; and it has remained so under the American dispensation. Puerto Rican flexibility is well illustrated by the fact that, within a year of the annexation by Washington, a political party was formed to clamour for complete absorption. Today, the island's two main parties owe their existence to the differing solutions they offer on the status issue: one advocates

Statehood (i.e. complete absorption) while the other opts for the indefinite perpetuation of the ambiguities of the 'Commonwealth'.

'Puerto Rico, USA' can be regarded as the slogan of the former. The assertion is not ridiculous. The transition from New York to San Juan involves no 'culture shock' – to begin with, one simply notices a rise in the temperature. Driving along the highway linking the capital to Ponce on the south coast is a purely American experience. Only the lush tropical vegetation greening the hillsides and the occasional glimpse of some remote hovel strike an errant note. Miami (they say with pride) is recreated in the Condado section of San Juan. Suburban life finds its confirmation in stylish shopping centres replete with air-conditioned banks and gaudy dispensaries of fast food. Puerto Rico, USA, exists when you flick from television channel to television channel or from radio station to radio station. Sometimes the chatter is in English; sometimes it is in Spanish. Unbelievably, in Ponce's art museum you can look at paintings by Rubens, Constable, Courbet, the Pre-Raphaelites. America exists in the one million motor-cars shared among the island's three million inhabitants, in the paucity of public transport, in the basketball courts you see everywhere, in the fat policemen with hands poised on bulging gun-holsters, in the fiery chimney of oil-refineries and the glistening globes and pipes of petrochemical plants. You will be told again and again that, with the exception of the continental United States and Canada, Puerto Ricans enjoy the highest standard of living in the Western hemisphere. Dependence may not be dignified – but it pays! Pitying, contemptuous shrugs accompany references to the Dominican Republic, to Cuba, to Haiti, to Jamaica. Ah . . . the miseries of Independence. How fortunate, how blessed, is Puerto Rico, willing step-child of a great and powerful country.

'We are *American* now,' a Ponce city official said. For him, being 'American', Statehood was the only legitimate aspiration. Its realisation would confer a proper dignity. To carry on indefinitely as quasi-Americans was not pleasing. Nearly every Puerto Rican, he assured me, was impatient to assume the full responsibilities of American citizenship. Also, as a passionate believer in democracy, he could see no other way of guaranteeing its survival in Puerto Rico. Unfettered Hispanic culture, he seemed to suggest, was inimical to it.

The Commonwealth party is more cautious. They worry about the additional taxation which Statehood would bring; they wonder if most Puerto Ricans really grasp the full implications of Statehood. These anxieties shade off into fears about the cultural fate of the island – still 'Hispanic' after all, still Spanish-speaking – if it were to be completely absorbed by the United States. Look at what had happened to Hawaii . . . what was there left of the Polynesian way of life? Would Spanish, for instance, be driven into the wilderness? The Ponce city official had laughed at these fears. 'What is wrong with learning English?' he asked. 'If we have to learn English, we'll just have to. Learning English isn't going to make Puerto Rico disappear.'

The fears of those who oppose him may be exaggerated. But they are not entirely without foundation. While I was there, the Puerto Rican Bar Association was driven to protest when a US Army major decided that all personnel at the Armed Forces Entrance and Examining Station must stop using Spanish even in private conversation. For some, incidents like these are portentous: they signal the submergence of Puerto Rico, the extinction of any lingering individuality. For the ardent advocates of Statehood, they are no more than tea-cup typhoons. But the advocates of Statehood and Commonwealth share one sentiment. They both react with horror to the idea of Independence, the dying dream of a tiny minority, stained by terrorism (bombs have been planted in New York City) and undercut by hard-headed realities. Puerto Rico, despite its industrial revolution, despite the ease of migration to the mainland, remains a basket-case. More than half of the population depends on Food Stamps and other Federal welfare handouts. Puerto Ricans know they will never make it on their own; they know – and submergence may eventually be the price they have to pay – that they need to be protected from themselves.

Sixty miles to the west of Puerto Rico the Union Jack flaps limply over those scattered crumbs of the Empire known as the British Virgin Islands. Area: fifty-nine square miles. Population: eleven thousand. 'Tortola,' said a nineteenth-century writer, 'is well nigh the most miserable, worst inhabited spot in all the British possessions.' I wouldn't go as far as that. I can think of at least half a dozen more miserable spots.

Like Puerto Rico, the islands have an internally autonomous political life and no one seems to care much for the idea of Independence – though, one gathers, the British would be only too happy to oblige. 'Give we Independence,' remarked one of the indolent, beach-combing locals, 'and you give we a dictator. No, man. We doing fine just as we is.' After which observations he offered to sell me some marijuana. The Governor sits in his house up on the hill and has little to do. Faint rumours of corruption surround the local administration. The Chief Minister, one hears, has a fondness for acquiring property. But, if some of the locals have doubts about the propriety of his real-estate transactions, the expatriates have none. To a man, these languid, sea-loving folk lavish praise on his wisdom and devotion to duty. If, I was told by one of them, the chief Minister had done well for himself, that was only because he was a tremendously hard worker and an extremely clever man. Which, I am sure, is true.

Away from the water not much happens. Road Town, the capital, is one narrow, winding main street. Along it promenade the tourists and locally bred Rastafarians – even in Tortola they have identity problems. The chief architectural monument of the town is a white-walled jail crowned with barbed wire. What else can one say? What else can one do but wonder at an Empire reduced to this level of absurdity? that has condemned eleven thousand people to so silly an existence?

There is nothing to look at; there is no visible sign of agricultural effort. Liquor is extraordinarily cheap and, apparently, one of the hazards of expatriate life on the islands. There is talk of drilling for oil – but, then, there is talk of drilling for oil everywhere one goes. During my stay an art gallery was opened and a Society for the Blind founded. The sea shines. Yachts move dreamily. At night, boat-loads of 'boat people' descend on Stanley's Beach Bar and jive to the steelband under the watchful gaze of cinematically menacing blacks who wear dark glasses and talk little. The most dramatic happening on the islands occurred about one hundred and fifty years ago when an Englishman was hanged for mistreating his slaves. Nothing of consequence happened after that. The British Virgins sit amid their shining seas, awaiting nothing in particular.

Fall from Innocence

Through a grey half-light I had my first glimpse of the islands, disposed like dreams in a grey sea. The aircraft's ultimate destination was the rounded volcanic rump of Réunion, another thousand miles or so to the south of the Seychelles. Réunion, still firmly French, was a reminder of the inchoate political geography of the Indian Ocean; an ocean whose waves washed the shores of India, South Africa, Australia, Madagascar ... its waters patrolled by the great navies of the world, none of whom could claim a special primacy.

It was not a quest for the exotic which was taking me to the Seychelles: those scattered islands, islets and rocks of granite – the remains, some say, of a submerged continent – interspersed with reefs of coral, spread across several hundred thousand square miles of ocean, offering refuge of a kind to a population reckoned with rough optimism to be approaching eighty thousand. I was going there because the Seychelles, on a Disneyland scale and in a Disneyland atmosphere, had succeeded in reproducing in an astonishingly short period (ten years) so many of the dismal features of the post-colonial world. Coup d'état, mercenary invasion, army mutiny – in the space of a few years the islands had lived through an accelerated cycle of political temptation and folly. For me, following these remote events, the islands gradually acquired a fascination comparable to that exercised on geneticists by *Drosophila*, the fast-breeding fruit-fly.

It would not be altogether untrue to say that between 1502 – when, it seems probable, they were sighted by Vasco da Gama on his way to India – and 1964 – when political parties first made their appearance – not much of moment had occurred. In 1756, the French, for want of anything better to do, laid claim to them; and in 1814, along with Mauritius, they passed from France to Britain. In between there had been settlement by a few French planters each equipped with a modest entourage of slaves and by assorted piratical adventurers.

I emerged into a vaporous, windless morning. Beyond the roof of the terminal building rose the mountainous spine of Mahé. I stared at the striated cliff-faces of elephant-coloured rock crowned with forest, surprised by the scale, by the splendour. The man from the Seychelles News Bureau was there to meet me. If you call him Gilbert and pronounce it in the French way that will do. He was youthful and smiling, with eyes narrowed by the tropical glare, with skin the complexion of tinned butter. He was one of the beneficiaries of the Revolution of 5 June 1977: a member of the youthful 'parastatal' aristocracy that had been created by it. We walked out to the car under the indolent gaze of a group of undeniably black, undeniably African soldiers dressed in camouflage uniforms.

'Tanzanians?'

Gilbert glanced at the soldiers. 'Seychellois,' he replied.

No one denies, so far as I am aware, the presence of Tanzanian soldiers in the Seychelles. They are the official guardians of the Revolution – which, in effect, means that they are there to guard the airport and the radio station. Yet Gilbert was always quick to negate any particular sighting, always perversely insistent that the soldiery we saw were of purely Seychellois origin. The Tanzanians did not appear to fraternise a great deal with the locals and looked queerly out of place and ill at ease.

We took the narrow main road winding along beside a blue, blue sea to Victoria, the toy-town capital of the islands. Across the water I could see the Air France jet shimmering on the runway, that eerie expanse of whiteness projecting like an oversized domino into the ocean. Built a mere ten years before, it had unleashed competing visions and versions of late twentieth-century reality on an unsuspecting and unprepared people.

Light-headed, somewhat unhinged by the nightmarish journey from Paris, I continued to be stupidly surprised by the height of the hills. It was easy to imagine that I was back in Trinidad and not on the western fringes of an unfamiliar ocean. Everything – the racial mixtures of the faces I saw at bus-stops, the small shops with glass cases and fly-blown jars of confectionery, the wooden shacks half-hidden among luxuriant bush, the more modern brick-built bungalows with louvres instead of windows, the flapping fowls narrowly escaping the wheels of the car – everything was touched with an odd intimacy. We went past a brewery, the first modest indication I had of industrial activity. Ahead of us glinted harbour installations, cranes, fuel tanks. We were entering the outskirts of Victoria. A handout from the Seychelles News Bureau called it the Queen City of the Indian Ocean, '... so prettily pint-sized [the writer went on to say] it could easily form the frontierspiece [*sic*] of a colourful storybook'. We passed the white-painted offices of Cable and Wireless – another focus of drama in the recent history of the Seychelles – the dark-interiored stores of Indian and Chinese merchants, the colonial Court House, the silvery clock-tower, said to be a replica of one on Vauxhall Bridge Road.

We left the sea and town behind, the road looping and climbing into the hills, threading its way to the western side of the island, towards the beach at Beau Vallon – where Adnan Khashoggi, an intimate of James Mancham, the deposed President, had once owned land. The vegetation was rich and wild. I stared at paw-paws drooping like elongated breasts, at the bread-fruit and jack-fruit and dark green mango trees, at the tangled vines and orchids and big-leaved epi-phytes; at the bougainvillaea and hibiscus, croton and marigolds and oleanders growing in untidy yards. Descending, we came in sight of the sea again. The hotel to which I was being taken had, not long before, passed into the hands of the Government, brought under the protection of yet another 'parastatal' enterprise – COSPROH (Com-pagnie Seychelloise de Promotion Hotelière). In a few days I was to become quite used to the pseudo-acrostic plague created by these bodies. I think – without particular effort – of SEYCOM (Seychelles National Commodity Company), SADECO (Seychelles Agricultural Development Corporation), NAIL (National Agro Industries Limited).

But not even COSPROH could spoil the tourist brochure loveliness of it all. The room in which I found myself that afternoon would have fulfilled the paradisal fantasies of most people. My veranda over-looked a sequestered cove screened by coconut palms and banks of yellow hibiscus. Farther out, the wind-blown water shone. I slept uneasily through the afternoon, startled into intermittent wakefulness by a louder crash of waves or by sudden gusts lashing through the palms. Towards dusk I made my way down to the terrace. Smooth wave-sculpted rocks were disposed along the shore, coconut palms decorated the slope of a green hill. I sat in the shade of a waxy-leaved frangipani studded with voluptuous outbursts of orange-white blossom. Seychelles cardinals fluttered like flames among the bushes. 'Don't you find,' an acquaintance remarked some days later, 'that there is an over-ripeness about everything here? A faint lasciv-iousness? It's almost embarrassing.'

Some boys were decorating the bar with coconut leaves: there was going to be a discothèque later that evening. The voice of Bob Marley complained from a pair of powerful speakers, hypnotically sombre amid the green gaiety. The manager of the hotel, a Seychellois Chinese, introduced himself to me. Our conversation turned to the tourist trade: in the Seychelles, it is an obsessive topic. Not even Socialist revolution could alter that. It was the Government's aim (he said) to attract 150,000 visitors a year to the islands. At the moment they were getting less than half of that number. Obviously, some of the shortfall could be explained by the recession in Europe. But the recession alone was not to be blamed. The foreign press, he implied, was frightening people away by painting too dark a picture of post-coup Seychelles. Still (he sighed, staring out across the twilit water) it could not be denied that mercenary attack and an army mutiny that had led to the seizure of tourists as hostages were not the best possible inducements. Tourism was a sensitive industry. A very sensitive industry indeed!

The omens were not good. In happier times British Airways had operated three flights a week from London. Now rumour had it that they were threatening to withdraw altogether. Rumour also had it that Lufthansa was clearing out. To compound the tragedy, the South Africans were keeping away. Lately, they had been feeling unloved. After the mercenary invasion of November 1981 – financed and armed by certain circles in Pretoria – the Government had retaliated by withholding landing rights from South African Airways. (Other trade continued to flourish – Socialist Seychelles remains heavily dependent on the food grown by their meddlesome southern neighbours.) As we talked, an enlarged sun sank with bloody splendour.

After dinner I returned to the thump-thump-thump of the discothèque on the terrace. Down there, on the edge of the ocean, the night was being danced away. It was a sad, half-realised scene, a pale reflection of the gaieties of the Mancham era when native and tourist connived at each other's fantasies. Mancham had had some intriguing ideas about cultural enhancement. For instance, a law was passed forbidding the erection of hotels taller than the surrounding palm trees. These hotels of palm height were also instructed to allow unhindered access to any Seychellois who wished to make use of their 'facilities' – provided (for even in so liberal a dispensation standards had to be maintained) they were decently dressed and behaved themselves; and, less romantically, could pay the bill. No fee was to be exacted for dancing. 'In that way [Mancham has written] our pleasure-minded people were made to see tourism for what it should be – an industry which could bring untold fun and happiness ...'

His approach was rooted in an older tradition of Seychellois hospitality. He refers to a fifty-rupee note adorned with a group of emblematic coconut trees. When examined from a certain angle, the fronds patterned themselves into the letters S-E-X. (I was given a tie adorned with the same motif.) 'This,' Mancham has written, 'admirably suited the island of love image which Seychelles had acquired during the Second World War when travellers had turned up to find that much of the male population was absent and the women friendly.' Under his guidance, the brothel-state was to hand. I sat out under the frangipani, breathing in the fragrance of the blossom, looking at the gyrating bodies on the dance floor. Cockroaches whirred out of the darkness and the waves broke white among the rocks.

But during that period other frailties, other temptations were maturing. That night, before falling asleep, I read a poem (composed in 1976, at the height of fun-time) dedicated to Albert René, leader of the Seychelles People's United Party.

> Hail SPUP, spearhead of the people's cause
> Which in its long march never did pause
> Bearing the banner of the rising sun
> To find our rightful place under the sun
> From a past bleak and dreary
> To a future full of promise and glory.

Until 1964 politics as such could hardly be said to have existed in the Seychelles. The franchise was restricted, confined to the landowners and professional élite. Assisted by a handpicked Executive Council and a tame Legislative Assembly, the Governor led a peaceful life. The Seychelles floated in a sunny and aimless isolation, as anachronistic as the slumbrous tortoises on Aldabra atoll. Mombasa, the nearest worthwhile landfall, was over a thousand miles away, a three- or four-day journey by boat. And the boats didn't come all that often. The islands' isolation, their removal from the realities of the twentieth century, was underscored when the Seychelles were chosen as a suitable place of exile for that troublesome Cypriot, Archbishop Makarios.

Reality, when it did belatedly begin to intrude in the middle Sixties, did so with vengeful rapidity. First there came the Seychelles People's United Party, the creation of France Albert René, a London University-trained lawyer. The SPUP announced that it had consecrated itself to the unceasing struggle 'for the total liberation of the people of Seychelles from colonialism and neo-colonialism'. It promised to create a Socialist state purged of all forms of discrimination and exploitation. The Organisation of African Unity granted its imprimatur. René was no slouch when it came to rabble rousing. 'The people of Seychelles,' he declaimed, '... will one day, somehow or other, kick out the British, kick out the Indians and kick out all those who have not ...' Etc, etc. Under the guidance of the SPUP, the Seychelles would be identified with all 'progressive' forces wherever these might happen to exist.

In response to all this frightening talk, there arose another lawyer, James Mancham, the handsome son of a local businessman. He set up the Seychelles Democratic party and possessed the not un-rare facility for mixing sex with politics. His fantasies were rather different from those of Albert René. 'My dream for the Seychelles,' he wrote in mournful exile, 'was a place of smiles and laughter with, under each coconut tree, a young man with a guitar.' Where the young women would be he did not say. In his mind's eye (Mancham cannot be accused of having had a political programme) he saw the Seychelles transformed into a sort of tropical Switzerland; it would provide a safe mooring for the ocean-going yachts of the sea-faring rich. His party turned its face against the Independence being clamoured for by René, suggesting instead some form of associate status with the United Kingdom. Mancham's party won every election that has ever been held in the Seychelles. Ominously, the losers murmured about corruption.

In 1971 there occurred a momentous event – the opening of the International Airport on Mahé, the main island of the group. Physical isolation was broken. Previously, perhaps a thousand visitors had arrived on the islands each year. A few years later, on the eve of Independence, their numbers would have climbed to nearly eighty thousand. Assorted celebrities and adventurers, in search of rest, recreation and lucrative investment, swooped down out of the skies. The Seychelles, perceived as a sexual and financial paradise, had become the place to go. Peter Sellers turned up with someone called Titi Wachmeister – in the fun-time, the islands were overrun by women whose bodies were lovely but whose names were hard to pronounce.

The Seychelles began to be courted. Mancham was invited to France by President Giscard d'Estaing. In proper statesmanlike fashion they discussed the development of fishing and agriculture. But Mancham, to his credit, was also interested in the development of closer cultural ties with the French. Accordingly, it was agreed that a pornographic film (*Goodbye Emmanuelle*) should be shot in the Seychelles. As if that were not glory enough, Roman Polanski was also persuaded to come out to the islands to make a film about 'high fashion'. As Mancham observed, the trip augured well for 'Franco-Seychelles friendship'. Alas, there would soon come a time when he would not be so sanguine about the French connection. Polanski duly arrived with one of his pubescent mistresses. On the night of their departure a policeman discovered the couple making love on the edge of the runway. The matter was reported to Mancham who was at the airport to see his new friends off. A charge of indecency was possible. Nothing, however, was done. The future President was amused rather than outraged: it was a suitably public affirmation of the new Seychelles style he was working so tirelessly to promote.

The economy, previously dependent on the slender resources of the coconut tree, was booming. Hotels were springing up among the palms; there were traffic jams on the narrow roads. In faraway cities Seychelles land was being bought and sold in a frenzy of speculation. Real estate values soared. Everyone, it seemed, wanted a share of paradise. A nephew of the Shah of Iran turned up. He wanted to acquire an island on behalf of the Shah and his Empress, a retreat to which they could retire when in need of 'rest and meditation'. In the event, the Prince didn't buy just one island – he brought three.

The British, nevertheless, continued to baulk at the idea of associate status. Despite the stagnation of his hopes, Mancham was triumphant in a third General Election in 1974, winning all but two of the fifteen seats. The Opposition voiced the by now standard charges of corruption and gerrymandering. With Independence looking more and more inevitable, the two parties, under pressure from London, were blandished into an unlikely coalition in June 1975. Their reward was internal self-government. Mancham was installed as Prime Minister while René was appointed to the less glamorous – but powerful – Ministry of Works and Land Development. Both men, in a sense, had got what they wanted. Mancham was now able to travel out of his spanking new international airport with enhanced style and prestige, attracting to himself queues of fair women; the more dour

René, the favoured son of the Liberation Committee of the Organisation of African Unity, could consolidate his power and await his opportunity.

In June 1976, the improbable coalition holding, the Seychelles was invested with full Independence. Mancham metamorphosed from Prime Minister to President.

On 5 June 1977, with Mancham, Honorary Knight of the Most Excellent Order of the British Empire, Officer of the Légion d'Honneur, absent in London to attend the Commonwealth Conference of that year, Albert René, voicing fears that Mancham was plotting the subversion of the democratic process, carried out his coup d'état with the help of Tanzanian soldiery. A policeman guarding the Armoury was shot dead. Political murder had at last come to the islands. Suitably enough, when his bedside telephone rang at 3.45 am, the ex-President was companioned by a 'guest' who was 'sleeping prettily' beside him. Suitably enough too, the caller with the bad news was his good friend, Adnan Khashoggi.

France Albert René,' . . . freedom fighter, kingpin of our liberation struggle and father of the Seychellois nation', had become Head of State.

Reality, African style, had caught up with the island.

'If some of our people cannot see that they are being hoodwinked into submission,' Albert René wrote in his party newspaper in 1971, 'then it is the duty of those of us who can see the light to show them the way.'

Ogilvy Berlouis was one of those who had seen the light; one of the small band of insurrectionists – dressed to kill in flashy combat fatigues – who in the early hours of 5 June 1977 seized various key installations in the capital. He had his reward. Nowadays he runs the Ministry of Youth and Development and lives in a well-appointed house on the hills overlooking Victoria. I met him in his office. A small, lightly bearded man, he affects a Guevarist informality.

'We joined the coalition because we believed in *unity*. From 1964 we were advocating Independence. Mancham was very much against Independence. Then in 1974 Mancham changed his mind. Once he accepted the idea we thought we could work together.'

– Despite your ideological differences?

'We thought we could *educate* them.'

– But you couldn't . . .

' fortunately we could not. The difference in ideology remained.

They didn't have any interest in the welfare of the people in general. Mancham was only for the foreigners investing in this country. They didn't mind if the poor remained poor while the rich got richer. So the coalition wasn't working and the people, as you know, decided there should be a change and all that.'

– The *people* decided?

'It was the *people* who reacted on 5 June 1977 and decided to change the government because they could see that the President was not fulfilling his promises and that the next General Election would be postponed. The people were wondering – "What is happening? What is *really* happening?" The people felt that their interests were not being looked after. We were still a colony a year after Independence.'

– You say the people decided and thought all those thoughts. But wasn't the coup carried out by a small group in the dead of the night . . . while, in fact, the people were asleep?'

'As you know, not *everybody* can be involved in such a matter. What you have is a small group of people doing *it* on *behalf* of the rest of the population.'

– If you were so worried about the subversion of democracy, why then did you decide to set up a One Party state?

'Well, we found out that the One Party state was *exactly* what was convenient for the people of this country.'

– How did you find that out?

'We did not believe that there was any point in continuing to have more than one political party in the Seychelles.'

– But why? You confuse me.

'It is not convenient for the Seychellois people to have too many parties.'

– But why?

'If the people of this country agree to the policy of our Party . . .'

– Do they agree? How do you know they agree?

'If the people of this country agree to the policy of our Party, why should they be bothered by another political group? It is not that we are afraid of having another party. If we have a One Party state that is only because we feel it is what is right for our people and because it is what *they* want. And, let me say, we still have General Elections in this country. We had one in 1978 and we plan to have another. Because there's only one candidate for President it doesn't necessarily mean that this candidate will be elected.'

– It doesn't?

'The procedure in *this* One Party state is that everyone can vote either yes or no. If the candidate is rejected then we have another election.'

– Why not have two candidates? Mightn't that be simpler and more logical?

'To some people, yes. But *not* to the Seychellois.' (Pause. His voice when he started to speak again took on a note of stridency.) 'What outsiders will say about our One Party state being wrong . . . *we will not listen to outsiders*. I would regard it as *external interference* in the affairs of Seychelles. We have our own system whereby the people can voice their criticism – they can criticise at their branch meeting. They are free to come to this office and complain. But, if the Government is doing right, why should there be any criticism against it?'

Along Independence Avenue, Victoria's main thoroughfare, one sees the developing modern profile of the Seychelles capital. Here you will find a couple of newish office blocks, the Ministry of Youth and Defence and, nearing completion while I was there, the building designed to house the State Monetary Authority – which, I was told, would be faced in black marble. At the eastern end of Independence Avenue, towards the harbour, there rises a piece of monumental sculpture, glowing white in the heat, commissioned to mark the two-hundredth anniversary of the town. It took me a while to realise that it was a representation of three birds with soaring, sail-like wings. They symbolised Africa, Asia and Europe (l'Afrik, l'Azi e l'Erop – as the Creole would have it), the three continents that had contributed towards the making of the Seychellois people. Going north from this monument, along the Avenue of 5th June – commemorating the date of the coup – you pass a patch of waste ground called Freedom Square and come, eventually, to the radio station. Security here is strict. Tanzanian soldiers lounge at the entrance, lazily suspicious of everyone who comes near. On the hill above the radio station is the Union Vale army camp, protected from intrusion by a fence of barbed wire. According to some, it has been used as a detention centre.

South of the avian monument is another centre of the town's social life, the Yacht Club – by no means so fearsome an institution as the name would imply. From the Yacht Club you can see at the top of a hill called La Misère the installations of the American satellite station, ~eat white globe floating like a moon against the sky. The tracking ~~t up in the dying days of colonial rule, was the result of semi-secret negotiations between the British and the Americans. Seychellois sensibilities had not been consulted. Mancham, exhibiting traces of a nascent national feeling, was a little hurt by this, though he had no objection in principle to the deal. Injured pride was tempered by schoolboy exuberance. 'At a stroke the Seychelles had gone from the eighteenth to the twenty-first century.' René was less welcoming, interpreting the deal as yet another imperialist imposition, a harbinger of every kind of evil. All the same, the tracking station was to survive the Socialist coup without apparent difficulty. It remains on its hill, scanning the southern skies, its great moon exuding a cosmic indifference to the fates of those below.

Victoria is a singularly characterless town. It betrays the emptiness and cultural isolation of the Seychellois past. One hundred and fifty years of British rule have made remarkably little impact. English, of course, is spoken but most Seychellois are not entirely at ease with it. It remains a formal language. French continues to be the more natural medium of expression for the élite; the less educated speak Creole. British dominion cut the Seychelles off from the living root of the French connection and never really replaced it with anything except the superficialities of colonial administration. The islands were too small, too far away, too deficient in the attributes that might have attracted settlers. One or two Englishmen may have acquired coconut estates. A handful of Indian and Chinese merchants ventured out. Their numbers were too small and their activities too minor to make any significant difference. The Seychellois lack not only a history (the islands must be one of the few colonial possessions not to have a fort) but a style. The 'planter's punch' ambience cultivated by the hotels is wholly derived from the Caribbean. Unblessed are the unexploited and unremembered! Mancham – perhaps unconsciously – sought to overcome this characterlessness by transforming the islands into a paradisal garden of sexual adventure. His efforts could, in their bizarre way, be considered an attempt at nation-building. Better a brothel state than nothing at all. Albert René also recognised that there was a problem and embarked on his own search for a Seychellois 'identity' that would make sense to the Liberation Committee of the Organisation of African Unity.

Socialism requires a past as well as a future. In the Seychelles the former had to be invented; or, at any rate, be subjected to mental reinterpretation. For René to make hi credible (if only to each other and the L necessary to concoct visions of oppression and suffering; to stimulate dystopic fantasies. Historical resentment had to be manufactured, the void had to be filled somehow. With so little to hand, the urge to 'revolution', to coup d'état, had to invent itself. 'For hundreds of years,' René proclaimed to the first Congress of his Party, 'the Seychellois people have depended on others – employees on employers – consumers on merchants – the whole population on foreigners.' They had been crushed by 'a system of religion which attributes all responsibility to God . . .' These abstractions are almost Buddhist in their mantric vacuity. In that airy dystopia, white had brutalised black, class had warred ceaselessly with class. Life, in other words, had been hell.

The picture painted was like a child's drawing of a house – recognisable but lacking in the particularity and concreteness of truth. Out of bloodless invocations such as these, a Seychellois identity, a national purpose, was to be forged. So there descended on the Seychelles the lethal abstractions which were to lead to 'Party Congresses' and, eventually, to coup d'état, political murder and the One Party State. Consider the language once more. '. . . the patience of the people ran out and in the early morning of 5 June 1977, a group of dedicated and courageous men . . . took up arms and overthrew the corrupt régime then in power . . . hand in hand the entire people, under the banner of freedom . . . march on towards true liberty, equality and fraternity . . .' The event described is hardly real to its perpetrators. It is hardly real because they are telling lies. But lies, reduced to the language of fashionable fable, became a marketable commodity and make those who tell them acceptable to themselves and to a world ready to believe anything.

The search for a Seychellois identity has led in other directions. Not ~~~isingly, it has assumed a linguistic complexion. Creole, the
~~ of the street, of the market-place, has been endowed with
~~ taking its place alongside English and French. The
~~ ~aper uses all three. They call this trilingualism.
~~ ~~garded – it being the tongue of the 'people' –
~~ ~as been designated the 'first national
~~ ~s the medium of instruction during
~~ ~doption has not been without
~~ ~d to be written, but other
~~ ~ing led a mainly oral

existence – over its spelling and pronunciation.

'Everybody says Creole is a dialect and not a language,' the Director of Information said to me. 'But what does that mean?' He glowered across the width of his desk. 'How did French begin? Wasn't it a dialect of Latin or something?' A faint air of triumph livened his austere countenance. After two hundred years, Creole had established its right to exist; it had come of age. Naturally, they would have to invent new words for certain scientific terms and so on. But why was that ridiculous? Which language didn't have to do that? The Seychellois were now a *nation* and Creole was an essential element of the national culture. On whose authority was it to be decided that Creole was a mere dialect? The Director of Information leaned towards me. 'Does God only hear you when you speak in English or in French? Doesn't He hear you when you speak in Creole?' I tried to suggest that it was not a question of communication with the Almighty, but, rather, of communication with other men whose languages afforded wider access to worlds of intellect and spirit than that allowed by Seychellois Creole. The objection was waved aside.

The Minister of Education and Communication was a no less ardent advocate of the cause. It was, he pointed out, a well-known tactic of colonialism to fool the colonised into believing that their way of speech was not the 'correct' one. That deception was known as 'cultural alienation'. It was clear that I myself had suffered deep cultural alienation. Did I know what was being done to a Creole-speaking child when he went to school for the first time and was taught in French or English? '*I* will tell you. That child is being *traumatised*. You are destroying his whole means of self-expression. You are destroying his whole means of understanding.'

My mind went back to my own schooldays in Trinidad where there was a clear distinction between the language of the street and the language of the class-room. Street talk played havoc with conventional grammar and pronunciation. It could easily be phoneticised into a semblance of autonomy. You moved, as the situation demanded, from the one to the other. It was no good, for instance, walking into a rum-shop and using the Queen's English. You would have been laughed out of the place. But I do not believe that I – or any of my contemporaries – were traumatised by our linguistic acrobatics. It all seemed perfectly natural. No doubt part of the explanation lies in the fact that the requisite 'political consciousness' did not exist in the 1950s. If you don't know you are supposed to be traumatised you tend not to be. It is an acquired habit. Nowadays, it is altogether different. It is beyond argument, an influential Jamaican intellectual says, that the first language of the Jamaican child is Creole – English-style of course. The phrases of discontent leap from his pages – 'cultural bombardment', 'mental dependency', 'deculturation' . . . and so on. To render these notions in Creolised English – or French – would, I imagine, require considerable ingenuity. Needless to say, no serious attempt is ever made to do so. Standard English is used to vilify Standard English.

'Identity' is an addictive notion. As a member state of the Organisation of African Unity, as clients of Tanzanian military might, the Socialist régime likes to stress its African credentials. This too has not gone down well with everyone.

'Do I look African?' asked a young woman I met. 'I'm not African. We are not African.' She waved at the people sitting round the table; she gestured towards the ocean glittering below us. 'Africa is somewhere way over there. More than a thousand miles away. What have we got to do with Africa?'

'Well – what do you belong to if not Africa?'

'Seychelles . . . what else? We're Seychellois, not Africans.'

'And what does it mean to be Seychellois?'

She laughed. 'That is a more difficult question.' Her ancestry was typically confused. At the turn of the century, her grandparents – they were traders – had emigrated from India. They had become converts to Christianity. At some point, Ethiopian blood (so she put it) had crept into their veins. Their ties with India were severed; the subcontinent was forgotten. To say you are Seychellois is one way of saying you are nothing in particular: a waifish confection, out of touch with Africa, out of touch with Asia, out of touch with Europe. Those who are afflicted by this malady of un-belonging all, to a greater or lesser degree, become unhinged.

L'Afrik, l'Azi (for the proletariat) – e (for the Francophile Creole aristocracy) l'Erop. 'Our cultural reality,' the avuncular Foreign Minister – Dr Maxime Ferrari – says, 'is also very related to Europe, above all to France.' Latterly, there can be no doubt that France has tried to instil new life into that moribund cultural reality. As is well known, the French and British have different ideas about these matters. The British do not have that sense of cultural mission felt by the French. 'Anglophone' does not pack the same messianic punch as 'Francophone'. Whatever the status accorded to English, whatever the communal rivalries between Creole and French, La Créolophonie remains a sub-species of La Francophonie. Mancham goes so far as to suggest that his overthrow was connived at by extremist Francophones in the Quai d'Orsay who saw the would-be rebels as possible conduits of a resurgent French pre-eminence. Certainly, France was one of the first countries to accord legitimacy to the coup. In addition, it quickly filled the manpower shortage caused by the expulsion of British officials and advisers. René, despite his University of London education, is not a card-carrying Anglophile. He once accused Mancham of wanting '... to adopt everything British – British language, British prostitution, British homosexuality and all'. To a leading light of the new régime the Chef du Service de la Francophonie is alleged to have said: 'Thank you, dear friend, for chasing out the British and for having returned Seychelles to its family.'

The Seychelles, in its quest for an 'identity', twists first this way and then that. But in no one direction is there a consummate satisfaction to be had. The people are confused and distracted.

'... the National Youth Service has ... made me a true and good militant ... Before I joined the NYS I was a good for nothing who didn't know how to plant and do other work, but now I feel I am prepared to do anything that I know will benefit others as well as myself.' (NYS student)

The National Youth Service remains the most fundamental and controversial innovation introduced by the new régime: an attempt to flesh out with substance the image of New Seychellois man. Next to it, the patronage of Creole pales into eccentricity. To take children away from their families, to confine them in camps (with minimal interludes of release) for two years, to put them into quasi-military uniform and subject them to all the rigours of barrack-room discipline, to attempt to instil all the ardours of collective egalitarianism, adumbrates totalitarian urges out of all proportion to the scale of Seychellois existence. As is so often the case, home-spun Third World 'socialism' collapses into unreflective cultism.

After some effort a guided tour to a National Youth service camp had at last been arranged for me. Early one morning Gilbert and I set off on our little excursion. 'Would you,' I asked him, as we drove through jungly verdancy, 'would you have liked to have gone to one of these camps?' He narrowed his eyes evasively – he with his fondness for double Camparis, his leisurely working habits, his devotion to his expense account . . . he who, a day or two before, had told me that the people were 'stupid' and, consequently, had to be herded and goaded . . . Gilbert, brother to a Minister, whose job bordered perilously on that of informer, one of the more novel vocations introduced into the islands by the Revolution.

'Yes,' he replies. 'I think I would have liked to go to a camp.'

No one was more in need of reconstruction. But I did not believe him.

The tarmac road came to an end. We bumped and shuddered along a rutted track, crossing narrow bridges spanning still, black-watered lagoons. Gilbert, who seemed unfamiliar with the area, questioned some labourers. Apparently we couldn't miss the fence: and we didn't. A wooden barrier blocked the access road. Two uniformed young women emerged out of a guard-house. Gilbert stated our business, the barrier was raised. We went past a plot of vegetable cultivation being watered by a revolving sprinkler. Ahead of us were low buildings of unpainted grey brick. We reported our intrusion to the main office. Our guides had not arrived. We sat outside in the shade of an almond tree, gazing out at the loveliest of coves, its waters calm and fringed by dense greenery. Under another dispensation there would have been colourful umbrellas here; bodies, hungry for the sun, littering the sand.

Our guides arrived – a middle-aged woman (she was called the 'village co-ordinator') and a younger man of Chinese extraction. We returned to the office, furnished in the dour, minimalist style characteristic of collectivist endeavour. A printed exhortation was affixed to the rough wall facing me. 'Washing One's Hands Of The Conflict Between The Powerful And The Powerless Means To Side With The Powerful'. This particular village – so the camp was referred to – contained over eight hundred children. Boys and girls were separated, though all shared equally in the common labours and duties. Both the sexes were organized in 'clusters'. Each cluster was further divided into three 'units'. This arrangement found visual expression in the star-shaped design of the buildings accommodating each cluster, the wings housing each unit radiating out of a central communal area like the spokes of a wheel.

Each unit had an 'animateur', an older student of settled progressive outlook, who provided ideological as well as practical inspiration to those under his care. Once a month the students might be briefly let out to visit their families; at Christmas they were given four days' leave. But, for most of the year, they remained confined within the fenced compound. Everything possible was done to promote the spirit of egalitarianism. The students were permitted only the most elementary of personal possessions. Pocket money was strictly forbidden. Instead, vouchers were provided, equivalent to about twenty-five rupees (under £3) a month. These vouchers they could spend as they pleased in the village shop.

Transgressors were dealt with by 'persuasion' and the techniques of 're-education'. If persuasion and re-education proved ineffective the authorities could resort to 'necessary punishment' – the infliction of a heavier burden of communal duty and the withdrawal of certain privileges. An especially grave offence could lead to expulsion. (Expulsion was no blessing in disguise: those who had not completed their two years in the camps were debarred from all further education.) To date, there had been some fifty expulsions from the village. The girls appeared to be particularly at risk. They were given pregnancy tests every three months – expulsion was automatic if the result was positive.

The village was not as neat as I had half-expected it to be. The sandy soil had a wasted look. Already, the cleared bush was reclaiming its own, subverting and satirising the aims of those who had only unexamined and reflexive notions of individual and social redemption. We stopped at a small clinic. Three lethargic boys were stretched out on cots. The presence of authority appeared to rob them of the powers of speech. One had cut his foot. Another, according to the nurse on duty, claimed that his eyes were hurting him. The third complained of recurrent headaches. Returned outside, I gazed at the ragged vistas of the compound. Here and there uniformed students moved slowly along the sandy lanes winding through the camp. The scene, despite the sunshine, was enervatingly colourless.

I looked into a girls' dormitory, a long room partitioned into cubicles by screens. Within each cubicle were two cots. Here a military precision and austerity prevailed. On each cot was arrayed the spartan equipment of its occupant. A tin plate. A mug. A spoon. Next to these – a beret, a brown shirt, a red scarf, a towel.

All the same. All equal.

From behind one of the partitions came a creaking of bed-springs accompanied by a spasm of coughing. One more, I assumed, was about to be added to the sick list. We inspected the communal kitchen. Hordes of flies had settled over the concrete work surfaces, feeding on the remains of vegetables that had not been cleared away. I looked askance at my companions. The village co-ordinator was apologetic. Unfortunately, the animateur had fallen ill a couple of days before. How fragile a thing is revolution: one sick animateur and the flies move in.

We paused by a playing field, a neglected rectangle of bare, beaten earth and wild grasses.

I remarked on the quiteness of the place.

'It's the time of day,' the village co-ordinator said.

I remarked on the sombreness of the faces I saw.

'What makes you think they are sad?' she asked. 'They lead very fulfilling lives here.'

Even Gilbert seemed thoughtful as the barrier at the entrance to the camp was raised and we returned to the outside world.

North-east of Mahé, a fifteen-minute plane-ride away, lies Praslin, the second largest island in the Seychelles group. I went there to attend the opening of a new hotel which just so happened to be owned by a brother of the Foreign Minister. The scale of the enterprise was modest; but since anything to do with the tourist trade is big news it was a well-publicised event. What was more, the occasion was to be graced by the presence of the Minister himself. Palm fronds bedecked with flowers ornamented the pillars of the open-air lounge. Tables were set out under the coconut palms bordering a sugar-coloured beach washed by a placid sea.

Assembled there in the descending dusk was a collection of travel agents and travel writers, each a courted prince of power and patronage, each come to reassess a paradise once suddenly found, then as suddenly lost, and which now yearned to see itself regained. For, after all the treason, all the empty words, all the killing, one humble truth still survived: without tourists, the Seychelles had no reason to be; without tourists, the islands would die. The Minister, easefully tropical in dress, cut a ribbon and made a speech. Many people, he observed with benign incredulity, seemed to have been infected by the idea that Socialist Seychelles did not want tourists. He was a little flabbergasted by that – because nothing could be further from the truth. Seychelles wanted all the tourists it could get. The President himself was as committed as anyone to the revival and expansion of the trade. Le Président lui-même! He was prepared to concede that some mistakes had been made ...

My attention drifted. Cameras flashed. The travel agents and travel writers showed polite interest and offered polite applause. Rather incongruously, a church bell tolled somewhere in the distance. The ghost of Jimmy Mancham haunted that Socialist twilight. Through the coconut groves came the strains of a hymn. Later that night I walked back to my hotel along the deserted beach. Moonlight gleamed on the leaves of the bushes and the palms. The dark sea was calm. Blackened garlands of sea-weed striped the pale beach which lay stretched out under the moon like an outsized zebra's hide put out to dry. Stray dogs shadowed my progress, now approaching, now retreating. The silence of the blue night, broken only by the splashing waves and the barking of the pursuing dogs, was unsettling. A primal immediacy imbued the scene.

It was here, on Praslin, in the last quarter of the eighteenth century, that the coco-de-mer palm was discovered. The macabre suggestiveness of this peculiar palm has always encouraged speculation. General Gordon – who visited the islands in 1881 – decided that Praslin was the site of the Garden of Eden. 'Surely,' he wrote, his mind obsessed by the errant Eve, 'if curiosity could be excited by any tree, it would be by this.' He concluded that the coco-de-mer – whose nut mimics the female genitalia and whose male inflorescence mimics the phallus – must be the Tree of Knowledge. Less convincingly (for it is not a native of the islands), he argued that the breadfruit was the Tree of Life.

The Seychelles have never fully recovered from this exegetic exercise. Gordon took it upon himself to devise a coat of arms for the colony. It showed the coco-de-mer supported on the back of a tortoise. Around the trunk of the palm is entwined a snake. The contemporary coat of arms is remarkably similar: the coco-de-mer and the tortoise are still there. Only the snake is missing.

Grenada – a Postscript

'Move, lemme get me share
They beating Grenadians down in the Square
Lemme pelt a lash, lemme get a share
They beating Grenadians down Woodford Square . . .

Way back in the early Sixties, Grenadians were making news in Trinidad. The problem at the time – about which the calypsonian (Lord Blakie) was singing – was illegal immigration. We in Trinidad felt that our small and overcrowded island was being overrun. Ugly rumours started to spread about the behaviour and personal habits of these unfortunate people. We began to fear the subversion of our entire cultural heritage and trembled at the changes being wrought in the character of our slum areas. Some of the methods used to identify the intruders could be a little cavalier. According to Lord Blakie, a suspect might be asked to say 'hog'. If he said 'hag' no mercy was shown. 'It was,' Blakie sang, 'straight in the police van.' I know how easy it would be to criticise the naïveté of the Trinidadian police. Pause, however, before you do so. Twenty years later, echoes of a similar approach to the task of identification can be detected among Grenada's liberators. 'You look into their eyes, sir,' a staff-sergeant of the Marines told a *Sunday Times* 'front line' reporter, 'and see if they are hostile to the United States. You can see it, sir.' Life sure can get tough. Yessir!

Trinidad, a large island by Eastern Caribbean standards and a comparatively rich one (we have oil), has always attracted immigrants from the smaller, impoverished islands to the north. Grenada, being nearest, has traditionally been the major source of this influx. Like all immigrants, the Grenadians were despised. They did, though, have their triumphs. Trinidad's most famous calypsonian, the Mighty Sparrow, was born in Grenada – but it is an aspect of his past which he has never stressed and which Trinidadians prefer to ignore. We considered ourselves immeasurably superior to those benighted 'small islanders' who, skulking ashore off leaky inter-island schooners, kept on surfacing among us in search of menial jobs and the more cosmopolitan excitements afforded by our wealth and our much larger multi-racial population. Generally – despite the periodic bouts of ineffectual persecution – they were tolerated; objects of an indulgent, harmless contempt. The Government, with one eye on the racial politics of the island, saw in these Negro immigrants a useful reservoir of anti-Indian votes. Our middle classes saw a useful reservoir of domestic servants. The Grenadian, simple, anxious to please, insecure, was considered ideal for this kind of work, altogether more suitable than the indigenous, indolent equivalent. Nowadays (so I am told) Guyanese, fleeing their bleak, South American homeland, have displaced the Grenadians.

In the immediate aftermath of the break-up of the West Indian Federation in 1961 (a Jamaican-inspired débâcle), Trinidad's relations with Grenada took a new and curious twist. The idea was bruited that, together with Tobago, the three islands should form what was called a unitary state. As ever, politics being politics, this was suggested with one eye on the racial structure of Trinidadian politics. It was, even so, an arresting proposition, one not to be casually dismissed. Nevertheless, it was doomed never to get beyond the stage of hazy theorising because, with the disintegration of the Federation and the heady scent of disparate autonomies pervading the Caribbean chaos, the times were no longer propitious. For, in each of the units of the dead Federation, petty baronies were already taking shape. These were in no mood lightly to surrender the opportunities that might soon be theirs. The British had lost their taste for Empire and were in an indecent haste to cut and run. All the barons had to do was affect a seemly patience. Decentralisation might be a fashionable political cry. In the Caribbean, the collection of 'haggard primadonnas' (so General de Gaulle once described the islands), bankrupt relics of the sugar boom of the eighteenth century, decentralisation was a foreshadowing of disaster. As is well known, those who will not hang together shall be hanged separately.

Grenada's political fortunes have evolved since then along not entirely incoherent lines. What has happened on the island over the last two decades could, with equal facility and depressingly similar results, have occurred in any of half a dozen Caribbean states. It has in fact been threatening to happen in several of them. Think of Jamaica, under the rule of Michael Manley, declining into a passable semblance of civil war. Or of the Guyana of Forbes Burnham, long surrendered to a caricature of the democratic process, of fake Third World militancy and of political murder. Or of Trinidad, whose army mutinied under the influence of Black Power ideologues. Or of the Bahamas, wallowing in the corruptions of the narcotics trade. Or of Anguilla, which broke away from its 'unitary' statehood with St Kitts and Nevis and only narrowly escaped falling under the domination of certain exotic 'business' interests. Or, even, of Dominica (whose Prime Minister, Eugenia Charles, has played such a conspicuous role in recent events), where lawlessness in the guise of Rastafariansim overran extensive tracts of that wild and mountainous island – the setting for Jean Rhys's memorable novel, *Wide Sargasso Sea*.

The list is long and could be extended. Each unit of the mutilated whole is a waif; each is adrift and afraid, vulnerable to predators from within and without. Grenada's tragedy is simply that the pattern of events enacted there within the last week or two finally reached a sort of apocalyptic completeness. The failure is not only a local one. It shows up the shabbiness and emptiness of the colonial past; a colonial past tawdrily and cynically disowned by the Common Market present, whose visions of responsibility focus narrowly on atavistic images of 'kith and kin'; on the blood ties of the primal tribe.

For some years after the break-up of the Federation, Grenadians were in thrall to a handsome lunatic, Eric Gairy, a self-declared Rosicrucian who once lectured the UN on UFOs. His hired killers, recruited from the island's jails, terrorised opponents of the regime. Gairy being fiercely anti-Communist, his opponents naturally tended to be left-wing. It was under his patronage that a so-called Medical School was set up for American students who weren't good enough to gain admission to the universities back home. Another messianic lunatic also showed interest in Grenada around this time – a preacher from Indiana called Jim Jones. Fortunately for Grenada, Jones was to discover a more spacious and secluded paradise in Guyana. Had Gairy survived, Grenada would have recreated on its soil a petty Duvalierism. If that had been its fate, everyone would have been reasonably content because Gairy would have been a menace to no one except his fellow Grenadians – just as Forbes Burnham in Guyana is a threat to no one except the Guyanese. Certainly, the deeply felt need to invade, to restore law and order and democracy and all other good things, would not have so afflicted Washington. What it has tolerated for generations in Haiti, it would also have tolerated for generations in Grenada. Political murder is not in itself objectionable to Ronald Reagan. He was, after all, prepared to go and be fêted by the Marcos ménage even after the killing of the Opposition leader at Manila airport. If Gairy had managed to cling to power we would have been spared Reagan's all to muscular altrium.

That, alas, was not to be. Grenada, lurching into coup d'état, was to take another fatal step along the post-colonial road. It was inevitable that Maurice Bishop and his associates in the New Jewel Movement, nurtured in the radical atmosphere of the late Sixties and early Seventies, should have espoused an amalgam of Black Power and Marxism; that Havana should have provided their tutelary deities. One can argue that, even granted all this, Grenada's threat was still mainly to itself. Admittedly, the Duvalierist state had transformed itself overnight into a 'revolutionary' state; admittedly, the Grenadian leaders were now issuing joint communiqués with Moscow; admittedly, a rather larger airport was being built. But the Caribbean operates at a high level of fantasy. The obsession with Carnival is only the most obvious symptom of this frailty. And, to save the day, there was the coup within the coup. Admittedly, a most distasteful business. Nevertheless, in General Austin, Grenada was not acquiring an even more 'hard-line' Marxist-Leninist. We really are in trouble when we start to believe in other people's fantasies. Grenada, through all the blood and mayhem, was merely reverting to a more recognisable image of itself: it was falling into the hands of a black dictator modelled on the Burnhamite pattern – a man of raw power, beyond the reach of ideology, devoted to compromise and survival.

Look into the eyes and you will see.

Acknowledgments

'Beyond the Dragon's Mouth', *New Yorker*, 1984.

Stories

'The Beauty Contest', 'A Man of Mystery' and 'The Political Education of Clarissa Forbes', *Penguin Modern Stories 4* (Penguin 1970).

'The Dolly House' (under the title 'The Process of Living'), *Winter's Tales 20* (Macmillan 1974).

'Mr Sookhoo and the Carol Singers', *The New Review*, September 1974.

'The Father, the Son and the Holy Ghost', *The Denver Quarterly*, Autumn 1971.

'The Tenant', *Winter's Tales 17* (Macmillan 1971).

'Lack of Sleep', *Encounter*, November 1974.

Pieces

'Living in Earls Court', *London Magazine*, August/September 1973.

'Flying the Flag in Brixton' (under the title 'London No-man's-land'), *The Illustrated London News*, June 1976.

'Passports to Dependence', *Sunday Times Magazine*, 30 December 1973.

'The Road to Nowhere', *Spectator*, 18 February 1978.

'On Cannibal Farm' (under the title 'A Stranger on Merseyside'), *Sunday Telegraph*, 9 April 1978.

'The City by the Sea' (under the title 'Taking Shelter in Bombay'), *Geo*, September 1981.

'A Dying State', *Spectator*, 4 and 11 December 1982.

'The Sanjay Factor', *Observer*, 4 and 11 January 1981.

'Bubbly' (under the title 'An Indian Encounter'), *Spectator*, 20 December 1980.

'Funeral of a Pope' (under the title 'Funeral in a Dead City'), *Spectator*, 19 August 1978.

'Legacy of a Revolution', *Spectator*, 22 May 1982.

'The Aryan Dream' (under the title 'The Iranian Disease'), *Spectator*, 27 May 1978.

'Victim of Ramadan', *Spectator*, 13 September 1980.

'The Bush Negroes of Surinam' (under the title 'Suriname: A Tableau of Savage Innocence'), *Geo*, March 1981.

'The Rise of the Rastaman', *Observer*, 27 June and 4 July 1982.

'Two Colonies' (under the title 'Nowhere in Particular'), *Spectator*, 3 October 1981.

'Fall from Innocence' (under the title 'Islands in the Sun'), *Spectator*, 12 and 19 November 1983.

'Grenada – a Postscript' (under the title 'Look into the Eyes'), *Spectator*, 5 November 1983.